NOTHING PERSONAL

ROBIN CHAPPELL

Illuminousity Press

First Illuminousity Press paperback & ebook editions June 2022

Cover and all Interior Design work by Robin Chappell
Header Typeface: HERCULANUM
Body Typeface: Times New Roman

Library of Congress Copyrighted
Chappell, Robert Alan.
Nothing Personal
1 Novel. 2 Fiction. I. Title

ISBN: 978-1-7374519-2-1   Paperback

ISBN: 978-1-7374519-3-8 ebook - Kindle

Illuminousity Press™
[a division of 21st Century daVinci, LLC]
Los Angeles, CA

If after reading this book and enjoying it, if you would be so kind as to leave an honest book review on my Author Central page, about what you liked and didn't… I would appreciate it!

This is the first Book (of Six) of Robin's coming out over the next year. If you would like to be added to his Mailing List for Books as well as Art and other Offerings, please go to robin@21stcenturydavinci.com. Of course you can Opt-out at any time.

—Review of Robin's Book first Book,
          "Dreams, Desires, And Dead Ends"

"Memorable, quirky sketches on life and love from a storyteller with potential."
          — Kirkus Reviews

This book is *Dedicated* to

All of My Lost Loves
(who weren't truly The One after all!)

and to

THE ONE

yet to come along.

(May You Come Soon!)

(Yes, I wouldn't mind a Fairy Tale ending.

Would you?)

ONE

The various luminous shades of pinks and whites of the newly opened cherry blossoms were everywhere. Competing with the glorious shades of green the blossoms were working to outdo was the clear, deep blue of the sky. Scattered bright white fleecy clouds sailed above it all, glinting off the Potomac River just beyond view.

But inside the high plate-glass window separating the sounds and colors of the outside world from those inside the building, a storm was brewing.

"Springtime in Washington," Angela sighed. "It's almost as nice as springtime in Paris, except — oh, I don't know. This doesn't have the ancient feeling that Paris has, that same eternal sort of feeling to it."

She said this as she sat staring into the space between the glass and the outside that was in front of her that she wasn't quite seeing. Her morning crumpet and coffee (both now cold) still sat untouched on the table in front of her.

"Well," her older friend said, sitting across from her with her back to the scene outside, trying to keep the irony out of her voice. "That was wonderful, Angela. Almost sounded like the beginning of a good novel."

With a concerned look still playing on her face, she added compassionately, "But you really should think about getting out more, my dear."

Angela laughed sadly at this and turned away from the window to face her friend. As she did, she suddenly recognized just how sad her reflection in the window had been.

I don't have much reason to go out much these days, she thought. But to Maddy she said, "Oh, I don't know about that, Maddy," without much emotion.

The sun still glinted off the Potomac outside. There were bright shards of sunlight everywhere.

With those crisp clear blue skies of springtime outside, I should be a lot happier. Those skies, those clouds almost seemed magical. Quite the opposite of her life, which was feeling rather dull and tarnished in comparison.

The water below this arching vault gently rippled and shimmered, its blue reflected glory only broken by the occasional luxury boat from nearby Washington Harbor gliding by, adding even more ripples and shards of light to it. Or by the students from nearby Georgetown University crewing with intent in their scull boats, leaving their needle-like wakes behind them.

On a day like today, the air was clear between their seats in this restaurant and the greening patch of Roosevelt Island across the river. The gleaming Towers of Rosslyn, Virginia rose beyond that.

All in all, a rather perfect day, Maddy thought to herself. Then, looking at her friend again: *All except for Angela's dreadful mood.*

The newly opened cherry blossoms glowing softly pink everywhere and swaying gently in the breeze were the very reason why this restaurant was named The Cherry Blossom in the first place.

The occasional midday couple strolling by, hands or arms locked in loving embrace, or joggers on the path beside it, could almost make one forget the the near constant flow of traffic along Rock Creek Parkway, making it the less than the idyllic scene it could have been.

At forty-two, Angela had already descended into the life of being the bored politician's wife. The woman who was formally referred to as Mrs. Barnes-Treworthy, Angela was the wife of a US senator. She still looked quite young for her age, her current mental state not withstanding.

Her longish and loosely curled cascade of black hair was a little tousled from her long walk from home not too far away in Georgetown. She didn't style it like most of the women of her class and status did, and liked that that made her seem just like any other bored housewife might look out for a walk from her home state of Connecticut.

Never one for appearances (except when necessary for State Functions or to portray the role of the Senator's wife), Angela could almost walk down the streets of just about anywhere in DC with relative anonymity. Her mood though helped in keeping her head bowed down for safety, just in case.

If it weren't for her face, that is. She could have been a model if her mind had been geared towards that direction.

Angela had come to be a senator's wife much later in life than most, having gone through an early career in public relations before being bitten by the bug of politics. She had joined the re-election campaign of her (then) state senator, found that she had a talent for it and then got more involved in politics than she had ever planned on doing.

Sitting across the table from her was her best (and perhaps only real) friend, Madelaine Lightfoot, who had a very different story.

Maddy (to only her closest friends) was a senator's widow, having played the role of senator's wife for some thirty years before losing her husband to cancer a few years ago.

She had been in politics — "since before I can remember," Maddy sometimes quipped. She had always been around it, always desiring to be in it. That she then married into it was no surprise to anyone.

"Old School" she called herself with a laugh. She was through and through about as blue-blood patrician-bred and raised as you could get. Maddy would breeze into any situation and immediately take the room over. Power dripped from her, even though her studied attitude put out a feeling of anything but.

This was their usual weekday ritual of morning coffee and crumpets at Maddy's favorite restaurant in town.

Of course it was only her favorite restaurant primarily because of the easy walk to the elevator from her apartment, and then the mere twelve stories down with a simple turn to the left. ("Never let yourself turn to the right," she sometimes joked.) She could then find herself at its ornate front door on the mezzanine level of the infamous Watergate Apartment Complex within moments. An "old woman must have her conveniences," she'd usually laugh when pressed about it.

Maddy this morning was (appropriate to her seventy-eight years), dressed in what she referred to as an "old ladies" modest floral print dress, attire unlikely to attract any undue attention to this once quite powerful woman. *Not that I really care that much about all that any more anyway,* she thought.

Angela, as she usually did, had dressed in the much more comfortable simple slacks and blouse that her life in the limelight as a Senate wife seldom afforded her in "public."

"More comfortably," she remarked to any friends she could trust (a list which was more and more being restricted to only Maddy.)

They had entered into a long silence that both mirrored and contradicted the life silently blowing, waving and barely heard honking outside. Angela's gaze kept returning to the outdoor scene, while Maddy quietly and sedately watched for her young friend to make her next move or comment.

The only sound for the last few minutes had been that of the clinking of fine china and silverware along with the muffled hum of the various conversations buzzing nearby. At this hour, the sparsely populated tables in this posh and clearly older-patron-centered restaurant were largely empty.

Maddy, for her part, sat comfortably in unhurried bliss. Turning to watch the peaceful scene outside, she treasured these generally quiet mornings with Angela, knowing in the back of her mind that Washington was usually anything but quiet this time of morning.

She had had enough of the "hurly-burly" of DC during her husband's career, and always when asked if she missed it replied, "This quiet is just fine, thank you," to anyone who asked.

Angela, though, might as well have been in the midst of the workaday madness, for all the stillness that she found inside herself. Fiddling with her silverware, nervously picking her cup up and setting it down again without drinking, she was nervous without any cause she could pinpoint.

There wasn't anything that should be disturbing her, so why did she feel so distraught inside?

Maddy waited out her friend's mood quietly, having grown accustomed to her unsettled demeanor. Wistfully recognizing the signs and portents of what her friend was going through, she had felt it herself many years ago. It had almost driven her to the kind of drinking that many other congressional wives had made into their lifestyle.

Turning back to her fidgety friend suddenly, Maddy finally made The Decision. *It's time*, she thought. *This will only get worse.*

"I have an idea my dear," Maddy said with a Mona Lisa-like smile. "You look like you could use a break from this city," she said cheerfully.

And suddenly.

Startled out of her reverie once again, Angela looked up frightened, realizing that what she had been feeling had been so transparently written on her face. "Whatever do you mean, Maddy?" she asked.

It was a politely and patrician-like phrased question that belied what she really wanted to do inside... Which was scream.

Flooded with the self-consciousness of her tone almost as soon as she'd said it, she came fully back to the present and said dishonestly, "I'm fine, Maddy."

"Don't worry, my dear. You'll be back in time for dinner," Maddy told her as she regally waved in the general direction of their waiter. *That is, if Franklin even comes home for dinner these days*, Maddy thought, maintaining her silence and sense of decorum.

Angela's husband, Senator Franklin James Treworthy III, had gotten into the habit lately of working so many long hours that his wife only saw him when she found him crawling apologetically into bed with her. If she didn't know her husband as well as she did, she might almost have thought that he was having an affair.

When Angela once brought the subject up to Maddy, her friend had said with an uncharacteristic snort, "Oh, he's having an affair, all right. An affair with Politics and The People. And that my dear, is not a thing that we can compete with, you and I."

On top of that, her husband had had a compulsion to serve driven into him from a young age. His father had instilled into the young Frank the idea that "We — your family and I — were given much in the way of wealth and prestige by the Almighty." And because of that wealth and everything that came with it, there was a "Duty to Serve" out of that which had been "given" to them.

This compulsion had driven Frank to volunteer to go to Vietnam, even though most of his friends were more than willing to allow themselves to be sent off to college instead of the jungles of Southeast Asia.

This was one of the things that had drawn her to Frank as soon as she started working with him. Oh, that and Frank's resemblance to a young Abraham Lincoln. Frank was not a traditionally handsome man, but he was tall and statuesque. He had struck Angela as someone of passion and commitment from almost before they had even formally met.

Frank fell in love with his young staffer for many of the same reasons that she was attracted to him. That, and she was gorgeous. Frank was smitten from first glance.

"I'm really fine," Angela insisted to her friend. "There's no need for you to—"

"Nonsense, my dear. I can see that there are a great many things are pressing on you."

Angela was now the one to snort at this, it represented one of her few faults in the eyes of the "Prim and Proper Police" surrounding her husband and his office. Angela felt that it was only some trifling emotion, and that Maddy was only doing what Maddy did — soothing Angela's sense of absurdity.

"I know this darling little restaurant out in Great Falls that I go to periodically. I think you'll just love it. Why..." Maddy said with a secret smile, "it even overlooks the Potomac." With her smile growing, she added, "Just like here," biting her tongue against the irony.

Smiling nervously, Angela merely nodded distantly. Almost ready to turn her nod into a vigorous "no," she caught herself. "Maybe it would be good to get away," she whispered, almost as if to herself.

"You don't have any pressing engagements this afternoon, do you dear?" Maddy asked her coyly.

"No," Angela sighed. And even if she did, she was beginning to not care whether she did or not.

"Good. Then we have a date," Maddy said, signing the meal cheque without even looking at it. She rose and walked away, leaving a slowly moving Angela to rise unseeing, and follow along in Maddy's bright wake.

T W O

Springtime in Washington...

When the trees are blooming in impressionist-inspired madness, drenched in blazing colors brushing the sky and littering the ground everywhere. When couples seem locked in passion everywhere you looked. And even the politicians on Capitol Hill are giddy with something other than power for a month and a day.

Where a young man's mind turns to love.

With temperatures in the 70s finally and after a rough winter with too much snow, all of that was now left in the recent past. The scattered blossoms littered the ground like a multicolored carpet here in the heart of the city, matched only by the office workers scattered like leaves over every square inch of the grass inside the large circle of trees and busy traffic known as Dupont Circle.

It was a convergence of a number of main thoroughfares and was one of the main cultural hubs of the Capital City. And with that city now crawling towards the encroaching madness of rush hour, cars were already clogging the length and breadth of Connecticut Avenue and its converging spider web of streets and avenues.

The lanes of traffic surrounding the Circle also enclosed where a little patch of country lay. The Circle itself was like a ringed moat of dragons in contrast to the seeming quiet and laid back atmosphere in its tree-filled center.

But even with rush hour almost upon them, most of the cars and trucks had their windows down (and with a few exceptions) were also enjoying the (somewhat) fresh and fragrant air.

Not even springtime, though, was enough to calm the frenzy in some denizens of the city. In one particular car circling the calm center, the air conditioner should have been on by now. That might have helped to cool down the hot summer argument heating up around the pressure of the relational warming trend which was about to explode with thunder and lightning.

Gabriel O'Connor and Carol Hodges looked as if they should have been the perfect couple. He was classically handsome, and she was (per her California upbringing) terminally gorgeous. They should have been the envy of everyone they knew. However...

"Why can't we go to Karen's party on Friday night?" Carol harped, slowly building to a fine whine. "My God, Gabriel. Why can't we have a social life? Is that really too much to ask?" she asked, pouring on the pity.

Sighing, Gabe waited a second before saying what he really wanted to say. Instead, he said as patiently and slowly as he could (almost as if he were talking to a child), "Because I work on Friday night." Turning towards her with a grim grin on his face, he asked her , "Remember, Carol?"

Sitting in Gabe's old Chevy Malibu rust bucket, Carol was dressed to the nines as usual. Her hair was perfect, her teeth gleaming model white.

In her mind she pretended that she was seated in a late-model Lexus, and not a car that was older than she was.

Gabe still had on his now quite rumpled (and no longer starched) white shirt and (no longer pressed) black uniform pants from the previous night's work. Sometimes these days, he could just forget to change.

Unless they happened to be going to a fancy restaurant. And sometimes, he just didn't really care even then.

"Right, I forgot. My boyfriend, the bartender," she said, warming up now with the acid dripping in her voice once more.

"Why can't you go out and get a *real* job, Gabriel? Why did you get your Bachelors degree in English? Just so you could mix and pour drinks for a living?"

It was a good thing for Gabe that the traffic was moving, however slowly. With his hands tightly gripping the steering wheel, Gabe kept his eyes straight ahead, not really seeing the traffic in his growing anger. Resorting once again to the parent lecturing their child tactic, he enunciated slowly, "Because I'm a writer. Remember? Writers need to have a job while they write, and that job, for me, is bartending."

Carol turned to him and replaced her scowl with a sickeningly sweet smile. "If you could only get yourself a nice, regular day job, say with some nice association on K. Street," she said, leaning in to wrap both her hands around his nearest bicep. "Then we could—"

And then losing it, her words turning acidic again "—go out at night. You know, like start having a social life again? Like, you know — regular people?"

Meaning, Not writers and other crazy, nutsy, artsy types. Like your friends, Gabe thought. *It always comes down to this.*

It's never enough for you, is it? Gabe also thought, doing his best to not verbalize one of their long-standing fight bon mots.

Frustrated and feeling the end of a relationship building yet again, he tried to not react to her taunt. Just as he was feeling himself lose the internal battle for restraint, she continued with, "Is that really too much to ask?" She was building towards her usual crying game, pouring on the pout.

With an all-too-practiced look, Gabe sighed and turned a stone-faced look in Carol's direction, cutting her off. They'd had this conversation way too often for his taste lately. As in every other week.

"What? We don't have a social life?" he asked ironically. This was all too much. "We spent practically all of last weekend in Ocean City. Remember? We went to that boring beach party at that over-priced house with all of your stuffy social and politically climbing friends. We stayed way too long for my taste, and even that wasn't long enough for you."

Letting her hands loosen and melt from his arm, she slowly turned around in her seat, putting on her "I am most displeased" queenly attitude on. Folding those hands neatly, primly and properly in her lap, she prepared to begin pouring all of the last month's worth of bile into what she felt was going to be one of her scathing retorts.

"Well," she said, now in full huff, "It's better to be a social climber trying to make something of your life, than it is to be just—" she paused before letting the acid fly with, " —hanging out with some perpetually adolescent drinking buddies all the time."

He let out a deep sigh and turned in her direction. "Me and my 'drinking buddies' as you call them, just happen to be artistically inclined, not money and status inclined. That's all."

Now totally bored with the conversation and waiting for the right moment, she laughed as bitterly as she could. "Yeah right. All of you writing—" and with a heavy dramatic sigh, she let loose the dog of war, "The 'Great American Novel.'"

Gabe turned towards Carol for the final round. "That's right. The Great American Novel. That's what every writer is writing for."

"Except that you never write, Gabriel. You haven't written a single page lately, have you? No. You just go out drinking with your 'buddies' and never write a thing. Gee. My boyfriend, the failed writer."

Both hurting and boiling inside, Gabe didn't know what he wanted more at this point; having a girlfriend, or peace and quiet. "Why do we have to keep having this same old tired conversation, Carol?"

"Because you never think about me. You only think about that awful Benny Hill... And all the rest of those slumming losers you call friends."

Almost laughing at this one but not wanting to give her the satisfaction, he said "His last name is Harrison, not Hill." Shaking his head, he added, "You know, your father watched way too much of that shit when you were growing up."

Gabe turned his eyes straight ahead, with the now slowly moving traffic close to unlocking. "And my friends are not losers. They all have regular jobs. Unlike all of your trust-fund-baby friends who have cushy jobs in their daddy's firms. We happen to work for a living. And we're the ones serving drinks and food to all those politicians and staffers in their dead-end jobs that you admire so much. We see them when they've drunk every last shred of their status and dignity away, and can barely make it to the rest room in time."

This is it, Gabe decided, and sighed. *This is the point that it always comes to in every relationship I've ever been in.*

Turning towards her after finishing his pique, Gabe saw that Carol was boiling herself now. But as soon as Gabe had turned towards Carol, he saw her grow suddenly and frighteningly calm.

Staring at him with her eyes now closed to slits (like a big cat ready for the kill), she finally went for the kill shot. "You mean... like your daddy, Gabriel?"

She knew how to cut him well when she wanted to.

That's it, he thought. Turning away from her as the traffic crawled and then stalled, Gabe nearly missed a street person walking through the street panhandling, as they stepped right in front of him and began pounding on the hood. But Gabe ignored him, focusing on his soon to be ex-girlfriend instead.

Controlling herself now seeing Gabe's expression, Carol turned emotionally on a dime. Playing the actress now and beginning to work it in earnest, she almost managed tears flowing to plead with him, "Gabriel, you've been writing that novel for almost five years now. When are you going to give it up and do something real with your life?"

And, pausing for her pitch across the plate, she continued carefully with, "You know? Like settle down? Get married? Have children? Like most of the rest of the sane and sensible world?!"

Dryly, Gabe returned, "I'll do you the courtesy of driving you right to your door this time, Carol."

Carefully avoiding what he knew would be Carol's fierce stare, Gabe let himself get lost in thought. Until the angry horn of the driver behind him brought him jarringly back to the present. He only had a mile or so of Life with Carol left, and he was tired of playing this game.

Moving ahead with the light change, Gabe continued driving in icy silence. Finally getting clear of the Circle traffic, he continued on Connecticut Avenue and on up the hill, past the last of the big hotels and towards her apartment building and its awaiting front door.

Turning into the little turnaround there, Gabe pulled up to the big double glass doors that Carol always seemed to think were so elegant.

Not even turning the engine off, Gabe just sat there without further comment, not wanting to let her start some new tangent. He did his own version of letting his hands fall to his lap, crisscrossing them on the wheel and just waiting for Carol to leave.

Turning in his general direction, Carol huffily searched for some last particularly cutting remark to mark their end, but nothing came to her. Finally taking the courage to look at Gabe directly and seeing the determined look on his face, she just opened the door and got out.

Turning back around before she completed the slam of the door, she leaned back in as if to say something, but found herself still at a loss for words. Instead, she gave him a disgusted look and huffily slammed the door as loud as she could, walked haughtily and regally to the front door and never looked back.

Finally letting his waiting breath out with the slam, his grip also loosened on the wheel and he lost all the strained pent up energy he'd been keeping inside. It was barely even noon yet, and Gabe already felt like going back to bed. Like he'd just worked a double shift and his body would just drift him off into oblivion.

"Why do I even bother trying?" he asked the air, then turned the wheel to find himself once again in the springtime Washington traffic.

Springtime. When young love goes astray of old expectations.

Pulling out into the flow, he didn't really know where he wanted to go at this point. *Call into work? Go home? Go for a drive up the Potomac and forget all about Spring? Right.*

Or... "Whatever. Drive," he said to himself. "Just drive," mimicking his hero Jack Kerouac.

I've got a car. I've got gas in my tank. I don't need to be back at work till tomorrow. I don't have to do anything. Just drive. Drive until I find myself... Wherever.

THREE

The limousine had left the Watergate complex slowly, turned out onto Virginia Avenue. As it drove past a number of tourists walking away from the Kennedy Center, Angela was amused to see some of the women in the group turn and strain to see if "someone important" was driving away. Ah, it had been such a long time since she had been that naive and curious.

Now she was merely jaded. She had met presidents and their wives, heads of State, and even Queen Elizabeth at one state function. Now that last one had left her in awe, but when she told Maddy about her reaction, Maddy only shrugged and said cryptically, "All things are relative." *If those women only knew*, Angela thought.

Reaching Washington Circle and snaking around it and into the perennially slow motion traffic there, the limo kept curving around to K Street There it turned right and headed down to meet the K Street tunnel.

Blending onto the rising ramp leading up to the Whitehurst Freeway, the limo continued weaving in and out of the smaller cars as it made its way up onto the elevated roadway, taking a road quite frequently traveled.

Whitehurst Freeway was really quite a misnomer. Spanning all of a mile or so between K Street and a small cloverleaf leading to either Key Bridge or M Street, it was really like a bridge, only included as an afterthought.

But it was still sufficiently elevated to start lightening Angela's mood.

With Georgetown passing below and around them, green was replacing stone as the color outside. The feeling of oppression that Angela could not seem to put a finger on, didn't seem so heavy any more.

Now she didn't even feel as if whatever it was, was something that she should even bother Maddy about, *although Lord knows*, she thought, *I've told her just about everything else regarding my life*. Whatever it was now seemed inconsequential with the act of leaving the city.

Looking upriver, Rosslyn loomed on their left, its new steel and glass towers gleaming from the still morning light. Frank would only say, "Time marches on," when she would bring this new city up as they were standing on the Kennedy Center Terrace at the intermission of a show there.

When she and Frank had gotten married, you couldn't even see Rosslyn from the DC side of the river. It was still merely a small town below the tree-line, a remnant of a Virginia of a very different age. Back then however, she thought, even DC was still very much a sleepy little Southern town, the doings of the Federal Government notwithstanding.

Turning and looking down river, the Potomac wended its way

south, past the Watergate where Maddy lived, and then past the Big White Box of the Kennedy Center. With the riot of cherry blossoms decorating even the most sterile stone as far as the eye could see, the sea of pink and white blossoms brought Angela out of her fog.

Going briefly under Key Bridge and then up and around and exiting Whitehurst onto M Street again, they found themselves briefly in the flow of Georgetown traffic. And then with barely a thought, they were crossing Key Bridge and heading directly into Virginia.

"Why don't I leave the city more often?" she whispered to herself, drinking in the scenery flashing by outside, her heart feeling lighter by the moment.

Maddy only secretly smiled from her side of the enormous leather seats, leaving Angela to her own thoughts. On the way to leaving the town she had called home for fifty years now, Maddy smiled in her younger friend's direction, as the limo sped up and took the turn onto the George Washington Parkway.

Soon enough, Maddy thought. *Soon enough.*

Somehow trying to find something to do with her life while Frank was consumed by his life on The Hill, just didn't seem to be something that Angela had felt was an urgent need before. And yet, it was weighing heavier and heavier of late, her life feeling devastatingly empty.

Frank's life always seemed so full of purpose, driven as it was by the power and responsibility of his being a United States Senator. *But then what of my life?* she often thought.

She had once participated more fully in his life on The Hill, continuing on as one of his staff even while she was his wife.

But (she had told herself), she had gradually lost interest (while in actuality she had been pushed aside). Except for his meager staff, Frank seemed very self-contained, until Angela had begun feeling almost as if she were intruding whenever she called. *That was too many years ago now*, she thought.

Looking out the tinted window now, Angela suddenly realized that they had already turned on the George Washington Parkway. If they kept going, the Parkway would eventually funnel them onto the Capitol Beltway, miles north from here.

Where **is** *Maddy taking me?* she thought, but didn't bother questioning her friend's intentions. She knew Maddy well enough to know that she would just tell Angela, "It's a surprise!" and leave it at that.

It seemed like ages since she'd felt this free, she now realized, and she was only leaving the city for the afternoon. Whenever she was with Maddy, she always felt a comfort that she hadn't felt for a long time when left on her own.

Her friend *was* comforting, not just as a mother figure, but because Maddy understood the weight of the duties and responsibilities of Angela's position.

Maddy had been a senator's wife for over forty years, buffeted by the demands and the constant attention. She knew and could talk about aspects of Angela's life that Angela dared not speak of with anyone else, and this had saved Angela's sanity more than once. Decorum and denial walked hand in hand in her life, almost from the moment she and Frank had come together.

"Isn't this much better?" Maddy asked quietly, rolling down the window and letting the cool, moist air off the Potomac infiltrate the car. *Maybe I should have done this earlier*, Maddy thought. *But she wasn't really ready. Before now.*

Remembering all too well, even after all these years how this straight-jacket life had felt for her, she worked to relieve that in Angela. At least Maddy had had children to leaven the boredom amidst the chaos of public life. Angela didn't have that buffer.

But as soon as her children, Evelyn and Michael, had left the nest, the very same emptiness had overtaken Maddy as well. She had involved herself with all the right charities, as had befit the obligation of a senator's wife. That had filled the gap for a while, but after "not long," even that wasn't enough.

But Angela had never had children with Frank to create those "years of purpose" in her life. She hadn't really wanted any, but had soon found that she wasn't able to get pregnant, even if she had.

She had been more than satisfied with her work; first in her husband's office, and then with the various charities that she herself had worked with. But that wasn't enough now either, for some reason she couldn't (comfortably) define.

She looked out Maddy's side window as they were passing the steeples of Georgetown University, perched high on its cliffs across the river. Angela herself had once had her sights set on going to Georgetown, once upon a time, being a good little Catholic girl. But somehow that had never happened, and she went to Brown in New York City instead.

A little further along (and with the sights of D.C. disappearing behind them), they were entering into the timeless scenes of river and trees. Offered a flashing blur of green on either side and clear blue skies above, Angela was able to carefully ignore their fellow travelers on this busy highway. Those cars were passing them like a blur, as she and Maddy rode in their stately and more slow moving limousine.

Angela hit the button that rolled the window down on her side, but unlike Maddy, rolled hers all the way down down to let the crisp breeze snapping by fill the cabin. Turning to her friend, she smiled broadly at Maddy, who was smiling wistfully and contentedly back.

Why hadn't she done something like this before? Angela thought again behind her smile. And suddenly Angela noticed that they were passing the three islands in the Potomac known as The Three Sisters Islands, just beyond Maddy.

The Three Sisters were small islands — almost more like tufts in the river with vegetation and some sparse trees growing out of them, more than actual islands. The Sisters lay in the middle of the Potomac a mile or so north of the Georgetown waterfront, now off to their right as they were traveling northwest. Moving closer to peer past her friend, Maddy was pointing to them and asked Angela, "Do you see those islands?"

Angela nodded and laughed lightly, wondering what Maddy had up her sleeve. "Of course, Maddy. I'm not exactly a tourist here."

"Yes, but have you ever heard the story of why they're called the Three Sisters?" Maddy asked.

Pausing for a second, Angela sat back in her seat, unsure of whether she wanted to answer. "No. I guess I haven't." She wanted to smile as if she were about to get an inside joke, but she couldn't. "Why?" she finally asked, curiosity getting the better of her.

Smiling at the possibility of her friend telling another of her stories, Angela smiled as Maddy paused, relishing the moment. Maddy did relish telling a story, Angela remembered.

"As the story is told," Maddy started, drawing it out, "back when there were only Native Americans living here...

"Up over there in what is now the Potomac Palisades, lay their hunting ground. The area was rich in wild life then, and the Powhatans lived quite well and peacefully.

"There were three very beautiful sisters in the tribe, as headstrong as they were beautiful. And all of the warriors of the tribe had vied for the right and honor to be marrying one of these sisters. But not one of them had been able to win a single sister's heart or favor."

They were now beyond The Sisters, where the roadway had risen high above the river, but Maddy continued with her story. Angela longed for fall to come each year almost as much as spring, for the colors that Nature lavished on these steep hillsides.

"Then one day, one of the neighboring tribes from further north began attacking the Powhatans. The sisters themselves were brave and fierce warriors as well..."

While Angela waited for Maddy to continue, she saw a tear was forming in her right eye. As a moment turned into a minute, Angela was about to prompt her friend to continue, starting to feel concerned.

But after another moment whatever had come briefly had passed, and Maddy sighed, continuing on more quietly than before. "When they attacked," she continued, "the Powhatans fought back ferociously.

"For some reason though, the other tribe fell back without really killing anyone. Taking advantage of what they saw as cowardice, the Powhatan warriors drove off the warriors of the other tribe.

"Before the men of the Powhatan tribe had left, the Chief caught the Sisters and gathered them up, telling them, 'All of you are strong warriors in your own right. But you need to stay and protect the other women and the children of the tribe.'

"One of the Sisters objected to this, saying, 'But Grandfather! Surely there are younger warriors not yet blooded who can stay and help protect the children and Grandmothers?'

"The Chief was hard pressed to say no. He hated to tell her, but, instead he said, 'Fierce daughter, there will be time enough for you and your sisters to prove yourself,' and he left.

"After a while though (being the headstrong women that they were), they rebelled and went off in search of ways to help their warriors against the other tribe.

"They didn't find the warriors of their own tribe though, but instead ran into one of the war parties of the other tribe, coming around from the rear.

"Captured as the other tribe had intended all along, they were taken back to the warring tribe's camp and there the warriors had their way with them, intent on breaking their spirits and making them war brides."

At this, Maddy paused and grew silent again. Angela was about to playfully excoriate her, when she saw that Maddy was somehow lost once more in her strange reverie.

Angela waited for her friend to continue, but after a minute or so of silence, turned her attention to the trees now flying by outside her window.

She was about to give up on hearing the end of the story, when Maddy quietly returned from her thoughts. "After that," she said softly, "the Three Sisters laid a curse on the warring tribe, that they would die out and their land would cease to grow food.

"In turn, the other tribe cursed the sisters. That they would never leave the spot where they lived, and they then killed the sisters, throwing their bodies into the river to carry them away. But instead, they found themselves in their last dying breaths in the middle of the river. And so to this very day, the Three Sisters stand guard over the river where their land once was."

Angela paused before asking any questions, not sure of what to make of this.

"So..." Angela said after a while with a puzzled look. Maddy could tend towards the cryptic side, but this was making Angela wonder about her friend's mental state.

Turning in Angela's direction and looking quite present now, Maddy had a "tsk, tsk" sort of look that always made Angela uneasy. A look as if Maddy expected more out of her. Not that this was a usual look, but when she made it Angela felt like a schoolgirl again.

Maddy leaned in towards her friend and said quietly, but strongly, "Even in our modern age, my dear, we can still be trapped by our society's expectations of us as women."

That still didn't clear up the point being made to Angela, so she just decided to play along. "I'm afraid I still don't understand."

Smiling, Maddy reached across the expanse of leather and patted Angela's hand kindly. "I'm sure you will if you think about it, my dear," she said, and turned away to look out her window at the passing trees.

Stunned into silence, Angela turned away to contemplate the scenery as well, which had suddenly begun dimming slightly as the foliage thickened and covered the Parkway. This little expedition that Maddy was taking her on was beginning to make less and less sense to her. The ride was nice, Angela thought, but she was left feeling uneasy again.

After Angela was caught up in contemplating the scenery, Maddy turned silently back in her young friend's direction, feeling both Angela's pain, as well as hope for her. *You have so much more than I had,* Maddy thought sadly of her friend, *And yet, in some ways, so much less.*

F O U R

Having gone on autopilot after driving away from Carol, Gabe did no such thing as just go off driving. Anywhere.

He found himself on a side street just off Connecticut a mere three blocks away from Carol's apartment building, having turned there and pulled in behind the first car from the corner.

He didn't feel like driving back to crawl into an empty apartment. But he found himself unable to drive anywhere else.

Carol, of course, was just the last in a long line of women who had either thrown themselves at his feet, or seduced him into a relationship that he didn't really want, and didn't really feel satisfied with.

Having an assortment of women was never really his problem. Having a relationship with a woman he felt could be his equal without making him feel guilty... *Now that is a problem*, he thought to himself.

He had never aspired to having children, and that was the only thing that many of these women seemed to want him for. Or to please Daddy. But not really because they were interested in him as a person, only merely as a father to their children or a bank account to keep them from working. (Or usually both).

Carol was now just another bad taste in his mouth. But Gabe probably wouldn't go a week or two at work before another woman looking for him to be The One would start chatting him up with the usual aims in mind.

He had long since stopped wondering how women always somehow seemed to know when he was once again newly single. *It's almost like gay men and "Gaydar,"* he once thought. *Uncanny.*

No, his life was not working for Gabe. In that much Carol was right. And no, he hadn't really written much of anything recently. While his inspiration had once upon a time come fast and furious, that hadn't been the case for quite a long time now.

Life was doing what he wanted to do, and that was all he was looking to do in the meantime. He had a nice degree from Georgetown. He could get another one of those jobs on K. Street that Carol so coveted, just about any time he wanted one.

But being an only child had had its benefits for the bookish, introverted Gabe. His parents indulged him, and since both of them had their own careers, he was left with plenty of time to read... And write.

And since he was on the tall, gangly and unhandsome side, "getting girls" had not been a priority.

And then all of a sudden, adulthood happened. All of a sudden, he was no longer "gangly and ungainly," but was still however tall. Girls began fawning all over him, but he didn't know how to handle it.

He had had one of those jobs that Carol was so enamored of, but which had only lasted two grueling years before he had grown tired of the office politics and quit.

It hadn't been without its perks, however. It had allowed him to get his current apartment, as well as affording him some writing time.

Then... Benny happened.

He was free from large bills and any more responsibility other than just showing up for work, then going out drinking with the guys— *Ok, so it's devolved into me and Benny going out drinking. So what?* he once told himself.

Benny. His "best friend/roommate" from college. Not the sort of person that Gabe had ever imagined himself staying friends with after college, but... what the hell.

Most of their other friends had managed to either get their girlfriend pregnant, or missed coming home to someone. Or...they'd just settled. Settled down into the only life that they had ever actually been prepared for.

"Yeah. Settled is right," Benny had once said. "Settled right into the mud and rug rat scene," and then he'd fake shivered in disgust and laughed.

More than once, one of Gabe's girlfriends had brought up the Peter Pan thing. "You're just such a 'Lost Boy,' Gabriel. Aren't you ever going to grow up?"

"There are some fates worse than death," he told one of them, laughing grimly.

He had that degree from Georgetown, with his double major in English Literature and (mostly to please his father) Business Management. He also had his nice condo that he had bought after getting that degree and getting that "real job" right after college. He had settled down about as much as he wanted to.

He just hadn't gotten married yet. Hadn't made children yet. "It's not like I went off and did the whole Kerouac bohemian thing," he had told Jessica, the last "let's settle down and have children" girlfriend that Gabe had had just before Carol. That was four years ago.

And Gabe could have just about any woman he might meet in any bar that he and Benny went to regularly. But the "tigers in the sack" types always went for Benny, the "irresponsible one." The women (not girls) that inevitably got attracted to Gabe, also inevitably saw him as "a catch," and went after him.

"The whole 'make him and break him' thing," Benny had said one time. And laughed at another time and had said "Good husband material," mimicking what he heard "Some bitch in a pack" say while cupping her hands over her mouth and dishing with her girls. She had been eyeing Gabe hungrily before attacking him and working to seduce him into said husband-hood.

So Gabe had indeed just driven. Just not as far as he would have liked to in his mind.

He had headed up Connecticut Avenue, passing the bridges over Rock Creek and then the Zoo, and soon found himself in Chevy Chase before he knew what hit him. Waking up as he was heading into Chevy Chase Circle, he continued to drive around and around that circle, until he eventually turned onto Western Avenue.

"This is ridiculous," he muttered to himself. Part of him just wanted to find a bar and get wasted. *Let em' tow the car,* he thought. *I don't need one. Hell, I don't ever go anywhere.*

But he didn't. He continued driving on down Wisconsin Avenue, heading back downtown towards Dupont Circle. There he could park the car in his building and go to any of a dozen bars within walking distance of his place.

I can even go to a gay bar, and not have to deal with another woman, he thought. And then, *Too bad I'm not gay*, he thought some more. Solve a few problems, not the least of which would be getting rid of Benny. Benny hated gays; or at least the idea of being gay.

Somehow he found himself turning on to Massachusetts Avenue just past the National Cathedral, and then much further down, turning onto Rock Creek Parkway. From there it was just a short way down to P Street and his apartment (which conveniently was just off Rock Creek).

Thinking hard about trying not to think, he almost missed this turnoff and would have soon found himself passing the Watergate. Screeching tires as he made a split-second decision, he just managed to get off on the sharp curve in time, leaving a line of furiously honking cars behind him. He wasn't normally this reckless a driver, but Carol was a last straw. Something had to change.

He had eventually made the circuit of the one way streets around Dupont and P Street, and found the ramp leading down to the garage of his apartment building and parked. Turning off the ignition, he just sat there in silence. "What the hell am I doing?" he asked himself.

Gabe managed to open the door to his apartment and had successfully gotten himself inside before loosing any semblance of energy and momentum. Exhausted now, he threw the keys in the general direction of the end table that they lived on, not watching whether they landed or not.

Flicking on the lights instead of opening the thick curtains that were still drawn, he headed directly for the couch. Being a sparsely decorated bachelor's pad, this was about the only place to sit.

Throwing himself down on said couch, he reached down to

casually pick up the book he'd left laying there several days earlier. Tilting it above his head and pretending to read it for several minutes, Gabe finally closed it, letting it fall like a brick to the floor close to where it usually resided these days.

"No wonder I never make it to bed," he said, and fell asleep, exhausted.

FIVE

My life is so dull and repetitious these days, Angela began thinking again, careening into dark cloudy days of thoughts that lasted only minutes. Sure, Maddy helped to ease that, but then she went through periods where she felt overwhelmed by Maddy's regal-like presence.

For her part, Maddy would let her young friend call her when she wanted to resume going out. Maddy had other friends, but they weren't as ... engaging as Angela was. Lively. Maddy's other friends were like herself, only much older. Only Maddy had kept more of her energy than her friends had.

Why didn't she insist on being part of Frank's team, just like in the old days? Oh, right. That witch of an executive admin had pushed her out. *Why didn't I fight that?* she thought gloomily.

Because she had given up fighting. She let her husband work without interference from his wife, and Angela had become less and less interested in the agenda that Frank's staff had laid out for him. Always hewing to the Constituents' wishes. That was (supposedly) the job of a politician.

Oh, Frank had his pet projects that he was always working on. This is what kept him working at the office until late almost ever day. And

Frank insisted that he be on the floor of the Senate as much as possible, "Representing the People" as he said.

Sometimes lately though, Angela was becoming worried when Frank did finally make it home. He seemed exhausted, and sometimes even a little pale. She had begun to wonder if that witch, Evelyn Carothers, even bothered to keep her boss fed. Angela would have made sure of that. If she were still allowed to interfere, that is.

Angela was lost in her reverie, until the limo started slowing as the traffic was coming into the usual bottleneck surrounding the Maryland-Virginia Beltway Interchange. *Why is it that no one ever seems to know where they're going when they get here*, she thought, rolling up her window against the growing exhaust fumes.

Reaching the Capitol Beltway, Angela expected the limo to make the right turn heading north over the Great Falls Bridge and on into Maryland. Across the Bridge here, they would no doubt turn again onto Chain Bridge Parkway, the Maryland side equivalent of the George Washington Parkway and continue on south back into Georgetown. Maddy would drop her off at her house and Angela would be left to wonder what this short trip had been all about.

Except that the limo didn't turn right heading into Maryland. Instead it curved around to the left, which would dump them onto the Beltway heading west, keeping them solidly in Virginia. Was Maddy planning on taking them out into the country? Say, in the direction of Winchester and Skyline Drive? She had said "for the afternoon," but Angela was left wondering what sort of adventure this was after all.

She didn't have to wonder long about the direction, as they exited almost immediately onto Old Georgetown Pike, a two-lane winding country road which just about everybody treated as a four-lane highway.

Completely confounded now, Angela decided to allow Maddy her little excess as it were, and she soon found herself lost in the lush scenery and riot of spring flowers flowing that flew past her window here as well.

Rolling down her window once more to take in the fragrant breeze Angela thought, *It's a nice ride*, relaxing back into the seat to drink in the rolling beauty that was almost a blur at high speed outside her window. *I have nowhere else to go*, Angela told herself. *And if Frank does decide to come home early, it would still be well past nine before he would.*

And then she wondered suddenly why it even mattered to her at all. Whatever time her husband wandered home in the first place, was apparently out of her control anyway.

Maddy for her part was smiling to herself again, watching her friend finally unwind from her inner turmoil. *It won't be long now, dear*, she thought, turning her attention to the panorama outside her window as well.

Henry knows where to go, Maddy thought, letting herself drift into the sound of the wind coming in her window. *God knows he's done it enough times over the years.*

After what seemed to Angela like another half an hour of traveling, the limo finally turned right and left Old Georgetown Pike somewhere in Great Falls. The road they had turned onto a very roughly paved (if "paved" was what it should be called) road that was marked with large and very insistent No Trespassing signs in a periodic multitude on either side of it. Other than that, this appeared like any other private residence drive out here.

Except that it wasn't.

Awakened from her own reverie by both the turn and turn of events, Angela shot a very puzzled look at Maddy, who merely smiled secretly back at her once again.

"Are you taking me to some secret military base?" Angela asked playfully (she thought). In reality, her question had a nervous edge to it. Angela trusted Maddy and so didn't raise any objections, but this trip was getting curiouser and curiouser by each turn.

Maddy smiled for a couple of moments more, before saying (cryptically again), "Just you wait, my dear."

After another mile or so down this road, the trees thinned out into a clearing and a modest parking lot appeared off to the left.

Modest that is, except for Angela noticing that there were quite a number of limos (small and stretch) as well as town cars of modest size scattered about, with the occasional behemoth parked off to the side. Angela strained out her window, trying to take it all in. *Where is she taking me to?*

Shortly after this, their limo pulled into and around a (relatively) small circular driveway in front of what seemed like a (relatively) modest Tudor styled building.

Except that the size of this modest building didn't match the number of vehicles parked nearby.

And then there was the lavish Baroque-style fountain in the middle of the circle, complete with cherubs and swans gamboling in stone around frolicking gods and goddesses in positions that Angela thought might even make gods on Tantra friezes in India blush.

Rising up out of the middle of all of this was a central god-like swan reminiscent of Zeus in the Greek myth of the rape of Europa, which had water alternating between gurgling and erupting with a jet stream of water out of its mouth. Angela felt herself blushing at this, thinking that this was the most phallic and quite obscene sculpture that she had ever seen.

This whole fountain was almost the size of the fountains in front of the Library of Congress and the adjacent Capitol buildings downtown. It was quite more than it should be for a modest restaurant out in the country. It struck Angela as looking more like it belonged to some of the Tuscany hills villa estates in Italy that she and Frank had visited years ago.

And this is just a mere twenty miles north of DC, she thought. And then she also suddenly thought, *And this is just the OUTside.*

This grand fountain reeked of obvious wealth, and along with those who appeared to be in attendance ... All of this belied the illusion of anything approaching its rustic nature. That and some of the trees surrounding it were huge pines and oaks speaking of this modest establishment having resided here for many years if not centuries — and not being a recent addition to the landscape.

The simple sign that Angela saw framing the massive and ornately carved double doors that appeared to be the entrance, read modestly The Rendezvous Inn, without any further flourishes or other information. To Angela the signs and the setting screamed "seriously exclusive club" to her. What did all of this mean?

Looking at the now beaming Maddy, she was about to start asking her multitude of questions that this whole scenario brought up, but instead tried to quiet her mind, sighing deeply.

This place also screamed "mystery" to her. "Welcome to my secret little getaway," Maddy finally said, settling into a Cheshire cat-like smile. As if she were, indeed, one of the owners.

With her eyes still on Angela, Maddy said, "Thank you, Henry," to the air, as the door to each woman's side magically opened as if on cue.

"Where are —"

Maddy only beamed and gave her friend a grand royal flourish gesture towards her door.

From their respective sides, Maddy regally and then Angela hesitantly, stepped out of the limo with a helpful hand of a doorman who suddenly appeared on each woman's side.

The doormen were dressed as if they belonged to an embassy or some other similar high state official residence, and not some small rustic restaurant. Any more opulence to their uniforms and Angela would have thought that she might be stepping into a fairy tale at a castle, rather than a mere afternoon lunch.

Finding herself almost stunned into silence yet again, she whispered, "Maddy—"

"As the sign says," Maddy merely responded cryptically again. "The Rendezvous Inn."

After having assisted each woman completely out of the limo, each of these men bowed deeply and formally to their respective guest, as if they were arriving royalty, referring to both women as "Madame."

Angela turned around in a circle, as if indeed she were a fairy tale princess, in a fairy tale dream.

Not thinking she could get any more awe-struck, Angela realized that the town car had disappeared and the way was clear to the entrance. Quickly joining Maddy at the ornately carved door, she whispered before they entered, "What is this place? And why haven't I ever heard of this restaurant before?"

Turning to her friend and holding out her hand, "It's a very private club, with a very private — and quite exclusive — clientele," Maddy said matter of factly this time. And then with another Mona Lisa smile she added, "One must be introduced to it."

As they were about to pass under the sign (which now presented itself to Angela as an arch), the doorman suddenly appeared. He was dressed as if he were a Beefeater in London allowing entrance to Buckingham Palace.

He approached as if out of nowhere, and opened the front door. He beckoned with an Old World flourish once again, bowing low to make way for them to enter. He smiled discreetly, bowing his head in deference as the two women passed him to enter.

"Thank you, Jean Luc," Maddy added, continuing on inside the doors as if she owned the place.

Inside the seemingly small entrance that they had just passed through, the space expanded quite rapidly beyond the door. Having just left the bright, sunny woodland atmosphere outside, it took Angela's eyes several moments to adjust.

When she could see better, Angela found herself inside what looked from the outside to be the the whole of the restaurant. But inside she found that this — rotunda? — was merely the beginning. It was largely empty, but with a grand mural painted in the arc of the dome, and what looked to Angela to be ancient wall hangings surrounding them below that.

To add to the royal flourish, there were knights dressed in medieval armor stationed at regular intervals, all around the cavernous room. "What are they guarding?" Angela whispered in awe.

"Sometimes my dear, a suit of armor is just a suit of armor," Maddy said with a loving wink, taking Angela's hand in hers once more and leading her further inward.

They had not gone very far when Angela found herself at the top of a long, broad, steeply descending staircase that led down into a cavernous space into which the light seemed to disappear below. If Maddy hadn't suddenly taken her hand, she might have lost her balance and fallen headlong into this darkness.

Suddenly Angela realized that this restaurant was actually a much larger building than she could have ever imagined. It appeared to be built into the very hillside itself — that the building which she had seen from the outside was merely the entrance to a much more ominous... What?

"Oh, my—" she whispered again, sounding even to herself as if she were a little child in a cathedral. What had she allowed Maddy to get her into?

Realizing that she was staring off into this space and that Maddy was no longer by her side, she looked around and found Maddy waiting patiently at the bottom of this staircase, looking up at her and still smiling and waving for her to follow from the shadows below.

Growing silent in her inability to take all of this in, Angela turned once again to find her friend standing beside her, as if she had magically ascended the stairs once more and was once again smiling that maddeningly Mona Lisa-like smile. It was now Madelaine Lightfoot's turn to gesture grandly towards the bottom where she had just been.

"Come, my dear," Maddy said in a hush. "Wonder and privilege awaits."

Was Angela being mesmerized? Was her friend actually some kind of a witch or a wizard, initiating her into far more than a mere restaurant? She shook her head, as if to ward off the spell.

It seemed to Angela that, like Alice, this was a rabbit hole that only got larger and larger the further she tumbled emotionally into it. It had both the feel of ancient mustiness and mystery to it, but mixed with the smell of it being regularly cleaned within an inch of its life with only the finest of oils.

Angela had only felt this way before the time or two that she and Frank had visited Europe; and taken tours of ancient castles and had been treated to the Royal Touch.

Without Maddy there to gently warn her with a touch, she would have been heading for a real tumble, as she was still looking everywhere but where her feet were taking her. Shock and awe were making her face comically child-like in her unfamiliarity.

Having both had children and having been here many times before herself, Maddy for her part took hold of the still bewildered Angela, deftly guiding the two of them down.

At the point where the stairs gave way to yet another expansive circular domed foyer and meeting space, Maddy stopped. Following in Maddy's wake once more, Angela walked over to meet Maddy some distance away again.

With a child-like awe, Angela asked Maddy, "Are we there yet?"

Slipping her arm around Angela's and subtly taking charge, Maddy patted her hand gently and began leading her further down the rabbit hole.

At this next level, the walls on either side of them were studded with ornate paintings now, in even more ornate gilded frames. The ceiling above her seemed to be gilded in gold as well, although she couldn't tell whether this was fake or not. The dark cavernous nature of this room only accentuated the ancient feel to the place. Burgundy velvet and gold inlay seemed to be the color scheme.

Also filled with what seemed like potted plants and small potted trees (which were actually growing in and up from the floor), this large room was also interspersed with the suits of medieval armor, only this time equipped with spears and shields.

This atrium once more had the feel of a castle to it, rather than a mere restaurant. As if this place had been here for centuries. Angela was feeling more dwarfed by the feel of this place than she had been even in the Dome of the Capitol when she had first arrived many years ago.

It also had the feel of St. Peter's, but was decorated once again with much the same motif that was evident in the Fountain outside. The scenes in the paintings were of frolicking gods and goddesses, having sex in just about every position imaginable, with the occasional human interspersed usually at the mercy of the gods.

Angela imagined she could feel the power of many a large gathering that had graced this space in the past, yet it was now largely empty. They were alone except for several staff appearing and disappearing around them, seeming oblivious to their presence and with their eyes appropriately glancing downward; they seemed engrossed in whatever their tasks were.

Suddenly, however, she noticed one person who was actually directing her gaze at them. A small woman who reminded Angela of the stereotypical gypsy women she'd seen in some old films came over to greet them formally with a very deep and warm bow.

When she spoke finally, it was with a heavily accented French voice, raspy as if from decades of over-indulgence from smoking Le Gallois cigarettes. "Madame Lightfoot. How have you been?"

The Greeter, as she was known, both formal and informal through her years of service and having given many such greetings to an obviously well-loved patron, was not on a first name basis with Maddy. But she seemed very close to it.

"Madame Toussaint," Maddy bowed, greeting her back and returning the favor, as if to an old friend.

Turning towards Angela, Maddy added, "I would like to introduce you to my friend, Madame Treworthy. She will be one of your latest, and I hope, also one of your long-term guests."

Madame Toussaint bowed quite formally, as if being introduced to a princess or a queen. "Madame. I am so glad to meet you. Madame Lightfoot has graced us with so few initiates in the past, I am sure that you are of the most rare personage."

"Initiates?" Angela thought. *What kind of a secret life has Maddy had?*

Turning to Maddy once again, Madame Toussaint said, "I will inform Antonio of your arrival."

To Angela, she added, "I do hope that you find your dealings with Le Rendezvous to your pleasure and your comfort. Please inform me if there are any deficiencies at all in any of your stays with us."

Bowing once again, Madame Toussaint turned and retreated to her office, her greeting officially done.

"Thank you," was all that Angela could manage to whisper in her direction.

"Come, my dear. You must be famished by now," Maddy gently

told her, directing her toward a waiting hallway leading towards a brightly lit doorway off in the distance.

Numbly following her friend's lead, Angela began walking in her wake and found herself once again being guided down this long, dark and very French corridor.

As they walked, Angela noticed that the decor here was at once both very ornate (being filled with many objets d'art of different periods), but in some ways also austere at the same time. The lushness of the grand foyer had transitioned to the stateliness of an embassy again.

Angela felt as though she had stepped into one of the most exclusive art museums in the world, or that by continuing down the hall, she would come to yet another grand staircase. Or had somehow been transported to make some grand entrance at a state reception.

Except that she felt more and more like a child rather than visiting royalty.

Awash in strange feelings that she couldn't completely fathom, Angela thought she had seen it all. After having been the wife of a U.S. Senator for so many years, she had grown accustomed to Franklin's family and their grand blue-blood soirees and fetes, and yet here she was still feeling awed. As if she were standing in a place that kings and queens had regularly visited, and that even she was slightly out of place here.

"What *is* this place?" she finally managed to ask in hushed tones in Maddy's direction. She almost felt unsure of how she should even act in such a place as this.

"I know, my dear," Maddy told her nonchalantly and a little loudly. "It was a trifle overwhelming to me as well when I was first brought here." Stopping, turning and smiling at her friend's feeling of overwhelm, she added, "But you'll get used to it."

Winking and taking her young friend's hand once more, "I did."

After walking further down this long hall than she would have assumed they would need to walk, owing to the apparent size of the building she had seen from out front, they finally stepped across a threshold and into a large, dark and cavernous banquet room. Or so it seemed.

Maddy slowed to a stop, and Angela followed her lead. As if by magic, a tall, thin, balding and very French-like man, dressed formally in a maitre d' suit appeared behind them.

Maddy turned and bowed formally to this man as well.

"Antonio," she acknowledged.

"Madame," he returned, bowing deeply and long. Once he had risen out of his obeisance, he turned his hand into an "apres vous" gesture, pointing toward what appeared to Angela as the dining area. He turned crisply, and Maddy followed.

Angela once again stood as if frozen in place. She was past asking questions of her friend, but was also still awed by her surroundings. Eventually she followed.

She entered what appeared to be a smallish room, although she could now hear that there was an indefinite buzz to the place. She was detecting a low-pitched faint murmuring as if there were a great many voices all around them.

This mysterious sound only intensified as she and Maddy walked towards a wall of glass appearing on the right, above a row of intimate and lushly appointed booths. These were separated sufficiently to give each one a sense of its own privacy.

She suddenly realized that what she was hearing was hushed conversations in progress all around them. The rise and fall of these hushed intimacies sounded much like that of either a waterfall or ocean surf, with the occasional peal of wild laughter breaking through and ringing out of the hush. As her eyes adjusted to the seeming darkness, Angela now saw that there was the flickering of candlelight everywhere, adding to the intimate setting.

The scene that was appearing to Angela out of that former darkness was backlit by the mural that the right-hand wall seemed to glow with. It seemed to be of stained glass and depicted a woodland scene, in motion as if it were on a huge, wall-like TV screen.

Suddenly, Angela realized that this was no mural, but was actually a huge plate glass window. It rose from just behind the booths she had previously thought were the full extent of this dining room, and continued up to meet the ceiling that she was only just now perceiving. This room, too, she realized, was a dome-like cathedral of immense size, hinting as to being some sort of grand cavern she could even now barely guess the size of.

As they continued their journey and got closer to the light now obviously streaming in from the outside, Angela began to make out figures in the semi-darkness around and below them.

Men and women were spread throughout this maze. But then she also began recognizing that there were one or two same-sex couples around here and there, most of whom were in closely intimate discussions and oblivious to anyone else.

As they continued their grand entrance, Maddy would occasionally glance at one or another of the couples at a table they would pass, nodding acknowledgement discreetly and occasionally getting a slight rise and bow from some in response.

Angela for her part, was also occasionally recognizing one or the other of the couple that she and Maddy knew, but not recognizing the person that they were obviously there being intimate with.

There were married men and women here who were carrying on close and physically intimate converse with persons who were neither their husbands nor their wives. And like as not, carrying on with more touch than words. Very intimate touch in the case of one couple, she noticed, who were all but climbing over each other.

She looked away at the realization that hands were in very intimate places that in public would attract both notice and police. Her shock returned and deepened to the point of numbness, when the obviousness of the reality of this place began choking her emotionally.

Once inside and sitting at the booth that the maitre d' Antonio was gesturing to, their guide through this maze of intimate display finally had them at their table. He bowed deeply once more, and disappeared as silently as he had come.

Angela turned slowly to find that Maddy was already seated, as if this was her throne. Angela slowly slipped herself into the plushly appointed side of the booth across from her.

Looking now at the window to her right, she noticed that what she had thought was streaming light in from the outside, was actually muted with a film that gave the scene outside both a soft, surreal glow with an out of focus hush of its own.

Even with that film, it took Angela's eyes time once again to adjust to the high contrast difference between the outside, and... Her attention wanting to be drawn to something familiar, she took in the scene outside.

Just beyond this window were similarly large and ancient trees as she had seen out front. But by rising slowly and slightly from the booth cushion, she found that she could look — down. The trees she was seeing were rooted in the ground a hundred feet or so below her, almost perched on the level of the river itself.

Curiouser and curiouser, Angela began to stretch further (and in a very un-lady-like fashion), lifted herself up to see as far as her view downwards would allow.

What she could also suddenly see however, was that the whole building was perched high atop a cliff overlooking the Potomac. And that the Falls and their huge boulders were spread out seemingly far below. With her still child-like gaze of wonder, Angela found herself pressing her face close to the glass to stare out at the scene below, trying to take it all in.

I feel as if I could almost reach out and touch the rocks of Great Falls below us, she also suddenly realized. That indeed, this portion of the restaurant was on a shelf cantilevered out over this View.

But those trees, while allowing her the view out, effectively blocked any view from below to indicate that there was even a building here. Feeling uneasy (but in a very different way now), she quickly pulled herself back in and found her seat.

"Impressive. Isn't it?" Maddy asked her, her Cheshire smile now a very satisfied one. She was secretly quite happy, as she had managed to reintroduce awe to her young friend. *Surely this will help elevate your sour mood,* Maddy thought.

Turning away from the window, Angela let her eyes focus on the interior that had seemed beyond her perception earlier. By elevating herself from her divan once more, she could see more detail as her eyes adjusted away from the scene outside.

To her left, there was a path below them that had previously been barely perceivable in the darkness, that was like a nautilus shell descending down into the pit of darkness in the center. She almost wanted to lean over the close-by low wall for a clearer look.

But somehow the sounds that were echoing softly up from below her were enough to tell her that she did not need her curiosity to be confirmed and have her intruding in affairs that she was still coming to grips with that seemed to be happening all around them.

This space she was in seemed both huge, as well as very, very intimate to her at the same time, as if it was some sort of womb. She also soon saw the very distinct vault to it, which accounted for the sound of hush amidst the labyrinth.

As if she sensed what her friend was thinking, Maddy leaned in and said (in an equally hushed voice), "Where angels fear to tread."

Angela's eyes were now both accustomed to the light pouring in, and were also still naively wide open as well.

She has quite the haunted look, Maddy thought. *Was I wrong in bringing her here even now?*

"Why have I never heard of this place before?" With the mist of knowing in her eyes, "I mean... Why?"

Quietly appraising her young friend for a long time, Maddy smiled again before resuming, deciding to go for the full explanation. Of the place, and of their reason for being here. "The nature of this place is not such that ... even a senator's wife is necessarily going to—" Maddy gestured with air quotes "—'hear' of it. Its very presence is a well-guarded secret. It is one that is known only to those who are needful of knowing of it."

Still wearing a completely befuddled look on her face with a tangled mass of emotions behind it and even more tangled thoughts behind that, another realization crossed Angela's mind. "So... Why are you *initiating* me now?"

Looking at Angela very knowingly, Maddy said, "Why have you been in such a frightful mood lately, Mrs. Treworthy?"

"Mrs...?" Angela was taken aback by Maddy using that formality again with her after all these years.

Even now she was still finding herself unable to tell Maddy everything. Even to admit everything she was feeling perhaps even to herself. It simply seemed to just be beyond her. "I... I just don't know anymore, Maddy. I guess I'm just tired of being a senator's wife."

"Yes? And?"

Blushing at this bold statement and looking down suddenly, Angela began taking an extraordinary interest in the place settings on the table resting near her hands. "And..." shaking her head, "nothing. I guess."

Trying to brush the thoughts she didn't want out of her head, she repeated, "Nothing," shaking her head insistently and altogether too defiantly.

Maddy, while still having a compassionate look in her eyes, steeled her voice to force the issue. "My dear Angela. How long have we known each other now?"

With her head still bowed and her emotions churning like the river below, she was trying her best to be nonchalant. "I don't know. Fifteen, sixteen years. Why?"

Silent for another moment, Maddy dipped her head down closer to the table and looked up, trying to catch Angela's downcast eyes.

Feeling her friend's focus, Angela reluctantly lifted her eyes up sheepishly to meet Maddy's gaze. Her innocent look evaporated into a frown on seeing Maddy's earnestness. She was ready to laugh all of this off, but some emotion suddenly caught in her throat.

"And would you say that, as your best friend, I might know you fairly well?" Maddy asked.

Afraid of what was coming, Angela asked with a sinking feeling, "Ok, Maddy. What are you getting at?"

Looking pleased to have finally breached her friend's outer protective wall, Maddy sat up erect and looked Angela directly in the eye. With a look of brutal honesty that Angela had only seen once or twice, Maddy said with a tinge of sadness. "I've seen many other wives of congressmen go through what you're going through now, Angela."

Looking askance and trying to find something terribly of interest outside the window close by, Angela could only ask, "And?"

Leaning across the table in what seemed suddenly to Angela as a totally uncharacteristic and unladylike expression, Maddy made sure she got Angela's attention before speaking again. "You've been a senator's wife for what? Almost twenty years now?"

Not wanting to admit what Maddy already knew, she replied with a reluctant "Yes."

"And you've done all the congressional wifely things — heading ladies auxiliaries; working for all the right charities; attending all of the right dinners of state required of you. You've also worked in your husband's office, studied all of the legislation that Franklin had deemed important for you to know. Advising him on what you'd gleaned to balance out all of the nonsense his other handlers and advisors trot out for him."

Beginning to feel the weight of all of those years and activities pressing in, Angela was surprised to find that she almost felt like screaming.

Pausing, both for effect and out of compassion, Maddy continued to look at her friend intently in a take-no-prisoners stare. Seeing the pain and remembering back to her years of responsibility and emptiness, she stated softly in a voice that spoke daggers of loss, "And now you're bored out of your mind."

Sitting back in a way that almost suggested a man of power herself, Maddy continued. "Without being able to go with Franklin overseas as often on congressional trips now that spending on junkets have become so tight and without feeling like going overseas alone, you feel trapped. You're still an alive, competent woman, but with no challenges left.

"And—" Maddy seemed to go in for the kill, "now you're feeling empty."

"Yes," Angela whispered, with a volume which was almost more of a breath than words. With the internal dam of denial about to break, she looked up at her friend with tears forming in her eyes. The weight of all that she had been denying was about to come crashing in. She looked to her mentor for an answer.

Tersely Maddy continued (with a hint of her own underlying pain), "Of course, you could always go out and get a job. Be another Barbara Dole, for instance. Or even Hillary Clinton for that matter. Use your experience and connections to do more than merely act as a figurehead to whatever charity or good works organization you're working for."

Bouncing now back and forth from the emotions of wanting to cry and wanting to shout, Angela was feeling trapped at the seeming absurdity of her situation. "Being the wife of a U.S. senator, you'd think I'd have more options..." she said through her tears, feeling the saltiness washing what makeup she wore down her cheeks.

"Angela, my dear. You do have more options," Angela heard Maddy saying, rather matter of factly. "What you need is an affair."

Looking up meekly, unsure of whether she had really heard what she thought she had just heard, she didn't know how to respond. *Maybe it was a joke?* Angela thought.

Except that looking up fully now, she saw that Maddy was intently waiting for a response. Any response. Looking out of the corner of her eyes once more in the direction of the riotous green and other colors outside Angela suddenly thought, *Maybe I'm dreaming all of this. I'll wake up, and this will all just be—*

Looking away from the glass, she saw that her friend was still looking quite intently at her. She was beginning to realize that this wasn't the dream that she hoped it would be, but was distinctly a reality.

Her previous mood broken, she was brought forcefully back with the shock that Maddy was being quite serious. "I'm sorry, Maddy. What did you just say?" she asked with a hard laugh.

Maddy, smiling once again and looking younger than she had ever before, repeated what she had said. "I said, Angela Walker Barnes Treworthy. What you *need* is an affair."

There it was. The utterly ridiculous statement that she thought that she had heard. Coming out of the mouth of someone whom she would never have thought — never in a million years — would be saying such a ridiculous thing.

*She **must** be joking,* Angela thought. *That's just it. She must be* *joking. Except*—

"You need something to take your mind off how much time you have on your hands."

Looking around them nervously to see if someone had heard what Maddy had just said, Angela noted instead that nothing had changed. No one around them was listening. In fact, no one even appeared to be in the least bit interested in listening.

The scattered couples she saw around them were only interested in each other. The walls still stood. The sun still shone outside the large window next to her and didn't dim. No apocalypse was about to begin.

She sat in silence. And Maddy, showing a patience that Angela would never have suspected, sat in silence waiting for any reply.

Every once in a while Angela now recognized, that one or more of the couples that she had been noticing here and there around the room, had risen from their tables. They were leaving by one of the various side doors that she now noticed were very much in evidence around the shadowy edges of this enormous room.

Some of these doors opened with a light suddenly stabbing into the darkness, extinguished only by the shadows of the figures exiting and the door closing again. Some of them only opened on the appearance of the darkness of what Angela could only guess were corridors leading to other areas. *How big is this place?* the thought suddenly came.

She also realized that there were no checks being left and no money was changing hands (as far as she could see). And even more couples were still arriving every so often as well.

Angela looked soberly around the room, realizing for the first time this afternoon that she didn't really need to whisper. That everyone here had secrets to keep. And that she and Maddy weren't alone.

Indeed, she was now comprehending (with increasing clarity) that this was the whole reason for the being in this place in the first place — in the keeping of and manufacturing of — even more secrets.

Feeling slightly dizzy from all of this, Angela turned once again to be met with a once again Cheshire cat-like smile from her friend. To Angela it said, *Do you see now?* Angela was still feeling incredulous though, as if she had indeed stepped through the Looking Glass itself.

"But why an affair?" she asked Maddy wearily now. "Why not suggest that I get a job? Or adopt another charity to do good deeds for? Or maybe even adopt a child?"

She was even feeling that she was heading towards the exhausted side. As if the great expenditure of energy that she had been bending towards keeping this secret from even herself, had exhausted her supply and she needed to sleep now.

"I mean... Why an affair of all things, Maddy," she asked, feeling on the verge of tears again. "I mean, after what Bill Clinton has just gone through?"

Adopting another attitude that Angela hadn't seen before, Maddy looked more directly at Angela than she ever had before. Angela was seeing the steely-eyed look of a strategizing politician, not a senator's wife.

Except that she was being calculating without being cold. It was still chilling to her that Angela had never seen this side of her friend before, but only the matronly look of friendship.

This was the look of power. Real power. And it scared Angela more than just a little bit, coming from this friend she thought she knew so well.

"My dearest Angela... I know what it's like. To be an intelligent, independent and capable woman, but always being relegated to playing the good wife. The helper. Denying my own aspirations. Setting all my will aside in public to help support my husband. Always standing by your man.

"Not all of us can be a Hillary or Tipper. And even they haven't had the power that they wanted. God knows, Hillary has tried. Sometimes I think that that was the whole reason she married Bill in the first place. As a stepping stone to power. And now look where it's gotten her.

"Who knows? Maybe she might even be a senator some day, but that's all in the future for now."

Still somehow at a loss to see the connection, Angela still had to ask her friend yet again, "But— Maddy. Why an *affair*?"

Sitting back and losing the edge that Angela had seen, Maddy softened, retreating inwards once again. "If you were the mothering sort, of course, I'd suggest adopting a child. But you're not." Her piercing blue eyes looked up again, and were now starting to make Angela feel very uncomfortable once more.

Maddy, sensing that she was losing Angela, softened her gaze and lowered her head slightly. She laughed a giddy little laugh. With a certain wistfulness seeping into her eyes now and looking up, she said quietly, "I know how hard it was for you to find out that you couldn't have any children of your own."

With a look of questionable reason, Maddy seemed to be almost on the verge of tears now herself. "But to tell you the truth Angela, dearest. As much as I love my own children, I was never really meant to be a mother, either." She smiled away the tears, saying, "And I sense the same about you."

Angela, taking this in, felt herself about to melt into tears. She realized that what her wizened friend was saying was true, whether she liked it or not. That she had as much as known this without being able to acknowledge it. That she was even now realizing that this was a part of the pain she had been feeling; that stab of emptiness.

Taking a deep, almost rattling sigh, she was finally accepting all of it. Frank. Her life as a senator's wife, with the hopelessness that she had been feeling...

"But, Maddy," she asked much more softly again. "Why cheating on my husband? Is that really what I should do? Is that what you would have done in my—"

Sitting back suddenly on to her throne, Maddy struck another totally uncommon pose for her. Placing her arms with her hands locked behind her head, Maddy locked eyes with Angela and admitted, "Yes, as a matter of fact. I would, and I have."

Angela thought now was that she was about to die. Her jaw was falling open as she tried to say something, but couldn't — several times. She didn't know whether to laugh or cry now, feeling more completely lost than ever.

"Surely, you're joking," was all she could finally manage to get out.

Without any hint of irony, sarcasm or jest, Maddy said levelly, "No, my dear. I most assuredly am not."

Maddy's admission finally hitting home, Angela's mind was racing. With her mind more than just a little upset, she couldn't figure out what to say next. "I— I couldn't do— that."

Matter of factly once again, Maddy countered with, "Of course you could. I did."

Relaxing her arms, and again uncharacteristically crossing them across her chest, Maddy asked seriously, "Don't you ever wonder what he's really doing in the office till all hours of the day and night?"

All of a sudden, Angela felt embarrassed. "No. Of course not. Why should I?" she said, a little too defensively.

"But suppose he *is* having an affair?"

Almost bursting out laughing at this, Angela didn't even know why. She had never really entertained the idea that her husband would have an affair. It was just so — not Frank. She had pursued him. She had fought to win him.

Of course, that was a different age. Or so she thought. "
rank? He would never—"

"And just how did you meet your husband-to-be?"

"You remember! I—" Angela started to say "at work," but stopped. "I just—"

"Met him when you first joined his campaign for the state senate, lo these many years ago. And he could still be doing the same thing today. God only knows there are enough possibilities running around in short skirts with great ambitions."

Fear suddenly began seeping in as Angela started considering this. She began going over and over in her mind, searching her memory for any possible signs of her husband's potential indiscretions.

After a few moments of reconstruction, she could recall several of Frank's assistants, aides — and yes, even a few interns — that she had felt might have been interested in her husband. And then she brushed any concerns aside again.

Frank was so single minded when he was at work, she could even tell he was distracted when she called. She had watched him at work, phone in one hand or cradled on his shoulder, creating a neck ache and one or both hands shuffling papers, going through the piles on his desk that he called "organization."

And then she realized something else and replied, laughing, "Oh. He's having an affair of course. Like you told me earlier."

"An affair with politics and power," Maddy said, nodding. "No other lover is ever going to gain his attention as much as politics. Including you, my dear." She sighed. "Unfortunately."

All of Angela's fears, exasperation and boredom were suddenly blowing into a gale force wind in her mind, and they were rising to the surface like so much flood wreckage. *This is why I've been feeling like I was drowning*, she thought.

With all the years that she had felt that she was both wanted and unwanted, she ceased to wonder that he had never wanted any children. She couldn't even remember the last time that she and Frank had even made love.

"The political life," she said, now with enough venom in her voice that Angela didn't know whether to laugh or cry again.

She leaned in to reach for Maddy's hands for comfort. "When I first married Frank, I reveled in the glamour. Always being in the spotlight. Being known. Not just being... one of the crowd. But it's gotten stale. My God, Maddy. I can't believe now how stale it's gotten. Even on the campaign trail..." she started to say, and fell silent.

Maddy said nothing and let her work through her pain.

"Maybe if I had only spent a little more time with Frank..."

"I understand completely," Maddy said, patting Angela's hand lovingly.

Shaking her head sadly, Angela continued. "Lately though, it seems as if he's always working, always meeting with this constituent or that lobbyist. Even when we have a vacation, it's usually still just some thinly disguised form of work.

"Going back home," she said, choking back her tears and throwing her arms helplessly in the air. "Home. My God, what a concept!" she said, laughing grimly. "Home is still meeting with constituents. And even more constituents. Honestly, I don't even remember why I go back there with him any more."

Pausing and raising her finger dramatically, and waving it in the air, almost choking on what she was saying. "Yes, I remember now. To be the good wife! To present the image of the perfect political couple, in order for Frank to be on a good footing for the next election."

Both women were both laughing and crying now. Angela for her pain, and Maddy for her remembrance of her same realizations, all those years ago.

After having dried her eyes with the napkin at hand, Angela asked only half seriously, "Maddy? Why did we ever want to be politicians' wives?"

Only answering with a knowing smile, Maddy waited for Angela to finish having her catharsis.

Angela, at a loss now that all of the anger and disappointment that she had felt pent up inside of her had finally begun seeping out, allowed herself to now fully break down in full tears, uncaring of who might see.

Maddy for her part, resisted the urge to rise and go over and comfort her friend. If Angela was going to change anything, she was going to have to do it herself.

After a few minutes, Angela reached for the napkin again to dry her eyes. She couldn't help herself, but she felt on the verge of laughing wildly again.

Instead, she sighed. Suddenly freed from the burden of not knowing what it was that had been bothering her so much without her actually allowing herself to be knowing, it was almost as if she felt that she was so light now that she was in danger of floating away.

She had been bowing her head for the last few minutes. When she looked up, she felt the most glowing and loving smile radiating from Maddy. More than she felt she had ever experienced before.

Reaching some point of resolution in herself, Angela started to ask tentatively (for the fun of it), "So...", and then stopped herself, laughing again at the whole absurdity of the thing. Angela asked her friend, "So. Just how does one go about having an affair? Just out of curiosity, that is."

"Especially when someone like us might be recognized, you mean?" Maddy asked. "Especially in the age of Monica Lewinsky?"

"Well, yes. That too."

Pleased that her friend had finally reached this critical point, Maddy began, "Well, now. You need to start by not going after someone who knows who you are. And who thinks that they have something to *gain* by *knowing* who you are."

Pausing to wave the waiter over, she said brightly, "But first, let's start with one of the simpler items in this whole — situation."

As the waiter arrived with their menus in hand, Maddy answered brightly with, "Let's order lunch. Shall we?"

S I X

Gabe was waking up to a darkened room that was much darker than when he had drifted off to sleep. Starting out of sleep from yet another ex-girlfriend dream, he'd almost fallen off the couch until he remembered where he was. And also that he wasn't in his bed. Yet again.

He groaned as if he'd been out drinking all night, even though he hadn't taken a single drink. Plus he also realized, it was still day out and not night, the sun peaking out from under the bottom of the curtains.

Am I getting a cold? he thought, and then decided, *Maybe I need a drink and I'm just going through withdrawal. Bad sign in either case for a bartender.*

Gabe had once been someone who wasn't even much of a drinker. That was most definitely his friend Benjamin Harrison's fault.

Benny was a drinker and a heavy one at that. And for all Gabe knew, he'd probably been one from the moment he could hoist a fifth or a mug to his mouth. Carol was right on that one point: Benny had been a bad influence on him from the word go.

But Benny was the only other one of their friends who hadn't taken the plunge — i.e. gone and gotten married, had children, gotten a regular job, etc. He'd become his only friend by default.

Yeah, by default all right. By de fault of you never wanting to go out and meet new people, one of his other ex-girlfriends, Karen, had once told him. All of his girlfriends after a while sang that same old chorus of the grow-up song and dance. If he didn't hate the idea so much, he might almost agree with them.

Benny was a failed playwright in his own estimation. "Not gonna be followin' in the Bard;s footsteps any time soon," he used to joke. Once upon a time. "What's the use in thinkin' when all my time's spent drinkin'," was one of his favorite jokes. Except that it had long since ceased being much of a joke to Gabe.

Sighing and rolling over, he slowly got off the couch and reached up and turned on the light on the end table there. "Shit," was all he could manage to say and think. "Good thing I'm not on schedule to work tonight."

He hesitated to look in the direction of his answering machine. He knew no doubt when he did, the message light would be blinking.

Whether the message was one from The Globe with their boss wondering if he could come in tonight anyway, or one of Benny screaming into the phone, "Where the hell are you, dude?"

Or perhaps Carol? Leaving one last excoriating message for him as a rejoinder to his misery? In any case, he really didn't feel like finding out.

Not really wanting to, he slowly eased himself off the couch with a groan. *No reason to be so dramatic*, he thought. He wasn't hurting (at least physically) and he was in pretty good shape even for being twenty-eight years old. "All of that up and down with the bar glasses," he'd once joked to one of his now long-forgotten female escapades. Funny how many of them he'd forgotten in the meantime.

Of course he was not like Benny. For Benny, his life was filled with nondescript, "What's her name?" sex as the standard order of the day. And God knows, he always seemed to find his mark.

Gabe had been through his one-night-stand period, but then grew tired of it and began having relationships again. *Maybe it's time to go back to "no expectations" sex myself*, he thought. *Follow in Benny's footsteps for a while. No expectations, no regrets.*

Except he was wanting more. Not the "settle down and make babies" more, but... Something.

Hauling himself up off the couch, he headed towards the kitchen and the fridge. *A little afternoon libations should solve the crisis for now*, he thought rather blurredly.

As he walked past the several diplomas on the wall he no longer saw (they reminded him a little too much that he had once had high hopes), he carefully avoided the still standing picture of himself and Carol sitting on the breakfast counter.

"Why do I even put them in picture frames anymore?" he once asked to know one in particular.

Once on the other side of the recent madness, he flipped the frame over so he wouldn't have to avoid glancing in her direction. He'd deal with removing the photo of the late and great Carol later, putting the frame away (until another woman reluctantly took Carol's place in the same frame later).

Opening the fridge, he reached in and hefted out his pitcher of the always available "cool aid" — the tradition of which was handed down to him via his father who had the similar habit (much to his mother's chagrin).

Gabe switched back and forth between it being gin and tonic and vodka and tonic, always (sort of) freshly made usually for just such an occasion (his transitions in and out of relationships of late becoming a ready source of "pulling for the pitcher").

Only this time he automatically poured a tall glass, and then uncharacteristically, set it back down on the counter without even taking a sip. Pulling the bar stool over and sitting down, he put his head in his hands on the countertop and wondered, *What the hell **am** I doing?*

Thinking back to the grand plans that his mother and father had had for him, he laughed grimly. Lifting the tumbler of "cool aid" up as if in a toast to them, he muttered, "But then I guess, Da, your life didn't exactly fall out as planned either. Did it?"

But then thinking back to his Irish heritage he said, "Or maybe it did. And I'm just following in your own blessed footsteps."

He didn't look forward to going back to work. He'd be confronted by Benny, and with Gabe's lack of a poker face, would be outed by his friend and made to confess his sins (or lack thereof).

"Maybe I should have become a priest," he said to the empty kitchen yet again.

S E V E N

Having had a wonderfully satisfying meal, Angela was finding herself as close to relaxed as this whole afternoon would find her. Digesting her thoughts while trying to digest her food had not been easy however.

She was still however in a state of shock at this whole afternoon's sudden twist. Her realizations of her growing dissatisfaction and Maddy's subsequent bombshells had nearly exhausted her.

Turning to stare once again out the huge window to her right, she drank in the scenery, using it as a balm and a block to the turmoil boiling inside her head.

Returning to the remains of her meal, she glanced up to find Maddy intently staring at her. "How long have you been looking at me like that?"

Smiling her most compassionate smile yet, Maddy asked, "Does it matter?

"The only thing that really matters my dear, is that I understand what you are going through. I went through it myself many years ago. Unfortunately though, I had to go through it all by myself. There was no one else that I thought that I could turn to.

"It was a very different age back then. I didn't know who I could turn to. Or who I could trust."

Her eyes turning inward for a moment, Maddy sighed and then laughed abruptly. Looking back up after a moment, she focused once again on her young friend, who was now taking the role of looking concerned and compassionate herself.

"Even though the 1960s had happened, I'm afraid that the 1970s still weren't exactly peace and free love in my circles. Women who had affairs, however discreetly, were still unheard of." Pausing and smiling with a mischievous grin, "And very much frowned upon if found out, shall we say."

Laughing a nervous laugh, Maddy suddenly sighed furiously. Looking up again, her defenses were down completely, in a vulnerable manner that Angela never thought she'd ever see in her.

This afternoon is absolutely full of surprises, Angela thought.

"So I did what the loyal politician's wife did — suffered in silence. I kept up the Good Front."

Then a deliciously wicked smile crept into her dour expression. "That is, until I met Remy."

Like two school girls leaning in to whisper sharing a wicked little secret, these two women, one in her late 70s and the other in her early 40s, drew together conspiratorially across the table and across the years. Angela whispered, "Who?"

Maddy suddenly looked many years younger, and had both a present gleam in her eyes, and a girlish faraway gaze as well. "I met him at a formal embassy affair. I had known him before, of course. I had seen him all over, but had never met him.

"But... His reputation proceeded him."

Getting almost beside herself with her curiosity working overtime Angela, (like a teenager sharing a delicious secret) prompted, "So... Who was he?"

By now, Maddy's eyes were beginning to glaze over with a sheen of tears. "Oh. Only one of the most romantic men in the world." Pausing now out of nostalgia, she finally said softly, "George Remy."

"George Remy?" Pausing for a second, Angela tried to remember who— And then all of a sudden asked incredulously, "You mean, The George Remy? As in the French Ambassador George Remy?"

Sitting back a little less misty and a little more in control now, she smiled broadly. "Yes. That George Remy."

Angela found herself without anything to either think or say. The shocks just kept on getting larger.

"So you see, my dear," Maddy leaned back in again intently. "It is possible. Even in our circles."

Angela had forgotten whatever feelings of boredom and frustration she had been feeling, so caught up in this exquisitely delicious secret Maddy was sharing. All of a sudden, pieces of the puzzle of her life were falling into place, and she was no longer on the same level that she was this morning.

"But... Where would you go to, to — you know — enjoy his company?" Angela asked, as if she were asking her mother whether the tooth fairy was really real.

Sitting up with a most mischievous smile arcing across her face and gesturing grandly once more with her arms opened wide, Maddy smiled serenely. "Why... Here, of course. Why exactly do you think that I brought us out here today?"

Looking around herself suspiciously and now feeling completely confused again, Angela stared dumbfoundedly. "But... This is just a restaurant," she said, with all innocence once again.

The thoughts of what those other patrons surrounding them had been doing in this restaurant had not crossed her mind at the moment. Pausing at a total loss even after all that she had seen and heard here, she was still not wanting to understand what had become completely obvious. "Isn't it?"

Smiling conspiratorially and caught between sighing and laughing again, Maddy said, "Ah! But it's so much more. Why exactly, my dear, do you think they call it..." and flourishing grandly once again, "The Rendezvous Inn?"

Angela needed time to take this last addition in. Her head had been spinning before the last few minutes, but she was to the point of being unable to think at all. In fact, she was feeling almost numb.

Of course she had already as much as guessed — had already seen acted out all around her — much of what Maddy was telling her. Her head had been spinning before.

"It is **the** discreet place for meeting for either an afternoon's liaison," Maddy continued, "or for an entire weekend, should the opportunity arise."

Leaning back again and retreating into the haze of memory, she added, "some of the most special moments of my life were spent here." After a few moments of reverie, Maddy returned to the present and leaning in to take her friend's hands firmly in hers, looked directly and compassionately into Angela's eyes again. "And now that possibility is available to you as well."

"But... How did you hide it from Henry? Was it only for a short while?" Still having a hard time grasping the consequences, she blurted, "I mean... Your affair?"

"Oh no," Maddy said definitively. "It lasted until almost the day George died, a little over three years ago now." Beginning to be overcome with other emotions surfacing now, it was Maddy who turned her head away to contemplate the landscape outside.

Sensing her friend's need for privacy, Angela returned to her own thoughts. *Three years ago,* she thought. *That means that they must have been together for more than forty years. And nothing ever leaked out to the voracious press.*

Amazing, she thought. *Absolutely amazing.*

Gazing intently at her friend's hands and suddenly noticing the varying colors of age on them, Angela resisted the temptation to interrupt her friend's reverie. *If Maddy could do it...* she found herself thinking, and then started shaking her head. *But I can't,* she finished. *I can't do that to Frank.*

All of a sudden, she could feel her friend's intense gaze had returned. Looking up, she saw a mass of conflicting emotions playing across Maddy's face, belying the look in her eyes.

Hesitantly, Angela almost didn't want to ask, but did. "And Henry never found out?"

"Oh," Maddy paused, and as if she had become the age that she was finally, began showing the palsy of regret, turning her attentions to playing with her napkin.

Angela caught the sense of her friend's guilt and regrets suddenly coming out. Maddy's mannerisms were betraying the toll that this affair had taken. She wanted to ask her friend how the older woman had dealt with that, but didn't.

"Oh, I'm sure that he had his suspicions. But it kept the impression that we were a happily married couple alive, and that was all that was really needed. The happy image to keep the voters happy. And I wouldn't be at all surprised if, sometime before I die, I find out that Henry had also had an affair. Hell, perhaps even several over the years."

"So..." Angela hesitated again. "You didn't end up having an affair because of something that Henry did."

"Oh, no. Henry was always the perfect husband and father. Perfect that is, if you didn't count the workaholic tendencies. And that other tendency that still exists to have your three martini lunches or even dinners. Back-room politics are still the same, even cruising towards the twenty-first century."

Cruising, Angela thought. *Not a word I would have suspected to be coming out of Maddy's mouth. What else don't I know about this woman?*

"We were living in Washington and George and I — I discovered after the fact — were not alone in our little private dealings. Most people in the limelight were successful in keeping their private affairs out of the public eye. There were rumors and innuendos of course, but it was only a suggested reality. The Press back then were not who they are today," she said.

Feeling a little exhausted, Angela was beginning to seriously think about what her friend was proposing. This had been a very long lunch indeed.

"But I haven't met anyone who I would even dare to think of having these sort of — dealings — with, Maddy. Or even the vaguest idea of how or where to even find them."

Changing mood on a dime yet again, Maddy's behavior returned to the younger, giddy Maddy. Gleefully once again the girlish conspirator, she smiled in a proud of herself kind of way. Maddy dipped out of sight momentarily, triumphantly reaching into the satchel at her feet.

When she popped back up, she had something she had fished out of it. Rising with a flourish again, she plopped her find on the table between them.

Oh. My. God, Angela thought. "That isn't what I think it is. Is it?" Surely Maddy did not really mean what she thought she meant.

Gazing down apprehensively at the table beneath her, Angela saw that what Maddy had dropped so ceremoniously onto the table was a newspaper. But not just any newspaper. It was one of those free papers she had seen around Dupont Circle and in her favorite bookstore. They were distributed all over DC. Mere advertising rags that were both salacious in content and considered themselves to be alternatives to the Big Papers.

Shocked and completely confused now, Angela didn't even bother reaching for it. Instead, looking at it as if a small dragon had suddenly appeared on the table and was about to eat her, she slowly raised her eyes to the still beaming Maddy. Angela couldn't even begin to know what to say to her friend, whom she thought knew her so well.

Eyeing Maddy as if she were truly going mad (or senile), she watched as Maddy, with another flourish, opened the folded paper up and Angela's worst suspicions were fulfilled.

"It's one of those free newspapers they have here in DC," Angela stated flatly, her voice filled with as much apprehension as she could muster. And the least likely idea she could ever imagine that her friend would suggest to her as a possibility. "Why are you—" Angela started to ask.

"Well, I have just the solution," Maddy continued giddily, unconsciously interrupting her and seeming oblivious to Angela's utter consternation.

"I've been told that these—" gesturing in place of finding the right word, "have the kinds of advertisements that are quite popular now."

Incredulous again at this even stranger turn, Angela said flatly with her heart sinking into her legs, "They're called personal ads, Maddy."

"Yes! That's it," Maddy said triumphantly, like she was a child who had just opened a present. "Personals."

"Maddy. Surely you *must* be joking this time," Angela said, as if this paper in front of her would just go up in a puff of smoke if she touched it. "Please tell me you are joking."

But she saw that Maddy was still smiling her Cheshire grin in earnest. When Angela still had consternation on her face, Maddy got a curious expression on her face, continuing with, "Well, I must admit, they can seem a bit on the... interesting side."

Continuing to be shocked and amazed at Maddy seeming to be completely serious with this, all Angela could say was, "My God. You're not joking," and wanting desperately to put her head in her hands.

When Angela had the courage to look up again, Maddy had taken on such an earnest look, that Angela had to laugh. But it was clear that Maddy was deadly serious about this suggestion.

"Come on, Maddy. What sort of man do you really think I'm going to find in these ads?" Pointing to the offending article, "What sort of man would advertise for a clandestine affair here. And would I even want him to look at me?"

And with a sudden shivering revulsion adding, "Much less touch me? I mean... Have you really read this trash?"

Naively, Maddy replied, "Strictly for amusement, of course. This is about as spicy as a woman of my age can get these days. I mean, some of these ads almost read like pornography. That's about as risque as I get these days."

Lowering her voice dramatically to a masculine sort of growl, Maddy revealed another part of herself that Angela thought surely no one must have ever seen before: The Actress.

"'Let me massage all of your tension away'," Maddy said, looking for a second like a drag queen. And then returning to something more closer to her natural voice continued, "And other such similar nonsense."

"Madelaine Lightfoot!" Angela gasped, laughing a nervous laugh, finally unsure of how she could ever be surprised by this woman again.

"Oh, of course I wouldn't be so insane as to recommend you respond to trash such as that," Maddy said, prim and proper once again.

Roundly relieved at this, Angela told her friend, "Well, I'm glad that you at least know me a little bit."

With a "pshaw" type of flourish, Maddy continued, "Don't be ridiculous, my dear. Of course I know you better than that."

Feeling admonished and a little guilty, Angela blushed about the idea of thinking her friend was serious about this. "I'm sorry, Maddy. It's just — I mean — I never had any idea that you..."

"You mean about George?"

"Yes."

"I know. But we all have our secret lives that none of us know about the other. Especially in this town. Intrigue reigns supreme my dear, even in this capitol of the Free World." Adding for emphasis, "*Especially* in this Capitol."

Opening the newspaper again, Maddy folded it back to an already creased page, turning it around and pushing it across the table for her young friend to consider. Turning quite serious suddenly, "Just think about it, my dearest Angela," she said. Who knows," and winking lasciviously added, "Maybe it will inspire other ideas."

Accepting the newspaper from her friend, Angela picked it up off the table gingerly, as if still fearing that it might somehow burn her. Looking up after scanning several of the ads, her expression was a glaze of fear mixed with incredulity at what she was finally starting to contemplate — and a little bit of nervous anticipation at the prospect.

"Oh, I don't know about this, Maddy," Angela said, her voice quavering. "I'm not sure I'm ready for—" and waving around to indicate their now almost empty surroundings, "Any of this."

Picking her coffee cup up and peering over it calmly, Maddy took a sip with a sparkling look of hope glancing at Angela's shaking head.

Neither was I, my dear. Neither was I.

E I G H T

Several days later, Gabe was rolling into his home away from home (otherwise known as Work) once more.

The Golden Globe bar and restaurant was like many of the several other dozen bars on Capitol Hill. It largely had the same crowd, and the same ambiance — meaning booze and a TV set perched high on the wall over the bar. This TV though instead of sports, during the day was set to CNN, and then at night usually to whatever sports game was in season — with half-time breaks back to CNN.

It was a little different from most of the other more trendier (and less ancient) bars though. It had become quite dusty with age, and also had smoke-laden, heavy red velvet curtains in the windows that lent it the air of an English pub. It continued surviving largely because of that ancient vibe.

Many of the old-school patrons who tended to inhabit the place, whether politicians from The Hill or their staffers and sycophants, or reporters and general assorted other political hangers-on — also called it their home away from home as well. Some of them used the phrase in a way that was not at all ironic.

To Gabe, it was a job. Nothing spectacular; just a regular job (with some fairly good tippers for The Hill). It was nothing really to brag about, and certainly not what he considered to be more than a convenient, well-paying rut.

He had stumbled into bartending several years earlier as a means of making money while he finished his graduate degree. Then he stumbled into Benjamin Harrison on a bar binge right after his dissertation.

Benny was already a long-standing tradition at the Globe, and he talked Gabe into applying to work there. And when Gabe got really angry with Benny, Gabe referred to it as having been snookered into working with Benny. Just so he could have a regular drinking buddy and the excuse of relaxing after work.

The years had rolled on, and Gabe had taken on more and more hours. He had also put off seeking other prospective employment elsewhere in the meantime. Gabe half suspected Benny of putting in a not-so-good word to keep him at the Globe, but he couldn't prove it.

Many a girlfriend had commented (some rather snidely) about Gabe and Benny being "lost boys." One in particular had even hinted (rather angrily) that Gabe and Benny were "more than just friends."

Gabe had just laughed at that and dumped her quick. Benny was about as far from being gay as any man could be, and the idea hadn't come up ever since.

Since Gabe had decided to not return any of Carol's frantic calls over the last several days, he picked up whatever shifts he could beyond his normal forty, glad for the routine keeping his mind off her.

This was easy enough for now, because no one else wanted to be working inside this spring. Even the regulars were thin, lost to the bars and restaurants that had outdoor seating, or windows that actually opened.

Only the lonely drinkers who had nowhere else to go and didn't want to be seen drinking for hours outside, seemed to still be here in any quantity. With the sun kept at bay from bursting into the dark room by the awning outside and the heavy curtains inside, there was a certain anonymity available.

With the TV droning in the background behind him, Gabe served drinks without even having to ask the regulars whether — or what — they wanted. "Pay without thinking, drink without 'shrinking'," Benny had once said. Not that that would stop Gabe from thinking. And Benny would never think about therapy.

It was currently the slow comfortable time between late lunch and the early evening rush, with the late sun sneaking its way into the cracks between curtains and clean glass. On the screen behind him, the news was reporting on the latest break in negotiations in the latest crisis in the Middle East, but there weren't many eyes glued to the tube. Only to their drinks, with some muffled conversations buzzing quietly like bees in various places around the room.

As Gabe was wiping the bar down for the umpteenth time this afternoon, he suddenly paused, dropping his soaked and stained rag onto the countertop. Walking to the back room to find his "best friend" the always quick to disappear Benjamin Harrison had managed to pull his vanishing act once again.

Looking down at the pile of dirty rags in the box at his feet and then looking over at the now gone stack of should-have-been-there clean ones, Gabe sighed and cussed under his breath.

Since this was a regular occurrence, it didn't really surprise Gabe, but just pissed him off. Carol and all his other girlfriends had all these expectations of him, that he would grow up and get a regular job. But he couldn't even depend on Benny to do his current job, much less anything else.

He went down the line of the bar and made sure that all his regulars' drinks were in good condition, and then turned preparing to go stomping downstairs to the cellar where Benny usually took his time off (which happened at the drop of a hat — any hat).

This time Gabe turned the corner and missed a piece on the TV crawling to a close of the latest Mid-East Peace negotiation. It was being replaced with a lighter piece on the latest Rose Garden legislation signing soiree that had happened yesterday.

With the President beaming his photo-op smile and shaking hands with a group of senators and their wives, a certain bored politician's wife with the political sense to force a smile when she saw that the camera was being turned in her direction, was among those attending.

Angela Treworthy smiled warmly back as the camera zoomed into to focus on Senator Franklin James Treworthy, III and his lovely wife's moment with the President.

But once the President's attentions had moved on, her smile all too quickly faded as the camera moved on along with the President.

Standing at the top of the stairs leading down into the bars nether regions (basically the store rooms), Gabe yelled, "Benny! Benjamin Harrison! Where the hell are ya?" into the darkness. Gabe always hated this.

Being the stereotypical, red-headed Irish lovable scoundrel type, Benjamin James Harrison was kind of like an older version of a certain actor from the old TV show of a family that became a band from the 1960s. Not quite as aged as the actor, but definitely not aging very well himself either, hard drinking and definitely being alcoholic, the years of that drinking were taking their toll on Benny.

Benny was always either on the make, on the take, or on the hide. Working in a bar wasn't necessarily a choice for Benny at this point, and he tended to disappear quite frequently, often to take a nip. Also quite clearly annoying Gabe to no end.

With a second of hesitant silence, the voice of unreason floated up out of the dimly lit semi-darkness testily, "Comin', already."

Turning away and heading back towards the main room, Gabe was approaching being too tired to really be that annoyed. With another girlfriend gone, his attention span wasn't really sufficient to get too worked up. Still...

Waiting about five seconds, Gabe still didn't hear the pitter patter of flat feet coming up the stairs, and he was just annoyed enough to go in search of Benny.

About to turn the last corner before getting into the dish washing room, Gabe was almost to the first stair step when he heard Benny pounding up the steps out of the darkness. Gabe put his hands on his hips in preparation, turning his most practiced stare at his friend and leveling a tired, "Jesus, Benny! Where the hell you been?"

"Aw, come on my man. Lighten up. Rush ain't here yet?" Benny said as he came into view.

"Yeah, but I don't want Bernie having to ask me where you are. You know?"

With a clever, knowing smirk crossing his face, Benny merely told Gabe, "Got it covered, my man. Don't sweat it."

Not entirely liking this expression that he'd come to view with great unease, he just shook his head. "Come on, Benjamin. We've got to get ready. You know? Rack up some bottles? Fill my beer stock? Give me some rags to clean up the later sloppy seconds and thirds?"

Still grinning, Benny tried passing Gabe, ready to give the old fake boxer's one-two to Gabe's shoulder. But Gabe's arms, now folded solidly across his chest, suggested to Benny this was not the time. "Don't sweat it, Gabe. You know we're gonna have a light one tonight. It's only gonna be the old shits that're gonna be coming in. At least till the sun goes down, that is."

He was right, Gabe knew, and it was kind of depressing. It'd be even more depressing though, to be out walking the streets of The Hill or Dupont Circle, seeing happy couples enjoying the gorgeous weather in the near summery dusk. That, Gabe knew, he couldn't take right now.

"So..." Benny was about to add.

Throwing his hands up in disgust and walking away, Gabe said, "Don't even mention it."

Already mischievously smiling, Benny's smile suddenly grew even wider. "What? You not gonna tell your old bud Benny what's up with you?" Starting to brush past Gabe, Benny mock said to himself, "Not like I can't see it on your face."

Scowling, Gabe just turned and began walking back to his place behind the bar.

Catching up with him in the anteroom, Benny wrapped his nudge with a smile. "What? You gettin' private on me all of a sudden? Maybe this rich bitch's turnin' your head just a little too much."

Turning on his friend angrily, Gabe said, "Look, I told you not to call Carol a rich bitch. Understand?"

Taken aback by his ferociousness for a moment, Gabe turned

quickly, embarrassed. But only for a moment, and then his stone face snapped back into place.

Getting all the information he wanted and putting his hands up in a mock defense, Benny smiled broadly. "Whoa, buddy boy! Didn't mean anything 'bout that." He cocked his head before moving in for the kill. "Looks like you're falling in love with her."

With a touch of anger returning, Gabe began losing it again. "Who says I'm falling in love with her?"

"You been dragging your sorry ass around here for the last few days. That don't look good." Trying the seriously-hurt act, Benny said, "I'm your best friend, bro. So I thought like, you know, you'd let me in on what's up? So," returning to twinkling in a blink, he asked, "What's up, dude?"

With his face a tangle of emotions now and no longer wanting to deal with his friend, Gabe turned to make the final corner to walk back into the bar proper. There he met the same old faces still sitting there, staring into the same old emptiness at the bottoms of their glasses.

Gabe, in a similar state, went back to wiping down the counter absentmindedly to avoid acknowledging his downward slide into the same fate as his customers. It was also the same fate that, as Carol had so ably pointed out, had driven him to drink like his father had. Hopefully his fate would be slightly different enough that he wouldn't drink himself to death.

Taking the last few steps as strides, Benny started to step along side of Gabe but stopped as soon as he caught Gabe's look of desolation. Hesitating in a very un-Benny like manner, he quickly recovered, mock punching Gabe in his right arm.

Gabe barely even noticed, so Benny hit him again, this time a little harder. Gabe glared menacingly in Benny's direction, but remained silent.

"Oh, come on man! Haven't I known you way too long not to notice?" Benny said, starting to get a little angry himself.

"It's nothing, Benny! Just leave it alone." *Why do I have to shout with you so much?* Gabe was ready to demand.

Turning dismissively, Benny told him, "Yeah, right! Suit yourself," and started huffing and puffing back towards the dishwashing room.

"Nothing," Gabe repeated distantly to himself. Unfortunately he failed to wait until Benny was out of hearing range.

Benny turned on a dime at this, and was at Gabe's side in a New York minute. "Well if it's nothing bro, must be female problems. Am I right? Ol' Carol Miss-Goody-Goody-Gucci-Shoes not puttin' out for you, huh?"

It always came back down to that with Benny. The root of any problem, with anyone, was always sex. Either you weren't getting any, or you weren't getting enough.

Going back to wiping the same old bar spot, Gabe sighed, not wanting to give Benny any encouragement. "I said, I don't want to talk about it. All right?"

Leaning on the bar and leaning in for emphasis, Benny squeezed his eyes shut, miming getting some heavy duty inspiration, opened them and reached out, and snapped his fingers. "In that case, let me guess. She laid that old get a real job bullshit on you again. Am I right?"

Getting both his goat and his attention, Gabe finally looked up. "You don't stop, do you?" he asked, really wishing he hadn't taken this shift today.

"Ohhhh, ho, ho, ho. I get it. She dumped you. The little bitch musta

dumped you," Benny accused Gabe gleefully. Mock punching Gabe
again, Benny gave the fists of victory to the air above the bar, wearing
his got-ya look and screaming "Yee-haah" silently.

Better get it out, Gabe thought. *Now the little bastard's figured it
out, he won't let up.* "Wrong," Gabe said without any enthusiasm. "She
didn't dump me, I dumped her. Ok?" Gabe said, turning to face the
still-grinning Benny.

Benny tried to hide the smugness he was obviously feeling. "I hate
to say it, buddy boy—" he started in.

"Then don't, Benny. I don't want to hear it. All right?"

"Look, Gabe..."

"I've got customers to tend to," Gabe said, turning and walking
away. "Oh, and by the way. You've got a job to do, too. Before rush
hits? Ya know? At least pretend that you work here? Am I right? I need
bar rags and bottles."

I'll get him later, Benny thought. *Liquor the boy up, and he'll spill
like an oil gusher. Big time,* he added, chuckling to himself as he
walked gleefully to the back room, grinning like a madman.

NINE

The sun was highlighting the trees on the other side of the Potomac with a golden glow, telling Angela that it was getting late. Lunch today had quickly expanded into Happy Hour, and Angela and Maddy had begun to turn the corner food-wise into dinner.

The staff at the Rendezvous were well trained however, to allow the patrons (who paid a rather hefty price to be members) to take their time eating (and drinking) and leave the plates on the table until the patron asked that they be removed.

Maddy's plate had been cleaned off a long time before, owing to her usual small portions. She had never been a big eater ("Helps me keep my girlish figure," she would always inform anyone who asked).

But Angela's plate was a different story. Still filled with only half-eaten food, she had been picking at the remains long after they were cold, and Maddy had indulged her this contemplative time.

The afternoon had been lost to periods of Maddy reminiscing to Angela with tales of George Remy, stories of similar afternoons and evenings, both here at The Inn and on the French Riviera as well.

And there were other long periods where silence was the main entree. They either sipped coffee or, later, sipped their wine (Angela loved a deep rich Burgundy, and Maddy preferred Merlot).

Angela was slowly becoming reconciled with this idea of infidelity through Maddy's romantic tales about her life with her Ambassador. Hence the reverie on Maddy's part and the quiet desperation of Angela's having been tamed from a frightful storm into only a drenching summer rain.

Not that she was feeling comfortable with the idea of cheating on her husband. Frank had done nothing wrong to Angela. In fact, he had been an almost perfect husband to his wife, except for the lack of attention and the long hours at work.

God knows, Angela thought, *that's not grounds for divorce.* And paused, thinking, *Or other things.*

If that were the case, half of America would be divorcing. *But then again*, she thought, *half of America **is** divorcing. And who knows how many of the other half aren't having affairs to keep the disquiet they were feeling quiet?*

*Perhaps an affair **would** do my marriage good*, she thought, laughing as soon as she thought it.

"Why does it have to come to this?" she asked her sometimes wise seeming friend across the table from her.

Maddy, coming out of her own reverie, looked up and said quietly, "It shouldn't have to, my dear. But it does."

"Frank has been the best husband that I could have asked for. Yes, he wasn't the most romantic man I ever dated, but he was the kindest, and in his own way, the most passionate. At least then."

"Ah, the fire of youth," Maddy said, returning to her most lucid. She looked piercingly in Angela's eyes, and said sadly, "Unfortunately, passion is something that most people lose in their old age. And romance? One is lucky to have that with most men even from the start. Romance is more for the woman's part of a relationship than the man's. Most men only want sex anyway."

"So Henry wasn't the romantic sort?" Angela asked, pretty much already knowing the answer.

"Henry? No. Henry didn't have a romantic bone in his body. But, yes, he was a good man. And he was a good father. As much as he could be, that is," Maddy whispered.

"It was a very different age when Henry and I started the whole mating dance. Women were supposed to be housewives and mothers, and security was the order of the day in marriage; not romance and passion. You were considered extremely lucky if you had all three in a marriage."

"Perhaps I might have been happier had I grown up and married in the time that you did," Angela said wistfully.

Maddy reacted strongly to this, leaning in once again in a very masculine pose. "I was much more prepared for that kind of life, Angela. And it still didn't stop me from being disheartened and eventually unfaithful."

Turning more compassionate once more and softening considerably, her eyes turned moist and she smiled sweetly and more femininely. "You shouldn't be hard on yourself, my dear, any more than I was. This happened. And as much as certain people would like to make you think the worst of yourself, we're only human. If we don't get our needs met, we begin to have an empty space inside.

"In my case, George was there to help me feel fulfilled. Perhaps you may yet find your own George Remy, now that you're looking. Find the man that will fulfill you as well."

"Oh, I don't know, Maddy." Holding up the free newspaper still gingerly, she said, "I'm not sure that I'm ready to step into this new world. I was just getting used to the old one."

"'O brave new world, that has such people in it?'" Maddy said, quoting rhetorically. "Or women."

"Not this woman," Angela said, this time with feeling. "Oh, Maddy. I'm really not ready for this whole thing."

"Not yet perhaps, my dear. But do think about it," Maddy said, grandly gesturing around the now largely empty room. "The Rendezvous will be here for you when you're ready. And perhaps we shall lunch here again in several weeks," Maddy said formally with her Mona Lisa smile once again. "Should you need some more encouragement, that is."

They had finished off their glasses of wine, had some coffee in silence, and Maddy had her driven back to Georgetown. Because of the traffic on the Parkway and then on Foxhall Road leading into town, they arrived on 32nd Street well after dark.

On the way, Maddy had left Angela to her own thoughts, watching the turmoil coming in waves of calm and anguish across the younger woman's face. *If she needs to talk, she'll talk*, Maddy told herself, stopping herself from offering any more advice. This was something that Angela would have to come to on her own.

When they were in front of Angela's house, she hesitated to get out. There were so many questions coming and going in her mind that she wanted to ask Maddy. Maddy sat patiently, waiting for her to make whatever decision she was going to make.

Sighing deeply, Angela started to cry. "Did you really go through what I'm going through when you considered doing..." She hesitated to even say it, since they were back in Maddy's limo and she was unsure about the driver, so she just said, "This?"

"Yes, I went through something similar," Maddy said. "But it wasn't something that I considered until the opportunity arose."

"When he came into your life, you mean." *Meaning the French Ambassador*, Angela thought.

"Yes, until George came into my life. You can say his name. I don't need to have any secrets in here," she said, nodding her head in the direction of the driver, Henry. "We have an agreement surrounding these matters."

"I'm not sure I can trust my Henry to be so agreeable," Angela whispered.

"You'd be surprised, my dear. Discretion is always part of the job description when it comes to being a chauffeur for the rich and famous. Otherwise, they wouldn't last very long."

Patting Angela's hand, Maddy smiled and then leaned in for a hug. Looking over Angela's shoulder, Maddy whispered into her ear, "You will come to your own arrangements and agreements in time." Then pulling away from her friend, she squeezed Angela's hand once more.

"In time, everything will be decided," she said cryptically. "And the burden you bear now will be washed away by whatever waves of passion may come your way."

"Why, Maddy," Angela said with complete surprise, "I never knew you could be so eloquent." Catching herself, she quickly tried to retract what came out as an off-hand comment. "I mean..."

"I know what you meant, my dear," Maddy said with a smile. "There were many things I got from my years with George. Heavily accented French romanticism being only one of them. You'll see. You may not have any idea now what this seemingly twisted and wrong path may provide."

Her fears calmed by this for now, Angela told her friend, "Thank you. For everything. I am so glad we met and I'm honored to be your friend."

"What are friends for?" Maddy asked, as Angela opened the door, preparing for her future.

Leaning back in, Angela said, "Thank you for the wonderful lunch and et cetera. Our next Rendezvous adventure will be on me."

"We'll do brunch before then," Maddy said.

With a final wave of her hand, Angela closed the limo door as Maddy watched her friend walk soberly away.

Sighing and sitting, contemplating her friend as she got her keys out of her purse and opened the side garden door, Maddy wondered if the Rendezvous was a mistake.

Angela already seemed overburdened as it was with her predicament. She hoped that Angela would make a decision to at least experiment. It had done wonders for Maddy, and had helped her survive the last years of her husband's run in Congress.

And Henry's death soon after.

No sooner had Angela closed the garden door before breaking down into a fit of sobbing. She was glad that she had given the housekeeper and her driver the day off, so no one would be there to witness her breakdown.

She knew Maddy was right. It wasn't going to get any easier. And lately Frank stayed longer and longer at work in his office. Often times it was approaching midnight before she heard him come in the front door.

When he finally managed to make it up the stairs, he was often looking haggard and drained. The various times Angela had mentioned this (and almost pleaded with him to see a doctor to examine his condition), Frank would brush it off.

"I'm fine," was all he would say in that blue-blood Connecticut accent, calmly indicating the discussion was over.

Angela had in the last few months stopped calling him on his physical state, and had since worried silently. She hadn't made mention of this aspect of her own mental state because she felt that she already over-burdened her only real friend anyway.

She walked into the now darkened kitchen and hesitated a moment before turning on a light. She almost felt like marching herself upstairs and putting herself to bed.

On the verge of crying once more, Angela thought it would be pathetic to do what she felt like doing. *I shouldn't have to feel this way,* she thought, *feeling like a lonely teenager. Thank God for Madelaine Lightfoot. I don't know what I'd do if it weren't for her.*

She had tried to make other friends, most notably with other Senate wives, but she always felt as if they thought she was in competition with them. Even the wives felt like political rivals. Leaving the kitchen and not turning on any lights, she made her way upstairs. Theirs was a modest house compared to many another politician's residence in this city. Other politicians had literal mansions, capable of (and often) entertaining parties of a hundred or more.

But Angela never felt comfortable in a truly large house, and Frank (who was not the large party sort) had agreed, even though his family had a thirty room mansion in Hartford. As with many hardcore socialite parents and siblings, Angela often thought of Frank as being a misplaced only child.

Of course, there was a reason for Frank's stand-offishness. Vietnam.

He hadn't come back as damaged as some of his friends had, but he liked quiet. *Odd for someone being in Congress*, she thought when she first met him. But he had the same kind of feel that she could imagine Lincoln having. Not quick to act, but when he did...

And he was not exactly what you would call bold or vigorous in his office. He rarely sponsored any bills, and when he did it was usually as a co-sponsor to a friend's bill.

No, Frank was a steady, hard working Senator. He did the best he could, considering if it had been up to him he wouldn't be in the limelight. That was his family's leanings and they had apparently leaned hard on him to run.

Although he wasn't one to bask in the spotlight. he did love interacting with the his voter base. This brought out the Good Servant in Frank. He was a good man.

But he was also a workaholic, the result of which was that his wife rarely saw him outside of bedtime.

Walking into their bedroom, she took the now rumpled piece of newsprint out of her purse, and found a place in the deepest part of her bottom dresser drawer to hide it in.

And then she prepared to go to bed, not knowing exactly what she was going to do or how she was going to react when Frank eventually made it home. Hopefully, she would be long asleep when he did.

T E N

About half a normal rush later, the Globe's traffic was already starting to wind down and clear out. Benny, however, was just winding up.

Gabe had been hard pressed to find something to do while the few patrons who were interested in being inside on this warm spring night slipped in and out of the bar. He'd spent large blocks of time just staring into space. Yet when a customer would call his name, he'd respond quickly, eager to have something to relieve his boredom.

Sidling up to him, Benny restarted rapid fire the earlier conversation about Carol. As if it had just broken off five minutes and not five hours before. "Ok, ok. So I won't say anything. I mean, she's a real piece of work, but..."

"I thought you weren't going to say anything?"

"Well, now that you ask."

"I didn't."

"Look, Gabe——"

"Look Benny, I know what you're going to say, and I'm not giving you the satisfaction of saying I told you so. And that's that. Understand?"

Getting a mock sorrowful look on his face, Benny's eyes betrayed his glee. "Gabriel, my man. How could you think I would say such a thing?"

"Because I know you all too well, Benjamin."

"Well Gabe, it just means you have more options now. That's all. Am I right?"

Deflating from the lack of fight from Benny, Gabe let a tired look steal onto his face. With the current quite soaked bar rag in his hand still, Gabe contemplated throwing it at Benny for the proverbial New York Minute. Instead he pitched it into the laundry bin at Benny's feet.

Hoping to cut the argument brewing in Benny to the quick, Gabe folded his arms over his chest and walked off in search of a customer to serve. "I don't want to think about it right now."

Following after him, Benny went on the attack. "All right. It was no business this afternoon, and no business this evening, so it's gonna be dead tonight. So I'm sure ol' Bernie's not gonna wanna pay us for nothing. Early night tonight, and time to play. Especially since there's no cat to pay."

"Don't you think we ought to let Bernie decide that? I mean, he is still our boss, you know?"

With a downright wicked grin plastered on his face, Benny informed Gabe, Already taken care of, my man!" in his forced sing-song way, "Nooo problemo, bro. Bernie's all taken care of."

Gabe was in no mood to even think of what new dirt Benny had on their boss so he just sighed, resigned to the inevitable.

A cab ride with Benny could be an ordeal for Gabe just about any time, but when Benny was in his trolling for information mode and had a captive detainee for questioning? Gabe knew that he'd made a mistake tonight of all nights, just as soon as they'd gotten into the cab on Pennsylvania Avenue

Benny was a New Yorker originally, so it was nothing for him to hop in a cab. It didn't hurt that he'd lost his license permanently several years earlier after a ferocious (even for Benny) binge. And since the cab system in the Capitol was designed by Congressmen to make it filthy cheap to hop a cab anywhere on the Hill...

A cab ride to their (well, Benny's) favorite bar in Dupont Circle cost almost next to nothing, allowing Benny to be generous to the cabbies. It also helped that said bar was a simple four-block walk down P. Street to Gabe's apartment... He could usually slip out early and Benny wouldn't notice.

Gabe usually left his car in the basement garage these days. When he was occasionally questioned about it, he'd say, "To keep it in mint condition, of course," to which the usual reply was, "But it's a rust bucket."

So Gabe would respond to that by saying (when he was in a really good mood), "That's a precious patina," and the questioner would get the point. As long as there weren't any (major) holes in the body, it would still pass DC inspection.

It also usually didn't help to drive it to work anyway, as it was often a futile exercise trying to find reasonably close parking to The Globe anywhere on Capitol Hill. He could walk to the Dupont Circle Metro Red Line stop on Connecticut and be down at work within forty minutes (if there weren't any problems).

It also prevented Benny cajoling him into going on a joy ride, especially after work or they'd gone drinking. Gabe wasn't about to lose his license. And especially in his mood now, he was just as likely to drink away his troubles after work anyway. So why have the temptation?

They were close to Dupont Circle on Massachusetts Avenue now, as Benny picked up where he left off just a minute earlier. "In an hour or so, you won't even remember..." he started saying without losing a beat from where he was. In a dramatic fit, he was pausing and snapping his fingers and putting his index finger to his head, looking up and concluding with, "What's her name?"

Not in the mood for his antics, Gabe got out "Benny..." in a very weary voice. He was wishing he'd just bowed out and not come. Or was perhaps looking to grab a quick one and then disappear.

On a roll though now, (and not catching Gabe's drift), Benny was unstoppable. "No, my man, I mean it. Bitches are disposable. Get tired of one, get another one. Right?" This was his usual rant after one of Gabe's breakups.

"Benny..." he tried to interrupt, but Gabe couldn't win.

"Gabe, why do you gotta do all that sensitive shit? Why can't you just be the man, play the field, and... You know?"

Putting on his best New Yawk accent, Gabe replied with, "Because. I am a sensitive guy. Ya know? And as much as you hate that sometimes, comes with the—" and pausing now for his dramatic effect and using Benny's favorite phrase to describe Gabe's attitude, "English Lit shit."

About to say something else in response, Benny is suddenly snapping to and turning to shout, "Yo, cabby. Right here." And as the cab was coming to the curb, he rolled on with, "Like I said. Have a few brews, and you won't even remember the bitch."

"Benny."

Paying Gabe no attention as he went into his magnanimous business mode without even looking at the cab driver, Benny tossed a crumpled twenty-dollar bill he'd just managed to fish out of his pocket onto the front seat, past the driver's outstretched hand.

"Keep it," was all Benny managed to say before popping out the door and plunging into the throng of hopeful patrons at the bar's overcrowded entrance.

Gabe was about to get out and follow him, when the driver turned to him and rumbled in a thick Jamaican accent, "None of my business, mon. But maybe you should—"

Exhausted from the cab ride and constant Benny-speak, Gabe only manages a weak, "Yeah. I know," before scooting himself over and out the door.

The cab driver sat for a second before moving, then shook his head, mumbling and snorting to himself, "Americans."

Picking the bill up and smoothing it out on the dash board, he slipped it into his shirt pocket, and turned back to find an obviously shit-faced couple getting into his cab.

"Where to?" he asked hopefully. They looked as if they were going to Potomac and he could get away from The Circle for a while. If they didn't throw up in his back seat, that is.

The Dupont Circle nightspot that was Benny's "Favo-right Establishment" was called The Killer Queens because it usually had "beavies of bouncin' babes." The Queens was Benny and Gabe's second home away from home.

A very different kind of bar from the Golden Globe, The Queens was as frenetic and jumpy as the Globe was quiet and staid. And with the clientele, there would never be velvet curtains here. The Bar was all glass except for the major sign hanging in the window. Queens was a bar to be seen in, and not to hide away in, like the Globe.

Everyone here furiously came to See and Be Seen. And when the summer nights hit and they opened those massive glass French door windows right onto Connecticut Avenue, people would hang out the window as well, wreaking havoc between the bar and the DC Liquor Commission.

Until then, the sign for the bar hanging in those French windows read KILLER QUEENS. It featured two very scantily clad and well-endowed women in bikinis — one on each side and leaning in and on the wording — framing the name.

With the crowd overflowing and spilling out all over the sidewalk outside and into the street on this warm spring night, Gabe struggled to keep up with the shock of red hair bobbing through the crowd. Without even glancing in his direction, Benny waved at the bouncer, who in turn started waving Benny through without another glance.

Benny was almost to the door when he found himself in the midst of a sea of blond mermaids, all of them pretty much dressed the same in their Little Black Dresses, and virtually indistinguishable to Gabe's eyes. Their hair flowed down to there, and their micro minis rose up to (sort of) there; they looked like a walking ad for the Queens of the bar's name.

His forward momentum enticingly stopped, Benny gave his full attention to this apparent swim team, getting swallowed by this throng of women seeking his obviously already well-oiled attention.

Being Benny, of course, he used his wiles and his access to get them in the door and past the others waiting...as if the bouncer weren't already contemplating it, with their looks.

Even for a Tuesday night, this was a still a large crowd for The Queens, and Gabe stood a little back towards the edge of the shoving mass, watching the various couples, singles and groups jockeying for position in the street flow.

He was on the verge of letting Benny flow on into his oeuvre and disappearing himself off into the spring night life for a walk and eventually home. But he hesitated for far too long of a moment. Benny looked back into the crowd before disappearing himself into the mayhem and waved Gabe inside vigorously, pointing to the swim team surrounding him and making obscene gestures.

Gabe sighed and follow him. He'd never hear the end of it if he didn't at least put in an appearance. At least, thankfully, he didn't shout out Gabe's name with all the obscene gestures.

Reluctantly following his friend inside, Gabe took a deep breath and plunged into the crowd. Being instantly recognized and waved on in by the burly bouncer Jimmy, Gabe could see him counting the numbers none too secretly.

Finally arriving at the door, Gabe grabbed the hand that received him and gave the customary shake, with a quick, "Hey, Jimmy." Between being both regulars here as well as fellow bartenders, Jimmy was quick to allow Gabe access as well with a, "He's already inside, dude. You're missing out."

Wearily, "Yeah, I know," Gabe sighed. "Thanks."

Jimmy slapped him on the back as Gabe crossed the threshold and began swimming upstream into all the spring testosterone madness. The place was already packed and throbbing, with no single inch of floor space to be found without flesh covering it.

The Globe was 40/50-something and The Queens was definitely 20-something. It attracted just about all of the college kids from all over town at one point or another, and was an infamous pick-up joint.

Gabe followed in Benny's wake as he often did. With Benny, it was either shaking hands with, or calling out to about half the people in whatever room he found himself in. "Working the crowd," Benny used to tell Gabe, as if Benny were a politician, and Gabe was one of his assistants.

Hearing Benny more than actually seeing him, Gabe stood amazed in the madness that one man could actually manage to be heard above this kind of a din. But that was Benny.

Finally finding Benny glad-handing and shouting greetings to both men and women as he parted the crowd like a Gen-X Moses, this was obviously Benny's element. Still surrounded by the group of women he met in line, Benny was chatting up the names, and as soon as he saw Gabe's head again, he began furiously signaling.

Introducing them all to Gabe as soon as he was within shouting distance, Gabe didn't catch any of Benny's chatter. Used to this big show though, he played along, nodding dumbly in the direction of each of the (looking the same to Gabe) beauties' directions. Each of them smiled the same vapid smile full of bright flashing teeth back at him, and Gabe thought, *Like swimming with sharks.*

With most of their phone numbers or business cards already in his hand, Benny started kissing all around and began moving off, already trolling the bar for other prospects.

As Benny moved towards the bar, a space parted there for him just in time as he moved into it, once more like magic. Holding two fingers up as he sat down, the bartender merely nodded, and Benny dropped another twenty on the counter.

Gabe often wondered how Benny the Barback (who shouldn't be making all of the money he drops, since a barback is just the glorified dishwasher at The Globe), could possibly manage to have as much money as he does. But Gabe refused to ask for fear of the answer. Instead he just watched as Benny seemed to rule wherever he went.

As Gabe again reached within shouting distance, Benny got in a few more hand shakes before the beers arrived. It was a testament to the regularity that Benny and Gabe spent in The Queens that the bartender wandered over with their drinks already in hand, not needing to ask any more than Gabe did with his regulars, what they were ordering.

Handing Gabe his beer, Benny nodded acknowledgment to the bartender before turning and launching into his certified pep talk at Gabe.

"So you let one fish go," Benny shouted above the din.

Turning with his beer in one hand, he gestured broadly around the crowd with his other. "There's plenty more where she came from, bro. With your natural good looks, and your position of esteem in our little world here, you shouldn't have any trouble hookin' up with another one."

Pausing to nudge him in his right arm, Benny concluded with his usual, "Am I right? Or am I right?"

Although Gabe was in a better mood, he still shook his head as he turned to Benny. "I swear, Harrison, that 'fishes in the sea' shit's older than the hills," he shouted. "You're a writer. Can't you come up with anything better than that?"

"Hey! What do you want? You paying me for my most excellent advice?"

His eye suddenly caught by a woman wandering by who had barely glanced in his direction, Benny was off his stool in a New York Minute. Happily forgetting his best bud and wandering off in her general direction, Benny's eyes were already locked and loaded on his target. In hot pursuit with his beer still in his hand, he disappeared into the throng towards the back of the bar.

Sighing and thinking to himself, *Incorrigible*, Gabe merely shook his head in disgust. It happened far too often to get angry with Benny, but it still pissed him off. Benny would "go fishing" at the drop of any hat (or any hint of an invitation, whether it was real or not). Sometimes he was likely to be leaving Gabe in mid-sentence.

Now it was Gabe's turn to empty his thoughts "inta his beer." Taking his first long draught, he settled in for another lonely night. Even with the mad hum and music thrashing around him, he still managed to feel as if he were completely alone.

Gabe and Benny's other friends, when they managed to slip away from their wives and families, weren't much better than Benny was.

"Maybe Carol is right," he said to the empty feeling but still raging room around him, so deep in his misery that all of the madness surrounding him had dimmed to a dull roar outside his head.

Benny was still on the hunt when he left, the target that he had so locked on had rebuffed him only a couple of minutes later. Unused to women not taking his charming character (once he poured on the charm with a bucket), Benny wasn't so eager to try and start any more pep talks with Gabe for the evening.

Which more than suited Gabe. He'd had enough of the Benny-monster trying to make a man out of him for yet one more night. If Gabe weren't so wrapped up in work, he'd promised himself that one day soon, he'd like, maybe find himself another life other than tending bar at The Globe.

He didn't do it often, but Gabe had decided earlier in that night that he'd drink himself into oblivion. After all, his apartment building was only a drunk's stumble away. He could make it there crawling, he once joked. Location, location, location...

A half an hour later, Gabe had left the Queens' monster crowd still raging and thumping in loud pounding music and full hunt mode, and not looking back, headed for home.

But he hadn't done the oblivion thing. He'd finished off his one and only beer and left, wading back through the crowd of wanting to be here women and men doing the mating dance.

Lost in his own thoughts, he got himself to the street and started navigating through the throngs of couples being couple-ly all over. Along with the groups of single women on the prowl, he eventually found peace with the open street surrounding him.

Not watching particularly where he was going, he suddenly found himself up against one of the many Free Paper boxes that were in great profusion everywhere around The Circle blocking his way.

What the hell, he thought, *time for some amusement tonight*. Reaching in and grabbing a copy of the very same free newspaper that Angela had been given earlier that day by Maddy, he crumpled it under his arm and headed for home.

Ambling over to P. Street, Gabe was confronted by a similar but more diverse crowd. Only this one was a little less intimidating since it merged into the groups of gay men heading towards the various hangs of P. Street. It was an older crowd, and not tending towards the large clumps of eager single women.

"What the hell," he said to no one. He didn't feel like going home yet, and yet he didn't want to be confronted by another Carol eager to make babies.

Weaving his way through the different crowd, he made his way down the basement stairs into one of the many gay bars along the way. Unlike many straight men, Gabe wasn't afraid to get a drink in a gay bar. And most of the other patrons knew that he wasn't there for them and so they left him alone.

Occasionally another guy would try and hit on him, but his non-response soon left him alone again.

Several beers later, he was stumbling up the steps and out of the bar, making an unsteady beeline across P. Street in the general direction of his apartment building.

It was a large and now terribly upscale building, which Gabe had moved into owing to his earlier days in corporate life. All of the front desk people called him by his last name with a "Mr." attached, which he still found both amusing and a little upsetting.

Tonight, he stumbled into the lobby and merely waved in the direction of Antonio, the night shift desk clerk, as Antonio waved a giddy acknowledgment back. Antonio was a young and very gay George Washington University student who Gabe knew had a severe crush on him. Gabe finished swimming his way over to the elevators and finally managed to punch the dancing UP button after a few tries.

Once the elevator came and he was inside, he didn't exactly have the same kind of luck pressing the button for his floor, and so took a tour of the several other floors before his own, finally landing on the right floor almost by accident.

Finally at his apartment door, he managed to fumble his keys out of his pocket and insert the right one into the right lock, before stumbling into his apartment. *Maybe's time to move out,* he thought vaguely, the beer haze he was clinging onto desperately blurring the door when it surprised him by opening.

He'd only had a couple of beers, but the toll of the day was catching up with him and he knew he wasn't going to make it much farther than the couch. Again.

It had been a short night at The Queens because he didn't want to really be there. Thankfully, he had only seen Benny periodically as he came back to the anchor that was Gabe to get another round.

Truth was, in this part of town if a man didn't walk up to a woman and offer to buy her a drink, he wasn't exactly going to get harassed by the women. He'd gotten tired of that everywhere else.

He also knew that he could get just about any woman's attention he wanted. If he wanted to, that is. Being a bartender, he made damn good money. Almost too good an amount of money. And all the women who knew him, knew that only too well.

But he also had a very withdrawn attitude about him, and unless some woman made him her pet project and he accepted what she offered, he wasn't sought after either.

Unlike Benny. The Bad Boys always seem to have women begging to be had by them.

"Fuck em' all," he mumbled once he was finally inside, turning the light on just inside his front door as his body was heading towards the couch.

So as he had satisfied himself that he had almost forgotten all the unpleasantness about— "What's her name?" to quote the Benny Monster, he found himself upside down again, luckily staring at the ceiling from the couch this time, and not the floor. (He'd also had his share of nights where he woke up finding himself pointed the wrong direction and barely able to breathe.)

He had once again managed to make it to the couch before collapsing onto it, falling from his drunken stupor into a leaden sleep.

ELEVEN

The next morning was business as usual for the floor of the US Senate. No big measures on the docket; no discernible orations that had to be waded through. Although as always, there were hidden agendas.

Bill after innocuous bill had been brought up and routinely voted up or down. These were all of the non-debatable items that no one could argue with, because they had already been agreed upon in committee before they reached the floor. Without fanfare they either passed... or they didn't.

Sitting in his big padded leather seat and going through the motions, was the esteemed senior Senator from the grand State of Connecticut, Franklin James Treworthy, III. Admired by most of his colleagues for being both highly amiable and not quick to judge, his seat was one of those perennially almost guaranteed to win re-election.

This was largely because he both was a team player that didn't need the spotlight, and because his state was small enough to not need that much pork. The Groton Shipyards in New London were the only real national concern, and they were largely sacrosanct because of the

Navy. Most of Connecticut was either Blue Blood Central, or bedroom communities for those commuting daily between The Big Apple and home.

Frank Treworthy was the sort of quiet, unsung type of man of Congress who never rocked the boat. He could always be counted on to cast his votes without any animosity developing out of competing interests.

This morning was his turn to deliver a speech before the floor, and everyone knew it would be a highly predictable and much-deliberated sounding speech. In other words, it was one of those speeches likely to ruffle few, if any feathers.

Few members of the Senate ever interrupted Frank's speeches. Most of his speeches were devoid of any passion, but just making his points. They were also usually, blessedly short, and many of his fellow politicians liked that. If they were even in attendance, that is.

This morning was another matter. Frank was going to be making a rather passionate plea for one of his favorite causes — the peace process in a small West African country in which he had been stationed during his Peace Corps days after Vietnam. Thinking at the time that being in the Peace Corps would appease his parents' desire for public service, he was wrong.

Even after his tour in Vietnam, they still insisted that he, the lone brother still not in the family business, should take some sort of public office. Frank's grandfather had been a Senator, so therefore Frank needed to continue in that grand tradition as well, whether he wanted to or not.

Surprising even himself, he had developed a passion for what he did once he got on his first campaign trail. He was a withdrawn sort even before his experience in Southeast Asia, but there was something about being in front of an audience that brought him out of his shell. He had actually grown to like giving speeches before the constituents, both surprising himself and pleasing his relatives.

But now, Frank was in his early fifties (although some of his colleagues were thinking he was in his late sixties). He was tall and thin, reminding some of Abraham Lincoln, and dressed conservatively with his rapidly graying completely gray hair. Even though he was one of the untouchable incumbents in the Senate, his passion for the job had long since waned.

He was holding on in large part simply because his family expected it of him. And also in part, he'd occasionally had to admit to himself, because he wouldn't know what he would do with his life in its absence. He was never one to take vacations. Or play golf. Or tennis. The Senate was his life. Not even his marriage gave him very much satisfaction any more.

Looking uncomfortable even after all these years, he sat upright and prepared to be called to the national stage once more. Half listening as he heard the Chairman of the Senate call his name, he began making his way down the aisle and to the steps to the right side.

Once at the podium, he looked out on his fellow senators, a growing minority of which were women, and began with, "Ladies and Gentlemen of the Senate." He carefully arranged his papers knowing at the start that this was going to be a hard sell.

"We cannot make a decision so lightly on a matter of such regional importance. Barundia is staying true to the accord they signed with their neighbors in Sierra Leone, and it is up to us to back them." Pausing briefly as the usual murmurs began rising from the floor, the

Chairman banged his gavel, and the murmurs subsided. At least for a while.

"Ladies and Gentlemen," he began again, "As unpopular as it seems to this body," Frank continued, "I propose another fact-finding and arbitration mission, before we take this final vote on emergency funding." At this, several loud shouts sounded. Raising his voice again, Frank pressed on. "Especially to the formerly rebel-held territories—"

But this time, he was interrupted by one Andrew Stanton, the Senior (quite portly and of well-heeled status) Senator from West Virginia, who rose abruptly to "take umbrage."

Stanton had always had a less lenient attitude than most of his colleagues toward the esteemed Mr. Treworthy while on the Senate Floor, even though they still considered themselves friends while interacting off the Floor and in the Halls of Congress.

"Would the esteemed Gentleman from Connecticut like to explain to this august body, how we could possibly justify another, quote-unquote exploratory mission to this God-forsaken country to our legions of still-angry electorate? This is not, after all, a country of any strategic importance in the world body politic."

There was a sound of voices murmuring a variety of responses to this, which was met with the resounding sound of the gavel of the Chairman for silence, pounding a Call to Order.

Bowing his head, Frank took a moment to collect himself before speaking again. Stanton was obviously grandstanding for the CSPAN cameras and the electorate at home, and this didn't sit well with Frank.

With a pained expression crossing his face briefly, Frank continued after a long moment. "My dear colleague from West Virginia. If you would please let me continue..." he said, sounding tired of the fighting. "I ask so very little in the way of funding from—" and pausing, Frank added with an uncharacteristic dose of sarcasm to his response "— 'This august body...' and I would highly appreciate it if..."

"Give it up, Frank," an unnamed senator shouted from the back of the chamber, prompting the Chairman to gavel once again "for order and civility, gentlemen."

A cacophony of other senators' voices were beginning to murmur their agreement with Stanton, however. Even the ones who wholly detested Stanton's heavy-handed weight in the Senate felt this was not a real Bill.

Hearing his looked-for approval, Stanton began puffing himself up to continue, as if their cries were ones of tacit approval and not merely grudging acceptance.

"We still have an angry electorate to deal with on budgetary issues. They — and I as well — believe that this country—"

It was Frank's time to interrupt. "If the Gentleman from West Virginia would defer, I don't believe many from his great state even know that the country of Barundia even exists," he said, his weary look belying his sarcasm.

"Whatever you want to call it, Mr.—"

And at this, a number of their esteemed colleagues started laughing. There was seldom a major floor fight between these two, and the tension was all they needed now.

Most of the Senate, if they cared about any other state (besides their own that is), could care less about some obscure country in Africa.

"Burundi," Stanton started to say, but Frank broke in to correct him. "The name of the country is Barundia, Mr. Stanton. Not Burundi. That's another country. "

With scattered, cautious laughter starting to creep into the Hall at this, Frank and Stanton were following their usual back and forth on these sorts of issues. To some of their colleagues, it was only natural. To others, it had grown tiring a long time ago.

Stanton, as if he hadn't even heard Frank's comment, continued, "— Has been ever so kind to oversee the peace effort to this stage. They — and I — believe that our efforts would be more kindly served dealing with the Middle East crisis at this time. I dare say—"

But with an increasingly tired look in his whole demeanor, Frank deflated and continued listening as Stanton droned on for the cameras.

Tired of just about everything else in his life as well, he barely acknowledged this to anyone, barely even to himself. And most certainly, not to Angela.

Later that morning as the Senate was breaking for lunch, Stanton walked up to Frank in the halls just outside the Senate Chamber, and lightly clapped him on the shoulder. Frank was luckily turned away, and so Stanton didn't see Frank wince at this.

Turning to him, Frank said, "You know, Andy. I just wish for just once that you'd just let something I bring up for discretionary funding pass. It really wouldn't hurt your beloved electorate to spend a little bit of money on something other than the military or pork projects for your own state, now would it?"

To which the jolly Senator "Pork" admonished his friend, "Relax, Frank. You know it has nothing to do with you."

Frank's response at this was to just shake his head and walk away, not wanting to even deal with Stanton right now.

Later, sitting stiffly but comfortably in his office, he was finally surrounded by the real tools of his trade — his paperwork and his telephone. They were the only things that ever really made Frank comfortable with this job.

He had never really been comfortable giving speeches on the Senate Floor. In fact, if it weren't for the crowds' adulation back home, he wasn't even really sure that he would be comfortable giving any speeches at all. And even the power of adulation had recently wearing paper thin for Frank.

He had been thrust into politics by a family that had had a long history in the profession, going back into the nineteen-hundreds. Coming from Old Money, it was expected that he would either go into politics or the family business. And he liked dealing with business finances even less than he liked giving speeches.

Later in the day, the Senate grudgingly granted Frank a very limited amount for a personal trip with himself and several aides.

Lately, he was feeling so tired and unable to gather much excitement about anything. And going up against Stanton once again wasn't helping his attitude. If it didn't have anything to do with getting the pork for his home state, or a media op to increase his stature in the Congress, Stanton didn't usually bother Frank.

But this was a different era than when Frank first got into office. Back then, most of Congress didn't care whether or not the US budget ran into debt or not. "Debt is the price of doing business," the old adage went. When oil was plentiful, no ruckus was raised over spending while America ruled the world. But those pre-Berlin Wall days were gone.

Now, "the Electorate" was screaming every time taxes were raised and money was spent that didn't need to be spent. Every dollar in every budget counted. And if you didn't bring home the Pork...

Glancing at the ancient grandfather clock in the corner of his office, he noticed that it might be time to call Angela. He didn't look forward to having to tell her that he was going to be going over to Africa yet again — without her — but he had to tell her sooner or later.

Looking around his office of thirty years, his eyes rested on framed bills he had negotiated through Congress, his diplomas, and his pictures. His wedding picture with a much younger version of himself and his then blushing bride ten years his junior. *God, she was gorgeous*, he thought, not recognizing that he was thinking in the past tense.

All the other pictures of his political as well as private past were sprinkled in and around his office walls. Pictures of himself shaking hands with Presidents Carter, Bush and then later, Clinton were there. Along with the obligatory pictures of his nieces and nephews, although he was never really internally a family sort of man; they were there mainly for show.

There were several photo ops there as well of the occasional ground-breakings in his state over which he had presided.
nd on his desk, his eyes finally rested on a picture of a much more solemn and slightly aged Angela, taken just a few years ago in some portrait studio in Northwest DC. There was also another picture on his desk, of the two of them on one of those rare vacations that they had taken together... What? Ten years ago now?

The years only seemed blunted and blurry now. Like so much of his life was seeming to blur lately.

Sighing, he spent several moments letting his attention waver between the vacation photo and the studio photos on his desk. *Whatever happened to us?* he thought fleetingly. And then, just as suddenly, quickly shut the thought out of his mind.

As he contemplated and then picked up the heavy handset of his faux 1950s style rotary phone and hitting the number 1 on the auto-dialer below it, he waited for the ringing to come. *Maybe she won't be home and I can have another few hours of peace and quiet,* he sighed while he waited for the ringing to end and her voice to come through the handset.

At this moment, one of the perkier interns in his office staff chose to wander in with more paperwork for his attention. Cute but not pretty, she had been having aspirations toward her middle-aged and distinguished state senator for some time. She waited patiently just inside his door for him to recognize her presence.

Although most of the interns on the Hill had learned a lesson from the whole Clinton/Lewinsky affair the previous year (that they weren't going to get anywhere with their high-profile superiors), this young girl (and she was still very much a young girl and not a woman as of yet), had somehow taken a very different lesson from the President's woes. She still thought that she had a chance of catching her father figure's attention and approval. That she could turn that attention into something more.

After a few moments of Frank paying more attention to his phone than to her, she bounced further in with the papers she had been waiting to deliver at just the right time. She gingerly laid them on the desk in front of him and waited.

Still intent on his ringing home phone however, Senator Treworthy merely looked up and gave the broadly smiling intern a perfunctory glance and nod.

With his not even responding with a smile though, just a glance, the intern bounced out of the room, somehow secure in his attention and some girlish intent on a future that was never going to happen.

While Frank had barely even noticed, a new set of papers for him to look at had been placed in front of him. He was vaguely aware that it was the new intern, but that was the extent of his awareness. Too consumed by his work and his wife (per usual), he had little attention for anything else.

Not even his aching, tired body was grabbing sufficient attention to distract him away from the earnest business at hand. If his job were going to be bearable at all, he had to give it everything he could.

"Good afternoon. Treworthy residence," came the familiar, soothing deep ranged and heavily accented voice on the other side.

"John, this is Mr. Treworthy. Is my wife there?"

John Masters had been his servant and chauffeur for almost twenty years now, having become employed with his house almost as soon as the Treworthys had taken up residence in Washington.

Frank almost felt as if they should be on a mutual first name basis with John by now, but protocol is protocol. He had almost on many occasions, asked his butler--chauffeur to call him by his first name, as Angela did, but Frank somehow couldn't manage to change his upbringing to reflect that sort of desire.

In some ways, John seemed as if he should be one of the family. But both men kept their distance, honored the upbringing of their respective eras. Frank was still the employer, and John was still the employee. Some things almost never change. In many ways, this particular senator was one of the most lonely men on the Hill.

"Yes, sir," John said. "She is upstairs currently. Shall I inform her of your call?"

"If you could, John. Please? Thank you."

My life might have been so much different. Frank thought while he waited for Angela's voice to arrive, and shuffled the papers on his desk. Sitting with the receiver in his left hand and his right massaging his forehead, he didn't like arguing with Angela, although lately it had become a regular routine. He had just gotten to one of the position papers on his current focus in Africa, when the voice on the other side said (without introduction), "Are you going to be coming home at all tonight, Frank?"

To the point, he thought painfully. *Always to the point*. He had once admired that attribute in his wife very much. But lately... "I'm planning on it, dear. But I do have a little more work to do..."

He could almost hear her exasperation over the phone, as Angela just sighed. "Frank... It seems as if lately that's what you always say."

Pausing where she was standing in the kitchen as she waited for his standard response, her marriage to her marriage was crumbling rapidly. *Any positive response to her question would do the trick*, she thought. *Anything, Frank.* But she was not expecting one anytime soon.

He had been talking to her for a while, getting wearier by the second, but he couldn't let her know the real reason why.

After a few moments of silence, she merely got a muffled "Hmm," out of her husband. She couldn't tell whether it was even a response to her jibe or not.

"I'm sorry, honey. I wish I could," he told her, looking out of the window next to his desk now and barely seeing the riot of colors in raging splendor there. "But you know we're trying to wrap this thing up in South Barundia..." he said, his voice drifting off. With another moment more of silence, Angela could feel what was coming.

Already hearing her husband's mind wandering back to the paperwork she knew was in front of him, she was preempting his saying goodbye with, "Do we at least have any money at this point for me to go along?" She asked him this after a long pause on the phone, and this brought him back to the present.

With his hand now firmly around his head, he said, "You know that's not possible right now. The voter vultures are just looking for something like this to pounce on. Angela..." he started to say, as he set the paperwork down.

Interrupting him, she said, "It's not as if we're broke. You have money and I have money." She could almost hear him close his eyes.

She also knew that he didn't really like for her to go on these foreign trips unless it was to Europe. And this, she gathered, was anything but.

Now leaning very heavily on the kitchen counter on her end, Angela was not even concerned now with whatever John heard. "When was the last time we had a real vacation, Frank? Or even that we just went away for a weekend somewhere? Or even for that matter, had a weekend?"

Now it was Frank's turn to sigh. "I promise you, sweetheart. As soon as this session ends, we'll go away for a while."

"'For a while,' Frank? You mean for a weekend? A week? Two weeks?" His head was beginning to pound as he reached into the top drawer of his desk, rummaging around amid the papers and other detritus there for his medication bottle. Brushing past another medication bottle, he pulled the one he was looking for out and closed the drawer.

"I don't know yet," was his usual noncommittal response.

A few more seconds of silence was accompanied by Angela's usual reluctant response, "I guess I'll see you when you get home."

"I'll try to not make it too late tonight," he said, returning to scanning the papers in his hand.

"I guess that that means no," her exhausted response came back flatly. The all-too-frequent moments of silence began once again to stretch towards minutes.

"Angela, it's a very tense situation there. I don't even want to be going myself, and you'd be highly unhappy. It could also be very dangerous."

"So then, why are you going, Frank?" she asked pointedly.

"Because it's my job, Angela," he said, a little too roughly with his hand going unthinking to his head. "I have to convince my opposition here that we have another crisis brewing, but I can't do that without more extensive press coverage. And to do that, I have to go there to bring attention to the region. The Press is too focused on the Middle East right now."

Sighing over the phone lines, Angela was pleading now. "Frank. Can't it wait?" Just a few days even, she wanted to ask.

Still cradling the receiver on his shoulder, he returned to leafing through various documents spread out on his desk as he talked. Frank's attention was already refocused more on the documents than the conversation, his mind already gone to the next page.

"Look, honey. I know that this is the third time in as many months that I'm going on a junket, but it's reached a delicate stage, and I need to go. You know how important these small countries without a voice are to me."

"Franklin Treworthy, do you know how important your wife is to you?"

Hearing the usual response breaking thorough his mental dam, he put the papers down. Turning his head toward the window with a look of pain crossing his face, "Oh, come on Angie. Please don't start pulling that on me again."

"All right, Frank," she conceded. "Never mind. You win," and she almost added, *as always*.

Sighing heavily and tearfully into the phone, she added, "Will I at least even see you before you leave?"

As the sound of Angela's voice trailed off and she placed the receiver down, Frank in turn set his down on his desk first, and then noticing where he placed it, reached for it and placed it into the cradle. Equally unthinking, he returned to shuffling papers without looking at them.

Suddenly clutching at his chest, he turned to the right side top drawer of his desk, fumbling it open. Grabbing that medicine bottle again, he fumbled to open it.

The label on it read **Nitroglycerine**. He blindly reached for the glass on his desk that held three-day-old water, almost knocking it over.

He turned his attention to it only for the second it took him to grab it. That glass of water seemed too far away for him to reach in time.

But once he managed to, he quickly popped and downed both water and pill.

He sat back and waited, hoping he had once again caught it before...

After a few moments, the pain subsided, and his breathing deepened. Wiping the sweat that had formed off his forehead, instead of lying down like his doctor warned him to do, he plunged back into his work...

Desperate to find that certain document that would give meaning to all of this effort.

TWELVE

Back at their home, Angela slowly placed the receiver gently back down in its cradle. What she really wanted to do was rip the cord out of the wall, pick the phone up and throw the whole damn thing out of the kitchen window.

Looking around her efficiently organized and barely used kitchen, she suddenly realized that the emptiness that she felt today wouldn't be filled with either fixing lunch or brewing more coffee. It wouldn't be filled with going for a mid-day walk or jog in Rock Creek.

Her finely appointed mansion was in one of the more respected parts of Georgetown. What once had been a help emotionally in those early and more desperate days when she had first come to Washington, now wasn't. Those frenetic earlier days had become a dead end that gave no comfort to her whatsoever.

This mansion now felt like it was a prison, with bars of loneliness that caged her in, reminding her that her once fairy-tale marriage had long since crumbled into the dust of the years past.

Those earlier days were filled with distracting activity, entertaining new friends and dignitaries alike in their modest banquet-hall-sized dining room (which she barely even sat in these days). Except for those rare dinners in which Frank actually made it back home by a decent hour, she rarely even took a meal in here.

She had once taken enormous pride in this house which had seemed more like an embassy at times. Now it only served to remind her of how lonely her life had become.

The expansive gardens outside were kept up these days more for show than for utility. She rarely sat outside these days, not wanting to feel as if she were some nun in some faraway, desolate convent somewhere.

Built to resemble a larger version of a fine Tuscan home, its walls were indicative of the character of the neighborhood, which did house many embassies. Not as large as most of the other distinctly mansion-sized ones around it, it was still a personality in the neighborhood.

Trudging back upstairs and returning to her bed, Angela fought to hold back the tears, knowing that she wasn't going to see her husband until late that night, if at all.

He barely even bothers to acknowledge me anymore, she thought. "I don't even know why you even bother to come home at all," she told the air, falling back on the bed. "After all, I'm just a distraction from your more important matters."

Fighting the feeling of hopelessness rising up again like a flood and coming to a decision, she pulled herself off of the bed. Feeling drawn to Maddy's suggestion and steeling herself once again, Angela walked over to her chest of drawers and, kneeling down in front of it, hesitated again.

"Just what the hell am I doing," she muttered to herself, as if she was almost praying at the altar of her despair. "Does it really come down to this?"

She laughed at herself through growing tears. "Shit. Now I'm even talking to myself."

In response, her hands slowly opening the bottom drawer. Rummaging around under her old work clothes — *why did I stop working in the garden?* — she was struggling to even remember the last time she had actually knelt down in the dirt.

"I should go back to gardening," she said to no one.

Finally finding the neatly folded but now dirty newspaper there, she gingerly pulled the ink-stained newsprint out of its hiding place. Almost as if she might get burned by it, she picked it up and laid it on the floor beside her instead of in her lap, gently closing the drawer.

Remembering that the door to the hall was still open, she jumped up suddenly running to close it. Silently pushing it closed with a faint click, she turned and put her back to the door.

John is probably downstairs. She blushed in her now resurrecting Catholic school-girl guilt, still afraid that she might somehow draw his attention. *As if he would even be so concerned with what I'm doing, or even pay attention unless I asked him to,* she thought guiltily to herself.

Once a Catholic school girl, always...

Returning to the dresser, she bent down to pick the newspaper up. Taking it by her fingertips only, she returned to the bed and placed it on top of the covers. Once again, she gingerly opened it up to its full size and then stopped.

Backing away from it, as if waiting to see if it would set fire to the bed, she finally laughed nervously. "What the hell am I doing? I'm acting like I'm a teenager again, and I have to be careful to read 'Lady Chatterley's Lover' in the dark of night."

Standing there drinking in her fear, she suddenly realized that she had come to the point that Lady Chatterley had come to. Except that there wasn't some handsome gardener for her to have her indiscretions with now. "We really haven't come very far at all. Have we?"

Blinking back her tears and finding new courage in her despair, she remembered the delicious nature of reading *Lady Chatterley's Lover.* Reaching down to pick up the paper, Angela took it firmly and sat down on the edge of the bed, relaxing finally into her decision.

"I'm a grown woman now. I'm the wife of a US senator. If my husband even half-way paid attention to me..."

Opening it up to the already earmarked section, she began reading the "men seeking women" section. Scanning down the ads, she was horrified to see some of the very ads that she was afraid she'd find there. There were the usual testosterone-fueled macho nonsense that jumped off the page at her, but there were a few (not many) more measured ads as well.

Calming herself down, she began reading some of the other ads that she didn't have the same violent reaction to. *Some of them are actually quite nice,* she thought, surprised at what she was finding. One or two of them even sounded quite romantic.

Of course, they're all probably complete lies, she thought. And then she realized, *If I weren't already married, I might even consider calling some of these. They don't sound all that bad.*

Except that even as she thought that, she realized that all of the ads here (even the macho ones), were essentially looking for the same thing — a relationship. And a long-term relationship at that. Not at all what she was looking for.

*And just what am **I** supposed to be looking for?* she wondered. *I'm* *certainly not going to find any dashing ambassadors in here.*

Continuing to flip further, she happened onto the "Seeking Other Needs" columns. Reading down the list of "hunks seeking hunk-ettes," "woman seeking women," and the bondage/master/mistress ads, she quickly folded the paper up in as many folds as possible, finding herself thoroughly disgusted.

Crying now without reservation, she asked aloud, "Maddy... What the hell am I supposed to do?"

Walking over to her desk, she carefully opened the bottom drawer and pulled out a spare shopping bag she always kept there, opened it up and stuffed the folded paper into the bottom of the bag.

She folded the bag and its offending material up as many times as she could, and when she was satisfied that no one but the most persistent of voyeurs (or snooping reporters) would ever see what her guilt had tried to hide, she put the whole package in her bottom drawer again. She resolved to dispose of it somewhere other than her home, at the earliest possible time and in the least public fashion.

"It's a good thing that we don't have any nosy reporters going through our trash cans." At least that was some solace in this whole miserable affair. Having shut the door on her momentary weakness, Angela returned to her empty bed to lie down.

Remembering John again, she sat up and reached for the phone. Tapping the intercom key, she waited for his melodious Caribbean accent to come on.

If only I knew I could trust him, like Maddy seems to trust Henry, her chauffeur. I just never know what is going through his head. Even after all of these years. I guess that's what makes him such a good servant.

"Yes, mam?" he finally answered, curtly.

"My husband's not likely to get home until late again, John. And I won't be needing you any more today."

"Are you quite sure, mam?"

"Yes, John. You deserve the rest of the day off."

"Very good, mam. I will see you again in the morning."

Replacing the receiver down, Angela once again settled her body back onto the bed. Her body resting but her mind roiling, she tried to cry, but suddenly found that for some reason, she couldn't.

THIRTEEN

At the Globe, Benny and Gabe were in full flying mode, mixing drinks and delivering them as fast as they could.

It was Friday night, and unlike the other days of this week, this was an especially hectic shift. It seemed all of the lonely people on the Hill had spilled out of the various Senate and Congressional office buildings and were drinking off their week.

And trying desperately to drum up their date for Saturday night.

Many hours later, the evening was finally wearing down towards last call, so Benny finally had the opportunity to grill Gabe about his opportunities the night before.

"So what happened, chick magnet? Did'ya score?"

Wiping the counter again for the last time, Gabe turned to look at his friend with a look of thinly-veiled disgust. "What do you think, Benny?"

"Don't know. All I know is, I turn around after my little fishing trip and... My man's gone. Didn't think you had any time to score, so..."

"No, Benny. I didn't. I had a drink and I went home."

"Why? You afraid to spend a little time in a pick-up joint?"

"Benny, I spend way too much time in *this* pick-up joint right here as it is," Gabe said, losing patience. Turning and throwing the obviously soggy rag into the laundry bin, he added, "I'm just getting a little tired of it, that's all."

Benny, finally realizing that this isn't going to work, shrugged. "Hey, what do you want then?"

"Right now, I just want you to let me finish cleaning up here so I can get out at a decent time. Ok?"

"Hey, I'm just trying to be a friend. You don't gotta jump down my throat, you know."

Stopping in mid-swipe with another towel, Gabe looked over at Benny and got a strange look on his face. "Benny... Why do I call you my friend? We're just so— Gee, I don't know... Different."

"You've known me too long, bro," Benny retorted, mock punching Gabe gently on his arm. "Sides, you've loosened way up bein' 'round me. If you'd stayed as stuck in yourself as when I first met you back in school, you probably woulda killed yourself by now."

Pausing, more serious than Benny usually liked to be, he recovered quickly to his more jock self. Brushing off his friendly concern with his hands flying wide into his self-congratulatory am-I-right? stance, he smiled just a little too broadly.

Gabe, looking both half disgusted and half amused, sighed. "Gimme a break."

"Besides, who makes you laugh? It certainly ain't the women you been seein' the last few years."

Returning to wiping the bar absentmindedly, Gabe began withdrawing again. "I'm tired of looking, Benny. Tired of the same old Washington women. All of them just looking for a husband to take care of them. I want someone to take me for who I am. Is that really too much to ask?"

The always buoyant Benny changed to a more sober attitude, now that Gabe was obviously starting to deflate. He began walking away when inspiration hit, and he snapped back at his friend with a smile.

"Hey! There's ways around it, bud. Howsa bout you doin' one of them personals ads? You never know what you might find."

Gabe brightened at this, finding a way to return fire. "What would you know about personals ads, Benny?" Digging deeper with an uncharacteristic smirk, "I thought you didn't need to resort to shit like that," he shot back.

Hesitant for his New York Minute, Benny recovered. "I don't. But I just thought that you might."

Changing direction once again: "Besides, there's probably some crazy chicks answering those ads." Becoming inspired: "Yeah! I know. So go after one of them 'just sex' ads. You know, 'meet me in the woods for midnight nookie?' That sorta shit."

Turning sober once again, Gabe realized that talking down to Benny's level wasn't going to get him anywhere. Both laughing and sighing, he said, "That's psycho material, Benny. And besides. Don't you remember? We're living in the land of AIDS?"

"Hey, that's what protection's for. Right?"

Gabe merely glowered at Benny, catching sight of one of his customers gesturing to him out of the corner of his eye. Mixing up the customer's usual, Gabe took it down to him.

Returning to his spot, Benny hadn't even moved an inch from where he was. Ready to return to his line, Benny leaned nonchalantly against the bar. "Ok, so maybe that's not your approach." With a sudden flash of a grin, he added, "So do the 'lonely but afraid to commit' routine. You know? The—" leaning on the bar and doing a fake suave Benny interpretation of some other guy's romantic advances, "'Let me massage all your tension away' type of ad."

Laughing, almost in spite of himself this time, Gabe shook his head. "Benny, I swear I don't know about you. Hell, I might as well be advertising for some lonely widow, or horny housewife type."

Almost before the pin finished dropping, "Bingo!" Benny exploded, pointing at Gabe with both fingers blazing.

Completely uncomprehending this time, Gabe exhaustedly asked Benny, "'Bingo,' what?"

"Horny housewife, Gabe! You know all about that. Right?"

Laughing bitterly, Gabe slapped Benny none too gently on his right cheek a couple of times. "That's a real winner, Benjamin. As if I'd go through *that* again," Gabe said, and walked away.

Caught off guard, Benny quickly turned on his heels and followed him. "You just gotta be a little more picky this time, my man. That's all," Benny said, shrugging.

Turning and confronting Benny, Gabe was fed up with this. "You're incorrigible. For that little shit suggestion, you owe me another round of beer. Make that several more rounds."

Turning and walking to a customer at the other end of the bar, Gabe left behind a covertly smiling Benny.

FOURTEEN

Angela was once again in Maddy's limo, only this time heading north on Foxhall and blending onto Water Street. She was still being silent and moody, having fought with herself over her potential infidelity.

Maddy, for her part, was still letting her friend struggle with what she needed to. However she needed to. When she had picked Angela up at her home, she didn't like the pale look she saw in Angela. She had obviously not been sleeping very well, and Maddy didn't want her beautiful friend to grow haggard and old before her time. Wanting to let her speak when she was ready, Maddy rolled her window down to let the still moist and fragrant air of spring rush in.

Out of the blue, Angela asked, "How did you cope with this idea? Before you were being wooed and courted, that is?"

Glad that Angela was at least moving towards the idea, she said, "I was from Iowa. It was unheard of for a wife to be unfaithful."

"Unheard of?" Angela asked, turning around.

"Well, if a wife became unfaithful, it was heard plenty I'll tell you! Talked about from one end of town to the other," Maddy said turning to face Angela with a wicked grin. "So, yes. If it happened, it either stayed unheard of...Or else you were run out of town."

"It wasn't talked about. But you heard about it."

"Sometimes," Maddy said. "If they were unlucky."

"But—" Angela started to say.

"We live in a very different age now. Our indiscretions are not gossip, because most people do not gossip. Or at least, not loudly. Most of us have too many of our own secrets to keep under wraps.

"Now if we still lived in a small town..." Maddy started to continue. But looking at Angela, thought against it.

Angela turned to look out her window, trying to think what to ask next. Her mind had calmed a lot in the last several days, and it was no longer racing the way it had before.

She hadn't fully accepted the idea of having an affair at this point, but she wasn't being as dismissive as she had been previously.

Frank had gotten more distant since their argument, and his hours spent at the office increased to the point where he was only coming home to sleep, coming into the bedroom late and waking Angela sometimes out of a sound sleep.

He was scheduled to leave for his African fact-finding mission tomorrow, and they hadn't really spoken of it since.

Angela was prepared to explore the idea of the Rendezvous Inn as more than an expensive lunch getaway, but was putting her foot in the water there tentatively. One toe at a time.

She would spend a weekend day and night there and get used to the idea of a different bed first, before the possibility of a different lover.

After their lunches (both food and liquid), Maddy rose and went over to Angela and took her hand. "Let's go for a little walk. Shall we?"

Angela knew there was so much more to this little Inn, but perhaps still wasn't prepared for just how much more. Maddy led her out the side door that Angela had seen so many couples leave by, and thought she was prepared for what lay on the other side.

They walked out the door from the semi-darkness and into the Tuscan Hills of Italy (or so it seemed). Beyond this door lay a garden of the most splendid variety and exquisite cultivation, with trees and flower beds in profusion everywhere. She felt as if she were Alice, and she had just crawled out of the dark rabbit hole and wandered into the giddy airiness of Wonderland.

"How...large is this place?" Angela asked Maddy, stupefied.

"Not as large as it seems," Maddy replied, delighted to see Angela's mood change so fully so quickly.

Today is definitely worth it, she thought. Seeing her friend basking in the otherworldly glow of this remarkable place, Maddy wrapped her arm through Angela's, and began guiding her friend through a tour.

Arm in arm they walked through the garden down the expertly manicured brick walkways, where not a blade of grass sprouted anywhere as far as Angela could see.

Pointing with her free hand, Maddy gestured off to the left to indicate a row of cottages that wouldn't be out of place in any European countryside. "You can rent those for the afternoon," she said, and then leaning in to mischievously whisper, "Or of course, for the whole weekend."

"They must cost a small fortune," Angela whispered.

"Yes, they can be. But it's well worth it," Maddy continued. "Not for the everyday excursion, mind you. There are also less pricey rooms in the corridor where we have always come in through," she said. "These are for special weekends. At our level of affordable, that is."

Stopping and turning toward Maddy, Angela had a worried look on her face. "Oh, I don't know about all of this, Maddy. I could blow my entire family's fortune with one weekend a month here. How am I supposed to afford to maintain an affair over the long term?"

"I'm assuming my dear, that whatever man you decide to take up with also has a residence of his own as well?"

"I guess that depends on whether I would want to meet him somewhere at his discretion," Angela said, trepidation once again taking over.

"Look on the bright side, my dear. If you keep it anonymous, the only place you need to worry about is here. And this establishment has its own safeguards in place to deal with unwanted intrusions, shall we say." Maddy said that so matter of factly that Angela hesitated to ask anything further.

"Shall I introduce you to one of the more intimate settings here?"

Angela blanched, but nodded solemnly as her friend started walking away. Sighing a very deep sigh, she once again followed in Maddy's wake, this time drinking in the explosion of color and form everywhere around her.

"It is worth it," Angela muttered to herself. "But how—"

She heard Maddy shouting "Yoo-hoo," in her old lady's voice from where she was a ways off. Angela started walking briskly to catch up.

FIFTEEN

Walking into his apartment bleary-eyed after a Sunday early shift, Gabe silently locked the door behind him. Crossing over to the end table next to the couch that had his answering machine on it, he unfolded the copy of the free paper he'd collected after getting off the subway.

Looking at it now, he was wondering what he was doing with it (besides reading it, that is). He shook his head somewhat wearily, and folding it up again, dropped it on top of the machine, not wanting to even bother checking for messages.

Continuing on into the kitchen, Gabe began to get the ingredients out of the fridge for mixing up another pitcher of his own kind of "cool-aid."

Going for the juice instead of the already pre-mixed whiskey sour though, he only poured himself a half glass and reluctantly closed the door. *Time to start knocking off the hard stuff too early in the afternoon*, he thought. *Just a hair of the dog.*

He was standing deep in not a lot of clear thinking, and walked back into the living room again and stopped. Taking another swig of juice and swirling it around in his mouth, he started instinctively turning toward the fridge again. But knowing better, he kept heading towards the living room instead.

It's a good thing I don't own a TV, he thought. *Or otherwise I'd be in real trouble.*

Crossing over to the end table, he stood staring at the folded free paper, not ready to pick it up yet. Hesitantly and almost as if against his better judgment, he pounced on it, like a snake that might strike if he didn't grab it first.

With his glass of juice balanced in one hand and the paper in the other, Gabe just stood there yet again, almost in mid-thought. Unable to even commit to opening the paper, he almost but not quite, let it go to fall back onto the table.

Beginning to walk away, he found himself returning abruptly and walking right back to the table to pick the paper up that he still had in his hand. Setting his drink down on its coaster, he reluctantly opened the paper up and thumbing through it.

Being familiar with where the ads were, he was still taking his time as he cruised through the rest of the paper; pretending to not be in the process of looking for what he was really looking for.

Plopping himself down onto the couch, he eventually (and reluctantly) found himself at the back of the paper where the personals were. Overcoming his reluctance, he started glancing at the "women seeking men" section, finding very little of interest to him.

Flipping it over to the "men seeking women" section, he briefly glanced down at the various approaches other men had taken. Continuing to flip through the pages, he got to the category labeled

"Seeking Other."

Curious, he began reading the more raunchy None of the Above ads. With ads like — "Girlfriend out of town? Want a man to take care of you?"; "I need a voluptuous older woman to pamper..." And then there was the "Three's more than company...It's a party!" and Gabe's fears were becoming more than adequately justified. Quickly having his fill, he dropped the paper onto the floor at his feet, heading toward the bathroom.

Forcefully opening the shower curtain, he turned the hot water on full force, and began stripping off his smoke-filled clothes. *I feel like I need to wash myself off after reading that*, he thinks, stepping into the now steaming stall. *And I'm a guy.*

The next morning, he was grappling with remembering where the alarm was that was ringing so insistently as he struggled over to the right side of the bed.

Finally pouncing on the sleep switch for the third time, he realized he had to get up. He didn't really have to get up just yet, but he was reluctant to have his life become a cycle of sleep/work, sleep/work.

He had heard the phone ring about an hour earlier and had had the sense to turn the one in the bedroom off weeks before. "Probably just Benny. The bastard," he mumbled.

Benny had this uncanny knack of going out drinking all night long, and still getting up the next morning after barely having slept. And *then* still ending up being more obnoxiously his usual bright-eyed, annoying self. And that was even after "fucking some bitch's lights out. Dude. All, Night. Long." *Uh, huh*, Gabe thought.

Wondering as he lay in bed mustering the energy and drive to get out of it... *Why do I have Benny as a friend again?* And then he wondered after that, *How many more times do I need to ask myself that question before Benny becomes my ex-friend?*

Stumbling out of bed and toward the shower again, he also thought, *Maybe I'm even hungry this morning.*

About an hour or so later, Gabe was feeling almost human again. He'd had some coffee, had managed to fry himself up some eggs, and had settled once again into his favorite chair.

Still bleary-eyed though with his second cup of coffee in hand, he rose out of the chair and hesitantly walked over to the patch of the living room floor which had disturbingly become (in some strange way) his end table. He reluctantly reached down to where he had dropped the free paper the night before.

Picking it up and easing back into the chair, he was once again hesitating to open it. But after a few more sips of coffee and then draining the cup, he finally felt ready to tackle his foe.

Opening the paper up to the earmarked section, he began reading the "None of the Above" ads once more. He was not feeling a whole lot better about reading them now than he had the night before, but at least he was willing to read them this morning.

There amidst all the kinky ads, was one that he had missed. It read: "Single White Male seeking married woman for afternoon liaisons. Clean and disease-free, I want to make all of your fantasies come true."

I guess that doesn't sound too bad, he thought. *But I could probably do a lot better.*

Setting the paper down in his lap, he thought back to his only other encounter with a married woman. It was back in college, and that was not that too terribly long ago.

And although he had finally managed to put the whole affair and its untimely end behind him, he still felt wholly unprepared to try to engage in yet another extra-marital affair. Unless that is, she was largely out of the marriage and their indiscretions would be just prelude to her divorce.

Except that he didn't want to be The Excuse or the jumping-off point either. Gabe had heard of very messy divorces where the marriage breaker ended up hurt (or worse).

His mind wandering now, Gabe thought back to college. He hadn't really been very experienced at that point, and he was still much the gawky, awkward teenager, even though he had been approaching twenty.

Mary Ann hadn't been all that married when Gabe first met her, but she was still legally bound and living under the same roof with her husband. Her husband had had his affairs, and she had gotten used to his wandering eye; accustomed to it and then numbed.

She was in Gabe's Early English Lit class at the local college, in large part to escape her boredom of being home alone all of the time.

After a semester or two, she had grown to like school. Not exactly the type of woman that Gabe thought that he would ever be attracted to though. Mary Ann was both older, and on the plumper side as well, and she wasn't exactly what anyone would call beautiful. But she was pleasant to be around, and for a while, that was enough for him.

She and Gabe had begun talking after class one day and agreed to go out for some coffee somewhere. Going to school in a large town afforded a lot of activities to do, but it also allowed a certain amount of anonymity as well. Gabe and Mary Ann had coffee a few times before

Gabe invited her to study with him in his dorm room (which ended up being a big mistake).

Gabe's roommate at the time was Benny. The one and only Benjamin Harrison.

Having Benny as a roommate afforded Gabe another level of privacy though in a way. Benny being Benny, he was hardly ever there. So there was no one there to interrupt (Gabe thought) when Gabe and Mary Ann fell into bed one day after passionately discussing some thirteenth-century poet's work.

It wasn't the first relationship that Gabe had had, but it was the first one that Gabe felt was actually an adult relationship.

Maybe the fact that Mary Ann was married and that this was an illicit affair helped. That Mary Ann was much more experienced in relation to sex than Gabe was, also probably helped as well.

Before, Gabe had always felt as if he and his girlfriends were groping for some reason to fall in love, as much as groping each other. With Mary Ann, Gabe was finding himself falling in actual love and not groping for the feeling.

This was fine for a while, except that Mary Ann was almost twenty years older than he was and very reluctant to get divorced to marry someone so much younger. And so much different.

Gabe's parents, while not exactly what one would call intellectuals, were nonetheless educated. Gabe had grown up in a house where reading was everything, which is what prompted him to announce to his parents that he wanted to be a writer. Coming from his Irish middle-class background, his parents were both pleased and also hesitant at the same time.

Mary Ann, on the other hand, had come from what she had herself called "trailer trash purgatory," and her going to school was more of a fluke than anything her family would have considered something she could do.

"They'd laugh in my face if I told them I was going to college. I barely managed to get through high school, and I was the only one of my family that had," she told Gabe one day as they were lying in bed.

Gabe was lazily tracing the folds of her stomach, occasionally finding his way down further. "Wouldn't they be proud of you?" he asked, being unable to conceive of a family not being proud of that.

She laughed lightly, and then stroked his face. "My God, Gabriel. You are sooo young," she said, kissing him on his cheek and then grazing his lips. "Aren't you?"

Almost more offended than he was aroused, he asked in a hurt voice, "What do you mean?"

She screwed up her face into what she later called her granny look and said like an old lady, "Trailer trash knows its place." And then switching back to her normal voice (which had a country sort of lilt to it) said, "No matter what happens. I can't leave Hank. I'd never be able to survive on my own."

"But—" Gabe started to stammer, "I can get work. I can support us," Gabe answered, now tending towards a whiny sound that showed his emotional age.

"And that's why you're so young," she told him. "You and me could never get married, honey. Just wouldn't work. You'd get bored with me real quick, just like Hank got bored."

"That's not true," Gabe protested, now seeing where this was going. Allowing her hand to go down his chest to his crotch, she purred in his ear, "It's been nice while it lasted." She had made love to him while he cried and did his best to stay hard, trying to act like a man.

And then Gabe made the mistake of telling Benny about Mary Ann, and it was on the way to being over — quickly.

Benny had (of course) found an excuse to wander into their dorm room at the absolute wrong time. "God damn it, Benny!" Gabe had shouted that day. Gabe had managed to push Benny out of the room while Mary Ann managed to get dressed. It was the last time Gabe ever saw Mary Ann, in school or otherwise.

"Wow, dude! An older woman to boot," was what Benny said, right before Gabe hauled off and gave him a right hook to the jaw. That was also the last day that Benny and Gabe spoke for several years after that.

It was only after Benny finally managed to have some humility to apologize to Gabe in their last semester at school, that Gabe wanted to have anything to do with Benny again. By then though, Gabe only had a half a semester (or so he thought) to put up with Benny.

Gabe moved to DC and finished his degree at Georgetown and had been working his regular day job, when he and Benny ran into each other again at a bar in Dupont Circle.

Both of them had changed, but it was Gabe who had changed the most. He'd become more withdrawn over the years since school, and had become mostly a hermit, only going to work and the occasional bar outing. When he became too depressed to stay at home, that is.

After years of not having seen each other, Gabe was willing to entertain another friendship with Benny, however reluctantly. Even then he knew it was a mistake.

It was Benny who had convinced him to go to bartending school at nights, just so Gabe would have something to get him out of his apartment.

As a bartender, Gabe had come out of his shell being around the buzz of the bar scene. Women started to notice Gabe (sometimes even over Benny's pour on the charm shtick — and sometimes because of it). For a while, Gabe was more popular with the ladies than even Benny was.

Which of course galled Benny to no end.

After a while, with the money he was making tending bar, Gabe managed to quit his stifling association job with the intention that he would write during the day, and tend bar at night. That way, he could finally fulfill his dream of writing that first novel of his.

It hadn't happened that way of course. That had lasted for all of several months.

He had also had a slew of girlfriends — some beautiful, and some not so beautiful during this time. Most of these women had started out being sympathetic (at least to Gabe) to his dreams of writing, but all of them usually came around to the same bottom line question.

So each relationship had come to the same end. Nagging him about getting a real job, each of them drove him to breaking the relationship off. Sometimes sooner rather than later.

He had gotten to the point after each one of swearing off anything except for casual sex. But in the end, even the most casual of sex ended up becoming a relationship. And then Gabe would find himself back in the same old quagmire again.

"And here I am once again," he mumbled to himself. "Only now, I'm resorting to this," he said as he looked back down once again at the piece of anathema resting in his lap.

"Maybe I should just go and become a priest, like my mother always wanted me to be." Throwing the unfolded paper to the floor in front of him and watch it fly into a messy pile, Gabe walked over to the bedroom to cast off his worn bathrobe and get dressed.

Leaving the apartment a short while later, he walked up P. Street on his way to his favorite coffee house, to douse his system with the third cup of his drug of choice for the day.

Alcohol was a drug of choice (he told himself). But coffee? That was the real drug to consume. Both were actually supposed to be the liquid mainstays of writers, but he'd begun having his fill of alcohol with the bartending lately. He'd begun having too much of the sadness and hopelessness that was inherent in the booze junkies he dealt with at work thrown in his face recently.

At least I don't smoke, he told himself. He'd had enough of those effects for the rest of his life by simply working in a bar. Plus his father had been an inveterate smoker. Of course, Gabe also swore off booze as well (the other habit of his father), but that hadn't worked out nearly so well recently.

And maybe Carol was right. Maybe he was becoming a little too much like his father even for his own liking. Falling into the same old traps that led his father to an early death.

As he made his way up P. Street, Gabe was still boyishly handsome enough to get stares from many of the residents of the area (P. Street was well known as the Gay Quarter of DC). But today, even if women were the ones who were scanning him with desire, he would still have been just as unaware of their intent. Caught up in the fog of his own dilemma, it could have been raining outside or even snowing and he wouldn't have noticed.

Crossing 20th Street on his way to the Circle and coming out of his shell, he began noticing his surroundings. Crossing a street in DC while being in a fog was the quickest way out of your misery, he knew, as most of the drivers careening around The Circle weren't generally looking where they were going. Any more than many of the pedestrians who those drivers barely missed.

In the past, he'd sometimes thought of just walking out into traffic and seeing what would happen. But he wasn't to the point of being in that much misery quite just yet. Even though sometimes it felt as if he were careening that way.

So today, he gave all of his attention to crossing the street and not being the next "Breaking News" report on the local TV channels that evening.

Finally reaching the Circle, Gabe was confronted by the same office workers that he tended to see when he was working. Only today there was a smattering of couples spending their lunch hour under the still flowering trees, basking in the sunlight, or lying on the grass or on the now thickening carpet of pink and white quickly fading in intensity, holding each other close, whispering secretively those things that lovers like to whisper. Gabe was almost to the point of returning home.

Looking around him as he strode on the walkway in between these showings of spring, he thought, *Great. Now I can't even go out for coffee without having my misery thrown in my face.*

Walking more briskly and determined, he crossed the inner courtyard of the Circle. The fountain there featured a voluptuous maiden in full alabaster nudity with breasts so perfect they and she seemed to call to him, which only made him stride along with even more purpose.

Lowering his head and even more determined now, he was past the overflowing display of lovers and scenery and was making his way onto the continuation of P. St on the other side, feeling safe now. Sighing and resting easier, he was able to block out the occasional passing couple making lovey-dovey, and able to navigate his thoughts easier.

He made his way the last few blocks over to and approaching 17th Street. He determinedly turned left, cutting across the street now temporarily empty of traffic. *Not too far now*, he thought, ironically now fully awake after his "dangerous" Circle crossing.

Finally arriving at his destination, the sign above the entrance read "The Java Hut." It was hanging low and making the steep steps to his favorite coffee shop even more treacherous, but at least he was here.

The Hut was the local hangout for the punk/alternative music crowd, and although Gabe was totally out of place there looking like a preppie, he somehow felt at home. It was almost a subversive act, coming in there dressed the way he was. And it was a great place to not have to deal with too much attention.

It was the punk aesthetic to practice non-involvement (meaning, non-interest). Once you proved you weren't freakable (able to be intimidated) they mostly left you alone if you paid them the same attention.

The first time he walked in, Gabe got very unfriendly stares all around. He later figured out that the stares were to determine if he was undercover police. When he didn't blanch but ordered coffee and then sat down to write, he was left largely on his own.

He was out of place here and he knew it. The occasional tourist would wander in not knowing what to expect, and then would immediately wander back out again, as quickly as they could, afraid to stay for very long.

Gabe had long since developed some perverse delight in being outside of the outside crowd. It made him feel at home for some completely strange reason. It also helped that this was the one place that he could go in the Dupont Circle area and be relatively anonymous.

Today Gabe walked in and stepped up to the counter to the usual counter grrrl (dressed in black and dripping in the usual Goth punk aesthetic, ripped and tattered clothes and studded with jewelry in just about every place that Gabe could possibly see or imagine — and no doubt quite a few that he couldn't).

This person — Kaaren (Gabe eventually found out) immediately turned away to make him his regular cappuccino, without even asking. Just as he would for many of his regulars. she had taken to doing this for him.

Kaaren turned and handed him his steaming mug, smiled ironically but warmly at him, and Gabe laid his money down and walked away, without waiting for his change.

With her regular customer's back towards her now, Kaaren flashed a smile at him that was not in the least bit ironic. She had gotten quite used to this one of her regular freaks, but was damned if she was going to tell him that. Ruin her cool, that would.

But she was finding him easier and easier to look at as his visits stretched into weeks and then months. No matter how strange he was.

Retreating around the back to his usual table and setting his notebook and mug down, Gabe settled into his favorite couch. *Maybe this is really my home away from home*, he thought with a laugh. *If only I could fit in a little bit more, maybe I should try and work here.*

Opening up his beat-up old spiral notebook and laying it on the table, he flashed on one of his ex-girlfriends asking him sarcastically, "Why do you always have to take that with you wherever you go?"

"Because I'm a writer," he'd say reminding her. "That's why."

He reached into his jacket and took his favorite cartridge fountain pen out and laid it on the paper, in expectation of inspiration forthcoming.

Grabbing his still steaming mug and taking a long draught on it, he licked the foam away from his mouth. Kaaren was passing by him on her way to the kitchen as he was, and held herself back from bending over and doing the licking for him.

In a moment she was gone through the swinging doors to his left though, and Gabe remained blissfully unaware of her intention as he uncapped and finally put pen to paper.

"Single White Male in search of no-commitment nookie..." he started to scribble, and then stopped. *God*, he thought, scratching this first laughable attempt out. *Am I really that influenced by Benny's deplorable bullshit?*

Shaking his head sadly, he ripped the paper out of the notebook, wadded it up thoroughly and rose from the couch to pitch it into the nearest trash can. Congratulating himself as it hit dead center, he laughed and resettled himself back onto the couch to continue.

Several fits and starts (and scratch-outs) later, he began writing in earnest. Scribbling furiously, he barely noticed his secret admirer turning and peeking around the corner, watching him from her counter area.

He liked what he wrote, but re-read it and went to another sheet ripping out the first one. *This one is it*, he thought quietly after finally putting his pen down.

Taking a long draught of his coffee this time, he picked the notebook up again. Reading it over, he felt satisfied with what he'd come up with, and wadded his previous scratch page up scoring another direct hit on the waste can.

Now to get it to the Washington Weekly office, and see what happens, he thought. Sitting back into the lumpy couch, he reached for the mug again to finish it off. *I just might have something here.*

Downing the last of his cappuccino and taking the mug back over to the counter, he left it there instead of on the table like most other the customers did. With Kaaren having made her way when he hadn't noticed back into the kitchen doing something, he left it and walked out.

Coming back out the swinging doors from where she had been covertly watching his last efforts, Kaaren walked over to the trash can where all of Gabe's previous efforts had ended up. Taking the crumpled sheets of paper representing his drafts out and taking them back to the counter to smooth them out, she began reading.

Gabe's first attempts drew a very distasteful frown and then harrumphing, her disdain obvious and her worst fears being soothed as she read the final copy. Then her trademark smirk changed into a smile, and she shook her head sadly in contrast.

Crumpling the paper up again and tossing it into the trash at her feet, she scowled, "Preppies." And then smiling once again, returned to cleaning as another more amenable looking (meaning full Goth attire) customer came in.

Gabe was once again walking briskly through Dupont Circle, with his notebook firmly under his arm, finding himself once again confronted by the multitude of couples, both straight and gay. This time however, it didn't seem to bother him as much as he headed for the subway and work.

He had something to occupy his mind now. *And it did feel good to write*, he thought, as he began navigating the traffic to get to the station.

Even if it was only a personals ad.

SIXTEEN

A week later, Angela was standing and looking out the window while Frank was behind her packing for his trip. Angela was feeling shredded by what she couldn't hardly reveal even to herself, and had long since ceased trying to keep her marriage alive.

As if from a distance, Frank was telling her, "It's only going to be for a week, Angela. I really wish you wouldn't make this into such a big item."

Looking up from his suitcase, Frank softened a bit. "Look, I know that this is the third time in as many months that I've gone over there. This time it's really crucial though. We're at a very delicate stage."

Almost as an afterthought, he added to the air surrounding them, "The facts have to come out."

Turning around but staying where she was, Angela told him, "I hardly see enough of you as it is, Franklin. Even when you're at home much less than when you're flying off to the jungle, or the Middle East, or...Wherever you're flying off to this week.

"Where are all those family values that you're always touting to the folks back—" she said, putting a particularly hard accent on it, she scowled at him saying, "home?"

"Hmmm?" he said, having returned to his packing. Now in travel mode, Frank seemed oblivious to her inflection and her sarcasm. His mind was already on his trip and its importance to him, her comments barely registering.

Suddenly snapping back, as if he finally heard and understood her, "Oh, come on, Angie. Please. Don't start pulling that number on me now," he said, raising his voice about as much as he ever did with her.

Crossing over and sitting on the edge of the bed just out of his reach, Angela began to nervously switch between folding her arms across her chest and placing them limply at her sides. Not knowing what to do or say to get him to understand the anguish that she was going through, she finally surrendered to being limp and exhausted.

"You know how important these negotiations are." Pausing to level an accusatory glance in her direction, he added, "Or at least, I once thought you did."

"Oh, of course I do, Frank. I'm not the air-headed campaign worker that you married. Remember?" she asked sharply, almost ready to add, *Of course they're important, Frank. But only to you.*

Instead beginning to gesture forcefully, she said, "But after all, I am your wife. I'm important too. Have you thought about..."

Pausing to take a breath, Frank got a pained look on his face, looking around for a chair to sit on. Not looking fully at Angela now, he could only say a haggardly, "Honey, you know you're important to me."

She almost told him, "If only you would come over here and put your hand lovingly on my arm. Wrap me in your arms. Something."

Something that might give me some reason to thank Maddy for her earnest interest in helping me find love. but I already have love, she thought.

Looking up finally and with some semblance of remembering, he said, "And you were never an air-headed campaign worker, Angie. If you had been, I wouldn't have asked you to marry me."

This was almost the touch that she longed for. Except that he only sat there in the chair, not bothering to get up and rise to the occasion that was about to be missed.

If only he had known. If only he had been able to tell her what was truly at stake here. If only...he had told her that he was in so much pain.

Except that he didn't. He hadn't. He...couldn't.

Ready to go into full pleading mode in order to get a scrap of reason for his going without her, Angela begged, "So why don't you take me with you this time? I swear, I won't get in the way. I'll even use my own money to go."

Returning to his ingrained way of dealing with his "angry wife," Frank resumed his politician stance to create the necessary emotional barrier for him to deal. "Look, you know that's not possible at this time. The voter vultures are circling every campaign, looking for some carcass to pounce on and begin a feeding frenzy in the next election. I can't afford to give them even the least little whiff of anything to use against me right now," he rolled off as his excuse, barely looking as if he were even present now.

Exhausted from fighting and not seeing her husband's exhaustion for what it was, Angela stood up and threw her hands up in a dramatic gesture. Crossing over to the window once again and shaking her head in response, she said without emotion, "Whatever, Frank. Have a good trip."

Without even turning to say goodbye, she heard her husband pick up his bag and leave. Unable to let herself cry anymore, Angela stifled the tear about to escape her eyes, putting her hands to her head and sniffing it back.

A while later Angela still stood at the window, looking outside, not seeing the green there.

She had watched John put Frank's suitcase in the trunk of the town car and open the door for her husband. Frank had at least turned around to wave goodbye before getting into the back seat and driving off. But that small gesture wasn't enough.

Sighing deeply as if to release herself from her self-imposed attempt to become a statue, she tried desperately to hide her sense of desolation, even from herself.

Past the point of crying, she returned to sitting on the bed, only slightly aware as she did so that she was sitting in the indentation still remaining from where Frank's suitcase had been.

Suddenly feeling the urge to call Maddy for some consolation, instead she found herself walking over to her dresser. She found herself kneeling down with her hands rummaging through the bottom drawer until she felt the rough brown paper of that grocery bag.

Hesitating as she was suddenly aware of what she was doing, she began to rise from where she was, ready to strip off her clothes and return to bed.

But before she did and making a very conscious decision, she sank back down to kneel at the altar of her coming indiscretion. Opening the drawer and slipping both of her hands underneath the work clothes there, she was feeling the roughness again before revealing it to the light of day and hesitating once more.

Stop, start, stop...This should be an easy decision to make, she thought, her heart tightening at the thought. She had lived in a loveless marriage for almost the last ten of the twenty years they had been married. To a politician who would probably be re-elected, regardless of the scourge of divorce (which wasn't really the black mark that it had once been for a politician's career).

She should be able to make at least this decision in her life. After all, all the other decisions in recent years had been made for her.

But she was feeling lost without the only role that had been left to her. And she was feeling lost even in staying or admitting to it.

She had sufficient funds to keep herself living in comfort for a while, until she acclimated to single life again, but she couldn't admit defeat. And she couldn't stay living with the way things were.

"Why can't I just leave you?" she asked the absent Frank, slumping hard against the polished wood.

Her sister had told her to do it months earlier when she had seen the signs. Angela had merely brushed the suggestion off.

Maddy had asked her once before if she was happy in her marriage, and Angela had cheerfully answered yes. What was so important to cause her to stay where she wasn't happy?

I still love Frank, she told herself. Although she was now cringing at the past tense she was feeling around that thought.

That was the answer. He was a good man, and although she knew it would hurt his pride more than his heart, she also knew that she didn't want to hurt him.

He had been very good to her early on in their marriage. When she had moved to Hartford after graduating from college and working a while in New York City, she had volunteered one summer for the senator's re-election campaign. She saw him, fell in love with him, and began spending every waking moment in the campaign office just to be near him.

Working long past the time the other volunteers had since left, Angela had found a new life. And a new love. Nights calling constituents and strategizing with the other staff in the office, became weekends calling and entertaining. All for the Cause.

She had become his right hand, supplanting his senior advisor whose tenure had been on the wane. The weekends at work became supplanted with moments of tenderness, and then massaging his shoulders...And finally ending up in his bed. It wasn't too long after that before they were engaged.

Now feeling disengaged, she was pulling out the folded copy of the free Weekly with which she'd replaced the copy that Maddy had given her. Her tears began flowing, staining the outside of the bag she held.

"Why did you let it come to this?" she demanded, unsure now of whether she was speaking to Frank...or to herself. But there wasn't anyone else in the room to answer the question; what once gave her life meaning, now only gave her pain.

Her influence on Frank and his decisions had waned after their marriage, as new campaign staffers came in to supplant her. Frank's new chief of staff had slowly edged her away from the process.

Angela fell into the role of the dutiful wife, finding herself more and more isolated over the years. The waning influence of feminism, she once justified to herself. *Frank would never do anything to hurt me. It's just politics.*

Still, they grew more and more distant as the years slipped by.

Meeting Maddy at a Senate Democratic fundraising luncheon one day became her only salvation.

She had isolated herself even more, taking more and more vacations without her husband, remaining the dutiful wife for the cameras. But now, that world for her was crashing down.

Still on the floor, her knees folded under her, she carefully opened the paper to the section that she was dreading to look at. Not focusing fully on the page, she suddenly looked sharply at the door, fearing someone would catch her in the act of infidelity.

Half expecting her husband to come back in and find her in this compromising position, she hesitated to return her gaze to the page. Relaxing after a few moments of quiet hum from the nearby city, Angela looked down to the rough newsprint once again.

Closing the drawer and pulling herself up, she was clutching the paper in her right hand as she softly returned to the bed to sit. Feeling like that teenager with the adult novel once more, she found herself thrilling to even the most obnoxious and horrendous ads on the page, wondering why. After all, she wasn't the Catholic schoolgirl any more. And many of these ads felt quite obnoxious and below her need to pay any attention to.

Scanning down the third column, one of the ads there suddenly grabbed her attention. Different from most of the other ads, she sensed some sensitivity to this particular ad that she hadn't expected. So different that she read it over several times, savoring every word.

What would it feel like? she wondered, dropping the newspaper to the floor. Another man running his hands over her body after all these years?

Lying down on her big, four-poster bed, the sense of Frank's suitcase was now lessening by the minute. Her hands going down to the sash of her bathrobe, Angela began pulling gently at it.

But hesitating once again, she merely laughed a bitter laugh. *All these years. And I still hear the nuns decrying any kind of physical touch to the body as being a mortal sin. Once a good Catholic girl, always a good Catholic girl*, she finished, sitting up again.

But all the nuns' loud voices echoing from her past weren't stopping her from thinking of having an extramarital affair. Some things were just a little too deeply ingrained, but not everything.

Reaching down to pick the Weekly up off the floor where it fell, she gingerly touched the paper for reassurance before fully committing to picking it up, as if to make sure that it wasn't going to burn up in her hands. Pushing past that fear, her hands grabbed the paper more firmly, pulling it back up into her lap where it rested for a few more minutes as her mind continued to grapple with what she was actually considering.

My, God, so it's come down to this, she thought. "Whatever happened to happily ever after?" she wondered aloud. "Maybe it's just been a fairy tale after all?"

Of course Maddy had made it firmly clear that she hadn't considered having her affair lightly either.

"In Europe," she had explained the last time at the Rendezvous, "people of power had always taken mistresses, consorts, and lovers of various stripes. It was just a matter of course. The idea was that people of power had marriages of convenience that were largely loveless, and they were made merely as acts of consolidation of power."

Handing her the fresh copy of the Washington Weekly that she now had as encouragement, Maddy had many choice words to say from a very European perspective, concerning the whole Clinton- Lewinsky affair.

"Americans are so childish in their parochial attitudes," she had once said to Angela. This was long before she had brought up the idea of Angela having an affair. *Or had Maddy been preparing me for her later suggestion all along?* Angela thought suddenly.

"But that's not the case in America," Angela had said. "Marriages here were meant to be for love."

"Nonsense, my dear. Marriage for love is such a late twentieth-century conceit. What do you think dowries were for?"

"Gee. I don't know. Gifts for the father of the bride?" Angela had asked naively.

Maddy had only gently laughed at this. "Marriage was a contract. That's all. And the dowry was the transaction price for the sale."

"Sale," Angela spit out.

"Yes. For the taking of the bride off the hands of the father."

"But..." Angela had started to object. But then thought better of it. She had never considered this before. *After all, palace intrigue isn't a new concept*, Angela had thought.

Sighing, *I suppose that I've been more than just a little naive, even after having been in the political ring for this long.*

Feeling more sure of her decision the longer that she thought about it, Angela more confidently opened the paper and scanned for the ad that had intrigued her.

Yes. This seems the sanest of all of them. Laughing and biting her lip, she mused, *A sane ad for an extramarital affair. Seems like a contradiction in terms. Or at least of everything I've ever been told.*

Picking up the phone, instead of dialing the number in the paper, she dialed Maddy's home number. When Maddy's answering machine clicked on with her message, "You have reached..." Angela quickly hung up, doubt creeping in once more.

Dropping the paper to the floor again, Angela strode into the bathroom, consciously washing her hands of the newsprint and of any dirty feelings coming up from her contemplation of an affair.

"What am I going to feel like doing, when I actually find the nerve to go through with this?" she said, lathering her hands thoroughly.

Drawing the shower curtain back, she bent over to turn the water on and returned to the bedroom to place the newspaper back in its bag for later. For either further contemplation...Or appropriate burial in the garden.

She would take a shower first, and explore running her own hands over her own body to see what pleasure she could give herself first. Without resorting to... The Other Option.

What's worse after all, she thought, returning to the bathroom. *Having a little bit of self pleasure? Or an affair?*

"You're going to burn in Hell, Little Missy!" she said, hearing Sister Mary Elizabeth's voice echoing in her head from so long ago, while turning the water on.

SEVENTEEN

Gabe was cleaning up after a fairly heavy evening rush, when Benny sidled up to him with a curious look on his face.

"Ok, Gabe. What's up? You find yourself some nookie last night after all?"

Gabe, suddenly aware that he had been feeling just a little too happy, frowned. "Why does it always have to come to that with you, Benjamin. Hmm?"

"Well?"

"Well, what?"

Dropping down into his "tweens you and me" look, Benny was oh so curious. About pretty much nothing. "Oh, come on buddy boy," he jabbed verbally this time. "Don't I always tell you all about my little dips into the female ponds?"

"Sometimes a little too much, Benny" Gabe said, and went back to wiping the bar down.

Thinking a little more about it but with the business about Mary Ann still fresh in his memory, he was hesitant. "I've been thinking about doing one of those ads," he said reluctantly.

"My man! I knew you had it in you." Raising his eyebrows, all ears now, Benny pressed on. "So? What's it say?"

"Well," Gabe began, suspecting he'd regret it later on, "I'm not going after another 'girlfriend' type again. Not just yet."

"All right," Benny said, sparking alive. "Gone after the tried, and looking to be untrue."

Once a bad Catholic, always a bad Catholic, Gabe thought. "Benny, you're always making it sound so nasty."

"Yeah," Benny said lasciviously, starting to swing his hips as fast and furious as he could. "Doin' the nasty and making it nice."

Shaking his head in disgust, Gabe forcefully threw the towel into the laundry, instead of at Benny's head. "God help me. I'd almost thought about asking your help in writing this, but I should've known better. I think I'll keep what I've already written."

"And you're gonna let your ol' friend Benny approve it, aren't you?" Benny said with a fake hurt look on his face, brightening into a Benny-smile in a Benny heart beat.

Just shaking his head and glowering at Benny, Gabe began walking away, snorting unbelievably at his friend.

"Just write it right," Benny admonished him. "And don't be bein' too much of a 'writer.' Right? Don't make it some English Lit project, ya know? Put some serious sex into it. After all, that's what you want. Right?" Doing the mock Benny punch, "Am I right?"

Taking his apron off and throwing that in the laundry too, Gabe kept walking away. "I'm not sure what I want at this point."

But one thing Gabe did know he wanted: to be left alone by Benny. Possibly for good.

Walking up the escalator at Dupont Circle, Gabe was feeling quite exhausted. He was also back to feeling doubtful about this whole personals thing. *Why does life have to be so complicated?* he wondered.

He was almost ready to turn away from the direction of home and head for The Hut, ready to sit down and write something. Why is writing all of a sudden so hard? I wrote this little personals ad. It doesn't take much to write down a few ideas, and then...

As he was crossing The Circle, the digital clock/temperature on the bank at the southeast corner was reading 1:02. He'd barely make the last Red Line train heading north from Metro Center.

He was feeling both exhausted and a little restless as well. But coffee at this hour was a bad thing. Not unless the ideas were flowing and he was ready for an all-nighter.

Instead of turning and following the pathway around towards 17th Street though, he decided to spend some time sitting on one of the circular benches surrounding the inner circle of the park. At least at this hour, he wouldn't be confronted by dozens of kissing couples. *Well, maybe gay couples*, he thought. He'd have some time to think. Did he want to have time to think?

The always voluptuous and silently still statue of The Maiden in the center of the park was dark and unlit at this hour, but she was still luminescent. Now glowing in the strange orangish glow of the sodium vapor lights of the city, she was no longer the alabaster-looking statue that she was during the day. In this light, she had a soft flush to her that made her almost life-like.

Voluptuous in a very pre-Raphelite way, she— It, he reminded himself, It — reminded him of the voluptuousness of Mary Ann.

Although Mary Ann hadn't been slender like this statue, it got him wondering what had ever happened to his first love. Gabe hadn't exactly had dozens of lovers in the meantime, but Mary Ann still stood out in the background. Since she was married, she hadn't put any expectations or requirements on him like most of the other women he had been with since.

When Mary Ann was with Gabe, they just *were*. The long afternoons that living with Benny had allowed for him to spend with this woman had meant a lot of healing from Gabe's childhood.

He no longer felt lonely with Mary Ann. He felt — loved — and for the first time in his life, it was an adult, intimate love.

Continuing his meditative walk around the fountain (now quiet and not flowing) and away from this reminder of his past, he was again confronted by a couple on one of the benches on the far side this time.

They were essentially almost having sex right there in the park. Almost eating one another's faces in the process, their legs were intertwining in a way that suggested that if they weren't already having sex, they soon would be.

Gabe didn't know whether to be more disgusted that someone would be having sex here in the park at night, or that they would be doing it at all with all of the homeless people curled up on the benches surrounding them. Homeless who, if they woke up, would no doubt watch if they did.

But they didn't seem to notice anyone but each other.

Gabe both longed for that again, and dreaded the consequences. He was almost to the point of believing that he was doomed to this cycle of have and then have not for the rest of his life. It wasn't comforting in the still heat of this night.

He quickly continued on, deciding that tonight was not the night to have a meditative time in the park. Lumps of blankets moving on the grass was one thing, but on the benches was another.

So once again, he had had his mind turned towards something he wanted to avoid for now.

Perhaps it was time for him to quit The Globe and take a trip. Find somewhere sans Benny, and sans any hint of expectations. He'd been wanting to go to Paris for a while now, but he knew that he'd be confronted with all of this there as well.

A nine-to-fiver kind of job again isn't sounding too bad either at this point, he thought, as he headed down the last stretch of P. Street towards home.

The Globe was in between rushes and Gabe knew that Benny was going to begin grilling him as soon as he could.

Gabe turned around after having deposited his last money in the till, only to find Benny right behind him. "Jesus, Benny! I wish you wouldn't do that."

Laughing, "What? You think someone's gonna rob you or something?"

Sighing, "I just wish you wouldn't do that whole leprechaun routine. Just a 'Hey Gabe,' would make me feel a whole lot better. You know?"

Grinning and unable to control himself, Benny launches into his "discovery process" of the evening, questioning, "So...You gonna keep ol' Benny hangin'? Or what?"

Brushing past him, Gabe retreated to the comfort of responding to one of the patrons at the end of the bar. Another obnoxious Hill lawyer or lobbyist, he sighed. But anything was better than dealing with being grilled at this moment by Benny.

When he turned around to fix this guy his drink, Benny was no longer in sight. If Gabe was needing Benny, he'd look around and the Scoundrel he needed would be gone.

When he was hoping for a just a little bit of quiet in between being on the fly with Benny doing His job and allowing Gabe to do his...Then all of a sudden, he'd find his friend standing behind him.

His friend. Quite frankly, Benny was beginning to annoy the hell out of Gabe. *Maybe I should just tell him off,* Gabe thought, but also knowing that it was impossible as long as they worked together.

"Please let some up-tight bitch with looks come in soon," he muttered to himself. "That'd get Benny off my case for a while."

"Talking to yourself again?" Benny said suddenly, scaring Gabe once again out of his wits.

"Harrison!" Bernie, their boss, screamed from the back.

Saved by the Boss again, Gabe thought. He watched Benny, his smile wiped from his face, turn to trudge to the back of the restaurant to find out what their boss wanted this time. "You're gonna get your ass fired one of these days," Gabe said to Benny's back, shaking his head and wondering.

Benny was subdued when he came back into room, and didn't look Gabe in the eye for the rest of the shift.

As they were cleaning up after close, Gabe cautiously asked Benny, "So, what did Bernie want?"

"The asshole wanted me to clean up a mess in the back. That piece of shit Priscilla dropped a can of oil she'd just opened in the kitchen, and instead of..."

"Well, Benny. That is kinda your job, you know. If you hadn't dropped that whole tray of drinks a couple a months ago, you might still be serving instead of being a barback."

Getting a nasty mischievous grin on his face, Benny cupped his right hand around his mouth conspiratorially. "That accounting class my old man made me take in school? Came in real handy when I looked at ol' Bernie's books last year. Nice to have a little job security insurance. If you know what I mean?"

This stopped Gabe in his tracks. No wonder Bernie never fired Benny. The leprechaun had apparently scouted out some private information about the Globe that Bernie obviously didn't want to get out.

Some things suddenly clicked into place in Gabe's mind — things that had been bothering him in the back of his mind for some time. "Last time I tell you any of my secrets," Gabe laughed ironically.

With an almost evil, twisted little look, Benny whispered, "Just a few little security measures, my man. That's all," and clapped Gabe on his back. *The Devil you know*, Gabe suddenly thought.

Changing direction almost in mid-sentence again, "So, you gonna go to the Queens with me tonight? Or you got a hot date from that ad of yours?"

"Later, Harrison," Gabe said, while Benny just grinned. *Better to lead him on,* Gabe thought. *Or he isn't gonna let me get finished tonight. No matter what he has on Bernie,* Gabe finished thinking and went back to cleaning.

It was a cool night when they finally got out. Gabe had only managed to bring a windbreaker with him (just in case). Once outside, it felt to him that even that might not even be enough.

Benny of course hadn't bothered to bring anything, and so was wrapping his arms around himself against the cold. It was especially cool after such a hot night in the crowded, muggy bar.

"Goddamn weatherman!" Benny muttered. "Why can't they get the temperature right?"

"It's not their fault," Gabe said, as he was hailing a cab coming up the street. "And besides, I told you to bring a jacket today."

"Hah!" Benny said, as he was opening the door to the cab. "As long as there's hungry hacks on the Hill, I won't be cold for long." Gabe didn't say anything, but merely followed his friend into the back.

"Connecticut and the Circle, my man," Benny tosses off at the driver before turning towards Gabe, that mischievous grin taking over again. "You gonna make me drag it outta ya?"

"Nothing's happened, Benny."

"Aw, come on Gabe. Nothin'?"

"Well, I've gotten a couple of responses," Gabe allowed, without wanting to elaborate.

"'A coupla responses'? Is that all?"

Not wanting to respond, Gabe thought, *Maybe I should have gone home tonight.* It was hard enough going through this humiliating process as it was, much less having Benny grill him about it constantly. *I shouldn't have even told him I was considering doing it.*

Sighing, Gabe relented. "I've gotten three so far. But that's it."

"So? What'd they sound like? Any of 'em sound like they might be babes?" Benny asked, almost sounding for a moment like he was being supportive.

Turning fully to face Benny, Gabe put his serious face on to tell Benny, "Maybe I can get out at the Circle and just walk home."

But it was almost as if Benny hadn't even heard him. "With that piece of English Lit shit you wrote, you should've had 'em comin' out of the woodwork lookin' for you," Benny said, not even attempting to gloss over his sarcasm.

"Look, Benny..." Gabe started to say, exhausted already and not wanting to fight about it.

Seeing that the confrontational approach wasn't going to work this time, Benny smiled and lowered his voice conspiratorially again.

"Next time bro, let me write the ad for you. All right? I'll get you plenty of babes for you to go out with."

Trying to take the edge off the conversation, Benny turned to the burly black cab driver in the front seat. Scanning the driver's hack license hanging on the passenger side visor, Benny said, "So...Abe," (after noticing the name Abraham on the license). "Ya think my friend here should have any problem finding women to take him out behind the barn?"

Studiously trying to keep his mind on his own business, the driver looked up briefly and coolly in the mirror for an instant, and then returned his gaze to the road.

Trying to avert his gaze out the window to avoid the embarrassment he's beginning to feel, Gabe thought, *Sometimes, Benny can get downright good ol' boy.*

Not getting any response from the driver, Benny screwed his face up sourly, quickly returning his attention back to Gabe. Pretending to not have noticed the slight from the driver, Benny whispered "So'd you call any of 'em yet?"

"I tried calling one of them. She gave me a pager number, but I just couldn't..."

"Give the number to me. I'll call her for you."

"Yeah, right," Gabe told Benny, trying for as much dripping sarcasm as he could muster at this hour.

Not getting the kind of contrite response he was hoping for, Gabe continued, "That's all right, Benjamin. I think I'll do the calling on my own ad."

Getting a serious look on his face, Benny gave up just in time for the driver to turn on to 17th Street, only a few blocks away from The Queens. Deciding to lighten the discussion up, "Turn on Connecticut, dude," he instructed the wearying driver.

"My man. I just don't know why you always got to be so heavy." Thinking the driver was going to miss what he probably went to fifty times a night on any weekend, Benny did his usual, "Whoa, whoa, whoa. Pull up in front of The Queens, bro."

Pulling to the curb after maneuvering around the crowd spilling over into the street, the driver threw the cab into Park and turned around, just looked at Benny without any obvious expression and said, "Twelve."

Going from jolly to perceived threat in an instant, Benny quickly pulled a twenty out of his pocket and dropped it on the seat next to the driver with "Keep the change" and exited the cab to cruise on towards the prowl.

Before Gabe was able to follow, the cabbie turned to him. "It's not my business, but...you should lose that guy," he said in a confidential voice. "He's—"

Already feeling that every cabbie in DC knew Benny all too well, Gabe merely nodded sadly. "Got a reputation? Yeah. I know." Starting his slide out of the back seat, Gabe hesitated, ready to tell the diver to just take him home.

But then he'd hear no end to it tomorrow from Benny. And after that moment of hesitation, he continued sliding out of the cab and towards the curb and the waiting madness roiling there.

As he started to walk towards the bar and the madding crowd, Gabe again contemplated the impulse to turn around and just continue on towards home.

Benny probably wouldn't even miss me, he thought, as he found himself waving to the bouncer, out of habit more than any desire to go in.

Well...so much for that, Gabe thought as he found himself already in the human flow and being buffeted towards the front door anyway. He suddenly found Benny at his side, grabbing him by the elbow and reeling him in.

"Miguel," Gabe said, acknowledging the different burly bouncer at the door, and continued walking into the din and past the line.

EIGHTEEN

Before Angela had left her house that morning, she had taken off her wedding band and laid it carefully on her bathroom sink before she left. Then she worried about the indentation that all those years of wearing it had left. And then that led to, "Oh, what the hell am I doing?"

She had casually walked down to M. Street and hailed a cab. Getting into the cab, she thought about jumping out while they were still in Georgetown traffic, and throwing a Ten Dollar bill on the seat with an apology.

But she didn't. She watched as the cab crawled through the mid-morning shoppers and tourists. She began relaxing again as soon as they were out of the traffic, but tensed up again once they hit the streets of Rosslyn and her deed of treachery became more real.

Having given John the whole day off, Angela was wandering through a section of town that she normally didn't go to, off the beaten path from the safe sections of DC.

She had decided to take the trip to Arlington on the subway over to an area called Clarendon in Virginia, which was just a short way from Georgetown and Rosslyn. It was a part of town where she was sure that she would be less likely to be recognized in.

And then at the last minute, she hailed the cab instead.

Getting out of the cab, she just began walking. So far, Angela hadn't seen anyone that she knew. *It's not as if Frank or I are nationally recognized figures, by any stretch*, she thought. *But just in case.*

And it's not as if Frank is going to change either, she also found herself thinking. He'd been as affectionate as he could be when they were younger, but that affection had dried up over the years.

He had only grown more and more distant as the years rolled on. She knew that he still suffered from what was now called PTSD from his years in Vietnam. She tried to understand, and had kept up her dutiful wifely attempts to soothe him.

But now, that was in the past. Since she rarely saw her husband these days, it wasn't as if it even mattered apparently.

So this was both an adventure as well as a serious search for anonymity that drove Angela to go so far afield from her normally accustomed areas. And this was particularly adventuresome for her, since she had spent much of the last week either pining for Frank to return, or dreading the time when he would.

While this wasn't a particularly bad part of town by any stretch, the area where she was in now had seen better days. More Bohemia than Suburbia, it gave her a certain thrill to be here. She felt like she was back in her college days, slumming it like no other congressional wife would ever dream of risking doing.

In a way, it was even liberating, this going outside the bounds of what was acceptable. Dressed as she was, she knew she stuck out in the crowd, even though she knew she wasn't very extravagantly dressed. And even though it was mid-afternoon, she was still not as alone on the streets as she might have wished for.

Spying a small coffee shop that looked more upscale than most of the ones she had seen so far, she dashed across the street at the first opportunity.

With a bright yellow striped awning hanging outside of the entrance, this coffee shop felt about as out of place in this neighborhood as she felt.

Pretending to window shop at a small trinket store next door, she took quick glances through the window to assure herself that there was no one in the coffee shop she had chosen that might recognize her. Indeed, there were only an elderly couple sitting at one of the tables, and a man reading a newspaper at the coffee bar.

As casually as she could, she ambled over to the door beneath that awning. Opening the door and crossing the threshold, she stepped inside and suddenly realized how bright it had been outside. She had to blink a little as she closed the door behind her, before her eyes would adjust to the dimmer interior. In another time, she thought, this would be a nice coffee shop to come to with Maddy.

It was relatively small and intimate, yet not as dark and dingy as it had looked from outside. Considering the grungy appearance of the more bohemian shops she'd walked past in the neighborhood, it was downright bright and cheerful.

She ordered a latte and began walking to the back of the shop, nonchalantly perusing for — *Yes!* she gleefully thought.
here in the back and in a nook across from the rest rooms, was probably one of the only pay phones left in DC. *Located in the back of the shop and shielded from view of the street*, she thought. *Just right*

for my covert deed, indeed.

Trying to seem as unassuming as possible, she paid for her coffee and thanked the counter lady, taking her drink to a table near the back. After noticing the strange look on the woman's face before she sat, Angela realized that she hadn't taken her sunglasses off after she came into the shop. *No wonder it's so dark in here*, she thought. *I'm not being very anonymous. More like I'm trying to not be recognized.*

Then, taking advantage of the fact, she almost decided to keep the sunglasses on, enjoying the idea of being a secret agent waiting for her contact to arrive. Going further in her imaginings, she pretended that this small shop wasn't in Virginia at all, but in Paris. She was an international spy, and needed the cover.

Laughing at her sudden flight of fancy, she sighed. "Yes, Maddy. I really should get out more," she said to her absent friend.

Taking her glasses off, the outside street scene seemed to just blaze with light. Inside this shop, the quiet seemed even more amplified, what with the strong visual bustle of cars on the street outside but without any noise to accompany them.

Taking a fresh, carefully-folded copy of the latest free paper out of her purse, Angela unfolded it, making sure to not reveal the inner treachery that she was about to surrender to. Pretending to scan one of the articles, she finished most of her drink.

Returning her cup to the counter, she tried again as nonchalantly as possible, to sidle to the back of the shop. Once again being a little too visibly secretive, she saw the counter lady shake her head sadly and disappear into the back of the shop.

Unfolding the newsprint to reveal the personals section with the phone number she had circled, she fee felt even more nervous than she had been all afternoon long.

Why am I so nervous, at my age, to do Anything out of the ordinary? she chided herself. *It's not as if I'm in any way some nationally recognizable person. Quite the Opposite.*

When she had looked at her reflection in her bathroom mirror at home that morning, convinced that she looked like just about any other ordinary housewife. She was not even sure that anyone would consider her to be even close to pretty at this point. *No wonder my husband has lost interest.*

Sighing and unfolding the paper, she also wondered if any other man would find her attractive.

Now that she was over forty, she once quipped to Maddy, "Isn't it all just downhill anyway?"

Maddy had given her a (playfully) very nasty little look at that one. "My dear, you worry too much. And by the way? If you are over the hill, what does that make me?" And then Maddy paused for emphasis, "Dead?"

Angela had cringed after that one. Maddy could always make her see the absurdity of her fears and self-judgments.

When Maddy had seen the look of horror that had come over her face, her older friend had turned on a dime, and broke out laughing. Sighing in turn, Maddy gave her a playfully excoriating look and said to her, "No, Angela Barnes Treworthy, you are most definitely not over the hill." Her look also said, "Pshaw. Don't even think of it."

Standing in front of this phone, her doubts assailed her again. "What am I doing?"

As she took the receiver gently off its cradle, she found her hands were shaking. Hanging the phone up immediately without even dialing the number, she thought, *This is absurd. I'm a grown married—woman, and I'm acting like a trembling teenager.*

Then she had to remind herself what it was she was doing here. Yes. A grown married woman. That she wasn't just making any phone call. *That* she could do from the comfort of her own home.

And why couldn't I have? She suddenly thought. *No one is listening in to my conversations there.* She hoped.

"I can't go through with this," she finally told herself out loud. *I don't know why Maddy even had to suggest it.*

She had determined that she wasn't going to go through with this act of betrayal, and yet, her body hadn't moved from her hiding place next to the phone. *This is ridiculous*, she thought, but she didn't move a muscle.

Finally moving in the direction of the ladies' room, Angela gathered her collection of paper and purse and retreated to what she hoped would be a little bit of privacy to decide what it was that she really wanted to do.

Closing the door and turning on the light, she found much to her relief, that she was in a small one room bathroom without stalls or multiple wash stands. With hopefully more than a minute to contemplate her situation before being interrupted by another customer knocking on the door, she realized how tense she was feeling.

No wonder she had been shaking.

Unlike her expansive bath at home, the size of this rest room gave her an uneasy feeling. It wasn't much larger than the size of her closet. And as she turned to look at her image in the small and paint peeling old oval mirror over the incredibly small bowl of the sink, she didn't see a vivacious woman not past her prime.

What she saw was a haggard older woman who no man would want to spend time with. Maybe it was the harsh and not too bright single bulb in the fixture over the sink, but all of a sudden, she was feeling old. Very old.

Perhaps Maddy was right. Perhaps Frank did have a mistress he was spending his time with. A younger version of herself perhaps. Or a redhead. She would need to wrack her brains now to go over the staff that Frank had now to figure out who it might be.

One of his aides that had gone with him on this trip? Maybe a perky intern was plying her wiles with her husband, a la Bill Clinton and that Lewinsky woman?

Then she thought again. Frank had been looking as haggard as she felt she was looking like in that image of her in this ridiculous little ancient excuse for a mirror. He wasn't looking as if her were expending all of his energy on another woman.

No. For Frank, the job was his other woman, like she had told Maddy at lunch that first day at the Rendezvous.

Angela suddenly felt both utterly ridiculous and contemptibly sad at the same time. She had been brought to this point, not by her own actions, but rather, by her own inactions. She could have fought being marginalized out of the important role she had once previously enjoyed in his life.

Except that she didn't.

With Maddy as a friend, she had somehow felt very young. Not that Maddy was really all that old, as far as Angela was concerned, but in comparison.

And even more than that, Maddy made her feel important. *But that's what friends do*, she thought. *Don't they?* she asked herself and then laughed a bitter laugh. She laughed at herself once again remembering that she was still a Senator's wife.

Still, she was glad to have such a good friend in her life. As ridiculous as her friend's suggestion had been, she had made it out of grave concern for Angela's well being and welfare. Looking back on that first strange day in the country, she remembered that Maddy hadn't made the suggestion lightly, either.

Looking at her reflection in the haggard light of the mirror once again, she mumbled to herself, "When did I get this old?" And then the same refrain of a few minutes ago, "And why would anyone want me?"

Suddenly, she began to cry. The waves of hopelessness she had been feeling for some time now seemed ready now to engulf and drown her. Her longing for her old life — the one she had once experienced at the beginning of her marriage — began to crush her. The thought *Why didn't he keep loving me like he did?* crowded out any sense of hope.

And now I'm reduced to this. Trying to work up the courage to have an affair.

My God. What's wrong with me? Maybe it is time for me to see a shrink.

Angela eventually waded through and got to the final stage. When the voice of her mystery advertiser began, she felt so much warmth and compassion in his voice, she almost felt like crying again. This wasn't what she had expected at all.

"Are you lonely, bored, or just ignored? Is your husband not treating you well?" the deep mellifluous voice on the message began.

"This sensitive male is seeking a married woman who is unfulfilled, looking for conversation and covert relations, without any strings attached.

"Must be able to enjoy sensual massage and give and take in bed. Let me listen to you in the morning and make love to you in the afternoon. And possibly into the night."

What was it she had expected? she thought suddenly, this voice already making her feel like swooning.

He went on to describe himself physically, and then, just as soon as it had started, the message was ending. "My name is Gabe. I'm looking forward to hearing from you."

Then the mechanical voice kicked in suddenly and jarringly, as if it were breaking a spell that that voice had put on her. She wanted to hear that voice again. And again.

But instead the mechanical voice instructed her— "You may now leave a message."

When three beeps sounded for her to leave her message, they were as jarring as the mechanical voice had been after...that voice.

The man called himself "Gabe?" And then the voice of doubt came in again like a demon whispering in her ear. *But is that really his name? Or is it a fake name?*

Abruptly hanging the phone up back in its cradle without leaving a message, Angela turned suddenly, as if to catch someone watching her from the tables.

Only not only was there no one watching her horrendous betrayal, but the patrons which had been there before had since left without a hush, without her even noticing.

Blushing to herself, she now felt completely ridiculous. Even the old woman that had been behind the counter was no longer in sight. For all intents and purposes, she was alone here in this shop. But this somehow made her feel even more lonely than before, rather than secure.

Without retreating once again to the comfort of privacy in the rest room, Angela looked at the number in the paper again and re-dialed.

She listened through the message again — that voice! — and when the beeps sounded, whispered hurriedly into the receiver— "My name is Angela. My pager is 703 555-3812. I'll call you back as soon as I can when you page," she said and hung up.

There. The Deed is done, she thought rather melodramatically.

She suddenly found that she had been holding her breath, and let out a harsh exhale. She was in a panic that the Voice that had been on this message, sounded like the ad.

She had been prepared for a squeaky-voiced, almost perverted timber on the recording. That would have allowed her to comfortably deny that she needed to call again. She could then tell Maddy that this affair business was most definitely Not for her. And no, she hadn't had any desire to continue this charade any further.

But instead she found herself reliving in her mind, the sound of...that voice. The sound of purring perfection that she knew, just knew, wasn't truly who and what this man was. Couldn't be.

"For all I know, you're a married man, and you're only going to break my heart," regretting this as soon as she said it. She also regretted that she had said this aloud.

Poking her head quickly around the corner to take another peek into the still deserted coffee shop, all she could see was the counter woman, who had reappeared again. Who was not paying her the least bit of attention. Who had not heard her call of indiscretion that had had her shaking from head to toe in that secretive corner.

Would he even call her? she wondered. *Will I even call back if you respond?* Could she be traced through her pager number? Was she doing this to be found out by Frank?

"God, am I that much of a neurotic mess?" She didn't know what she was thinking or feeling anymore. She just knew that her situation had to change. One way, or another.

She put her sunglasses back on and with her eyes darting around the little shop to make sure the coast was clear, quickly made her way out and into the street without even looking in the direction of the counter.

Once outside however, she didn't even allow herself to barely breathe until she was as far enough away from the scene of her crime as she could be.

"What the hell am I doing?" she muttered, picking up her pace.

Hailing a cab running up the wrong side of the street, she darted across three lanes of traffic, and slid into the passenger seat and sighed.

"Georgetown," she told the driver, and slid down exhausted onto the faded and cracking leather seat.

Slumped down and feeling hidden, she wondered if she could call this Free Paper and explain to them that this had all just been a mistake. And could they please find her response to this Gabe and delete it. As if it had never been uttered.

Biting her lower lip, she found herself wondering what this "Gabe" was really like. Was that even his real name, or just some sort of scam? Was he some sleazy used car salesman who paid his PR person to write up something guaranteed to reel in any unsuspecting woman who responded?

Or was he really as sensitive of a man as he said he was — and sounded like — on that message? And if he was, why didn't he already have a girlfriend? Or a wife for that matter?

Was he a sensitive, but ugly type? A Cyrano de Bergerac-like ugly little gnome of a character? Someone who only had flings, because no woman would truly have him otherwise?

In Angela's experience, ugly usually didn't make any difference with many women. As long as he had money, that was all that mattered.

God only knows, she had known more than a few men in politics who weren't exactly Adonis. But they had money. And power. And many times, that was enough to overcome any bad breath or lecherous intent that they obviously reveled in.

Hadn't Henry Kissinger (one of the uglier men she had ever met) once said (in that still think German accent), "Power is the ultimate aphrodisiac?"

Angela had met enough men in this town to prove that was true. And sometimes, the uglier the men, the more gorgeous the women who they had on their arm. Truly eye candy.

The only thing she could do now was wait and see. Maybe he wouldn't even page her back. She hadn't exactly left him a very warm message in return for the oozing warmth of his.

Angela decided to forget about the whole business. She was sure that Maddy would ask her about it the next time they talked, but for now, she couldn't worry about it. If she did, she somehow felt that John would know she had done something bad or horrendous when he came in the next morning.

Would he say anything to Frank? she wondered. "Isn't part of the code of the chauffeur to be the confidant?" she sighed. But then why didn't I trust him to being me out here?

Maybe she should trust him. She hadn't felt that for the purposes of today however, that she could. Hence the illicit trip via cab to another part of town.

He had been his usual gracious and appreciative self when she had given him the day off. He showed no hints that he suspected her of anything more than just wanting a day off without any complications.

If only he knew, she thought giddily, and then mentally excoriated herself for committing this injustice to her husband.

Then reminding herself of what she had been brought to do, she dismissed both the giddiness and the mental anguish. *If I had been able to do anything else, I would have done it*, she thought.

What she had done was an act of desperation more than betrayal, she told herself again. Of course she was betraying Frank, but she was also trying to save her sanity.

She would ask Maddy the next time. Surely her sage friend would give Angela some sage advice on how to handle this situation. But could she expect the same level of trust out of her John as Maddy had been able to with her chauffeur Henry?

She would probably need his help driving her around to places she didn't want to have to explain.

Suddenly, she wondered, did she even need to explain it to him? After all, John was as much her employee as Franks. That she might need for him to drive her somewhere to meet this strange man, and be close by in case she needed him for an escape, was merely part of his job. He didn't need to know the particulars.

Otherwise, she might be giving John the day off too many times for him to not notice something was amiss. "Or I could just go for a lot of long walks, I suppose."

Why hadn't she asked Maddy these sorts of questions? "How exactly does one go about this having an affair?" Or perhaps she had. She was having a hard time keeping all of this in her head. This was all so new to her.

Then she wondered how Maddy had gone about all of this when she did back in the Seventies. *Or had it been George Remy who had initiated Maddy? Surely, he must have.*

She felt amazed at how easy her planning this conspiracy was beginning to feel. Once she had gotten past the initial shock of what it was she was doing, she was surprised to feel herself begin to get excited about this whole business. She was even a little thrilled at the deliciousness of the secrecy of it all.

Maybe she would call Maddy up when she got home. Her partner in crime — or her mentor in crime, was more like it.

For now, she was beginning to feel exhausted from her efforts so far. Or to think about it too much.

As they were passing over Key Bridge into DC, she was beginning to feel a little more confident. And sleepy.

Can't wait to lie down, she thought. All of this secrecy and intrigue was getting to her. She had put out a lot of energy to deal with all of the feelings and logistics she had had to today.

The trees still had blossoms on them, but the color of the season was rapidly coming to be a thousand shades of green. She looked forward to her little garden at home.

And secretly looked forward to seeing that riotously glorious garden back at The Rendezvous Inn. Again.

NINETEEN

"Maybe you just need to give him more time," Maddy was telling Angela. They were in her penthouse apartment in the Watergate, with the scene outside the large patio window now overcast. Rain had been falling intermittently all morning and you could barely see Roosevelt Island across the Potomac from the window. Even from this high of a floor.

It had been three days since Angela had left the message for Gabe in the personals ad voicemail. After having had such serious doubts before, Angela was now suffering an intense letdown.

"The least he could do is call," she said, as she continued pacing around her friend's living room. Stopping and turning toward Maddy, she wasn't sure what she was feeling at this point.

"Patience, my dear," Maddy said smiling from her ornate and throne-like divan. "After all," she said, turning to look out the window, "You were hesitant to even consider the possibility just one short week ago."

Turning her gaze in Angela's direction, Maddy smiled gently, raising her eyebrows. "Perhaps he has as many doubts at you."

Deflating somewhat, Angela returned to the couch to sit down.

Reaching for her tea cup, she found herself pausing in mid-reach, curling her fingers as if there was a cigarette there. "It's been a while since I've wanted a cigarette," she sighed.

Looking up, she found her friend still smiling at her. "I understand completely," Maddy told her. Standing up, it was Maddy's turn to walk to the cloudy view. "Maybe I should take you to Europe," she mused, almost as if to herself.

"I should be able to take myself, for that matter," Angela replied dispassionately.

"Yes, but then it wouldn't be so fun. Without your dear old friend Madelaine Lightfoot to buoy you up, even the City of Lights might not be bright enough for you."

Laughing despite herself, "Oh, Maddy." Turning toward her friend, she didn't know what these last few years would have been like without this woman. "Why do we take ourselves so seriously?"

"That my dear," Maddy said, returning her gaze back to Angela, "is a very ancient conundrum."

Frank had returned several days earlier after having stayed for almost a week longer than he had promised his wife. Since he had, things had returned somewhat to normal. Meaning she was still not seeing him much.

She had tried to talk to her husband, tried to engage him. Desperate to find some reason to forget this mysterious Gabe and his bedroom voice. But Frank only seemed even more weary and distant than he had before he had left.

This was worrying to Angela, but Frank wouldn't talk about it. "It's nothing," was all he said. She could sense he was lying, but there was nothing that she could apparently do about it.

This had only added to her sense of desperation that this mysterious Gabe would call and at least confound her suspicions about him.

"Maybe he's died since placing the ad," Angela said, growing melodramatic once again. If a man she hadn't met could sense how desperate, lonely and pathetic she was feeling, what chance did she have with her husband?

Smiling at Angela's new found dramatic urge, she turned to give her a "tsk, tsk" with her finger regarding Angela's self-deprecation.

"Now, now, You needn't go there my dear. Any man would be very lucky indeed to have you. Either as a wife, or as a lover."

Slumping back onto the divan and feeling as if she were a troubled teenager once more, Angela felt neither desirable nor lovable. She felt that if she were either of these, her husband would no doubt be at least a little bit interested in her. If not sexually, then at least wanting to spend more time with her.

"Maddy, now I've started down this road, I don't know what I'm going to do if it doesn't lead anywhere. I was worried sick about making this decision, and now it seems like it was all for nothing."

Turning playful once more, Angela sat up and asked (only half jokingly), "Do you know of a good Convent, preferably in Europe with a nice view I could retire to?"

"None that would accept a divorced woman, I'm afraid," Maddy said with a merry laugh.

"Why does it have to be raining so hard," Angela asked to no one in particular.

"Perhaps now would be a good time to reconnect with that husband of yours. Maybe even find that your emotional distance was merely a misunderstanding."

"Oh, I don't know Maddy," Angela said losing any hope. "I don't even know why his work has become so all engrossing."

"Tell him you want a divorce. Perhaps that would break through the barriers he has set up. Reach some sort of understanding. And then this Gabriel might not even be necessary."

"But what if he said 'Ok?' What would I do then?"

"Have a great weight lifted off of your shoulders?" Maddy replied, with a hint of sarcasm.

Nodding with a distant expression on her face, Angela turned towards the window and bean paying moody attention to the outer storm that was blowing.

It was very late when Frank finally opened their bedroom door as quietly as he could. Angela had finally managed to fall asleep, but even this quiet sound shocked her back to being fully awake.

"What time is it?" she asked, trying to orient herself to where he was in the room.

"I'm sorry," was all he said.

"Frank. We need to talk," she said.

He stopped moving at this. "Angie, it's two am. Can't this wait?"

"How many more years do you think you need?"

He sat down heavily on the bed and said, "I'm sorry. I swear I'll make some time—"

"Franklin, we don't have any more time."

The worry in his voice was competing with his weariness now. "What is that—"

"I don't hardly ever see you any anymore. Except for when you need me to put in an appearance somewhere, that is."

"You know I've had to let go of some staff in these—"

"And I guess having this conversation is not going to fit in your schedule. Is it?"

Rolling over to touch his arm she was now seeing in the semi-darkness, she sighed. "I could come back to work. At your office, I mean. Help take some of the load off...You know? The way it used to be?"

"But you're my wife now."

Releasing his arm, "I don't know what that has to do with it," she said brusquely. This was not going the way she had wanted to.

Turning to face her fully, Frank reached over and turned the light on the night stand on.

"Angela. What is this really about?" he asked, with a pained expression.

Sitting up and turning around to face him, she was shocked to see the haggard look in his face and especially, his eyes. She was about to say, "just never mind," and roll over to go back to sleep.

But she needed to get this out. "I need to have something to do, Frank. My life of just being a senator's wife is not enough for me anymore. And it's been too long for me being out of the work force for me to go back to work for someone else.

"At my age especially," she reluctantly added.

"And what about your friend Mrs. Lightfoot? Don't you two go out and spend time together?"

"Maddy is wonderful. And although the time we spend together is wonderful... It's just...Not enough any more."

"For a minute there, I was thinking that you were wanting a

divorce," he said, without any relief in his voice.

"Well, why not, Frank? I already feel like I'm a single woman anyway. I feel like you're married to your job, and I'm just the mistress you see every once in a while."

For some reason, this struck him as funny, and he laughed. A rusty and brittle sort of laugh, but a laugh nonetheless.

He sighed suddenly, and considered saying something and then stopped. "I just don't know what to say."

"Why can't you spend a little more time with me? Go on a vacation with me? "And I don't mean a vacation home to Connecticut. A real vacation. You know—"

"You know that I have a hard time being able to take off work. This Barundia situation in particular—"

Cutting him off in a fit of anger and frustration, "Oh, fuck your Project, Franklin Treworthy. Don't you think your wife is worthy of your time anymore?"

"Well," he said, growing paler with a look of shock on his face. "You haven't ever used language like *that* before."

Flustered and turning away from him to lay back down again, she added, "Maybe a divorce isn't a bad idea."

"Oh, come on Angie. It can't be that hard on you. It's not like I'm seeing another woman."

"Oh, but you are, Senator Treworthy," she said without turning back towards him. "You might as well be."

She heard him sigh a deep rattling sigh. If she weren't so frustrated with him, she might have heard the warning sign that it held.

Except she was in tears by now, crying in her exasperation as to what to do. And not to do.

After a few minutes of silence, she felt his touch on her back. There was a tremble in it that almost broke through to her.

With another deep sigh, he began talking quietly. "You know why this 'fucking project' as you described it is important to me. Barundia is not much better than it was when I was there in the seventies. No minerals or gold, thank God. But it still has hostile neighbors that would like nothing better to do than take their country to add to their territory."

Turning back over to face him, she steeled herself to tell him what she needed to tell him. And then didn't. "Frank," she said in a whisper. "You can't save the world."

"No, but I can save a small part of it."

She could almost forgive him for his not being there, hearing that part of him that she originally fell in love with pouring though. She could hear his anguish. But at this point, her anguish was almost drowning her.

"Don't you love me any more?" she asked plaintively. She cringed at the sound of her "teenager" coming through, but this was part of what had been there in such anguish recently.

"Of course I love you," he said, hurt sounding like breaking glass in his voice. "Why would you think that I didn't?"

"Because I'm not a saint. I'm a woman. And women need to hear their husbands tell them that they love them from time to time." She reached out to his arm again, running her fingers from wrist to elbow. "We need to be shown that our husbands love us. Is that so hard to understand?"

She cringed again, as she saw a distinct look of pain cross his face. He almost turned away, but just cast his eyes down instead.

"I'm...just...I'm so tired these days."

"Then maybe it's time for you to retire." She was feeling as if this was all of a sudden going somewhere. That she had a chance to bring him back to her. "You're only 50, but you've had a hard life, Frank. Between your tours in Vietnam, and with—"

This time he did turn away. "You know I can't talk about that," he said, now in a barely audible whisper.

"You didn't need to go into the Peace Corps. Everyone would have understood after you came back—"

"I needed to go into the Peace Corps," he said with a bit of ferocity she hadn't seen in her husband before. He began to say more, but then standing, began moving unevenly towards the bathroom. Without breaking stride, he said to her, "I can't talk about this anymore, Angela. Go back to sleep."

Closing the bathroom door behind him, she felt as if the last door to their marriage had just been closed. She would stay with him, but she would try out this indecent proposal first. Maybe a good old fashioned roll in the hay (as Maddy had described it) would help to sustain her.

Until her husband had his Negotiations taken care of. And then perhaps she could have her husband back? As Frank took his shower, Angela began crying for her marriage, until she had cried herself to sleep.

TWENTY

Gabe was busy pacing around his living room and stopping periodically to look at the small piece of paper he was holding in his hand. "Why can't I bring myself to do this?" he asked himself. "It's only an affair."

Finally pouncing on the phone, he quickly dialed the number before he changed his mind. With the sounding of three beeps indicating he could leave a number, instead of punching his number in, he hangs up. And again returns to his furious pacing.

"Shit," he said, fists clinched and reprimanding himself. "Why the hell is this so hard?"

Pacing to the window with the curtains that he suddenly realized he never opens, he draws them back from the glass to be peering down on P Street below. Shocked to see rivulets of rain streaming down the window pane, Gabe was confronted by the rainy day he hadn't realized was out there.

His apartment being on one of the middle floors protected him from knowing what was going on in the world. He didn't need to hear the shouts and raucous laughter of any nights he found himself at home. Or deal with the rush hour traffic and smog that came during the week.

He had taken to not listening to the weather reports unless he had to go out. And since he usually left the heavy curtains closed these days, he had no idea of what the weather was like unless he went out.

He had run back up to his apartment the other day when he could feel it was cooler. He had sensed the coming rain last night, but had brushed it off considering the other things in his life.

"Do I really have to go in to work tonight?" he asked himself. "There's got to be someone else Bernie could drag in to cover for me at the last moment." God only knew he'd covered enough for some of the other bartenders there recently.

What would Bernie ever do if Gabe quit? Let Benny bully him into allowing his Benny-ness back behind the bar? Gabe doubted that.

And besides, Gabe thought, that that would be too much like work for Benny anyway.

With a lull in the heavy bar traffic subsiding that night, Benny corners Gabe again, pulling Gabe into the kitchen for one of his "talks." Looking around to make sure no one was listening, Benny mock punches Gabe on the arm.

"So, Tiger. What they like? Any Babes yet? Or they got too many miles on 'em? You call any of 'em yet?"

Why did Benny think that Gabe was spending all of his down time meeting chicks? Because that's what Benny would do, Gabe realized.

Folding his arms and trying to remain as noncommittal as he could, "I haven't had any more responses than I have already, Benny" Gabe allows.

"Oh, man!" Benny was laughing sarcastically. "You gotta let me write the ad for you next time." Like hell I will, Gabe thought.

Knowing better but confiding anyway, Gabe continued, "I tried to call one of them, but I couldn't get myself to do it."

"Look, my friend. It don't take that much just to make a call. Give me the number, and I'll take care of it."

With Gabe glaring dangerously in response, Benny backs down, once again changing his tactics. "So... How'd she sound dude?" Benny begged, as if asking for crumbs.

"Very professional," Gabe said. And then with a smile creeping over his face suddenly, "And scared totally shitless."

"There you go, my man. She's in as bad a shape as you're in."

Gabe was getting tired of this. "She's probably married Benny. I can understand her not wanting to jump into it."

"So call her tomorrow," Benny said, going into mock boxing stance again. "Sweet talk her into your sweet, ever lovin' arms."

Trying to mollify him, "Maybe tomorrow," was all Gabe wanted to allow him. *It's time I quit this job — and especially this friendship,* he thought. *This is getting crazy.*

Pacing his living room now after waking up the next morning, Gabe has the piece of paper with Angela's number on it in hand. The paper was now well crinkled as it has obviously been wadded up, thrown, and then retrieved and un-wadded numerous times. Between pacing and tossing it back and forth, he makes another attempt to pick up the phone and dial it.

What if she's stone cold ugly? he thought. What if there's a very good reason that she's looking to be unfaithful?

Of course, being unfaithful was still very much in the news recently being reported lately as one of the new national pastimes, what with the Clinton affair dominating the news. So it shouldn't be that obvious as to why.

And remembering back to that voice; so soft and fragile sounding. Her voice didn't sound all that rough. Or deep, for that matter. It was definitely a woman's voice, and it sounded like she could be sexy, too. Once she calmed down, that is.

"This is crazy. Absolutely bat-shit crazy. I meet her, we either click or she runs away. Simple."

Puffing out a sigh of tense energy, he heads towards the phone, un-crumpling the paper as he does.

But as he's reaching for the phone, it rang suddenly, causing Gabe to jump. "Benny," he said, suspecting the worst.

Letting it go to voicemail; whoever called didn't want to leave a message. Just as well.

The quiet having returned, Gabe sat down and grabbed the phone, pulling it to him on the couch.

Dialing the number, he hears the three beeps signaling the pager equivalent of "leave a number." Punching in his, he hangs up. But instead of setting it down, he found himself leaving it on his lap; as if she's going to call any second.

TWENTY-ONE

Frank had gone on his next junket once more, leaving Angela to contemplate and pursue her indiscretion fully and frantically.

She was in the kitchen when her pager went off dramatically beside her. Even though she had been waiting impatiently, the sudden "BEEP, BEEP, BEEP," almost sent her through the high vaulted ceiling.

There it was. The Number. It could be a wrong number, she thought, staring the pager down. And once she dialed it, she would feel alternately foolish and then frightened, afraid of the unpublished pager number now in the hands of a stranger.

As soon as she thought this she realized that, yes, her number would indeed be in the hands of a stranger. He might be a tall, dark stranger, but he would still be a stranger. Yet again, she bemoaned inside that she had let Maddy talk her into doing this.

"Where's your sense of adventure, Angela?" Maddy had asked her. "Even if he ends up a horrible dud for a romantic partner, he might just turn out to be one of your best friends. You never know," Maddy had chided her.

"But what if he's a Mr. Goodbar," Angela asked Maddy, referring to the novel and the movie of the same name that came out in the 1970s. It had come out almost as if it were meant to be a Scare tactic aimed at all the Little Girls who were being quite naughty (or "sinful" to many) at the time. All the women who were going out in search of the "Zipless" You Know What, rising from Women's Liberation and The Pill.

"There's always your little Hideaway in Arlington," her friend had said. Yes. She could go there and call him from that anonymous pay phone there, and hope that he was home when she called.

But then, she began thinking that all of this was insanity.

She would be worried that Maddy were losing her mind in all of this if she didn't feel that, somehow, her friend were just playing the fool. (The wise fool, perhaps.)

Underneath her seeming erratic surface, Angela sensed some purpose that was unsettling in her friend's actions and suggestion. Not in any way malicious, this behavior of Maddy's seemed like a heightened sense of play. And just perhaps, that's why their friendship had lasted this long.

Returning to looking at the number, all she could surmise was that this Gabe lived in DC (by his area code). Other than that...

She wrote the number down and prepared to go to the privacy of her room to make the call.

Perhaps I should make **him** *wait this time*, she thought, and then realized that would just be a stalling tactic.

The stairs climbed and the door to her room closed quietly, Angela walked unseeing to the bed. The piece of paper was firmly clutched in her hand.

She sat down on the bed, but instead of reaching for the phone on the nightstand, she pulled her legs up onto the bed and lay down (with the scrap of paper with the number on it still clutched in her hand).

The next day, Angela rose from her bed where she had been curled up in a fetal position. Her dreams had mysterious strangers who rarely came out of the shadows, and she kept running from where she saw them.

One time, one of these shapes came out of the shadows, and it wasn't a tall dark stranger, but a cameraman with a big lens pointing in her direction with a blinding flash. All she could think in the dreams was crying out, Caught! I'm caught!

She had woken with a start after the last one of these and almost fallen out of bed to burn the piece of paper with the tall, dark stranger's number on it.

After that night, she had placed this piece of paper (ironically, she would later realize), not under the work clothes in the bottom drawer as she had the free paper, but in her underwear drawer. Thinking at the time, *No one will ever look here,* she parted the intimate wear and buried her secret beneath them.

Now carefully parting her "granny pants," she began reaching underneath her old and battered regular wear, and began digging through her lacies.

Once her hands had found the plain piece of paper at the bottom, she pulled it out like it was the holy grail now, and something might happen to it that she didn't want to.

Later, when she told Maddy about this, Maddy laughed. "You'd think the number had an area code of 666 on it, instead of 202." Then thinking again, Maddy added, "Well, some people might even think that those two numbers are one and the same anyway."

Returning to her empty bed, she sat down on the edge, sighing. *This one step won't kill me*, she thought. And then she considered whether she should go to some public pay phone somewhere to make this most private and potentially explosive call. But unless this Gabe was one of the most skillful private investigators, he wouldn't be able to trace the number. It was both an unlisted as well as a privately registered one, for security reasons (Frank being a Senator).

Between bouts of looking at the piece of paper in her hand and staring at the telephone, Angela eventually made her decision and carefully picked up the receiver. Dialing the number written there, she sat stone still as she waited for the ringing to begin. Sitting motionless while waiting, she felt as if she was about to receive word on the death sentence of her marriage, listening as the line clicked through.

But instead of the soothing voice she had heard of this Gabe, she was jarred to find the Voice on the other end the outgoing message on an answering machine, which droned out its monotonous and mechanical— "At the sound of the tone, please leave.."

Almost hanging up before the final beep, she held on, screwing her courage up to say, "Um, hello. This is..." and then hesitated. Squeezing her eyes closed tightly against the pain, she got out, "Angela," before it hung up. "You called me the other day...And I was — wondering, um — if we could meet. Somewhere discreet. Please page me again. When you get this message, that is. Well...bye."

And hanging up abruptly, she returned to lying down and crying to herself. "Of course I'll call you," she said roughly, and laughing bitterly, "If you even call me, that is."

Laying down once more on the rumpled sheets, Angela sprang up again, and reached for her pager. Holding it up to her face expectantly (as if Gabe were going to page her any moment now) she laughed once more at the whole ridiculous nature of this escapade.

"Oh, Angela," she said to her self in a bemoaning, self pitying tone. "Maybe it's just time you grew up and realized that being happy is for others. You don't have the right to expect it."

This though threw her into an even deeper depression than the idea of having an affair. She threw herself back down on the bed and prepared to lie there all day.

"Why am I acting like such a teenager," she then asked the air.

TWENTY-TWO

In the bar that evening, Gabe was crouching behind the counter racking glasses he'd just pulled from the dishwasher for the next rush. Standing up from his couch, he was met by the leering Benny leaning over from the other side of the bar waiting to catch him. "What's up Tiger? You're not avoiding your old pal Benny, are you?"

Still caught off guard after all this time, Gabe jumped again. Not sure whether he should hit Benny or just try and pretend he wasn't there, instead he let out a long sigh giving a tired, "Jesus Christ, Benny. I really wish you wouldn't keep doing that."

Undeterred anyway (even with the Good Catholic Boy using the Lord's Full Name), Benny continued. "So, like, what's up? Call any of the babes yet? I mean, you did get more calls from the ad by now, didn't ya?"

That's it. It's time to get another job, Gabe was seriously thinking, shaking his head hard. *As far away from Benny as I can.*

Sighing and giving up on fighting to not give an answer, he blew out his anger and said a simple, "Yes." He left it at that, and tried to walk away.

"So..." Benny said, following him. Acting about as coy as Benny ever could, "Do I gotta beat it outta you? I'd have to stop being your friend then."

Thinking of giving a stinging retort that Gabe knew would really hurt his friend, he just ends up throwing his hands up in surrender. "Ok. I called a couple of them. And yes. One of them sounded an awful lot like a man."

"Dude, you didn't?"

Almost yelling, "Of course I didn't, Harrison. Jesus. What the hell do you take me for?"

Laughingly throwing his hands up this time, Benny just smiled and said, "Hey, hey, hey. Just checking."

Hesitantly, Gabe continued on. "To tell you the truth, there was only one of them in the whole bunch I wanted to call back."

"So you called her, right?" Benny said, jabbing back. He wasn't about to give up now.

"No, Benny. I didn't," Gabe lied.

"Dude! Do I have to call her—"

"OF COURSE I CALLED HER."

"Ok, ok" Benny said, lowering his voice and throwing his hands up again. He hadn't seen Gabe this upset since that time back in college.

"Jesus," Benny had said at the time. "Jus' go out and get yourself another old broad to fuck." Gabe had almost flattened Benny right then and there.

All mock concerned now and changing tactics, Benny lightened up. "Whew. Got concerned there for a minute, bro."

"Why don't you get the fuck back to work, Harrison. And let me handle my own fucking love life."

Sinking back down to his knees to finish the racking, he continued with, "This is getting out of hand," he said to himself, hoping Benny would hear and leave him be for now.

The next morning after returning home from the Globe late, he found Angela's message on his machine. Writing it down, Gabe was back to pacing again. Looking repeatedly at the paper in his hand as he did.

He reached a decision point and pounced on the phone, dialing the number before he thought better of it. The number punched in and the deed done, he returned to pacing again while he waited (he hoped not as long as this time) for his phone to ring.

"If you don't call me this time, I think I'm just going to kill Harrison and go to jail. That'll put an end to all of this."

Sitting in her kitchen after having eaten a late breakfast, Angela was just to the point of relaxing when her pager suddenly shocked her back to the present with its explosive beeping. So startled by the noise, Angela succeeds in sending the morning paper she was reading flying.

God it's a good thing that John wasn't here to see me do that, she thought, trying desperately to calm herself down.

Grabbing for the paper on the floor where it landed, she picked it up and began folding and straightening it out on the counter before bothering with the pager. *His number won't go anywhere for now*, she thought.

Then she laughed, saying, "This is ridiculous," and reaching for the pager, saw that it's the same number from the other day. Closing her eyes to steady herself, she crossed over to the phone on the wall and began dialing.

fter what seemed like an eternity of rings, there was a click and then silence. No more ringing, and no voice on the other end.

Also hesitating after picking it up, Gabe tentatively asked, "Hello?" With more silence echoing from the ear piece, the voice on the other end finally whispered back to him, "Did you just page me?"

"Is this..." Gabe started to say, and then looking down at his paper in his hand asked, "Angela?"

The voice on the other end replied a little too formally, "And your name is?"

Ready to hang the phone up, he lets his hand with the receiver fall to his side. Gabe instead puts the receiver back to his ear, "Gabriel. Yes. My name's Gabe. Call me...I'm sorry, I thought I put that in my message."

Staring out the kitchen window in obvious sheer terror, Angela cringed inside. "Um, maybe you did. I don't remember," she said, trying to cover up for her feeling like she was a teenager once yet again.

"Um, if this isn't a good time..." the very masculine voice on the other end started to say. *He seems to be polite at least*, she thought, her mind now to the point of freezing solid.

After what felt to Angela like an eternity (but was only a second or two), she finally managed to get out, "No, this is fine." Returning to formality, "Look, before we go any further, I need to lay down some ground rules."

"Here we go again," she heard him saying audibly to himself on the other side.

"Excuse me?" she asked, her first impression of polite and formal upbringing dissipating quickly.

"Nothing," he said. The sound of sighing on the line eventually led to a cautious, "What sort of ground rules did you have in mind?"

Angela tried to adopt her very best business-like voice. She began with, "First of all, this is strictly..."

She started to say, "just about sex," but stopped herself. Involuntarily feeling her breath catching in her throat, she added finally, "An affair."

"Ok. Got that," the Voice said calmly.

"And second, you're not to ask me anything about me. Or my...personal life. This is just to be strictly—"

"I know, just sex."

Hesitating, Angela held herself back from crying for a moment, and carefully enunciated, "An affair," she said, correcting him.

In his apartment, Gabe was sitting up straight on the couch where he had landed now, and was trying very hard to not sound too ironic as he acknowledged, "Right. An affair."

How was I thinking this was going to go? he thought.

After another long silence from the other side of the phone, he eventually heard her say, "I mean it. You're not to ask any questions. About me, about my... other life."

Did he detect a crack in her voice? He sighed and tried to relax himself before finally saying as politely as he could, "Yes. I understand."

"No. I don't think you do," she told him bluntly, part of her wanting to hang up right this instant. Squeezing her eyes shut to keep the tears from starting again, Angela was the one to the start breathing slow to keep the desperation out of her voice.

Breathing hard and finding it harder than she thought it would be, "What I mean is, if you ask any questions, that's it. I'll just disappear."

With only silence coming from the phone for thirty seconds or so, she asked hesitantly, "Hello?"

Finally hearing him sighing on the other side, she realized that she was being shrill, and yet she couldn't stop herself. She was about to apologize when she heard him say, "Yes. I understand. Fully."

He paused for another long moment and his Voice said, "Where exactly did you want to meet?"

She could hear some softening in his tone, and her heart started beating again. *Maybe this is someone I can trust.*

Feeling sick to her stomach now, she tried her best to regain her composure and sound — reasonable? "Where would you suggest? And it has to be—"

"Yes, I know," he said. "Discreet."

"This is about just sex. Nothing personal," she said with some finality. Whether she was warning him of her limits or setting the boundaries for her own self, she was unsure.

"Right. Just sex," he parroted, adding a little too derisively. "Nothing personal."

TWENTY-THREE

It was still a glorious Dupont Circle afternoon. The blossoms were gone on the trees now, but the sky was still a bright blue. The heat of the DC summer was still only a memory in the back of the collective mind yet to be in the coming months, and for now it was still seriously springtime.

With the tattered remains of the lunch crowd still hanging out here and there on the grass and on the various benches ringing the park, it was a day for skipping work altogether. Certainly not one for going back to office cubicles, and there were obviously many here that were going to be doing just that.

Most of the crowd who had covered much of the circle earlier however, had returned to duty. Those still left were dressed very casually, some of them probably out of work. And of course, there were the usual homeless characters around.

But a carefully and now formally dressed Angela began walking into this foreign territory, glancing from side to side fearful that even with the huge sunglasses covering most of her face now, she'd somehow be recognized. Her fear was that some high society friend might just be crossing The Circle at her most vulnerable moment, catching her in the act.

Of course most of those whom she knew would most likely not ever be caught dead mingling with this common crowd. (Except at election time, of course).

They would not be found in such a place as this regularly, and most certainly not during the middle of the day. (However gorgeous it was out.)

Trying her best to look as if she had every right to be here, Angela instead looked completely the opposite. Dressed as if she were some secret agent once again, sneaking off to some drop point and not looking all that secret.

She was obviously very uncomfortable in these surroundings, even in the middle of the day, and she looked as if she was quite ready to run at the least provocation.

Gabe on the other hand, was striding confidently into The Circle from his side of town. With his gaze roving expectantly over the various women walking or sitting around, he didn't have to look very far before seeing his obvious (and highly suspicious) suspect lurking off in the distance.

Wow, he thought. *At least I hope you're the one.* He had started thinking that this was going to be meeting another Mary Ann. Pleasant enough, but still matronly enough to not want to introduce to any of his friends.

But this woman, even though she was ridiculously dressed and looking like she was some actress out of a bad Italian movie from the sixties, was quite beautiful.

He knew that she was married. He could plainly see the wedding ring glinting on her hand in the sun where she stood. *Are you some kind of eccentric cat lady?* he wondered. *Is that why you sounded so strange on the phone?*

Making a bee line for this person he could only assume was the "Angela" he was looking for, he began slowing to a glide as he got closer, suddenly feeling as unsure of himself as she appeared to be of herself.

Looking entirely unsure of who to approach, Angela began cautiously angling in towards the only man close by that she could see herself asking anything of.

He was, yes, on the tallish side. And yes, he was definitely on the handsome side as well. Thinking that this couldn't possibly be the man she was here to meet, she considered walking away from him.

This man seemed to glance in her direction hopefully and was also seeming intent on walking in her direction. What if he's not the man I'm here to meet and he thinks that I'm just flirting with him? Angela wondered, her mind preparing her to flee.

Making a decision and walking up to this person she thought and hoped was this man Gabe, she cautiously asked, "Excuse me, but I was wondering— "

"Angie, I presume?" that Man asked in turn. He looked sincere and was eyeing her in a very appreciative way, but she stopped right where she stood.

Caught between looking like a deer in headlights and her sense of propriety being kicked into bruised high gear, Angela was taken aback and stricken silent. Recovering quickly as her formal training as a politician's wife was coming into play, she replied curtly and icily formal, "Angela. My name is Angela."

Looking around to see if anyone was watching, she hesitantly and formally asked a quiet "And you're..."

"Gabe. I left that in my message? Remember?"

Still anxious and bordering on angry, she replied stiffly, "Yes. You did. As I noted earlier—"

"Why did you—?" he started to ask.

"Why did I what?" *This is not what I expected*, Angela thought.

"I mean, why are you looking at me that way?" he asked.

She couldn't believe that she hadn't thought about this before. "Because I'm old enough to be your mother. That's why," she said, without any irony.

Now caught himself, he was fighting feeling something between being crushed and being amused. All he could get out was, "Excuse me? You're kidding. Right?"

Hating herself as she caught herself doing it, she replied haughtily in a manner that her own mother or even her mother-in-law might answer, "Why would I be kidding?"

"You're...what? Thirty-three? Thirty-five at most?" he said, flabbergasted that she apparently wasn't.

Flattered but taken aback at this, all Angela could do was sputter. "No, I... Thirty-five? Do you really think I'm...Oh, God, never mind." And then still finding herself flattered as she saw that he seemed to be telling the truth, she asked, "You can't be serious. Are you?"

As if he hadn't heard, "And I'm twenty-eight."

"Well, I'm— I'm not exactly in my thirties," she said, laughing at the absurdity of this. Flattery. She didn't know it could still get to her like this. My God, it's been so long.

Innocently enough, Gabe asked her perplexed, "You're not?"

Enough of this, she thought. Just exactly what had she been expecting?

Turning to walk away, something stopped her. She looked at the trees for the first time, taking in the beauty that was around her. She saw the remaining couples still on the bright shining green grass and longed to feel that way again. Could she feel that way again?

Struggling to come to some kind of a decision, she was at a loss. Would he still be there if she turned around? Had she driven him off and would she turn to find his back quickly walking away from her?

Turning back and walking closer towards him, she asked him in wonderment, "You really thought that I was in my thirties?"

God, Gabe thought. *Could it really be that easy?* Confused now but wanting to be acting as if he weren't, he asked her, "Aren't you?"

"Not quite," she said, unsure of what it was she was feeling. "But, thank you."

"How much..." he started to ask, not sure he wanted to know if she were really in her fifties. "How old are you?" he finally asked, not remembering that most women never wanted to be asked their age.

"Remember about not asking any questions?" she replied, not wanting to tell him. *Better leave you thinking that I'm in my thirties*, she thought. And then suddenly began laughing inside at this ridiculous idea.

In fact, she couldn't figure out what was more ridiculous in her mind: whether this almost child would think that she was in her early thirties; or that she might even consider that he would want to have anything, much less sex, to do with her when he found out how old she truly was.

"Well, I didn't think..." Gabe started to say, almost ready to laugh. Trying her best to be firm and taking a liking to him despite her misgivings, she said un-self-consciously, "You can keep thinking that I'm in my thirties. If you like." Then feeling ridiculous herself, she added, "But, I'm forty-two."

Oh, such a vain woman, she heard that little voice deriding her inside her head, that she clearly remembered as being that of her grandmother's saying.

Seeing an opportunity and walking closer, Gabe began putting on the charm, lathering it into a froth. "Ok, fourteen years older. That makes you...what? An older sister? Maybe? Not exactly what I'd call a mother figure." *Benny would be proud of me*, he thought and sighed.

"Well, I..." she started to say, caught now between being extremely flattered and shaking her head to clear what was obviously meant as a romantic gambit. "I... Never mind. I—"

Unbelievable, he thought, but said to her instead, "You're scared shitless. Aren't you?"

Both stupefied and horrified by hearing this language (even though she was occasionally known to use it) at the same time in public, she stammered out, "I, I, beg your— Your pardon? Scared what-less?"

My God, she suddenly thought. I haven't heard this kind of language in years. But then she remembered her fight with Frank and thought, *Am I really getting that old?* and cringed inwardly. *Perhaps I do need to get out more.*

Gesturing around them to the now almost empty park, Gabe decided to really press it. "We're here in this large crowd, acting like someone might hear us. Or even care about what we're talking about."

Smiling suddenly for effect, he added, "I assume that you agreed to meet in this public place because this isn't exactly the sort of place you might be recognized in."

"And?"

"And, we're not exactly in bed yet," he whispered casually, but low enough to not be heard from very far away.

Stunned at this latest infraction of presumed intimacy and looking frantically around her now, she couldn't believe he was being so bold. And in such a public place.

Whispering desperately to him, she said, "Don't you dare say that so loud!" She could feel that her whole face was glowing hot from the embarrassment. And perhaps was feeling slightly aroused, despite herself.

Gesturing around them once again, Gabe tell her, "There isn't anyone around us within earshot, my dear. There's no—"

At no end of being shocked by what this man was assuming, she hissed, "Don't call me that."

"What?" he seemed to ask innocently enough.

Looking around them now rather heatedly and regretting that she had agreed to meet this man at all, she was now feeling both deathly afraid that someone might hear them talking and also regretful that she should even be in this position.

"You know what I mean. You called me— 'my dear.' We've only just met, and...you don't know me yet. And..." she said in a cascade of words and emotions. She was also again feeling at the point of tears from the combination of her frustration and also her embarrassment.

But she was also mortified that he should use a phrase like that, one that Maddy used frequently. She was mortified, but also more than just a little bit titillated at it. When Maddy used that phrase, it was just "old time" formal speech; classical British speak.

But when Gabe had said it, it sounded so... intimate. And Angela had missed Intimate for so long, that it struck a chord in her that was way too deep to be ignored. *Such complicated things, these feelings of ours*, she thought.

Gabe for his part, recognized that she was upset and that he had stepped way over the line with this woman he had only just met.

Regretting that he had been so forward and intimidating (not to mention, intimate), he put his hands up defensively and told her quietly, "Ok, ok. I'm sorry," he said, feeling like he was Benny for an instant.

He watched in fascination as Angela relaxed at this. Almost as if she couldn't help herself.

"But still," he continued, "We are talking about—" he started to say and dramatically lowered his voice (for effect more than anything else), "Sleeping together. Aren't we?"

"I'm not so sure this is going where..." Angela said as she started wringing her hands. Whispering again at the point of tears, she said suddenly, "Yes," and swallowed hard.

"It's just that— I've never done anything— Like this. Before." Her fear was beginning to be overpowered inside by her obvious hunger for this kind of intimate talk.

Moving in closer, he pitched his voice even lower. "And of course, you think that I sleep with married women all the time I suppose?"

Stopped cold by this, she found herself moving in closer as she considered it. "Well...Yes. I didn't know."

Taking a sudden odd offense, Gabe said, "For your information, I've only slept with one other married woman in my life. And that was when I was in college."

Not being able to help himself suddenly, his hurt began coming out.

"And besides," he said a little untruthfully, "She was the one who seduced me."

She hadn't of course. It had been mutual act of seduced. Much like this instance, he thought suddenly.

Shuffling in place in an awkward silence of shared pain, Angela finally managed to get out, "I'm sorry." She said this as she found her hands stretching out unconsciously towards him. "It's just that...I never thought I'd be doing anything like this."

Looking up at her sheepishly, he told her again (this time with much greater empathy and understanding), "I'm sorry, too."

Finally realizing just how much he had been hurt by the whole business with this Mary Ann, he gestured silently towards one of the park benches nearby. Reluctantly nodding and following him, they appeared to arrive at a truce.

Sympathetically, Gabe asked her, "So...If you're so frightened and unsure of doing this, then why are you doing it?"

Letting down her guard at this sudden act of kindness she was seeing in this strange man, she pauses, unsure of how she will react.

"Because my husband hasn't...We haven't..." And then losing it she stops, finding tears welling up from an even deeper place than she had realized had existed even before now. Her well of dissatisfaction was very deep indeed.

Surveying the bench he was now pointing to before sitting down on it, she was trying desperately to calm herself down. Her tears were a private thing, and not something she wanted to share with this strange but comforting man on their first meeting.

Their phone conversation had not gone well, but now this meeting was not going at all as she had expected it would either. *What had I expected?* She wasn't even sure now.

Sitting down quietly next to her, Gabe couldn't help himself and began moving in closer to comfort her. This sudden movement allowed her to regain her composure, and Angela began throwing her defensive wall up again. "Please, don't. Not here. Not now."

Backing away now that he was realizing what he was doing, he said softly, "I'm sorry." Scooting himself a little further down the bench until she relaxed. He continued, "Look, maybe we should go somewhere where we can talk more privately."

Stiffening suddenly, as if all of her fears were about to become justified, she asked icily again, "Exactly how private?"

Ok...That's obviously not going to happen on this first date, he thought, laughing ironically inside. Not that he had actually expected that it would. Then he asked himself, *Is this what you'd call a first date?*

"A coffee shop," he suggested carefully.

Horrified at this suggesting, she interrupted him before this went too far. "Oh, no, no. I can't. We can't. Most of the coffee shops I know are the most public of places to be seen in. Even here was a—"

Smiling cryptically, he told her "Not this one," and laughed, unsure of whether she would go for something as strange as The Hut. "I doubt that anyone you would know would be caught dead in this coffee shop."

"Why?" she asked, as a fleeting vision of some sort of opium din crossed her mind. *How much should I really trust this...Gabe?*

"Because hardly anyone goes in there over the age of twenty-five. That's why."

Shaking her head vehemently, "I can't take any chance of—"

Holding his hands up and trying to be as reassuring as he could, "Please. Don't worry about it," he said, thinking of most of the denizens of his haunt.

"Besides, even if anyone *did* recognize you, it'd be so uncool to be that interested in anyone like us, that they wouldn't probably even acknowledge it. Believe me."

Looking dazed at this suggestion but somehow reassured by the tone in his voice, Angela sighs a deep sigh, saying to no one in particular, "I think I've been too insulated in the last few years."

"Well, I'd say that that's probably a very safe bet." All of a sudden getting a bad feeling, he asked her, "Look, I know I'm not supposed to ask any questions, but you're not, like—" and lowering his voice a little too dramatically even for his own taste, said, "You know. Connected to the Mob." And then feeling silly, just had to ask, "Are you?"

With the ice finally broken at this, Angela caught herself starting to laugh hysterically, wanting to stop herself as soon as this reaction erupted. Desperately trying to cover her mouth and quell her obvious display of attention, she finally managed to calm herself down enough to speak without laughing.

"No," she said, her laughter now under control again. "You don't have to worry about that. Although some people might say that..." she started to say, and then stopped herself again with a giggle.

Her mood now lightened considerably, she started shaking her head now trying to keep from saying anything else. "Oh, never mind," she said, and continued chuckling softly to herself.

Totally confused himself now and wondering about her sanity, Gabe started thinking, Rich people. They certainly are different from us.

Waving to keep herself cool and laughing at herself now, Angela started to stand but sits down quickly, letting out gusts of sighs quieting down into a semblance of her normal self. *If this is what it's going to be like*, she thought, *maybe this won't be so bad after all.*

Instead she said, "Let's go. I do really think I need some coffee now." And still hyper-ventilating a little, she stood. "And just where is this little coffee shop of horrors that you want to sneak me off to?"

Now unsure as to whether (or even if) he wanted to have anything at all to do with this strange woman, Gabe pointed in the direction of 17th Street He was also almost thinking of suggesting that they go at separate times, just so he could (conveniently) loose her.

Harrison, no I am going to kill you for this little suggestion, he thought. *Maybe it is time to settle down and find some half way innocuous social-climbing* (in Benny's words) *"bitch." And then get that "real" job.*

As she started to walk in the direction that Gabe was pointing at with his puzzled expression, Angela thought, *Oh, my! I can't wait to tell Maddy about that last one. She'll be in hysterics. The Mafia. Now that's one she hadn't heard in a while.*

The sign reading "Java Hut" was hung so low over the cavernous dark entrance, Angela found herself at street level hesitating again. With Gabe behind her and gesturing down, he said, "You wanted to go somewhere where you wouldn't be recognized."

With Angela still hesitating to go down these so steep steps, two very punked out (and severely pierced) denizens began to unceremoniously shove their way past Angela and Gabe.

As they disappeared down into what appeared to Angela like near total darkness below, she turned to Gabe. "I'm not sure this is a good idea," she said, ice forming in her breath.

To herself she wondered, *Am I ever going to get used to this kind of covert action?*

To Gabe though, she said, "I can see why no one over thirty goes in here, all right. And I'm not so sure about going in there myself, actually."

"Don't worry about it. This time of day, there aren't enough PIB's awake for you to worry yourself. And you did say you wanted privacy. Right?"

As Gabe began walking deftly past her down the stairs, Angela was fighting the urge to flee again. Curious as to what a 'PIB' was — besides being a soft drink from her youth — Angela reluctantly followed after him.

Clinging to the railing of peeling paint on the far side of the steps, she finally managed to get her question out, "PiB's?"

Turning to look at her strangely, he told her sarcastically, "People in Black?" he said, as if that explained everything to her.

Finally at the bottom of steps that were in deep and stark contrast to the steps at the Rendezvous, Angela found herself at the door, hesitating once more. What had Maddy gotten her into, she thought once again.

As her eyes adjusted to the dingy sparking fluorescent lighting inside, she took a breath and carefully stepped across the threshold. She peeked around just inside before taking the final steps to what she felt was her awaiting doom.

Gabe was already standing over at the counter, casually ordering his drink from someone whom Angela was not even sure of the sex of. Turning back to the door to find Angela standing hesitantly there, Gabe waved her over.

Taking a few more steps in with the light changing as she did, Angela began relaxing (as much as she could). *It only appears to be a black hole from the outside*, she thought.

Joining Gabe at the counter, Angela began taking in the young person behind it. Dressed in a totally foreign fashion to Angela by way of a black torn tee-shirt and matching leather vest, Angela thought that Gabe was completely normal by comparison.

The — girl was it? Or was it a Boy? - behind the counter had more jewelry in, on, and through them (of a nature that Angela wasn't sure she wanted to know about), than she had ever seen before in her entire life. She had seen photos of punk fashion as it were before. This was even more strange than what she'd seen back in the early Eighties when she was in school.

And she knew that every ounce of horror and fear that she was feeling towards — this person — at this time was showing through in her expression. And also, that this person — She? — didn't really care.

Or rather, she did care. The look that Angela was receiving back was one of scorn and extreme disapproval and dismissal. This (young woman, Angela decided) obviously had no liking that she — Angela — was even **in** her shop to begin with.

Accessorized to the max with various piercings and studs everywhere, this Kaaren had a look of disgusted disinterest on her face. Looking from the yuppie Gabe that she'd grown accustomed to, to the high society bitch queen standing next to him — right in front of her — she almost asked Gabe, *"What the fuck, dude?"* But he'd been a loyal customer for a while, so she didn't.

"Whadda want?" was all Kaaren could bring herself to say to the Bitch. And then looking to Gabe with a very glowering look that said, *You're bringin' my shop down, dude,* she thought. *Maybe you should just stick to going to the corporate slug coffees from now on.*

Taking his wallet out, Gabe slides a twenty over the counter in Kaaren's direction. Slapping her hand over it with a bang on the glass, Kaaren does a disappearing act as if she's stealing it, walking contemptuously away.

"I'll pay for it today. We can talk about how we're going to handle this later."

"I'll just have a Latte," was all Angela could muster, eyes still wide as much as from the lighting, as the clientele contemptuously surrounding them.

"Latte, it is," Kaaren repeats from the brewing side of the counter, even though Angela thought that she wasn't even paying any attention to her.

Paying no mind to the power play between these two opposites, Gabe points in the direction of some very out of the way tables in the back of the place. "We can sit and wait for her to bring the drinks to us."

Sarcastically over the sound of the grinder beginning to make its noise, Kaaren throws a menacingly sarcastic, "Don't go too far," in Angela's direction. "Don't want to get lost now," Kaaren finished off, smiling just as menacingly, with teeth bared wide with even more silver and gold inside.

Not sure whether she's shocked or disgusted, Angela musters an "Oh, we won't" sharp retort in return. She'd dealt with enough sniping

Congressional wives in her time to know how to find the right seemingly innocuous, but slaying retort herself.

Arriving at the most secluded table he could find, Gabe pulls the chair out chivalrously for Angela to sit. Surprised but pleased, Angela sits, smiling as she does despite herself.

"Well," Gabe asked her after he had sat, "If I can't ask you any questions, what are we going to talk about?"

"Well, why don't you start by telling me about yourself," she said, as she started sitting primly and properly erect.

I can look as different as I want to as well, she telegraphed in her look to the glaringly disapproving punks at the table next to them. "Why this ad? Surely you could have any woman you wanted?"

Smiling shyly, Gabe only said, "I'll take that as a compliment." Leaning back in his chair and waiting for Kaaren to deliver their drinks, he tried to think about the best way to answer that.

As Kaaren arrives, she placed their drinks none too gently on the table, walking away in an obvious huff. Smiling at this, Gabe leans in for a second to think his answer through before revealing it.

"What can I say?" he finally said. "I've gotten tired of girlfriends who only wanted me to do and say only respectable things. Wanting me to live their version of The Good Life." Shifting his pose back a little, he divided their drinks from where Kaaren left them, and took his first sip. It was a little on the tepid side, as if Kaaren was expressing her disapproval through giving them the opportunity to drink quickly and leave. "Too many expectations, you might say."

"So you decided to avoid commitment and have an affair," Angela said, with a faint air of disgust in her voice. Whether this was pointed at either Gabe or herself, she wasn't quite sure.

"Exactly," Gabe agreed, sensing the disapproval coming from across the table now. But he decided to continue. "No muss, no fuss, no demands." Smiling just a little bit too mischievously, he added (leaning in and whispering), "Like you said. Just sex."

Looking frantically around them once again, Angela calms a lot sooner, seeing that no one was now within earshot, the punks next door having removed themselves to a table near the door.

Sighing, she gives him a playfully disgusted look with an, "I wish you wouldn't do that."

"What? You mean talk about what we're doing?" Leaning back in his chair and sipping on his coffee for a long moment, he finally told her, "Like I told you before. No one here cares. Except that I'm afraid that Kaaren is not finding it terribly amusing."

Lost as to who (or what?) he's referring too, Angela asked him, "Kaaren? Who is...?"

"Oh, I'm sorry. I meant the barista," he said, puzzled at the expression he's finding her giving him. "You know? The one who served us the coffee?"

"Yes, I know what a barista is," she said a little too sharply, to hide her not really truly knowing.

Gabe figured that, no, she doesn't really know, and pointed in the direction of Kaaren, now studiously avoiding acknowledging them. Shaking her head slowly, Angela said, "Oh."

"They don't give a shit what we're here for. Or why. So you might say this is perfect."

Blanching at the obscenity once again, "I really wish you wouldn't say that."

Confused again, Gabe asked, "What?" Realizing what she found objectionable, he was quicker to apologize this time. "Oh, that. Sorry. Just a habit."

Feeling misunderstood again, he told her confidentially and as soothingly as possible, "Look. I know you've never done this before. I get that. But I really am a good person, you know."

Leaning in toward Gabe, Angela had a solemn look on her face. Not sure of whether to laugh or cry, she decided to confess to him a little bit. "I wouldn't be doing this if my husband weren't such a workaholic," she suddenly allowed. "And that he takes his work more seriously sometimes than I think he does me."

Leaning back uncharacteristically herself this time, Angela was yet again feeling on the verge of crying. What the hell, she thought, feeling out of control. Let me just have this man take me to his home and do whatever he's going to do with me. Hopefully I'll like it. Hopefully he won't hurt me.

Opening his mouth and then closing it several times, Gabe suddenly realized that he was no longer in control here. The full impact of what he was about to do with this woman was coming to him, and he's unsure if he should even be doing it.

She's very beautiful. And fragile. Is she going to go home with me and then accuse me of raping her? Luring her into my den of inequity and then calling the police?

He'd already seen two sides to this woman, and hoped that his instinct — that this was someone he could trust to not cry "Perpetrator!" on him — was right.

Sighing, he looks up and gives her a hard look, hoping for the best. "So..." he asked her slowly. "How do you want to do this? Do you need to meet with me for a few more times before you make any decision? You know, until you feel comfortable enough?"

He was suddenly looking like a little boy to her, unsure of what he was doing. Not looking at all like he was someone she should consider dangerous.

He's so shy. So sensitive, she suddenly realized.

Before this moment, Angela hadn't really thought that this Gabe was indeed someone she might be able to trust. But his sudden vulnerability had caught her off guard. She was feeling her heart opening up to him, surprising her with the intensity of the feeling.

As she was actually softening to this possibility though, she said abruptly, "Maybe next time," and rising from her chair began walking away.

But stopping herself just a few feet away and just shy of the door, some part of her couldn't let herself leave. Her body was reaching a decision point which her mind could not make, as she returned hesitantly.

She returned to the table and sat down slowly, and she covered her face with her hands. She found herself saying, "My God. What the hell am I doing?"

Gabe, looking worried once again about the sanity of this woman he'd just met, found himself melting too. It was time to drop the games. The amount of doubt and conflict was obviously taking its toll on this woman.

Funny, he thought. He somehow hadn't realized the depth of how hard this whole prospect might be for her. Before now.

As compassionately as he could muster, he said, "I know this can't be easy for you. To come to a decision like this."

Standing again and combing her hair with her hands, Angela

reached a decision point. *My God*, she thought. *I'm actually going to do this.*

"Is your apartment close by?" she whispered.

When he nodded, she told him, "Take me there. Now. Before I change my mind." And she began walking in the direction of the front door, not checking to see if he was going to follow her.

Stunned at this sudden turn of events, Gabe could only nod in agreement, and found himself standing and following in her wake in the direction of the door.

Not even acknowledging the perplexed and now becoming hard to hide hurt Kaaren standing behind him as he did.

On the way to his building, Angela had insisted that he walk a number of paces in front of her. And that he try not to look back in her direction as they walked. She wanted as much anonymity as she could get after their meeting in the park.

She allowed him to be quite a number of paces in front at one point, and Gabe had to fight hard to not look behind himself. He began worrying that she just might bolt before he knew it, having had second thoughts about this along the way and slipping away without his knowing.

Well...if she does, he thought, *it's just not meant to be I guess*. The streets were relatively calm and the sidewalks sparse as he walked.

He occasionally stole a glance in one of the many plate glass windows that lined the businesses on P. Street As he did, he also caught glimpses of the yet again sunglasses-wearing and tightly wound figure of Angela following discreetly behind him.

As he walked, Gabe all of a sudden wondered, *Surely this woman knows someone who's openly gay*, he thought. *She can't be that sheltered.*

And here I am taking her into the heart of Gay-dom, possibly opening her up to being recognized. Except he didn't hear anyone on the walk down P Street calling out her name.

Then he realized, *Well, she probably isn't worried about a gay man at this point*, he thought bitterly. And I hope she isn't still worried about me. And then came the thought, Should I still be worried about her?

Once he reached the front door of his building, he suddenly found the figure of Angela beside him. He counted on her being able to walk nonchalantly into the building without the front desk person questioning her, so he held the door open as if she were a visiting dignitary and she walked on past the front desk regally without raising anything more than a polite, "Madam," and a curt nod.

Slowing as he made his way in and waving to the regular day person, Charles, he continued on towards the elevators and the patiently waiting Angela.

Punching the UP arrow button, he used the opportunity to turn slowly. She was there standing beside him, trying her best to not look in his direction. She looked dazed again, but at least she was there.

The elevator ride up to his floor was made in silence too. Once the elevator pinged their arrival, he held the door open for her without her acknowledging him.

Arriving at his door, she quietly placed herself opposite him as he keyed the lock and opened it (not seeing any of his neighbors who were no doubt still at work) noticing them. He stepped inside and held the door open once again for her to enter.

Feeling more like a doorman than a potential lover, he let her move past him. Fumbling around for the light switch that he knew was there, he worried that his darkened apartment was a little too dark.

Wishing now that he'd left the drapes at least partly opened, he wondered if she was going to ask to leave. But then again, he really didn't think that she would be coming back with him this time anyway.

Hesitating for a second at the door, Angela drew in a deep breath, as if she were about to plunge into some dark, deep and chilly unknown waters without any air. Concerned that this strange man's apartment was so dark, her fears were almost suffocating her.

Once they were both inside the door and it was shut behind them, the lamps around the room made it seem less dark. Being the gentleman he asked, "Would you like for me to draw the drapes for you? I know it's kinda dark in here, and since we're on the fifth floor, no one is likely to be seeing in."

Comforted by his concern, she was quick to react though. "No, that's ok," she said tightly, her chest still trying to catch up with her mind. "I'll get used to it," she said, more to calm herself than him.

She was more afraid of being seen at this point, than of this man becoming dangerous and needing to be shown for his nefarious deed should he kill her.

But Gabe seemed genuinely sincere and kind, and as she moved further into the room she found that her fears were subsiding somewhat.

Even with the lights on and the apartment suddenly not so dark, he could see she was as stiff as a board. So he, thinking of one of the only things he could, asked, "Would you like something to drink? I'm a bartender, by the way. So I can make you something to relax."

Turning a little too sharply at this, she couldn't keep the fear from rising in her eyes again. Cringing inwardly at her continuing cowardly turns, "I'm sorry, but I still don't know whether I even want to relax just yet."

But with her Catholic upbringing prevailing, she told him, "Thank you, anyway," doing her best to try and relax.

"Doesn't have to be alcoholic," Gabe added quickly.

I hope this gets better, he thought. *Otherwise, this is going to be a real short affair.*

Quickly retreating to the other side of the room where she saw photos and diplomas hanging, she sighed and said, "A Gin and Tonic, maybe?" *If he has family photos and where he's gone to school on his walls, I guess he can't be all that bad* she thought.

She blinked once and turned slowly, eyeing the couch in the middle of the room. But not knowing whether she should relax that much yet, she added, "Yes. That might be nice."

Easy enough, he thought. And then, *Finally.*

"Coming right up," he told her, as he disappeared into the kitchen. He continued talking through the bar and asked, "Ice?"

Relaxing a little bit now despite herself, Angela turned back to look at some of the framed pictures on the wall. Stopping at one of Gabe and two people who were obviously his parents, she said over her shoulder, "Yes. Please."

He looks so...normal. Nothing at all frightening. So why am I still so afraid?

Right, she told herself. *I'm contemplating having an affair with this man. This man who isn't my husband. And even after twenty years in politics, I'm not that jaded yet.*

It's only natural to be afraid, she kept telling herself.

Coming back to something outside herself, Angela was realizing that Gabe was still talking to her. Obviously trying to relax her, what he's telling her doesn't even register. Except that he's continued talking. Continuing on to a frame with a diploma in it, she was taken aback. "You've got a degree in English Literature?" she throws out loudly to him.

Frantically trying to finish mixing the drinks and get hers to her, he misses her question. From the kitchen he asked loudly, "What was that?"

Matching her voice to his, she asked more loudly in return, "I said, I was surprised to see that you have a degree."

Walking in with their two drinks in hand, he hesitates before handing Angela her drink. Not knowing whether he should be offended by her question or not, he asked as nonchalantly as he could, "Didn't you know that bartending is one of the requirements for being a writer?" Handing her drink to her, he gestured towards the couch.

Taking it gingerly, she can't help herself from reacting. "Oh, so you're a writer?"

As he took a sip trying to calm his own nerves down, he noticed that she was still standing over by the wall. It was his turn now to be caught off guard. "I'm trying to be. That was the argument that ended my last relationship."

Now having a more complete sense of this man, Angela found herself moving slowly towards the couch. She realized she'd sat down a little too close to him just as she began inching away discreetly. "I'm sorry to hear about that," she said, and regretted the comment right after she said it.

"So was I," he told her, sinking back into the cushions.

Leaning in towards each other, Angela was suddenly aware of how close Gabe was suddenly sitting, and carefully moved to the opposite end.

Draping his arm carefully and slowly onto the back of the couch between them, Gabe took a sip of his drink. Angela stared into hers.

"Is there something wrong?" Gabe asked. He sounded more like a little boy being reprimanded than a man representing a threat. "Don't you think I'm attractive?" he asked, the sound of hurt rising in his voice.

Her glass shook. "Believe me, that's not it at all."

She wanted to tell him that she found him very attractive indeed. *But that seems too forward,* she thought, and then laughed at the incongruity.

Sighing and rising, Gabe said as he began his usual pacing routine when he felt nervous, "I don't know. Maybe I was wrong, trying to do it this way. Maybe I should stick to picking up women in bars—"

Putting her drink down on the end table suddenly, Angela stood, placing herself in Gabe's path. An awkward moment passed as Angela realized she's initiated this sudden move. With the taller Gabe now looking down into her eyes, he seemed to be as much at a loss as she was.

Leaning towards her and finding her not backing away, he placed his lips slowly on hers, and found her lips parting to accept the invitation.

Angela felt as if she was being shocked by an electric charge as their lips touch for the first time. *God, how I've missed this!* She screamed inside from the pleasure, as any vestige of ice and doubt melted quickly away.

The sparks of electricity at their lips, start descending from her lips down through her breasts and find their way all the way down into areas that haven't been touched for even longer.

Feeling this woman melting under his touch, Gabe took the chance of placing his hands at her sides and allowing them to slowly wrap around her waist. Their kissing, tentative at first, grew more and more passionate as the seconds blended into minutes.

His hands traveled slowly down from Angela's waist toward her more sensitive areas, ready to remove them at a second's notice.

But not finding any resistance, he began massaging her back side down towards her legs and pulling her into his now bulging pants. Backing away slightly with his hands moving gently around to her front, he began unbuttoning her blouse slowly as they kissed.

Not wanting this to end, Angela continued to not object.

When he began kissing down the front of her now exposed neck and further down onto her chest, she moaned, "Oh, God. Take me into your bedroom. Now. Before I change my mind."

Easily picking her up and carrying her towards the open bedroom door, she squealed approvingly, "Oh, my God," sounding more like a teenager caught gleefully off guard and not like a mature woman.

"Are you sure this is what you want?" he asked her as he crossed the threshold.

"No," she answers honestly, her breathing labored. "But don't stop now," she said, and smashed her mouth hungrily back onto his as they near the bed.

Angela, now past the point of no return, found herself being gently placed on the bed, with Gabe now looming on top of her. As she began moving under him, she let her body relax completely with a deep wracking sigh. *How many years has it been?* she thought, feeling alive for the first time in what seemed like decades.

Pulling Gabe's shirt off over his head without unbuttoning it, she grabbed for his zipper as he was unzipping her slacks, pulling his pants off deftly to slide to his knees where they are keeping him aloft on the bed.

In turn, he pulled her slacks completely off and tossed them onto the floor. He finished the removal of his own pants and unhooked her bra, caught it in his teeth and flung it to the floor, too.

Arching her back to meet him and lifting herself off the bed to meet his mouth, he removed her blouse to join their combined clothes on the floor. Her body now completely alive and shivering from the sensation, Angela was now laughing despite herself.

Tearing the covers off the bed from where they were already in shambles, Gabe slid her up the bed while simultaneously pulling her panties off.

Angela was suddenly aware that she was now completely naked in an unknown man's bed, and her upbringing began taking over.

Desperately attempting to pull the covers up and over her without thinking, she watches as Gabe removed the last vestige of his clothing — his boxers — from where he was now standing at the foot of the bed, his erect penis taunting her.

Laughing ironically to herself as her more conscious self began asserting control over her mind, Angela slowly started lowering the covers, playful and surprisingly sensual, revealing her body inch by inch, but not fully.

Taking his cue, Gabe crawled onto the bed like some kind of wild animal on the hunt. With both of them laughing now and the tension broken, Gabe finished his crawl at her throat and began kissing her from there.

Kiss by glorious feeling kiss, Gabe made his way down from her neck and past her now tingling breasts and then under the covers, where Gabe arrived at his intended destination.

Angela heard herself moaning, "Oh, God. Yes! Oh my God!"

Catching her breath at this unexpected turn of events, Angela began dissolving into the deep hiss of pleasure; her own pleasure. *Yes. I remember now. This is what it felt like*!

"Oh, God," she yelped suddenly, all inhibitions now thrown to the wind, with the deed being done and her aching years of loneliness now seeming over.

She started giving herself over completely to this man she had met only a couple of hours ago, coming back to that place and that person she had once dreamed of being. She opened her eyes and found a deeply intense Gabriel staring into her eyes as she felt him plunge inside of her.

As her back arched up in the agony of pleasure cascading through her body, she wrapped her legs hungrily around his body and allowed him access to her soul.

Lying in bed a short time later, Gabe was still languidly stroking each breast in turn, with a limp and exhausted Angela contentedly enjoying the afterglow.

Having relaxed completely, her doubts now seeming completely gone, she asked, "So. Are you planning to be a bartender all your life?"

not even thinking of the response that was swiftly coming.

Stiffening, Gabe catches himself reacting at her simple question and forces himself to relax. "No. I want to write."

"Oh, I'm sorry. That's right," she said, trying to hide her reaction. "So...tell me what you're working on then?" she said, reaching beneath the covers to begin playing with his sensitive areas.

"Ummm," Gabe said, suddenly unable to concentrate. "I'm still developing the plot. I don't like to talk about what I'm working on while I'm doing it. It might jinx it, you know?"

No, she didn't know, but she decided not to get into it at that point.

Remembering what he had told her about the other women in his life, she asked, "And your girlfriends? I take it you weren't happy with any of them."

Laughing bitterly quite suddenly, he said, "That's putting it mildly."

"Is that why—"

"You're in my arms? Yes. I'm tired of women wanting me to be who *they* want me to be, and not who *I* am."

Turning over suddenly to face him, she looked up into his eyes, now relaxed enough to actually see them instead of not being able to get past his face. "And so married women wouldn't be wanting you to take care of them? They'd be safe?"

"Exactly. Like you said...'Just sex. Nothing personal.' No expectations. No demands."

Turning to face away again, Angela felt a strange look creeping into her eyes, stinging somewhere silently, asking herself, *So why is this suddenly so frightening to me?*

She turned further and nuzzled her back into this strange man who had just given her one of the best afternoons of lovemaking she had ever experienced. As she did, she tried to imagine that she was actually in the arms of Frank when they were first married. Perhaps this could somehow be a way to feel as if she wasn't being unfaithful to her husband.

Except every time she tried to imagine it was Frank who was holding her, all she saw was Gabe's face over her shoulder. This was both extremely comforting as well as having a feeling of danger attached to it. That he had apparently been so haphazard with his love life, only added to this feeling of vulnerability on her part.

Perhaps this could be just what she wanted. One night or an afternoon a week; and the rest of the week she could pretend that her life with her husband was a normal one.

A relief valve, she thought, *with my basic physical and sexual need for intimacy met, and the rest of my life wonderfully untouched.*

But part of her was now hurt at the idea of seeing Gabe only once a week. *Why am I feeling this?* she thought sharply. As she had stressed repeatedly to him, this was just an affair. And Gabe had agreed to that.

No reason to feel hurt. No reason to feel used.

Now dressed and walking Angela to the door, Gabe was feeling the awkward silence once again standing between them like a third person hanging over the whole afternoon.

"So...When do you want to meet again?" he couldn't help himself asking.

Angela, looking shy after all of their intimate moments together this afternoon, was silent for some very pregnant moments. Unsure even exactly what it was that she wanted now, she whispered tentatively those words no one wants to hear. "Can I call you?"

Obviously crestfallen after what he thought had turned out to be such a wonderful first time together, Gabe turned icy. "So that means I'm never going to hear from you again? Doesn't it?"

Wrapping her arms around him for a last passionate parting kiss, "I really enjoyed today, Gabriel. But...I don't know." Sighing with her indecision, "I'll just have to see. Ok?"

Nodding silently and opening the door for her, when the elevator door finally opened after what seemed like an eternity to her, she turned back briefly to wave at him once she was inside as the doors silently clanged shut between them.

Moping back inside his apartment and closing the door behind him, he leaned his back into it to close it loudly. After this afternoon of sex in bed and then the wonderful shower they had after with even more delicious sex in the rushing water, Gabe doesn't know whether to laugh bitterly or start crying.

The only thing he could allow himself to think of (ironically enough), was that this time it's a good thing that Benny wasn't here to catch him in this.

"Now I think I really need a drink."

TWENTY-FOUR

The next afternoon, Angela and Maddy were having a nearly silent lunch at the Rendezvous restaurant. Each of them was nibbling on their meal, with Maddy looking up occasionally to find an as yet still silently intent Angela intently not looking in her direction. Putting down her fork down abruptly for emphasis, Maddy can't stand it any longer.

"Out with it, Angela Treworthy. Was it nice? Was he a boorish pig? Speak to me," Maddy spoke, as if she were The Queen, demanding a report from her recalcitrant daughter.

Putting her fork down as sheepishly in contrast as Maddy had fiercely, Angela began to have a mischievous look spreading over her face as she allowed herself to remember what she felt while Gabe was holding her.

Caught in almost girlish embarrassment, she managed to get out a clipped, "Oh, he was all right. I guess." And shrugging like her thirteen-year-old self caught reading about Lady Chatterly, she found herself smiling in spite of herself.

Almost wanting to rap her friend's knuckles like a schoolteacher now, "All right?" Maddy managed to blurt out. "You've just slept with the first man other than your husband in how many years? And it was merely—" and pausing with a comically threatening look in her eyes and mimicking Angela's feigned teen-aged complacency, Maddy finished with (in a shrill voice), "All right?"

Angela, unable to catch herself, began looking frantically around the room again at this, once more to find that there was no one really listening. Releasing a pent up breath, she returned her eyes to Maddy's intense but playful glare. That this should still have such a Catholic response in her, caused her to laugh to keep from crying.

With some sparkle coming to her eyes, she looked once again sheepishly at her best friend, calmly but lamely admitting, "Ok. So it was nice." And returning to picking at her food once more to avoid Maddy's mock furious gaze, she added a quiet, "And now I've gotten it out of my system."

Taking another tack out of desperation, Maddy continued probing. "My dear, there is more to—" and curling her fingers in a very twenty-something air-quoting fashion, continued with, "'Getting it out' of one's system, than just one good old- fashioned roll in the hay."

She tried her best to match Maddy's savoire faire, and began, "Well, as you so crudely put it my dear Maddy—" Not having the ability to be the natural actor that her friend had shown herself to be, however, she quickly lost the thrust of her parody and merely said, "My God, I'm constantly amazed at what I'm learning about you in all of this!"

"Don't change the subject," Maddy told her protege, scowling at Angela's stubbornness.

"Yes, I've had my 'roll in the hay' as you so crudely put it. And now," she added, mock scowling back at Maddy, "I'll wait for Frank to get back and see if I can have the same with him."

Exhausted at her friend's thick nature, Maddy asked more quietly, "Have you tried recently?"

Deflating suddenly, her indifference melting away and on the verge of evaporating, Angela said, "Maddy, there has to be a way that I can get my husband interested in me."

And then blushing at the memory of the day before, she found her face curling into an uncharacteristic for Angela smile. "Gabe was interested in me."

Triumphant at this first revelation, Maddy burst out, "Ah, ha. So. He has a name! Gabe." Shaking her head at the effort, "Quite frankly, my dear, I wasn't even sure I'd even get that much out of you."

Suddenly aghast at the feelings that rose up inside of her, the clouds that had been parting were now once again threatening rain.

"Maddy," she started to ask, "What would I do if I said it was wonderful? And that I felt like a woman again? And..." with the dam finally bursting and her previous exalted mood gone completely, "And that it wasn't with my husband? That it was with some strange man that I had only just met. That I felt things with this man that I've never even felt with another man, much less my own husband." Her hands having managed to relax, they were seizing up again on the table in front of her. "How am I supposed to deal with that?"

Suddenly, as if realizing that she's lost, "Oh, God..." Angela said with the tears now starting to roll down in anguish as the rains came once again.

Reaching over and placing her hands over both of Angela's on the table, Maddy was almost succumbing to tears herself.

"My dearest Angela. Don't you think that I know what you're going through? That I felt much the same feelings racking me with guilt when I first began my life with George?"

Laughing lightly to keep back the tears, Maddy told her, "Only at that time, it wasn't the subject of just about any day-time talk show you could watch on TV." That had the desired effect of clearing the air; Angela felt lighter and both she and Maddy started laughing through the tears.

"At that time, I felt that I was the only woman in the world doing such a dishonorable thing. And even though I knew I wasn't, it most certainly felt as if I were most of the time."

"Are you telling me that I'm lost? That it won't get any better with Frank? My God, Maddy. How am I ever going to be able to look him in the eye again?"

With her jaunty look returning, Maddy smiled the Mona Lisa once again. "Oh, you will, my dear. Trust me." Patting Angela's hand lovingly and ever so maternally, she reiterated, "You will. You're not the first woman who has been unable to save a failing marriage."

Leaning in suddenly and riveting her eyes on Angela's, Maddy grew as solemn as Angela had ever seen her to be, adding, "Nor unfortunately, will you be the last."

Sitting up formally, Maddy had the most serious look that Angela had ever witnessed crossing her wise friend's face, as she said, "Angela Treworthy, you are one of the most honorable women I have known. I've watched you suffer in silence for many, many months now, wondering if I should do or say anything."

Soberly and finally assessing her plight, Angela asked incredulously, "Has it really been that obvious?"

"Unfortunately...yes. I probably knew your desperation long before you might have even been aware of it." Sitting back in an almost manlike pose, saying, "God knows, I'd seen that look in my own mirror many years ago."

"But—"

Leaning in and looking sternly at her young friend again, Maddy said, "If Frank were not so wrapped up in his career, you wouldn't be in this nasty predicament. And, if you weren't the woman you are quite frankly, you would not be so racked by guilt. You'd play the field and consider it your divine right, the only option available to someone in your position."

Relaxing into crying and letting her emotions out now, Angela grabbed for her lightly used cloth napkin. "I know you're right, Maddy. But it still doesn't make it any easier."

"Nor is it meant to be," Maddy replied soberly.

Rising from her chair and offering her hand to Angela, "Maybe your husband will have a change of heart. Maybe he will wake up one morning soon and remember himself to be the husband you deserve." Angela, taking Maddy's hand with one of hers, began wiping away her tears with her other.

"Until that time however, enjoy your friend Gabriel. Continue the illusion of your happy marriage. For the electorate and for your husband." Pausing for a few breaths, Maddy continued, "After all. This may not last long..."

Wrapping her arm motherly around Angela, "And then again," she continued with a glorious smile lifting her mouth, "It may last a very, very long time indeed."

Patting her young friend's, Maddy smiled sadly, holding back the tears of her own remembered sorrows.

TWENTY-FIVE

As Benny and Gabe left the Globe after closing the next night, Gabe was walking away with an unconscious smile on his face.

With a cock-eyed grin on his face and doing a double time step to get in front of Gabe on the sidewalk, Benny dropped into his mock fighting stance and punched Gabe playfully.

"All right, spill it," Benny demanded. "I know you got laid, bro. You been smiling too much tonight. So go ahead and tell me. Or do I gotta beat it outta ya?"

Sobering up at this, Gabe stopped dead in his tracks, suddenly questioning himself, *Has it been that obvious?* "So? What if I had? Do you want a blow by blow account?"

"What? I just want you to tell your old buddy Benny that you took his advice. That it worked out. That you got the babe. And that you fucked her lights out." Shrugging, he added, "That's all."

Relenting in spite of himself (and against his better judgment), Gabe sighed and admitted, "Yes. I finally met one of them. The one I liked the sound of."

Benny dropped into his victory stance and gave himself a ovation. And not being a very patient man, it wasn't long before Benny began prompting him with, "And?"

"It was nice. She was good looking." And then pausing with a slight look of pain passing over his face like a cloud over the sun, he added solemnly, "And I don't know if she's ever going to call me again."

Turning in Benny's direction, he ended with, "Ok?"

"What? You don't got her number no more?"

"Well...Yeah. But we left it that she was going to call me. After all, Benny, she is fucking married you know. Remember?"

"So maybe he goes on lotsa business trips? You even know what he does?"

"No. The agreement was that I wouldn't ask her any questions. Nothing about her personal life. It was supposed to be about just sex." Wanting now more than ever to loose Benny, Gabe started walking again, picking up the pace.

But not wanting to be left out of the loop, Benny worked to catch up, dropping back into step beside Gabe when he could. "Can't argue with the 'just sex' part dude. But..." And coming to a stop himself, Benny shouted out, "Whoa. No questions?"

Getting some twisted inspiration suddenly, Benny goes ballistic. "Hell, she might not even have a husband. Maybe she's just yanking your chain. You know? Just another controlling bitch type."

Poking playfully in an area that Benny knew was dangerous, he prodded Gabe with, "Not like you don't know nothin' about that type. Right?"

Stopping in mid-stride, Gabe shot back, "She's got a husband, Benny. She's got a ring. And I don't think she wears it just for show or to stay independent."

Recovering a little and trying his best to back away from Benny's line of questions, Gabe added, "I wanted some feminine touch. So I got what I wanted. What do I care about what she does with the rest of her life?"

Stopping as if he's terminally hurt, Benny went into recovery mode. "Don't get so upset, bro. I mean, it's not like the bitch means something to you. Right?"

"Don't call her a bitch, Benny. She's a nice woman in a bad way. Don't go comparing her to—"

"To the other ho's you been with?" Benny asked, as if he can't help himself.

Changing tack just as suddenly and laughing again, he held up his hands. "Ok, ok. Sorry I called the nice woman a bitch. But you only just met this 'nice woman' once, and you're gettin' all defensive on me." He leaned toward Gabe and asked, "Anything else I should know about her?"

Gabe kept walking.

Benny said casually, "So, hey. There's a party I know of next Saturday. Wanna go?"

"Gee, I don't know Benny. Whose party?" Gabe asked, afraid to know.

All of a sudden, Benny hesitated in a very uncharacteristic way that sent a shiver down Gabe's back. Finally, after shuffling a little, Benny said simply (not looking up), "Um, Eve."

Stopping in his tracks again, Gabe thought of all the people he didn't want to ever have anything to do with again, Evelyn Tait was the first on that list. "Eve," Gabe repeated, unsure that he had heard what he thought he had heard. "Talk about grade A bitch-queens...You want me to go to a party being thrown by my ex-bitch queen of all bitch queens? Really?" This was sort of the last straw in the Benny Stupid Hits of all time. "God, Benny. You never learn, do you?"

"Eve's been asking about you, you know," Benny said, with his eyes still glued to the pavement. Just for a Benny Minute; he turned playful again and dropped into his boxing stance. "So...Ya wanna go? Take your mind offa things?"

To himself more than to Benny, Gabe sighed and said, "Talk about bitches."

And then again, Gabe mused, *Maybe she's changed.* Then into Gabe's mind comes a Benny-type voice that said, '*Yeah, yeah. Right!*'

Just to get Benny off of the trail he's been on, Gabe agreed with a deep sigh. "I'll think about it."

Thinking he's scoring his point, Benny relented. "Yes! All right. See ya tomorrow."

"Yeah. Tomorrow."

Even Gabe knew that Benny couldn't get out to his ex-girlfriend's house for this party without Gabe driving him there. And Evelyn Tait was rich enough no doubt to provide Benny with a little incentive to bring Gabe back into her web.

We'll see indeed, Benjamin.

"God help me. Evelyn Tait." Sighing and laughing at the same time, "Like hell I will."

After the whirlwind romance and emotionally bloody and loud breakups with Eve, Gabe had almost sworn off women altogether. *Being gay has to be easier than this*, he thought at the time.

Eve was the ultimate social climber. Her father was always going after whatever deal, legal or quasi-legal he could find, and his daughter was no different.

Eve was also gorgeous. And sexy. And willing to do to a man just about almost anything. Any time. Anywhere.

They'd once had hot and heavy sex in the back of his Camaro in the parking lot of a club they had just been to. With people streaming past the car to get in line in the club. This turned Eve on, and even Gabe had to admit it was the best sex that he'd ever had in his life. Up until that point.

But Eve also had a price. She was volatile. And she could be sparked off at any time, by almost any thing. Like her sexual hunger, only worse.

Gabe had gotten to the point where that volatility wore quite thin, and she had drained him of almost everything he could think of; emotionally, physically, and monetarily.

Gabe had to wonder after he had told Eve off the last time, why she would want to have anything to do with him. He had called her just about every name in the book, and then some. This was totally unlike Gabe, which was why he knew he had to have nothing to do with her. Ever again.

And here she was, coercing (or most likely, paying) Benny to get Gabe back into her reach. There had to be some ulterior motive in this, and Gabe didn't even want to think about what it was.

Shuffling slowly into his living room after another long and grueling Friday night along with the walk home from the Metro, Gabe tried to throw his keys onto the table with the answering machine on it, but missed.

Absentmindedly hitting the replay button as he passed it, he continued on into the bathroom. As the first Beep! sounds, the sound of water being turned on started drowning out any message.

This standing up for days on end and working double shifts was getting to him. *I have enough saved up to quit. If this Angela doesn't work out, I'll go back to Hawaii for a couple of weeks*, he thought as the sound of the water started the soothing process. *Get me an island girlfriend I can leave behind me on takeoff.*

Passing back through the living room again as he's heading to the kitchen, the machine beeped. Hitting the playback button once more, he heard the first message began replaying...from his mother.

"Just a reminder, Gabriel. Your step-father's birthday party is on the 27th. Hope that you and Carol can make it."

A groan issued from the kitchen at this; the motherly voice ended with, "We'd love to see the two of you."

"No, Mom. *You'd* love to see the two of us," he told the machine. His mother, for some reason, had had high hopes for his relationship with Carol being "the one" for quite some time now. Even after he'd gone to great lengths to dismiss that hope.

And as for his step-father, he thought harshly. That was another story. He had never cared for the man who took his father's place.

Another "BEEP" sounded, competing with the sound of rattling plates and glasses as Gabe tried to muster up a snack to go with his drink.

But this time the silence was interrupted by the sound of Angela's voice wafting in to him from the tinny speaker. That brought Gabe racing out of the kitchen, rushing to hit the rewind button to start again.

"Gabe? Are you home? This is...Angela."

With food and drink the last things on his mind now, he plopped himself down on the couch to listen. "Would you like to— Would you be able to, you know, get together again? Tomorrow, maybe? Page me in the morning." She finished with a very hesitant, "If you want to, that is."

Reaching over to replay the message, another BEEP interrupted before he could tap the button. Benny's voice came on, and he listened only long enough to know that it wasn't the voice he wanted to hear.

"Look, Gabe, sorry 'bout that little problem earlier—" *Yeah, right,* he thought, hitting "rewind" to listen to Angela's entire message again.

After it ended, he hit the STOP button as he reached for the phone. Beginning to dial, he stopped, gently putting the phone back down.

Rocking for a few moments, he explosively bolted up from the couch, returning to the kitchen to finish his snack, suddenly happily whistling as he went.

TWENTY-SIX

It was another gorgeous spring afternoon in DC as Gabe anxiously waited for Angela to make her appearance. He was either sitting or pacing underneath a huge oak at the location in Rock Creek Park that she had mysteriously described that morning. And his anxiety was rising.

He had driven the entirety of Rock Creek Park before many times. There were parts of the Parkway where you could swear you were in the hills of West Virginia, or even Georgia while you were there — and all not more than a mere mile at most from the busy DC streets.

And while he had driven it extensively, he had never managed to notice this little side open space almost into Maryland. Perhaps he was too intent on getting somewhere, like most other Washingtonians on this Parkway.

With the prospect of meeting Angela once more, he had found the energy to take the bus up 16th Street, and get off near Walter Reed Army Medical Center and walk down into the park to this four-car parking lot to wait.

What was it about this woman, he wondered, after only meeting and having sex with her once — *Ok, so it was wonderful sex. And she's gorgeous. So what?* he asked himself — she had been occupying his mind every moment he wasn't in the thick of working. No other woman had had this kind of influence on him, not even Eve.

With the warm sunlight streaming through the trees and glinting off of the creek just a few hundred yards away, both the day and this place seemed idyllic. In this sort of locale, ordinarily Gabe would have been entranced by now, and laying back on the bright green grass looking up into the cool shades of green above him.

But in sharp contrast to the lazy afternoon vibe he might otherwise be feeling, Gabe was now pacing back and forth. He was agitated, waiting in a not so quiet reverie for...What?

Was she going to drive up in a car and pick him up? All she had said on the phone earlier was, "Do you know about that parking lot just north of the split of Blagden and Beach Drives in Rock Creek?"

Hesitantly, he thought, *No, but I'll find it.* But, he had said, "Yes. Of course," hoping he wouldn't regret this.

"Can you meet me there about one p.m.?"

"Yes," he had said, not truly caring where or when he had to go, or how long it took to wait there to meet this woman again.

And so, here he was waiting. And while he was waiting, he was catching sight of a Black family having a picnic in one of the adjacent picnic areas.

Watching as the kids romped, and the parents playfully interacted with them, Gabe was struck with how that hadn't been the life for him. He hadn't wanted children, only considered children because of this lover or that lover, who he was with who already had them.

Continuing his pacing and surrounded by woods all around, he wondered: *Did she want to have sex out here in the woods? Was this her idea of a second private meeting, fucking like bunnies out in the middle of nowhere?*

Somehow, he didn't think so. It might be his idea, but most definitely did not seem like it would be one of hers.

Returning to watching the family again frolicking close by in the shade, he began easing his pacing, walking over to sit under the shade of a nearby tree. *God only knows when she might show up*, he thought.

Just a few minutes later however, a large ominous black limo came trailing up the parkway at a slow pace, like he'd seen them going up Pennsylvania Avenue or on Capitol Hill. The black of the limo seemed to shimmer and sparkle in the heat, like the driver had spent hours waxing and buffing it to a sleek perfection.

And just when Gabe thought that it was somehow going to continue up Beech Drive passing him as if in a dream, it made a U-turn and began pulling into the parking lot within feet of him.

Wondering if he should wait to see what happened next or run in the opposite direction, Gabe didn't move.

Pulling to a stately stop, the limo just sat there. Getting out of the driver's side of the limo after a few moments, an older black chauffeur, dressed in a highly starched uniform and ramrod erect in posture, got out and walked in a stately stroll, moving as if the starch in his clothing were infusing his very bones as well.

With more curiosity than anything else, Gabe watched this vision unfold, but somehow still really didn't make any connection between this and the woman he was here to meet. Turning away and looking back down the parkway, his attention was quickly drawn back.

The chauffeur walked over to the handle of the rear passenger door and opened it, waiting formally at attention. After Gabe began looking once again in his direction, he began gesturing silently, first to Gabe, and then to the interior. Gabe still didn't know what to make of all of this and did not move.

Still eyeing this mirage suspiciously, Gabe began thinking that he was hallucinating this somehow. Until he heard a familiar voice calling to him in growing impatience from the darkened interior, "Gabe, it's me. Come on and get in!"

Shaking his head as if he were still in a dream and walking over towards the standing starched ebony statue, he stepped warily up to the dark interior and looked inside. As if he was entering some dark cave to face an unknown monster, he began slowly to get in.

Crawling into the plush interior, Gabe's eyes took more than a few seconds of blinking furiously as they were trying to adjust to the darkness there. Sitting down by feel with the door closing silently behind him, the interior lights suddenly flashed on, blinding him even further.

Gabe found Angela's hands reaching over towards him. Looking awkwardly at each other for a few moments of hesitation, Angela and Gabe finally collapsed towards each other. The spell broken, they began wrapping their arms around each other hungrily.

With the sound of the driver entering the front compartment but shielded from view, Gabe could feel the limo begin pulling away from the parking lot and back onto the parkway.

From where Gabe sat in the rear, the engine sounded as if it was a hundred miles away. Gradually, they both began to relax as the car began picking up speed.

After another few minutes of comfortable silence in each other's arms, Gabe was finally comfortable enough to risk asking her, "So, where exactly are we going to?"

"It's a surprise," was all she would say. But she said it with such a giddy thrill in her voice that he could tell that it was something special, and that she was enjoying the suspense. Pulling away from him with a wicked grin growing on her face, she asked him, "Ever made love in a limousine before?"

"No. But I'm really anxious to find out what it's like," he said, and slipping his left hand behind her back and his right underneath her, he lifted her to him and scrunched her onto his lap.

Beginning with kissing her lightly, he slowly began parting her legs gently and moved his hand teasingly further and further up her inner thigh and under her skirt. Eventually with his right hand finding its way to another sharp moan of pleasure, their breathing began mingling.

Getting dressed once more and each with a contented smile on their face, he teased her with, "Very nice."

Angela's contented smile grew wicked. "I thought you might like it."

"So you do this often?" he asked hopefully.

"Only once before. When I was first seeing my—" she started to say, "husband" but shaking her head slowly said, "Never mind."

Pulling her toward him, he asked her, "And you still won't tell me where we're going to?"

And then he thought, *Or are we even going anywhere? Was the whole idea just this ride?*

Rolling her window down just a crack to let the spring smell-laden air begin filling the space and looking out the window and smiling, Angela was enjoying the suspense immensely. "Remember. No questions," she said, with that wicked grin returning to her face. "We'll be there soon enough."

Rolling the window down on his side just a little, Gabe could finally see that they were already on the George Washington Parkway, heading north. The air blowing in the window carried that certain freshness that only seemed to happen in the springtime. He drank it in as greedily as Angela apparently did.

Blowing her hair up and around her like a cloud at sunset, stray strands of it found their way into Gabe's face, but he took no great pains to bother removing them.

Instead, breathing in her scent, he closed his eyes in apparent ecstasy.

Nuzzling into him, her hair began drifting slowly down as her body inched away from the window and into his shade from the breeze.

Although they were only a short distance away from DC compared to how far they had come, Angela and Gabe were enjoying every minute that they had together in which they didn't need to hide. There was no need to keep their visible distance now though until whenever they arrived at whatever mysterious getaway she had planned for them.

Once they were off the main roads and on Georgetown Pike, Angela rolled her window down further to allow them to take in as much of the spring breeze and fields as they could. There was a riot of flowers outside in a colorful blur, almost as entrancing as their lovemaking had been.

It had been a hard winter with lots of snow and ice, and this spring was the long awaited-for respite that everyone had been eager to enjoy. It had not disappointed.

Gabe turned to Angela with a thoroughly confused look, and she only smiled back, so happy that this was the man she had made this choice with.

In some ways, Gabe was very much an adult. But he also had a child-like side to him that she was now seeing. His puzzlement at where they were going was almost comical. He pulled away from her now with a look of whimsy, and leaned his head out for his hair to be caught blowing in the breeze.

Angela thought, *If only I'd met you when we were younger, our lives might have been so much different.*

He leaned back in and looked at Angela. He suddenly felt a sense of unspoken love radiating from her that he hadn't felt for a long time, making this an even more special springtime than in years past.

He had had spring loves before, but in the past they had been short lived. They had left him with only work to fall back on to ease the breakup.

This somehow felt as if it was going to be very different.

As the limo was pulling into the gravel driveway and driving on its way up towards the front door of the Rendezvous, Gabe turned to Angela and told her, "I'll pay for this today."

Smiling her own Mona Lisa grin now, Angela only came back with a bemused, "Well, we'll see."

What Gabe didn't know was that today's little outing would probably cost about as much as he could make in a slow week at the Globe, which was not a small amount. Angela wasn't going to tell him that though. At least, not just yet.

Calmly exiting at the front door to the Inn as the doorman was opening the limo door, Angela was finally getting used to all of this pomp and circumstance. Stepping out this time, it was as if she were finally in her element.

Gabe followed her much more cautiously, still unsure of what he had gotten himself into. Stepping out and following Angela's lead, he nodded as curtly as he could to the two — *guards? In armor?* — standing at starched attention on each side of the door.

Until he realized that they weren't moving. That they were only suits of armor that were propped up by the door for show. The two real Front Doormen appeared suddenly, moving around them, and doing the formal entrance with each door opened with grand esprit d'corps. The one on the right, bowed as they passed, and gave the grand flourish of invitation.

Truly embarrassed now, it was not the first time that Gabe was going to feel foolish this afternoon.

As they walked down the long main hall, Gabe continued to stare all around him like a kid let loose in a candy shop. He was continually being amazed by this woman, but this took the cake as far as he was concerned.

Gabe asked her "Do you come here often?" and he was suddenly feeling both quite stupid as well as naive for that cliche escaping his lips, and laughed suddenly. "I mean—" and then hesitating once again asked, "Or is that one of the questions I shouldn't be asking?"

Smiling warmly at this man she hadn't known for very long, she said "No, I don't come here often. A friend of mine just recently introduced me to this place."

"But do you always live like this?"

She just turned and looked at him and laughed. She remembered her own reaction when Maddy first brought her here.

She herself was still not quite comfortable with this level of obsequious wealth, but even with their embassy-like mansion, there was still a level of small-town Connecticut about it. It wasn't huge by Washington standards. In fact, it was in some ways quite modest compared to the homes of some of the other people they knew that they called their friends.

But this was a step up altogether, even for her. "No. Until two weeks ago, I didn't even know that such a place like this existed. Or even could exist."

"You're kidding?" he asked deadpan.

"No. A friend of mine introduced me to this place. Just before she suggested what was to me the unthinkable."

"You mean, me?"

"Or someone like you." Angela was about to walk Gabe into The Womb, and was sure that he'd have the same reaction that she had.

As they crossed the threshold, his eyes grew even wider still. Gabe was deep into having the same sort of reaction to all of this pomp and secrecy as Angela had had the first time Maddy had brought her here.

Only for Gabe, who was not at all used to this level of lavishness seeping through every crack and pore of this place, the effect was amplified greatly. He even caught his jaw dropping at several points, as when he realized that what he thought was some huge lit mural to their right, was actually glass with trees waving behind it in the sunlight pouring in from outside.

"Is everyone here..." he hesitated to say, lowering his voice, "having an affair," but she knew that that was what he was thinking.

But instead she leaned in and conspiratorially whispered into his ear, "Having sex?"

"Yeah," was the only answer he could muster, still feeling very child-like in his astonishment.

"No. I think they're having lunch," she said mock seriously. And then she leaned in and with another wicked grin spreading on her face, laughed lightly in his ear and whispered, "Poor Gabriel. I know what you must be thinking."

"Ok. What?"

"That I'm some woman of mystery, and this is a den of spies," she said in a dramatic whisper, enjoying his shock so immensely.

"Well...Not quite, but close."

Gabe took Angela by the arm, and gestured like a maitre d', "After you, madame," causing her to laugh.

At that point, another maitre d' came up and gestured down the ramp to their left and into the darkness. As they both looked at each other hesitantly, they realized they were each feeling a little foolish. Angela nodded her head and the maitre d' patiently bowed and gestured into the darkness.

At least Angela was accustomed to a certain amount of wealth and power. But this was all so very new, and in a way quite monstrous, to Gabe. He was still walking every step here with his mouth slightly open in astonishment.

She guided him down into the labyrinth of whispered intimacies, and when he asked a question, found that he was speaking in hushed tones as well.

After being seated at one of the inner "wombs" where they could talk and cuddle with a certain amount of privacy, the maitre d' left them, allowing time for all of Gabe's many — and hopefully acceptable — questions.

Trying to take in the enormity of this place, he looked up into the high vaulted ceiling above them, that still seemed impossibly high and far away (as well as dark and womb-like, lit only by the shimmering tendrils of candlelight flickering above them).

Looking as out of place here as she had in The Java Hut, all he could muster was a noncommittal, "Hmmm."

"I'm sorry for this need for secrecy, Gabe. I won't keep things from you any longer than I have to, but I just need to be around you some more."

"Look, I know you must be someone with money and power, and I really appreciate your trusting me enough to even bring me here."

"But?" she asked, curious.

Sighing and looking around him, he said, "I don't know. I guess— I just didn't expect something like this when I placed that ad. You know? It all just still feels a little strange to me."

Reaching over to take his hand in hers, Angela looked at him lovingly and was on the verge of telling him everything. But biting her lip instead, she told him, "I know. In time. When I tell you everything, I think that you'll understand why."

Releasing his hand and returning to the menu, Angela smiled secretively as he began studying his menu assiduously, trying his best to not feel so out of place.

After a while, the glamour of the place was dulling around the edges for Gabe, as the real point of his attention here was Angela.

Their food had since arrived and Gabe was once again struck by the opulence of the place. And how he didn't seem to fit into this level of society at all.

After a while he tentatively asked Angela, "So...What exactly is this place?" he asked, feeling Angela so close to him even though they were about a foot apart.

"Like the sign outside said," she mirrored Maddy playfully saying, "The Rendezvous Inn."

"Yes, I know that. I mean, I saw that." Not sure of how to phrase what he had been slowly picking up (such as the ambiance of the place), he tried once again. "But I mean, how can we come here and you're not afraid of being seen with me?"

Dragging out answering his question by continuing to eat for several moments more, she began answering carefully, "Because, that's the nature of the place."

"Oh," was the only remotely un-foolish answer that he could come up with, and he returned to finishing off his lavish lunch. *Which obviously I'd have to work a whole week's worth of double shifts at The Globe to pay for*, he thought. He'd been in the business long enough to know how much things cost. And that this place put the all caps in the word "*Exclusive*," as well as "*Expensive*."

Angela meanwhile was beside herself with glee inside. Outside however, she was playing the worldly sophisticate, for once feeling as if she were really indeed a "somebody" again. She knew in a way that this play act was at Gabe's expense, but she also knew that she would make it up to him later on.

"I brought you here," she continued, without looking up, "Because my friend introduced me to this place specifically in preparation for my...little illicit affair adventure." And looking up coyly, she added, "I didn't know at the time, but here. With you. Now."

He hated feeling dumb or naive, but he just had to ask, "But...Why here?"

Looking at Gabe for a long while and measuring whether she could indeed begin trusting him beyond sharing her body with him, she carefully chose her words. "This place," she said, gesturing around her, "was created a number of years ago, so that the rich and elite could have a playground to have their..." she stopped. Trying to think of a word that he could understand that would give the fullness of what she wanted him to know, she offered, "Liaisons?"

Looking truly dumbfounded now, all he could say was "Ok."

"Before the 1950s, it wasn't really all that necessary to hide the extra little goings-on without the company of one's mate, because it was the sort of thing that the rich did anyway. Behind closed doors.

"But with the coming of the 60s and the 70s apparently, those people that frequented establishments such as this had to become much more discreet in their dealings."

"So, that's when this place was created? In the 1960s?"

"Apparently it's been here for a very long time before that. But in the last few decades, it's become a necessity. What with the Press trying to peer into the very private lives of public persons.

"My friend told me that this place became even more of a discreet location to maintain in the last two decades. Too many things were no longer being forgiven. Like affairs."

"So.. How private can we be here?"

"Very," she hinted with her voice dropping. "That's why we're here." Giving him what had become to be known as "bedroom eyes," she leaned in and lowered her voice to a purr. "Oh, and Gabe?"

"Yes?"

"Every time we come here, it needs to be on me."

Curiosity getting the better of him but knowing the answer anyway, he asked like a little boy, "Why?"

"Because, unfortunately, you would probably be paying a month's worth of rent every time we came here."

"Oh," was all he could say yet again. He was afraid she'd say that. Raising their glasses filled with a fine Italian wine, Angela and Gabe toasted each other. "To an excellent meal," she said.

"Yes. And to...whatever else happens."

Gabe had ordered things that he would never have thought of ordering otherwise; lobster bisque, truffles, and spiced other things that he couldn't pronounce.

He looked over at Angela at one point and thought, *God, this woman is gorgeous. Doesn't her husband see this?*

Angela looked up at this moment and saw her highest hopes in a relationship, and she let her wine glass drift down to the table. She saw that Gabe hadn't noticed her look, and she was glad he hadn't.

This isn't supposed to be a real relationship, she thought. *I'm still in love with my husband.*

Gabe, looking up and catching her unawares, saw her doubt and interpreted it in the wrong way. *What's wrong here? She looks like she's just killed someone.*

"Are you ok?" he asked, as if he had done something wrong.

Finding herself gazing at the table, she looked up startled, asking him formally, "Yes. Why do you ask?"

"I don't know. You just looked...I don't know, as if something were really wrong."

As she reached for his hand, she wanted to tell him what she was feeling. That she should be feeling this with her husband. Except that she hadn't — for a long time. "It's ok. I'm sorry."

"Well, you don't need to be sorry. I was just—"

"Let's go for a walk," she said suddenly. "Have you had enough?" Gabe began looking down at the meal he'd just shared with this woman he hardly knew and felt lost. "Um, sure," he said, in a hesitant voice. "Have you had enough to eat?"

She smiled up at him, pleased with his concern. *Why was I ever afraid of this man?* "Yes. Now let's go for that walk," she said, and was surprised to find him behind her chair in a moment, pulling it out for her.

Angela looked at Gabe with a growing smile as he asked, "Shall we take a stroll through the grounds?"

It hadn't passed Gabe's attention that no check had been brought and no money was exchanged. He would have thought this was like a rich person's paradise, except that he knew that money would be exchanged, just not in a publicly traded fashion.

Once they stepped through the door and into Wonderland, Gabe had ceased to be amazed. This place was alive with all of the best and brightest gardening that money could buy. Gabe, walking arm in arm with Angela, couldn't help but be more and more impressed and awed as they went.

Passing persons standing, kissing, and even once, almost fucking right on the spot — *here, in broad daylight* — he didn't have to ask any more about the station and wealth of what he was floating through.

And he could only imagine what sort of world that Angela moved in and through. It was an almost crushing difference between them in his mind.

Thinking that somehow they were walking on a circular path that was going to bring them back to the restaurant, Gabe was a little unnerved when Angela stopped in front of a small one-room cottage in a row of such cottages, with the door standing wide open and inviting in front of them.

Perplexed, Gabe turned to Angela. Angela however was only smiling a much satisfied smile, as well as standing oh-so-close to him. "Shall we go in?" she asked lightly.

Oh, he thought suddenly. *We're not going back to the restaurant.*

Standing in the doorway of the cottage hours later, Angela and Gabe seemed from this vantage point to be out in the middle of nowhere looking out on some farm far, far away from anything.

The Dutch door's top half hung open. They might as well have been standing in the 18th century on one of the heaths of Scotland, for the feel and look of the place.

Instead, they were wrapped up cozily together in one big rumpled bed sheet, looking out at the carefully manicured lawn with another half-dozen other similar cottages sitting just out of view. This was a touch of the past that, as with many other aspects of the Good Life only available to the very well-to-do few, was an out-of-place and out-of-date extravagance.

Still unable to believe he was standing in all of this, Gabe took a deep breath. "God, this place is so peaceful," he said. "You wouldn't believe we're, what? Ten, fifteen miles from DC?"

Smiling contentedly to herself, Angela silently thanked Maddy once again for having introduced her to the idea of having an affair, and once again for introducing her to this place. It was costing her dearly, but she sighed deep down in her body in gratitude for the possibility of this place and this experience.

And she had done it again and again since meeting Gabe. He had made love to her so sweetly and for so long and so hard, she could hardly believe that it was real. Except that afterwards, there he was, cuddling her from behind and making her wish like mad that this afternoon could go on forever.

She had decided earlier as they lay in the first sweaty afterglow, that she would have to take Maddy on some long vacation to repay her for the gift of her introduction to this place. If even that could even repay her, that is. But she somehow didn't think that Maddy would accept the repayment.

"Yes. I am so glad my friend introduced me to this place," Angela replied after a few moments of basking in the sun with him.

"So am I. Of course, if I weren't here with you, I probably wouldn't be able to afford to be here."

If you weren't here with me, you'd most likely never know this place even existed, she thought, smiling and closing her eyes in quiet ecstasy. "But you are here. And it's worth every cent to me for you to be here with me."

Turning around towards him and careful not to lose the sheet and its strategic hiding of their bared essentials, she said, "You make me so alive. Somehow, I feel as if I'm catching up on all of those years of deprivation where you weren't in my life."

Turning back to look out on the garden and feeling suddenly

morose, she asked herself more than him, "Why can't my husband make me feel like this?" She turned her head to one side and said, "But then again, I'm not sure that he ever did."

Solemnly, Gabe asked, "Can we have another agreement? We started this with you not wanting me to ask you any questions, and for the most part, I've kept my word."

Snuggling even closer, she told him, "Yes. I know you have. And I know it's also been hard."

"Well, while we're together, I'd like you to pretend that your husband doesn't exist. Ok?"

"Oh, of course. I'm sorry," she said, turning around and reaching her arms out of the sheet and wrapping them around Gabe's neck. He in turn started letting his hands slip lower under the sheets, and grabbing her by her thighs and slipping his hands under her ass to grab her there, said mischievously, "Wrap your legs around me."

"What?" Angela said, laughing and somehow knowing where this was going, asked him anyway. "What are you doing?"

"Trust me. You'll like it," he said, as Angela raised first her right leg and then her left leg up and around his waist. All of a sudden, even in this garden of fucking, her sense of propriety also started to rise (along with his now hard erection brushing her teasingly). She said, "At least let's close the door," and her breathing starting to get shallow as she was getting excited.

In one smooth and fluid move, Gabe used them and their gyration to turn around to where he could close the top half of the door as they turned.

Continuing the circle with the door now closed, he used the opportunity, now that they were in full privacy, to place her back solidly against the door.

Gasping as he entered her, she let out a yelp of, "Oh my God! Why hasn't anyone done thiisss," she said with a sudden sharp intake of a hiss in ecstasy, "to me before?" as he began to thrust inside her.

Entwined much later beneath the sheets on the bed once more, both Angela and Gabe seem exhausted, but also in heaven.

"I don't think I've ever made love this many times in a single day before. Even in my so-called wilder, younger days."

"So I guess that means you're telling me that it felt good?" he asked mischievously.

Turning around and nesting into him, playfully slapping him on the cheek, "Of course, you silly boy."

Turning suddenly solemn, Gabe couldn't help himself in asking her, "So, if you're really that unhappy, why don't you——"

"Leave him? It's a much more complicated situation than that."

"Or otherwise, you wouldn't be risking having an affair. Something like that?" he asked, glad that he could ask at least basic questions now.

"Yes. 'Something like that.'" she replied playfully.

Turning back around to face him, it was her turn to become the serious one. "Gabe, please don't complicate what we have here."

"Any more than it is right now?"

"Yes. Any more than it is right now. Let's just enjoy the time we have together. Like you asked, I just want to forget about my other life when I'm with you." Kissing him oh so gently on his upper lip, she pleaded, "Ok?"

Sighing and shaking his head understandably, "Yes. Anything for you."

She both loved hearing that and had a silent alarm bell going off at his comment. He was obviously falling in love with her, as she was with him. But it couldn't go beyond what they had in this moment, and other moments like it.

Pulling him to her fiercely, she started to cry, glad that she was facing away from him at this moment.

Later, strolling arm in arm along the brick path leading down towards the river, they could see that the sunset was coming.

"So. You're really a novelist," she asked, toying with him.

"That's what the propaganda is," he said with mixed emotions. Turning towards him now, she could see the hurt in his eyes.

"What do you mean?"

"Oh, nothing," he said, brushing it off. *Don't want to spoil a perfect day.*

"So, you never told me what it was you were working on. If you had the time to finish it, is it something that could be close to being finished?"

"Not quite."

"Don't you ever find time to work on it?" she asked, out of curiosity more than needing to know.

"Yes, sometimes," he said reluctantly. "But recently, it's only come in fits and starts. It doesn't help not having any support other than raging criticism and drunken helpfulness."

Coming to a lone bench overlooking the river, he gestured to it. Sitting and enjoying the silence of this place and this view, a pregnant pause started developing between them.

"So what was it made you want to be a writer?"

Pausing to choose his words carefully, "I fell in love with words." Adding awkwardly, "And it didn't hurt that I was terminally shy. You know, the lonely artist's garret, and all that."

"I can understand that."

"So, how did you meet your husband? Or is that..."

Pausing and withdrawing her hands, with some pain creeping in, she relaxed. "He was my boss," she said, finding that she wanted ever so much to be able to talk about it, but was still finding herself feeling afraid to divulge too much. "I was maybe a little too young when I began working for him, and wasn't too steeped in the ways of the world.

"Then the long hours I spent working with him turned into nights and weekends. And then..." she said, letting it trail off into silence.

"I see."

"He was very passionate then. And charismatic. And then, it just became a job for him."

"Yes. That does seem to be the way of the world."

Turning suddenly with a strange look in her eyes, she paused while choosing her words. "In many ways, he was a lot like you."

Entwining her hands with his again and deciding to change the subject, she said, "So why don't you write any more?"

"I guess the world caught up with me, too."

Turning to face him squarely, she had to know. "What about these other married women?"

"Woman, singular. Only one," he emphasized.

"Oh, right."

Maneuvering his hand under her leg, Gabe swung it around and over his, pulling her closely onto his lap. Instinctively starting to move away, she began glancing furtively around. Seeing no one near and remembering just where she was, she relaxed, returning to be almost in his lap.

"You'll get used to it," he reminded her.

"I kind of doubt it," she said, sighing. She really wished she could be. "I'm just not used to being so overtly sexual," and glancing around them, "Even in a place like this."

Relaxing a little bit more, she asked, "So, what happened? With this other married woman, I mean?"

Thinking back, he started off talking faintly. "I met her at the school library...She was an older woman, someone that I knew in class and one day we began talking. She was also a very unhappily married woman at the time, but didn't think that she could make it without her husband."

Out of nowhere seemingly, Angela began crying. Gabe had no idea he'd get this reaction from her when he began telling her about Mary Ann. He pulled her even tighter into his embrace, placing his free hand over hers, intertwining her fingers in his.

Recounting old loss at this point didn't have the same reaction that it once had, but her tears at the mirror he was holding up to her touched him deeply.

Here he was, in this absolutely glorious garden, with a woman who was a fashion model compared to Mary Ann. And yet he was still feeling the sorrow over that first loss welling up inside of him as well.

"How much older?" Angela finally asked him, blinking back the tears and unsure of whether she really wanted to know the answer.

"I was twenty. And she was thirty-eight."

Unable to help herself, she gasped, "My God. And I thought—"

"She was my first real lover," Gabe continued, his eyes now far away.

Laughing quietly in a self-deprecating way, Angela said, "And I was worried about our age difference."

Coming back to the present, Gabe focused on her eyes now, wanting to kiss the tears away from this fairy princess. "There really isn't that much difference between the two of us, you know. Or at least not age-wise. You live in a world of power and money apparently and I obviously don't, but we've still both been hurt."

Sighing and wiping away the tears with her free hand, she leaned into him. "So, what happened?"

Withdrawing back into his memory, he said, "I was falling in love with her, and it became so obvious that my best friend and roommate Benny began pestering me about it." Coming back abruptly out of his reverie and with his face transforming with disgust, he said roughly, "And I made the mistake of telling him."

"Why was it a mistake?"

"He came back to the dorm room one day when he told me he was going to be out all day. Mary Ann and I were in bed, in the middle of what Benny always calls 'doing the nasty.' We were in the middle of one of the most passionate lovemaking sessions we'd ever had. She was so close to coming, when the door suddenly burst open. We didn't have a chance to do anything, and when Benny came snapping into the room and turning the light on, Mary Ann was frantic. She began trying to wrap herself up in the bed sheet and get her clothes on at the same time. And I could have killed Benny right then and there."

Incredulous, she pulled back from him. "He actually walked in on you?"

"Yes."

"Did you keep seeing her?"

"Seeing her? No. I never saw her again. She apparently dropped out of school, and...That was the end of it."

"Oh, my God. How could someone be so—"

"Callous? Hateful? I should have ended our 'friendship' right then and there."

"And so you told this friend—"

"To go to hell. That was pretty strong for me back then."

"And you never saw him again either? I hope."

Still feeling both crushed and ashamed, even after all of these years, he only managed to squeak out in a younger voice, "I couldn't. He was the only friend I had at the time."

Stunned by this admission, Angela wanted to hold him and comfort him for the rest of her life. In some ways Gabe seemed both so innocent and so masculine at the same time, she almost didn't know how to handle what he was revealing to her.

"You didn't?" she said flatly.

"He...'made it up to me' later by introducing me to quite a number of other women—"

"But it wasn't her."

"No. It wasn't."

Pulling him to her breast now, a tear began crawling down her cheek. She could also feel the dam breaking in him as well, with a rush of tears streaming down into a river running between her breasts.

"Why don't we go back to the cabin?" she asked, after a few moments of shared anguish and tears.

Only nodding his head 'yes' silently, he buried his face deeper into her cleavage. Without hesitating, Angela hoisted herself fully onto his lap. A reverse Pieta, but with Mary sitting in Jesus' lap, pain and anguish overlapping into the utterly sensual.

Once they were back in the cabin, Gabe had recovered from his sense of loss. *That was the past*, he thought, *and this is the present. And what a present.*

This time, they slowly began undressing each other, Gabe savoring the process as he delicately kissed her in all the right places. Angela moaned in pleasure, thinking, *Can it get any better than this?!*

Several long, languorous hours later, she was the one who was being cradled this time, with Gabe stroking her face and occasionally letting his fingers trace down the line of her jaw to caress one of her breasts, bringing another sudden sigh of pleasure from her.

In both of their minds, they were wishing this afternoon could last forever. That they wouldn't have to return to the real world where, if they met in a crowded room they would have to feign a lack of recognition.

Angela sighed deeply, and told him, "We have to leave early in the morning. I told John to come back and pick us up around 5a.m., just in case my husband comes back from his trip early."

They had spent the rest of the afternoon turning into night in bed, alternately making slow love as they both cried, and holding each other intertwined in silence.

As the light quickly faded outside, Angela got out of bed and went to the end table where she had asked to have candles and candlesticks placed for a later romantic dinner she had planned.

She was digging into her own money from a separate account that she kept on the advice (ironically) of Frank. "Discretionary funds that the press can't root out, just so you're not always feeling dependent on my family's money," he had said at the time, not wanting to tell her that his family had not approved of his "marrying below his station" when he had married one of his younger staffers.

She had just thought at the time that it was merely a prudent reserve for her to have to do whatever she wanted with for shopping and sundries. But here she was using this discretionary fund for being discreet in a very different kind of sundry.

Lighting the candles and making the faux antique cottage glowing with ancient light, Angela crawled back into bed, trying to figure out how to make this night last forever.

It was going to need to be an infrequent sundry, since her fund was not a deeply pocketed one. Not even after all of these years.

He asked her, "Are you still in love with your husband?" suddenly, out of the blue.

Taken aback at this, she didn't know exactly how to answer. This was one of those questions that were not really up for discussion. Getting a very severe look growing on her face, she said tensely, "It doesn't matter. Like your first love, Mary Ann, I wouldn't be able to live on my own."

And then she felt very defensive, and said quite coldly, "That's a question I need you to never ask me again. Is that understood?"

How could he ruin this, this, what we have together so quickly? she asked herself feeling her face begin to burn.

"I'm sorry," he said, turning over. "I shouldn't—"

"No. You shouldn't," she said. She began crying out of a fierce sudden heartache. Did she still love Frank? Or was she merely biding her time? *Maybe I should have gone out and got a job*, she thought.

Damn you, Gabe, she thought. "Why couldn't you just let us have what we have?"

"I've—"

Fallen in love with you, he so desperately wanted to tell her. But he knew that would not go over well.

Turning back over to look directly into his eyes, but keeping her distance across the massive bed, she didn't know what to do next. Should she call John and have him come back tonight?

And then he began crying once more.

She wanted to stay in her new resolve that this was not going to work out, but looking at him now, she couldn't. She wanted to move closer to him and pound on his chest angrily. And then she wanted very desperately to have him pound on her — except not on her chest.

How is this going to work? This can't—

Angela felt several things all at once. Anger at Gabe for asking such a personal question that she didn't want to think about. Anger at feeling that, no, she didn't really love Frank anymore, and in some ways hadn't been in love with him for years (except as a friend).

And finally, anger at the idea that she should get to such a place as this and feel as if she had no other options but this. She settled on anger at Gabe for even asking such a question.

"Why did you have to go and ruin today by asking me that?" she said, pulling away from him.

Seeing her anger and not knowing it wasn't just directed at him, he began drying his eyes on the sheet and quietly said, "I'm sorry. It wasn't really my place. I'm— just so sorry."

As she sat up, she both wanted to apologize and stomp off to the bathroom and start cleaning up.

Instead, she began crying again, and began pounding on his chest in anger and also wanting to straddle him and make violent love to him at the same time.

She'd never felt these things with anyone else before, much less with someone she had known for less than a week. What was happening to her?

What was she feeling? Trapped? Disgusted at herself? Surely she couldn't be feeling lonely any more, not with this man laying in her (temporary) bed.

But her life felt like it was spiraling out of control, even more out of control than it had been before responding to Gabe's personals ad. She had what most women could only dream of. A powerful husband who expected nothing much of anything from her. A wonderful friend in Maddy that had introduced her to this fairy tale place and all of its wonderments. Someone who had done everything she could to encourage and motivate her.

And now she had this wonderful man, who she had treated in some ways like a servant, and in other ways like a paid lover.

But there were things in his voice, and in his actions, that suggested that all of this wasn't — indeed would never be — enough. He had started to fall in love with her. And she unfortunately, had also started to fall in love with him.

Had Maddy warned her about this? "It may be for a short time. Or perhaps for a very, very long time indeed." She had been happy with her arrangement, with her husband and her lover. For what? Thirty years? She had obviously fallen in love with George Remy. Was still in love with him, almost five years after his passing.

As she looked at Gabe, now with tears at the corners of his eyes, she wondered if this had been a mistake. Perhaps she should have just remained unhappy. Perhaps she should have found some other hobby to engage her time, other than another man.

But this man. This man was so much more than she expected. Couldn't she have found some man who did only want just sex and nothing more? And could she actually love a man who would fall in love with her so easily?

She wasn't a raging beauty, in her mind. He should have been able to find someone else to have his will with, and not someone in her position.

But he didn't. And he was laying there looking so hurt that he had asked a simple question. It was asked out of his longing, and it had brought up too much for her to handle. She should just put him in his place and this should be the last time they got together. It was just too dangerous.

Instead, she found her body deciding to straddle this man. While she could see it in his eyes that he knew that this was what he would call "break up sex," that didn't stop him from rising to the occasion.

They left much later, and had a very silent ride back into the city. Staring out at the lights sparkling in the clear night, Angela wasn't sure how she was going to handle this. She was going to miss him, but this had to end with last night.

She dropped Gabe off on 23rd and M. Street, and he had such a baleful look on his face as the limo pulled away, she felt her eyes tearing up and a storm coming.

This was not going to be a peaceful night for her, and Frank would be coming back tomorrow.

TWENTY-SEVEN

Angela had called Maddy earlier that morning, frantic and unable to hide it. Maddy chalked it up to Angela and Gabe having had their first real date and Angela's feelings arising from the emotional force of being engaged now in a full affair. *I can hear her anguish*, Maddy thought. *Have times changed so little?*

Meeting Angela at her door, Angela flung herself into Maddy's arms. "I suppose I shouldn't ask how it went," she said when Angela's arms finally loosened. "Let's go to The Rendezvous for our—"

Angela's reaction was immediate and intense. "No. I can't. I can never go back there."

Sighing, Maddy prepared for the worst. "But why?" she asked, acting puzzled but knowing full well why. "Wasn't it nice being there with your Gabriel?"

"It was glorious, Maddy. But...I can't."

Ready to play the stern mother figure, Maddy stepped away from her young friend. *Not what I thought, I suppose.*

"Come," she said, offering a hand to Angela and preparing for another storm. "I have a feeling that this is going to be a long discussion." She guided Angela inside and closed the door behind her.

Once they were on the couch, Maddy said, "Come. Tell Madame Lightfoot all."

Angela felt that what she had to say was both ridiculous as well as deeply disturbing. Looking at Maddy didn't help her focus on the disturbing element very well.

"Gabe asked me if I still loved my husband," she finally got out.

Maddy gave her a "silly girl" look and said, "Is that all?"

Puzzled, Angela thought it was self-evident. "I told him not to ask me any questions," she said, as if that was the most logical thing in the world that she should be upset about.

"And you told him, 'Of course I do. That's why I'm having an affair with you.' Yes?"

"That sounds so ridiculous, when you're saying it," Angela said, finding herself sitting stiffly now that Maddy hadn't seen the logic.

"Then what exactly ruffled your feathers about that question?" Maddy asked her in all seriousness.

"He has no right..." Angela started to say.

"And it sounds like he hit a raw nerve."

Complicated feelings were rising in Angela's chest and pushing hard against her new resolve. She knew it was a fine question to ask her, considering where and with whom she was lying with at the time, but it (ironically) felt like an invasion of privacy to her. The next morning, it still did.

"Oh, Maddy...I knew it was going to be hard—"

"Just not hard in the ways you expected," Maddy finished.

"Yes," Angela said, still feeling hurt that he would ask her that, and hurt that she didn't answer him with a solid "Yes."

She felt another bout of crying coming on, and Maddy deftly had reached for the box of tissues on her end table before she had been aware of her emotional damn being about to burst. The sobs began as wracking hiccups bursting from her stomach, and proceeded into full blown sobs as she grabbed for the tissue box Maddy was holding out.

After a few moments of crying and dabbing away the tears, Angela looked at Maddy and laughed a short laugh which began cascading back into sobbing.

Maddy allowed Angela to wade through the catharsis on her own. *The emotional midwife will be needed soon enough*, Maddy thought sympathetically. *You must come up with some of your own answers, dear one.*

"What is wrong with me, Maddy?" Angela asked as the storm was close to passing.

Finally reaching over to take Angela's hands in her, Maddy paused, giving Angela as supporting of a look before answering as she could.

"There is nothing wrong with you, Angela Barnes Treworthy. You are involved in a battle with your own emotions, and you're not winning. That's all."

Angela couldn't help but let out one of the hiccup laughs before catching herself. Leaning over, Maddy reached out and pulled Angela's head to her shoulder as a mother might.

"And you're not, once again, going through anything that I didn't go through when I started my other life. Rest assured, Angela, you have a right to feel what you're feeling.

"I know it wasn't an easy decision on your part to engage in this sort of behavior, and I also know that if you let it, it will grow easier over time."

Smoothing Angela's hair, Maddy remembered back to her many

doubts. If George hadn't so actively pursued her, she would have ignored it.

"But, Maddy. Why would he ask me a question like that? That's the sort of thing that I especially didn't want to happen. This was supposed to be a pressure relief valve, not an excuse for a divorce."

"And just whoever told you that love was logical, my dear?" Maddy whispered.

A deep sigh began lifting her head from her friend's shoulder. "I can't go on like this," Angela said forcefully, "I can't go on feeling like a teenager at my age. I'm an adult woman..."

Leaning in and catching Angela's eyes, Maddy interrupted with, "Whose husband has withdrawn emotionally from you, leaving you bereft and alone. You do not share the same ambitions as either the airheads or the 'political strategists' who pass for politicians' wives—"

"And I don't have a family. My sisters have families, but I don't." All the years of frustration at not being able to fulfill her family's (and particularly her mother's) wish in this matter started rising to the surface now, and Angela felt on the verge of tears once more.

Sternly now, Maddy said soberly, "Having a family is not a requirement for being a woman. Ask any career woman today. Family needs to be balanced out with another purpose," Maddy was suddenly sounding more like a politician to Angela, than a politician's wife.

Her emotions from her own decisions now rising to the surface, Maddy said softly, "If I had been able to be in your shoes, here, now, in your time, I would have chosen another path myself."

Laughing through her remaining sniffles, Angela asked her, "So you would have become a Hillary Clinton?"

Laughing lightly now as well, Maddy responded thoughtfully,

"Perhaps."

"The power behind the throne," Angela intoned with as deep a voice as she could muster.

"Yes. Something very much like that," Maddy said with a weighty sound in her curt reply.

"So you're saying that I should have both a job as well as a boy-toy at my disposal?"

"Why not?" Maddy said, returning to her more giddy and light self. *He has a right to fall in love with you*, Maddy thought but would not say. *And you with him.*

Instead she said, "Let him cool his heels a few days. Perhaps he'll get the message and you can have another rendezvous."

"But what if he doesn't?" Angela asked, her fear rising uncontrollably in her voice. "I've told him I need to be discreet. What if he tries to call me at night when Frank is home?"

"Why, then you turn off the pager off at night."

"Or during the day—"

"Perhaps you should concentrate on the idea of Franklin even being home before you're asleep. That might be a more improbable situation."

"Oh, I don't know about this."

"Then call up your 'boy-toy' and explain it to him. Just to make sure he understands your position."

"Yes," Angela said, feeling far away. "But..."

"You're already starting to miss your young man," Maddy stated. "And it's been what? A day?"

"Less," Angela said, trying ever so hard in her mind to not feel Gabe's hands running lightly up and down her body.

TWENTY-EIGHT

Gabe got home later that night after work to find the light blinking on his answering machine again. Hoping that it was Angela calling to arrange another meeting...and that she had forgiven him for that stupid question about her husband, he hit the button and waited, He was no longer feeling in a rush for once to get into the kitchen and his pitcher of "cool-aid."

He didn't really get too many messages these days, what with Carol having gone through her vindictive "I hate you" type of messages and grown tired of them.

The other messages were mainly from Benny and his mother. The occasional message that came in from their boss Bernie, was usually asking if Gabe could come in to cover for another bartender who didn't show up. But that was it.

He also hadn't had the heart to call his mother back and tell her about Carol. His mother wasn't the sort to be calling constantly and nag about things, so he would eventually have to return her call with his disappointing answer.

"Hello, Gabe?" Angela's voice said after the beep, and his heart rose hearing her. But there was something strange in the sound of it as well. The long pause didn't bode well either.

He shouldn't have asked that stupid question about her husband the other night. After that, the room got right chilly, with the long ride home being equally cold.

Gabe had wanted to apologize profusely on the way home, but she didn't look like she was up for hearing it.

"This is Angela," she said, and then paused once more, for longer than Gabe liked. It sounded like a break-up call, even though technically they had just gotten together. He hit the pause button.

I've got to stop thinking about her like she's a girlfriend. She's my mistress... No, that's not it. Am I her "mister?" he wondered. *Is that even the right word?*

What is it about this woman? he asked himself. *Yes, she's beautiful. But a lot of my other girlfriends — women, I should say — were beautiful. Eve had been particularly gorgeous. Vicious in the end, yes, but drop-dead gorgeous. She could have been a model if she weren't so hell bent on not working, period.*

He had wondered at the time they'd been going out exactly what it was that Eve saw in him in the first place, but obviously it seemed he was worth it. Eve had even banished some of her best friends simply because they had flirted too much with Gabe. He thought that they were only trying to piss Eve off, like girlfriends do sometimes; the whole being catty thing, he thought at the time.

They were so different, Eve and Gabe, but perhaps that was it. He was a challenge. And it probably didn't hurt that women thought that he was good looking. He was awkward and still shy, but...

His finger hovering over the play button again, he took in a deep breath and lowered his finger. "Gabe, I need you to know how much your question about my feelings towards my husband hurt me. It almost felt like you had hit me," she said, as Gabe hit the pause button again.

Why am I falling in love with you so quickly? he asked himself. *I don't want this to end just yet. I've got to stop myself, maybe see some other women as well as Angela. Maybe that would help keep things in perspective,* he thought.

He didn't really feel like listening to the full message right now, so he rose off the couch and headed towards the fridge. *Clear my head,* he thought. *Or perhaps just dull the coming freight train if she doesn't want to see me again.*

"Whatever," he said, grabbing hold of the fridge handle.

The next day he arrived at The Globe and had been thinking about Angela and their little getaway all the way on the Metro and the three blocks from the Eastern Market Metro Station. He had looked up several times, wondering if what he was thinking about was showing on his face, but the usual Metro "pay attention to your own business" prevailed.

He occasionally caught another woman eyeing him, but it didn't look like anything more than polite interest.

Thinking about her body, about her hair that was so soft and didn't smell like it was drenched in perfume, like so many of his other girlfriend's hair had been. Even the sound of her voice. It was so quiet and refined, in comparison to...those other women.

Entering the bar, he was glad that Benny hadn't come in early today. He could use the peace and quiet, along with the soft background noise of the patrons' hushed conversations and the TV on low. He looked forward to Howard the chef fixing him some eggs and hash browns, since he'd been too groggy on waking up to fix breakfast at home.

What the hell. I spend so much of my time here, it might as well be home. He had to stop that. He'd missed taking the Camaro out for long drives while spring was flowering. But then at the time, he was still feeling too down after the whole Carol thing. He didn't really feel like doing anything but working.

If only I'd known Angela at the time, he caught himself thinking. And then realized (or remembered) how she had picked him up the last time: in a limousine with severely tinted windows.

Here he was, back to the stark realization that Angela wasn't a girlfriend. That he would most likely never enjoy the things with her that he enjoyed with real girlfriends. Angela was his "special friend" as they were saying now, although that usually referenced someone gay who was still in the closet.

Hell, I am in the closet. It's just a heterosexual, not homosexual one. Now he knew what it felt like to have to live that kind of lifestyle. And he was going to have to get used to it, if he wanted to be in her life.

So much for no strings attached sex, he thought grimly. First woman I meet to have it with, I end up falling madly in love with.

Benny rolled in about five o'clock, looking so smugly self-satisfied that Gabe knew he must have scored big at The Queens last night.

Even though Benny was incorrigible, he didn't usually skip out on a shift, or arrive so late. Of course it was only Monday, so the dishes weren't stacked sky high in the dishwasher room.

When Gabe had said he wasn't going to go to The Queens last night after work, Benny had gotten a strange look on his face and said, "What? No need to hunt for nookie any more?" he had asked in his own grating style.

He couldn't imagine Benny being jealous, but Gabe had been able to keep from spilling the beans about Angela in the previous several weeks since they had first met. And Benny, of course, hadn't apparently given up.

Gabe figured Benny was still keeping Eve's party in mind the following weekend, and he wasn't likely to screw that up. Just what exactly had the conniving Evelyn Tait promised him? Gabe wondered more than once.

Looking at Benny strangely, Gabe said, "Come on, Benjamin. We've got to get ready." Slapping Benny's back just a little too hard, Gabe headed toward the front door.

As Benny began following him, he grabbed Gabe by the arm just a little too roughly himself and Gabe turned quickly, looking ready to deck Benny.

But Benny's hands were flying up this time in a heartfelt attempt to placate Gabe, "Whoa there, buddy boy! That's it? That's all you're gonna tell me?" trying to be as light-hearted as possible.

Looking at Benny as if fighting an instinct to violence, Gabe turned away from Benny, working hard to calm himself down. "Maybe we should talk about it later, Harrison. You know? Like, after work? Like, in a less public place?"

"What? You gettin' private all of a sudden? Maybe this rich bitch's just turning your head a little too much."

Turning suddenly with a not-good look on his face, Gabe said, "Or maybe our friendship has been turning my head a little too much, for a little too long," with a seriousness that chilled Benny when he looked around and saw it.

Finally sensing a major change in Gabe he hadn't expected and being stopped short by this, Benny changed his attitude completely. "What? What the hell are you talking about? Dude. Haven't I been there for you? For years?" Gabe noticed that even Benny could obviously be hurt, even through all of his macho bravado shtick.

"What are you telling me?" Benny said, suddenly sounding as close to vulnerable as Gabe figured he would ever get. *God*, Gabe thought. *He's almost pleading.*

But taking the offensive, Gabe crossed his arms over his chest. "I thought I told you to stop calling her a bitch. But you didn't listen. Did you?"

Seeing something in his only real friend that he didn't want to see, Benny stopped himself short of saying anything else.

But falling all too quickly back into his old pattern, he held his hands up defensively, and said, "Whoa. Didn't mean anything by that, buddy-boy."

Unable to help himself, even after seeing a side to Gabe that did not back down, Benny continued with, "Goddamn man, looks like somebody's fallin' in loooove."

Gabe stalled for a second, a mix of emotions flying across his face. Caught in a windstorm he didn't see coming, Gabe tried to toss off a nonchalant, "Who says I'm falling in love?" at Benny, and began storming towards the door.

Once inside the Globe, Gabe thought that Benny would cool his jets. But, no. Calling after Gabe as his manhood recovered, Benny told

Gabe a a little too loudly, "Man! You got it, and you got it bad," raising a few heads around the room.

Smiling his usual Cheshire Cat grin, Benny began running to catch up. "The jig is up, O'Connor."

Cleaning up again, Gabe studiously avoided talking to Benny, while Benny was just biding his time. Each of them wove in and out of the bar area and into the kitchen, when Benny finally decided to make his move. "So. You still up for The Queens?"

Not answering at first, Gabe continued wiping the bar but slowly grinds to a halt. Unsure of whether he even wanted to talk to Benny after his confession to Angela brought up so many feelings of hurt he thought were gone, he finally relented.

"I guess. But I've got to make a call first."

Laughing his "I got ya!" laugh, Benny asked none too slyly, "What? To your answering machine?"

Straining to be civil and not haul off and hit Benny, Gabe just gave a restrained, "Yeah," as the only answer he could give without emotion.

"Well. Let me know if you change your mind," Benny dug back.

Only nodding, Gabe tried walking quickly away before Benny had a chance to "lock and load" again.

Leaving the Globe after their shift, Gabe and Benny's silence was only interrupted by a bunch of passing rowdies, all obviously already shit-faced and bragging loudly.

After a while, Benny managed to break the silence. "So. You really expectin' her to call?"

Deflating and not really knowing what he was expecting, "I don't know," was all Gabe could say.

"You know. Eve's still having her thing on Saturday. You still gonna come, aren't you?" Benny said, more hopeful than maneuvering this time.

Gabe stopped and folded his arms menacingly, "Look, Benny. I don't even want to see Eve again. Understand? You want to be calling somebody a bitch? Well, her name is Eve. Evelyn 'Daughter of the Devil Himself' Tait. That's who the real rich bitch is. And you'd like it so much for me to go to this thing. Wouldn't you?"

"Dude," Benny was about to break in, and thinking better of it, put his hands up in mock surrender. "So I won't say anything again." Turning playful once more, he said, "Man, you like so gotta get wasted."

Letting go of the last few days with a loss of energy, "Maybe I do," Gabe finally said.

Relieved, Benny for once said nothing, merely biding his time.

Fumbling his way in the door of his apartment, Gabe had obviously followed Benny's advice. Sloppy and barely able to walk, he tried making a beeline for the kitchen, heading straight for the fridge. Not that he managed to get there without a few bumps and later bruises in between.

Meanwhile, not noticing the flashing message light on the answering machine, Gabe did his drunken best at making a late night snack, clanging dishes and silverware in his befuddled attempt and almost dropping one of his best plates on the floor.

Staggering back into the living room with a too full drink barely in one hand and a sloppily laden plate barely in the other, he finally noticed the light flashing on the machine.

"Shit," he cried, doing his best to put plate and drink down before lunging for the replay button. Sending his precariously close to the edge drink flying, he grabbed for and luckily caught it before losing all of it on his previously clean rug. "Shit!"

Mumbling even more deprecations to himself, he stumbled back into the kitchen, came back trailing a rag with him and almost tripped over the coffee table, and found himself on the floor close enough to the spill to begin crawling to it. Gabe began wiping and then kneeling to collect himself, in a real state of disarray.

Throwing the fairly dry rag back in the general direction of the kitchen on his way to the answering machine, he finally found himself close enough to be punching the button. Plopping himself onto the couch to wait for the machine to go through its motions, he jumped when it finally screamed "BEEEEEP" at him.

"Hi Gabe, it's Angela. I'm sorry I didn't call earlier, but I've had some other commitments to take care of." Hesitating just a little too long, Gabe thought that maybe the message was over. But then, "If you want to call me later, my number is 555-8969. Talk to you soon," she finished and hung up.

Reaching for the phone where it sat, he knocked it out of the cradle and it took a plunge off the end table, ending up scooting itself across the floor towards the kitchen. "Shit!!" he let out again. This was not going right.

Crawling to where the phone was, he began dialing. On the wall, if he chose to look at it, the clock read 3:35. As in A.M. Bad mistake.

Very sleepily, the voice on the phone sleepily answered, "Hello?"

"Angela?" he slurred. "Gabe," was all he managed to get out.

"Who?" Angela said, as she struggled to put the voice to a name.

"Oh, Gabe. It's you." Pausing for a second and looking at her clock, "My God, Gabe. It's after three." And then waking up some more, "My God. It's four o'clock!"

"Sorry I'm callin' so late," the obviously sloshed voice on the other side responded.

Still lying down in the dark with the receiver cupped to her ear, Angela managed to get out, "Gabe, you're drunk, aren't you?"

Sighing heavily into the phone, he said, "Sorta."

Pausing again, this time to collect herself, she finally sat up. "Why?"

Now cupping his other hand over his eyes to hold back the tears, he mumbled, "You didn't call."

"Gabe, I had a — a function — to attend. Just because my husband is out of town, doesn't mean I don't have things I need to do."

"Yeah," was all he could manage to get out.
hen, "Look, I'm sorry, I'll call you back tomorrow."

I think that might be a good idea," she told him. Sighing and now becoming all too awake, she told him, "Good night, Gabe."

With the sound of the line clicking off, Angela carefully returned the phone to its cradle. Now completely wide awake and with a very concerned look growing in her eyes, it was obvious that she was not going to be getting much sleep this night.

Pacing back and forth in a most unlike-her way, Angela was already on the phone to Maddy early the next morning. Obviously in mid-conversation and still very much distressed, she said, "My God, Maddy. I thought he was different."

Maddy, in the most soothing voice she could manage this hour of the morning, asked, "Why, my dear Angela? Did you think that he was a saint?"

"No," she told her friend. "I just didn't think that he was the sort to get sloppy drunk. And thank God, Frank is still out of town."

On the other side of the conversation and sitting on her old-fashioned Victorian-style love seat, Maddy was trying not to laugh out loud. *Oh, the incongruency,* she thought.

Sitting amongst the furnishings of obvious wealth and talking on a similarly old-fashioned phone from a quite different era, Maddy was telling her friend calmly, "Maybe he isn't, my dear. Everyone has their lapses."

Angela's voice was still coming in quite shakily, "I'm still afraid, Maddy. What if he decided to call like that if Frank were here? Especially if Frank were to answer?" She finished in a terribly anguished voice, "I should never have given him my home phone number."

"Nonsense, my dear. I'm sure that this was only one time he would make such a gaffe. Please don't use this as an excuse to break it off. Not yet, at least. Give him another chance. Don't you think he deserves it?"

And then, Angela's anguish poring forth, "Oh, I don't know, Maddy. Maybe. Maybe I shouldn't have let you talk me into this in the first place. He's not the ambassador of a country. And at this point, I'm not even sure he's a gentleman."

"Trust your earlier sense of him my dear, and give him another chance. I really don't think you'll regret it."

"My God, Madelaine! I'm a senator's wife." Angela told her. "And he's just— a— bartender! He should be waiting on me! Not being — on top of me."

"Yes, Angela dear. He's just a bartender. But he's also a man with dreams of greatness. Very much like Frank and Harry were, only without the opportunities."

Pausing for added effect and emphasis she continued, "Only he didn't grow up with money and privilege, as did your Frank and my Harry. Only his dreams."

And pausing once again, she added, "Give him time."

TWENTY-NINE

The Globe was slow once more. Standing talking at the bar, Benny was in rare form.

"You gotta do something to get your mind off this rich bitch—"

Gabe was just about to tell him, "Benjamin, I told you—" when Benny knew to give in contritely, "Yeah, yeah, sorry. But like I was saying—"

"Benny, you say too much. Just do me a favor, and let me get back to work, cause I'm tired of talking about it. You obviously can't understand how I feel."

"But—"

"Butt out, Benny. When I need your—" and taking on a Benny-like heavily sarcastic tone with him, Gabe continued "—most excellent advice, dude — I'll ask for it." And then without another heartbeat's pause, having had just about all of the coaching that Gabe could take, "Understand?"

Not one to take no for an answer, Benny tried again. "But I've got the perfect solution for you, my man."

Gabe knew what was coming. Whenever Benny ended up trying to be cryptic, Gabe knew he could expect the worst.

Benny for his part tried to make it as seductive as he could, like the devil's solution, turning coy to make up for the reaction he knew Gabe was going to give him.

Folding his arms tightly across his chest and afraid of what was coming next, Gabe asked tersely, "Ok, Benny. What."

Smiling to himself with a wicked grin creasing his face, Benny tried going for the gold. Thinking that he was getting the point in, he snickered while he said, "Two words." And leaning in to whisper into Gabe's ear said— "Evelyn Tait."

"Benny. You have got to be kidding." Not sure whether to hit his friend or just walk away in disgust, he shook his head. "Evelyn Tait?"

Unable to imagine why, Benny began pleading. "Come on, Gabe. Her wild thing is still Saturday night." Turning coy suddenly, Benny added, "Saw her at Queens on Monday. She asked about you, dude."

Responding to himself rather than Benny, Gabe told no one, "Yeah. I bet she did."

Almost pleading now, Benny whined, "Gabe—"

"You're not able to let this thing go, are you? This is the arena you think you deserve, and I'm your ticket in. Am I right? That's what this is all about. Isn't it, Harrison? Tell me. What did the Devil herself promise you if you brought me? Huh?"

Putting on his best "poor misunderstood me" attitude, Benny just said a child-like, "Nothin'."

Gabe asked, "How is going to a party by the bitch queen of all bitch queens, going to take my mind off of—"

With his usual wicked grin, "We go, meet lotsa babes...Never know what might happen. You wow em' with your English lit charms..."

"This is you, getting into the 'rich bitch' arena. Right? And I'm your ticket? Through Eve Tait?"

Coming up with his best hurt self, Benny gave a shocked, "My man! This is me, doing his Benny-best to make up for the past. "I'm shocked," Benny said, feigning being hurt but barely keeping his smile from breaking in. "Besides, if Eve's a bitch, better the bitch you know. Right?"

Giving in highly reluctantly, Gabe knew when to give up. Realizing that this wasn't going to end, Gabe figured giving in would at least end the hard sell.

And maybe he was right. Maybe. "Ok, Benny. This once," he said, exhausted at all of this effort.

Having finally won, Benny was ecstatic. "Yes! My man—" Benny said triumphantly.

"I said once."

"You won't regret it. Get your mind off this Angie babe for few hours, and—"

Cutting in, Gabe said, "Angela. Her name is Angela, Benny."

Unperturbed and on a roll, Benny bounced back with, "Whateva, Gabe. You won't regret it. You'll see," Benny said ecstatically, floating off in an upwardly mobile — or was that nubile? — haze.

Whistling to himself as congratulations for his victory, Benny bounced off to the kitchen without Gabe even prompting him, for a change.

"I'd better not regret this, Harrison," Gabe said to himself, once Benny was out of earshot.

"Never mind. I'm regretting it already," Gabe said in a very tired cloud.

Driving out to Cabin John, Maryland, was a long drive from

Dupont Circle if you weren't used to it. Especially driving his rickety old Malibu. It was getting too old to take the turns, and gave jolts with the bumps and pot holes that the Park Service never managed to keep fixed out here.

Gabe had originally bought it not just for the look, but also for the name. Being the writer, he'd had visions just out of college that he would move to California, the land of the Beats, and all the other avant guarde writers in one of the two most unlike Nebraska places he could think of (the other being New York City, and he couldn't imagine living with all those buildings so close in after his home).

In the end, he ended up at Georgetown for his Bachelors, largely because his father still had hopes that his wayward son would change his mind and become a lawyer, far from the salesman type that *he* had been all his life. Gabe acquiesced only long enough to take the writing courses he had wanted to, keeping his father's hopes alive as long as he could.

And then his father had died while Gabe was in his first year, and that sealed the fate of being a lawyer. His father had died of cirrhosis of the liver, the result of a life of hard drinking on the road. Gabe swore he'd never end up like his father.

So of course, he ended up being a bartender. "Good Irish Catholic tradition, I'd say," Benny once told him, not seeing the irony for Gabe.

Gabe was steeped neck deep in misgivings. This trip into the wilds of Bethesda and then Cabin John was made even longer by Benny constantly chattering away in the passenger seat. Gabe had long ago found out that it was sometimes best to just shut Benny out of his mind and occasionally interject some monosyllable response into Benny's rant at the appropriate silence, to pretend he was still listening.

They were now wending their way up the snaky part of Mac Arthur Boulevard, with the Potomac flashing the occasional gleam in the moonlight through the trees on the left. They had passed the "hoity toity" (according to Benny, as Gabe tuned in for a second) section of DC behind and were about enter the "even more hoitier and fucking toitier" section of Maryland.

Gabe had always wondered how Benny had found his way out to that secluded college in Nebraska where they met, but he gathered (and didn't find it hard to believe) that Benny had been exiled to the place that most closely resembled the moon in contrast to New York City and the Bronx where Benny had grown up.

Gabe often wondered whether Benny had been disappeared because he had done something to someone, someone his parents never wanted to find Benny again. That would fit in with Benny's current behavior.

"How can people stand living out here with so many trees around them?" Benny asked Gabe suddenly. "All way too creepy for me," Benny said and honestly shivered.

Gabe was also seriously re-evaluating just how much longer he could keep this friendship up. Maybe it was time to shut Benny out of his life altogether. Telling Angela about Mary Ann and the unforgivable thing that Benny had done, had opened up all the old wounds he hadn't realized were still festering and close to the surface.

Tuning into to what Benny was ranting about for a second, only confirmed the growing divide. Benny was all about drinking, and picking up "chicks" — or, depending on his mood — "bitches." And Gabe was growing truly tired of listening to it all.

Having been given directions to Eve's new house, Gabe wasn't familiar with this part of Maryland. Benny would almost invariably tell him, "Hey, hey, hey! We shoulda turned back there," just as soon as they passed the turn they were supposed to take. This was making the trip even longer that it would have been, irritating Gabe to no end.

Benny, on the other hand, was sitting next to him in the ratty bucket seat ranting and raving about the women he was going to meet tonight and all the things he'd do "to make those rich bitches swoon and fight" for his attention. *Right*, Gabe thought, *Like they're going to be crawling all over you.*

Of course, Gabe could care less. If Benny met the bitch queen of his dreams tonight and forgot all about his best bud Gabe, Gabe would welcome the break. "All the best, Benjamin," he would say, if he even got the chance.

Even with his foul mood at the thought of seeing his least favorite bitch queen tonight, Gabe had to admit to himself that he was starting to relish this drive out to Cabin John. With the window rolled down part of the way, if it weren't for Benny's incessant high-pitched chatter, he'd really be enjoying this ride.

He almost wanted to turn off the headlights, just to see if it'd scare Benny or not. Realizing just as suddenly that it would only appeal to Benny's bad-boy nature, the desire evaporated just as soon as it came to him.

With the occasional cars passing by and the voice of Benny droning on and on beside him, it was putting him into a strange state. Reminding him of his rides to the Rendezvous, he could almost smell Angela's hair in the wind.

Funny. It wasn't until now, making the mistake of driving to this party that he didn't really want to go to, that he knew was going to be filled with people that he wouldn't normally even want to associate with (but Carol would absolutely feel in heaven around), that he realized just how much a part of his life that his mystery woman had become. Sighing only helped him drink in even more of the night air.

The Potomac was just a stone's throw away from him now as he came out of the sharp turn that put him onto the Cabin John Parkway heading north. The address that Benny had given him was just off the parkway, and even deeper into the richer part of Cabin John/not quite Potomac than they had been in so far.

Potomac was where all the nouveau riche of Maryland always moved to. He was sure that that was where Carol would eventually end up with whatever husband she managed to snag before her brittle beauty died, happy to live in what was called a McMansion in a subdivision filled with other McMansions.

These houses had huge empty halls residing on the edge of the death of the American Dream, the height of ego and the last cutting edge of conspicuous consumption for those needing to be rich or seen as rich.

Ironically, he mused, if it hadn't been for Benny's prodding about the whole personals thing, he would have never met the woman who was now dominating his thoughts.

Hell, he thought. *If I hadn't met Angela, I might even have eventually slid back into the arms of Carol*, he thought, shivering slightly.

If it weren't for Angela.

Pulling off onto the ramp that he almost missed for getting off the parkway without streetlights to guide him, he returned to the present enough to ask Benny, "What were the directions from here?"

"Dude, that's what I been tellin' you 'bout for the last minute or two. Weren't you—"

"Listening? No, Benny. I had more important things on my mind," Gabe said and left it at that.

He could see a puzzled Benny sitting beside him out of the corner of his eye, not wanting to admit to what Gabe was talking about. That was fine with him.

"Oh, oh—" Benny suddenly hooted like a little kid, "Turn here!" Benny shouted, as if Gabe weren't sitting next to him.

"All right, all right," Gabe said with a smirk. Benny was almost pissing in his pants to get to this party. What the hell did Eve promise him to get me here? Gabe thought at this, even more insistently than before. His very own bitch queen of the Bitch Queen's choosing? Had Eve promised to set Benny up for his maneuvering to get Gabe out here?

Another few turns, deeper and deeper into even more luxurious houses, brought Benny into a wide-mouthed stupor, and Gabe into a very crowded scene that he was sure wasn't representative of what this local area usually hosted.

They could see, even before the address became visible, exactly where the party was. Was Eve even going to have valets here to help with this crowd?

Finally pulling up to the street the house was on, Gabe turned off the ignition and began drifting the car to a stop. "My God, Benny. This is definitely severely 'rich' territory, even for Eve. I don't even think we're going to fit in for a second."

"Hey, I don't care if I fit in or not," Benny said, with his mouth still hanging open to the wind. He was in Benny heaven right now. "Just as long as I find something to 'fit in to,' if you know what I mean?" he said, as he closed his mouth and only opened it to give a suggestive lick at some imagined crotch.

Right, Gabe thought wearily. Sometimes Gabe almost wished that he could be like Benny, not taking anything seriously, living only for the next drink, or the next fuck. Live his life seemingly without any conscience whatsoever: that might be a relief from the constant doubts that plagued him.

Cruising up to the big stone slab at the entrance that read "Tait" on it in huge gold letters, (along with the number in a somewhat smaller but still significant size), the high-end expensive cars that screamed wealth and status were piling up around them everywhere.

"I don't know about this, Benny," Gabe sighed. Shaking his head, Gabe decided to drive further down the street to park his in-comparison piece of rusted, scrap metal Rust Bucket somewhere else.

Even Benny seemed to be cowed for once, and a little bit questioning at the sight of all of this obvious wealth. Uncharacteristically at a loss for words, Benny finally managed to almost silently whisper, "Riiiight. Let's park further down the block," to Gabe.

"Don't want to make an entrance getting out of this rusty old bucket of bolts and rubber bands."

For once, Gabe agreed with Benny. "Yeah, except that this is the end of the block," Gabe whispered back. Turning around at the dark end of the street, Gabe began cruising back past the madness, almost wanting to just drop Benny off and leave.

"I really don't know about this, Benny."

"Holy Shit, Gabe! Eve's daddy musta made a whole shit load since we last saw her. This is Bad Money Mojo, bro."

"Yeah," Gabe whispered. "Like I've said, Daughter of the Devil Himself, indeed."

Pulling out of sight of the minions with their mighty steeds, Gabe finally found a dark part of the street out of harm's way to park, a good four blocks away and on a side street that could barely fit a car before it died out in a dead end.

Pulling in and getting out, Gabe pounded on the roof to get Benny's suddenly distracted attention and leaned in. "I don't like the looks of this." He could see that even the voracious Benny was having his doubts as well.

"So maybe we should go back to where we know," Gabe asked hopefully, knowing what the answer would be.

With the possibility of dripping wealth suddenly gleaming in Benny's eyes even in the dark, Benny came suddenly to life. Turning to where Gabe was leaning in, he had the growing look of a kid on Christmas Day waking up to remember that Santa had left gifts downstairs under the tree.

"Dude. We have got the check this out," Benny said, looking in the direction of the still-arriving stream of cars heading towards Eve's, finally awed by something in his life beside himself.

Gabe was totally unconvinced. Looking at Benny with the hardest stare he could muster, he said, "I mean it, Harrison. If we go in and I'm ready to leave and you're not—"

"What," Benny said, his bravado returning to leaking greed. "Yeah, yeah. Right bro," he said, not even seeing Gabe any more. With dreams of monied babes gleaming in his eyes, Benny popped out of the car just as suddenly, smirking as he slammed the door.

"Come on, my man. Where's your sensa adventure? We gotta at least check this out." His mind was obviously already in full plotting and planning mode for his conquest of the party, fully recovered from his former awe.

"This is out of our league," Gabe said quietly, recovering sufficiently to return a jab by adding, "Even out of the league of your dreams."

But Benny was turning himself on, puffing himself up and preparing to do battle with the best and the brightest (not to mention, richest of them). Gabe watched as the smile that Gabe had learned to fear crept over Benny's face. "That's the whole point! Right?" Benny said, ready and already on the prowl.

Walking off in the direction of the crowd spilling in like a hypnotized man, Gabe followed in Benny's wake, knowing that this was most definitely going to be a mistake.

Shifting into cool, Benny turned to assure Gabe, "Dude. We go in, we check it out. If it ain't cool, we leave. Right?" And turning back again, he continued walking, step by step getting his swagger back.

"Just like The Queens. No prob," Benny said quietly, as much to himself as to Gabe.

Walking to catch up to him, Gabe told him again sternly, "Benny, remember. If we go in and I'm ready to go and you're not...I'm gone."

And of course, not getting any reply, "Right, Benny?" Gabe reiterated again, hard and harsh.

"Right," Benny said, obviously no longer paying attention to anything Gabe had to say. Target acquired, and ready to launch his missile, Benny's stride took him at a quick pace from his friend's side.

Seeing it not sink in, Gabe started pushing hard to match Benny's stride and then some, punching Benny on the arm to get his attention as he did. "Right, Harrison?"

His focus on riches ahead, Benny barely even reacted. "Right," he whispered.

"It's a hell of a long cab ride back to DC from here."

Still distracted, Benny only managed "Yeah. We'll see," and picked up his pace even harder. Giving up on keeping up, Gabe slowed and let Benny go on his way.

Now flowing into the sea of wealth waiting for them, Gabe's pace began slowing down even further as he seriously contemplated just coming to a stop and turning around and leaving Benny to his own devices and whatever excuse he would need to give to Eve as to why Gabe had disappeared.

It'd serve Benny right, Gabe thought, imagining Eve's wrath and fury. "I dunno. He was right behind me," he imagined Benny groveling.

Of course, Benny would soon recover. He always did.

As soon as Gabe thought there wouldn't be much at the other end of this driveway, he walked around the final bend in the flagstone paved drive, coming hard upon what Gabe could only describe as a building screaming MONEY! A RICH PERSON LIVES HERE.

Eve and her daddy done obscenely well, Gabe thought, dropping into Benny vernacular in his awe without even realizing it.

With all manner of cars from BIG to HUGE unevenly parked here and there, there were still even more cars pulling up and around this circular driveway before this house (if it could be called that).

Gabe was confronted by both a huge fountain in the circle and a waterfall mountain in the middle of it, and got the impression of countryside White House.

He also couldn't help but think of the Rendezvous Inn with the sight of all of this. But this wasn't Old Money. This was New Money, a different kind of wealth at its most obscene and excessive. More of an embassy than a house, Gabe thought, impressed despite himself. This place has wealth flowing from it like the water in that waterfall. Like the Potomac River with its Great Falls not more than a mile or two away.

Then, despite himself, he found himself saying out loud, "My God, she has a waterfall in her front yard." But Gabe took little satisfaction in this, knowing that Benny's cool could still be broken.

He began looking around, noticing that the crowd that flowed by him (and still getting out of their vehicles that cost small fortunes in and of themselves), were also dripping wealth. And power. Lots of power.

Realizing that Benny was nowhere to be seen, Gabe began following the path that Benny must have taken into the fray. *Didn't take him long to recover*, Gabe thought ruefully.

As this crowd of obscene wealth flowed around him and inside, he quietly took in the house and its surroundings. He cautiously began approaching it as if he were entering a lion's den before walking in the huge double front door. Once again he was reminded of the Rendezvous. But that place in some ways downplayed its power and purpose. Not here.

The layout of this place shocked him back to the present. It had a two-story tall living room with equally expansive two-story windows opening on an interior that could probably hold most people's houses.

And to boot, it had a tree growing in the center of it.

And not just a small tree, either. The house had been deliberately built around this already full grown tree in the midst of it. And that was just what he could see from here.

Even though he wasn't inside yet, the music was already washing over him as if he were at a concert, it was so loud. Pumping from some enormous sound system, he guessed; he couldn't even see the speakers.

Gabe felt like a pauper who had gotten lost and found himself on the wrong end of the royalty chain. He flowed through party goers dressed in designer fortunes who were paying him little attention, as if their even noticing him would be a serious breach of their haute chic etiquette.

Once more, Gabe realized what Angela must have felt walking down those stairs and into Java the Hut. Except this was more obscene than the Rendezvous. That place was understated elegance compared to this place.

Threading his way through the throng, it did not surprise Gabe that Benny was nowhere to be seen.

Walking in through the huge gated front door and taking the even more huge size of this place in as he did, Gabe clumsily bumped into the occasional disdainful glitterati, apologizing to their backs as he did.

Finally inside, Gabe was confronted with an opulence the likes of which he'd never seen except in magazines and on TV. He saw that not only was the living room the size of a house, but it was also a sunken living room, complete with a fireplace in the middle to rival that of a palace just beyond the tree.

Beginning to take in deep breaths to calm himself, Gabe tried to navigate through this literal horde, his hackles raised in distress. Even the Rendezvous Inn hadn't had this effect on him.

Catching up with a smitten Benny already chatting up some bling-blinged trollop on the far side of this cavern, he tried to shout at him, "You still think we're not going to drown in this sea, Benjamin?"

But because the music was pumping through unseen speakers as obscenely loud as the wealth dripping everywhere (and also because Benny was on the hunt), he conveniently didn't seem to hear Gabe until Gabe tapped him on his shoulder.

Looking as if a fly had talked to him, Benny turned only for an instant to shout, "Yeah, maybe. But if I do, I'll die happy." Returning to putting the moves on his at least listening latest adventure, Gabe realized his futility and began walking away.

Great, he told himself. Casually throwing a, "Remember what I said, Harrison..." in Benny's direction, Gabe saw that he was going home alone from this. "About that cab ride," he throws into the mix, knowing that Benny never heard a word.

Wading through the mass of beautiful people for whom he has no respect and   looking for an exit, Gabe finally found the back door, "Great," Gabe murmured. "Just great."

Without the grown child he called his friend to look out for, Gabe wandered around and through the bevy of women all around him, some talking amongst themselves, others on and often in the arms of (often older to much older) men. Unlike Benny, he was feeling completely out of his league, and was being suspiciously obvious about it.

With all the model-gorgeous women draped over their high-end executive-looking men all around him, Gabe was already looking back towards the front door, now barely seen through the throng, for his escape.

Deciding that he has had enough, Gabe was at the point of bolting, when he suddenly felt a svelte, slender arm slipping under his and intertwining around it like a snake around a tree. Without even turning, he knew that the body attached to the arm he was being engulfed by was the velvet figure of one Evelyn Tait, her scent just as seductively warning him as Angela's earlier remembered scent had comforted.

In her mid-twenties now and model gorgeous herself, Gabe turned finally to find Eve dressed in a slinky, barely covering slip dress. *This is the Devil herself,* he thought. *Forget her father.*

The Devil was supposed to be dark and black, but this devil (*Succubus?* Gabe thought), was perfectly blond, with hair down to the middle of her back.

When Gabe first saw her almost five years before, his first thought was here was the genie Jeanie, from that old TV show. *It almost glows in the dark,* he thought later, and it still shimmered even now, as if spun out of real gold.

Has to be colored, he thought back then. Until she was naked in his bed. "Only your hair dresser knows for sure," he remembered the old ad saying. "I don't think your hair dresser wants to see that," he said to her one time as a joke.

"Well, well, well, O'Connor," she hissed in his ear seductively. "Didn't think that Harrison would manage to draft your writerly self into coming out here. Into the jaws of the beast, that is."

Sighing in spite of himself, he could only manage a weary, "Hello, Eve."

She was wearing a white silk dress, that was barely covering all the essentials even more than the mermaid squad from Queens. The front scooped down so low, that he felt if it went any further, her navel would have been seen. And down her back went the plunging neckline as well.

"So. How have you been, Gabriel?" she hissed once more.

"Ok," was all he could bring himself to say. *My God*, was all he could think.

As she turned to him full on, she began wrapping her other arm around his waist, as if to entrap him. The Snake entwined, she leaned in and insinuated into his ear in as hoarse and sexy a whisper as she could manage, "Benjamin told me about that little slut you were seeing. Social climbing doesn't suit you well," she purred.

Right. That's why your Daddy did it and you do it so well too, Gabe was tempted to say to her. Instead he merely asked, "What's the point, Eve?"

Turning away from him and delicately but forcefully guiding Gabe away from the inside and towards that back sliding glass door now so conveniently open and leading outside, the sea of her guests were parting like the Red Sea before Moses. But they were sneaking exchanged glances and bringing their hands up to whisper behind them as they did.

Eve, ever so nonchalantly not deigning to pay attention to the stir she was causing, merely dropped, "Let's go somewhere and talk," into the explosive feeling mix. "Private," she added forcefully and none too softly.

Gabe, knowing that Eve was eating up all of this intrigue as to who he was, decided to fall into line. For now. "I guess you know the way," he said, pumping as much irony into it as he could.

"I always do," she said, ignoring his dig as she finished the glide out the door and away from her sycophants.

Letting her arm slip silently down his and finally grabbing his hand, Eve was now also somewhat forcefully pulling Gabe further and further away, silently, into their own secluded patch of garden.

Further and further into the soft, fragrant night. Seeing the boardwalk of the trail leading further into the darkness, he was feeling dizzy even looking at her and feeling as if the ground was disappearing underneath them.

Gabe followed in her wake, wary but unable to let the shimmering glow in front of him go. Eventually reaching an ornate gazebo far from the partying crowd, he noticed that the lights underneath the overhang were only on enough for him to make out the lighter shade of his temptress; hair, side of her face and now a hint of chest.

Releasing his hand, Eve glided over to a bench on the far side of the massive structure and sitting cat-like and seductively down on the crisply polished wood, patted the spot beside her without looking up. Gabe, standing his ground, was looking around, suddenly eager for another exit, but seeing only darkness beyond.

As his eyes adjusted to the lower level of light, he noticed that the Potomac was once again glistening not very far off from them, only this time it wasn't far below them at all.

He imagined that during the day, this gazebo had a perfect view of the falls just down river from Great Falls. And under a full moon, this would float like a fairy glade in the dark, feeling like the end of the world. The specter of all this wealth and its danger, once again screamed loudly in his ear to...*Run*.

Not so easily, he thought. But deep down he knew that he was slipping into the passion play that Eve had set up for him to fall into. "Seduction has its own incredible power. And grace," he remembered hearing once. "And danger."

"You're destined for greatness, Gabriel." Patting the bench again, this time a little more forcefully and insistently. Eve began pouring it on, continuing with, "You're so talented, handsome, and hardworking. All you need is a little help," she said, looking up through her eyelashes once more and pouring on the seduction.

She finished with, "With the right woman by your side, of course."

Of course, he thought. *It always came down to that.*

Turning away from her as if that might break the fairy spell that she was weaving, Gabe found himself turning once again suddenly. Almost as if he couldn't help himself.

"And, of course, that woman is..." he started, pausing for the intended ironic effect that he could muster but knowing it would fall on deaf ears, "...You?"

She slipped her glitter-encrusted glass slippers off slowly, with each foot. Then she began raising and then turning to one side to pull her right leg up to rest on the bench.

Eve then began turning her left leg, a little too much in the other direction, letting her left leg finally ride up to the bench as well. Even in the darkness, Gabe could see the opening slit exposed in the absence of her dress, exposing just a hint of the darkness that lay in between.

Gabe of course, had already been to that garden many times before. But that didn't mitigate the devastating effect that creating this piece of theater had on the bold pressure and increasing bulge in his pants.

"Why not?" she said, as she lowered her head seductively and began looking through her well tended eye lashes again. "You can take me, Gabe. Right here, right now..."

"And you have a life of wealth and glamour to offer me," Gabe said, not as forcefully as had wanted. "And just exactly what do you want in return?"

Arising from her throne and covering the garden of Eve once more, she began to glide ever so seductively over to where Gabe was still standing. She placed herself firmly in front of him, ever so close.

"Why...Just a strong man to be by my side," she said, as she reached out and down, and with fingernails outstretched, began stroking his already throbbing pants in just the right place.

God, she's good, Gabe thought trying not to moan, as his resistance was quickly melting away. He was working really hard to not moan with the delicate touch, and managed to get out a strained, "With an inheritance riding on it, perchance?" out of his mouth.

Eve flinched for a second but then recovered quickly. Moving close enough to be within kissing range and removing her hand from where it had been playing, Gabe sighed with relief.

Instead, she lifted it to his throat and for a second Gabe was worried as to what her true intentions were now. If he disobeyed.

As she let her hand drift down so that it landed enticingly on his chest, Eve began pouring it on purringly, turning playfully pouty, and then letting the actress out as if she was playfully deeply hurt and offended. He could also tell that she was working hard on her part to keep her cool and not lash out.

"Why are you always so distrustful?" she said in such a kittenish tone that Gabe (if he didn't know better), would interpret as playfully innocent. But like a big cat, she was playing with her food before going in for the kill. That kind of kitten.

He could hear the wind beginning to rustle the leaves in the giants above them that he could only barely make out now, perceiving the lower leaves in the glow from the house. If it had been fall or winter, the rustling would have been enough to shake him out of her spell completely. But since it was springtime, the leaves gave off a soft and enticing hush instead.

It took all his concentration to focus on that, instead of the hand now carefully working its way button by button down and then inside his shirt.

"Oh, I don't know Eve," he tried to say with as much disinterest in his voice as he could, (although it wasn't working). "It's just that I've learned that most women want something. Something that I'm not sure I'm willing to give."

He let out an inadvertent gasp of pain as that hand on his chest found a clump of chest hair, and grabbed it for a tight involuntary squeeze. Letting just a little too much venom leak through, Eve regained her sense of power enough to ask, "Why? Don't want anything to distract you from your holy cause of writing?"

He backed away suddenly, as if the spell she had been casting was breaking. "Now you're starting to sound like Carol," Gabe said, digging back. He knew that Eve and Carol had seen each other across the room at some party all three ended up at a few months back, and both of them being blond, the comparison was easy.

As if she suddenly realized the veil she had woven was dropping, Eve suddenly switched directions. Returning to her previously seductive tones, she said, "She didn't understand you, Gabriel." As her hand started dropping once again to his nether regions, she added in a husky growl, "Or know how to make you jump."

This was the wrong choice of words for her to use, and the spell started falling away. Now effectively broken, Gabe felt his resolve returning to intervene, growing stronger the more she tried to seduce him.

Finally managing a full laugh at her, he chided her with, "And you do."

When he saw fear rising in her eyes even for just the slightest of seconds, he knew she was getting desperate. But it was gone again just as quickly as it had come. God, she was good.

Pushing her way towards him, pouring on the last reserves of her power, Eve returned to the kittenish avatar, as she drew her mouth to his chest and then up to just under his chin. "If you'd let me," she whispered, and began to drop her head down to where his will could be devastated.

Having seen this move in movie after movie, he wondered if she knew how unoriginal this move was. But it still had the desired effect.

Pulling away and turning with all the strength that he could, he felt the cord snap between them. "What difference would there be now than when we were seeing each other before?"

With a disturbing shiver of coldness, she said ominously, "I was Carol then."

Coming up behind him and slipping her arms under his, her hands began gesturing grandly around them, like a goddess offering a mortal immortality and power over the whole world. All this could be yours. If only...

"Now I don't need to climb," she whispered ever so seductively. "I'm already there, thanks to Daddy. I have the lifestyle that I've always dreamed of."

Turning around and backing away from her, he decided to play some back. "And just what exactly would I need to do to fit into that lifestyle?"

Closing in on him and attempting to unbutton his shirt all the way down to the belt, Eve began pouring on the raw sensuality. A few buttons down and her right hand slid right in. But it wasn't to rake his chest.

"You're so suspicious," she said as he involuntarily gasped. "Why can't you just let go, and enjoy what you might have?" He knew her hand was slender, but he felt now sliding past his belt and into his underwear, searching for his penis.

Wracked with doubts now and feeling too much of the focused electricity flowing from her fingertips, he began to fall again. While she had his attention focused on other things, she deftly had his belt undone. His pants unfastened and his zipper at half mast, her lips hit his chest and his resolve all but melted. It began dripping away like wax that melted into her mouth. She had in the moment sunk to her knees and was in the process of finishing the seduction she had started.

With all the focus he could manage, he could only get out a strained, "You're gorgeous, and now you're even wealthy."

Maybe it wouldn't be that bad this time, he thought, his mind melting into a haze of sensation at what she was doing below.

She had started rising when he looked down and saw that her slip dress had conveniently now slipped off. And there she was, in all her glowing blond glory.

He had forgotten how both slender and shapely Eve was, her perfect little body calling its siren call for him to pick her up and take her right here and now. Like she wanted.

He was almost ready to reach for her and hoist her up, when just as suddenly, the face of Angela appeared in his mind out of nowhere.

He felt some sense sink back into his mind, resurrecting reason where animal lust had almost taken him over the edge. As if some part of him that had almost abandoned him, returned like a Prodigal Love, and he knew that he could never have anything except sex with Eve.

And "just sex" (ironically) had a way of becoming undesirable over time when he hadn't felt love grow along with it. The sex with Eve had been porn star sex material. *Until her utterly bitchy side came out and ruined it.*

He stepped back, pulled his pants up from his knees where he found them, and turned away. As he tried to button his shirt, he began looking frantically over his shoulder to see if there had been anyone watching.

He sighed, "There's still something missing, Eve."

Silkily following him and re-wrapping her arms around his neck, she said way too sharply, "Gabriel, you think too much." And like the gymnast she once had been, began lifting and wrapping her legs around his waist to regain her position of power.

"Maybe. Maybe that is the problem, Eve." Unwrapping her legs from his waist and freeing himself to back away, "You see, I do want to think. I want to feel. And you, Eve? Well, you just want to enjoy."

With a little evil thought coming suddenly to mind, Gabe began smiling maliciously in turn, unleashing his inner Benny. "You should be with Benny, Eve. Your daddy would like Benny. He's just like him."

With this last jab pushing her over an edge she didn't see coming, Eve's face began twisting into pure disgust. "Harrison. You must be fucking joking."

"No, I'm not. The more I think about it, you and Benny would be perfect together. Until you lost his interest, that is. Even the ultimate Temptress has her limits to tempt."

And with that, he saw the crack forming and the emotional lava about to erupt. "I need a lot more than you can give me, Eve. I always have."

Walking away from her this time, his confidence building as he continued on his way back towards her house and his real desire, she began crumbling into a mix of crying, raging and laughing behind him. He could see her standing there in his mind, her naked need to both please and control matched only by her perfect body glowing in the dark.

Doing her best to hurt him, Eve threw a hoarse, "This is it, O'Connor! You walk away this time..." at the retreating figure.

Whispering to himself as he walked away from the more and more desperate entreaties, he told her, "God, I hope so."

"Gabe!" she began shouting, more and more childlike. "Gabe?!"

Trying his best to not look back lest his resolve turn into a pillar of salt, Gabe went off in search of the Ever Disappearing Harrison Monster to give him one last chance for a ride back to the land of the Queens and away from the land of Rich Bitches.

THIRTY

Back to tending bar a couple of days later. Gabe was moving quite slowly. His heart not in swabbing down the bar any more. Not in serving his soggy customers. Not in— Well, not in much of anything.

The last couple of days he had spent going over his decision to turn Eve away, thinking that he needed to try calling Angela again, and generally regretting much of the last several weeks.

He had picked up the phone to call Angela dozens of times, and then each time thinking better of it, setting the receiver gently down again. He was hating himself for not calling her, not apologizing, and he was also frightened about what she would say if he did.

So here he was again. Back to tending bar. Back to wishing that he had the kind of reckless drive that Benny did, and then knowing that he was better off not having that.

Speaking of Benny...Running in late as usual, Benny stopped only long enough to slap the bar loudly, grinning with the usual wicked Benny grin on his face, shouting, "My man!" and continued on running his way into the kitchen.

Disgustedly shaking his head and pretending not to notice, even the sound of Emergency Vehicles roaring by close by outside on

Pennsylvania Avenue didn't seem to attract his attention.

Returning to lackadaisically wiping the bar, he didn't even notice when his usually taciturn patrons begin turning their attention to the TV mounted on the wall behind him.

here was a "LATE BREAKING NEWS" banner flashing on the bottom of the screen, interrupting the afternoon soap. One of his regulars yelled at him from the back of the room, "Hey, Gabriel. Turn it up!"

"Huh?" he asked, as several of the other patrons also began to point at the set behind him as well.

Turning towards the TV, Gabe reached for the remote where he kept it behind the lines of liquor bottles in front of the mirror. His finger ramped the volume up just in time to catch an announcer saying, "...as he was giving what for him was a very impassioned speech on the floor of the senate."

His attention gotten, Gabe returned to his wiping.

"The senior Senator from Connecticut, Franklin James Treworthy III, has apparently suffered a massive coronary on the Senate Floor."

Frank's picture was now replaced with CSPN footage of his last moments before he clutched his chest and began falling towards the podium, his face wracked with pain.

With the shot of the late Senator Treworthy on the screen fading out, the anchor was back, reading the hastily written script in his hand. "Attempts to revive the Senator, however, appear to have been unsuccessful, and he has been pronounced dead en route to George Washington Hospital a few moments ago."

Suddenly, the previous footage from the Rose Garden photo op with the President three weeks before was shown. As the image zoomed in to focus on Frank and Angela, Gabe stopped all pretense of working. All he saw on the screen was Angela, her face registering obvious (to him) disdain at having to be there.

In spite of himself, he did a Benny and whispered, "Holy fucking shit" to himself.

Just as he said this, Benny suddenly appeared seemingly out of nowhere, walking over to investigate. "Whoa, dude. What's up? You look like you just seen yourself a ghost."

His gaze now transfixed on the screen, Gabe didn't say anything for a long second. Then as if out of a great distance, he whispered, "That's her, Benny."

Still not getting it, Benny was only getting pissed. "That's who? What you talking about, dude? Her who?"

"That's her," Gabe repeated, as if that's all the information Benny needed. Coming back to reality abruptly, Gabe was changing from mystified to pissed as well. Turning on the now dumbfounded Benny, he just said plainly, "That's Angela," pointing to the screen.

Running through his own soggy brain, Benny started playing along. "Angela. Angela. Angela. I don't..." and then all of a sudden with recognition finally dawning, it was Benny's turn to be awe-struck. Which of course coming from Benny quickly changed into glee with a hint of admiration.

"Holy shit! You're kidding. That's the rich—" Benny quickly recovered with "She's a fucking senator's wife?"

And suddenly much louder, he started with, "Oh, my Gawd, dude! You're fucking—"

Recovering himself and catching Benny with a hand quickly wrapped around Benny's mouth, Gabe grabbed him and started moving him towards the back room.

Once there, Gabe was almost ready to haul off and hit him. "Jesus, Benny. You going to announce that to the whole fucking world?"

Benny, being as quiet as he could now that Gabe has just managed to manhandle him to the back in a New York Minute, leaned in to whisper furiously to Gabe, "Whoa! You been fucking a senator's wife, dude. And you didn't even know it. That's fucking—"

In shock again, "Yeah" was all Gabe could come up with, trying to come to grips with this revelation.

"Shit, indeed. And I thought that my find on Saturday night was fucking hot." Benny's expression changed back from shocked to mischievous.

His calculating mind at work, he went into "low down" mode. "Well, well, well. And now that hubby's out of the way—"

Gabe rounded on him suddenly with, "Jesus, Harrison. I didn't think that even you could be so crass. I mean, her husband just died," Gabe said, now truly disgusted and seriously considering walking away completely.

"If you say anything to anyone, Harrison, and I mean anyone," Gabe whispered, furious that he reacted so quickly and was caught off guard so easily around Benny.

"Hey! I'm just sayin'! I see opportunity when it knocks, bro. At least now you don't gotta go sneakin' around any more."

Gabe, now thoroughly exasperated, just began shaking his head and walking away. "Benny..." was all he managed to say.

Benny, suddenly realizing how close to the edge of friendship he's skating, began running after Gabe. "Sorry, dude. Just tryin' to help."

Turning, Gabe merely points in the direction of the basement.

"Why don't you help by getting that shit load of dishes from lunch down stairs already. How 'bout that, Benny? How 'bout doing your fucking job for once."

Continuing walking away from the now completely stunned Benny, Gabe was all of a sudden completely tired of bar life and all of the characters (and now most especially Benny) that it contained.

Being the closest he's been to walking away from his entire life, Gabe headed downstairs for a minute to take the information in about Angela. "No wonder she didn't want me to ask any questions," he said, mulling over in his head what to do next.

Pacing back and forth in his apartment the next morning, Gabe occasionally paused, and glancing over his shoulder, walked towards his phone. Stopping himself before reaching it and picking it up, he returned to pacing.

Not now, he thought. And then thought, *Maybe Eve was right. Maybe I do spend too much time in my head.*

Doing this several times more had him in even more of a frenzy than he was in the previous night. After recovering from the initial shock of the revelation of just exactly who he had been sleeping with and thinking back to how she had laughed at the joke he had made in Dupont Circle about her being part of the Mob, now Gabe wasn't so sure that it was any different. She was still inaccessible.

Walking over to his reclining chair and sitting, Gabe continued his staring match with the phone from a discreet distance away.

Inside the bar that afternoon, Gabe entered warily, waiting for the Roadrunner pounce. Not seeing Benny standing just inside the door, he started thinking, *One of these days I'm just going to haul off and flatten him*. When it comes though, he's still unprepared for the punch.

"So'd you call her already, or not?" Benny said accusingly out of nowhere, making Gabe jump.

Startled in spite of his best efforts to not be, Gabe realized surprisingly it doesn't have as much power as the usual Benny Pounce once had. *Too exhausted to care much at this point, I guess*, he mused.

Deciding to take the hard road, Gabe started with, "No. I couldn't bring myself to—"

But Benny being Benny, "Whadda ya mean, 'you couldn't—'" Benny shouted, and with a disgusted look, continued with "—'bring yourself to do it?' Dude—" Benny started to say, but Gabe cut him off.

"Benny, I don't need you to—"

"Dude, you been sleepin' with the—" and catching himself this time just in time, changed his regular phrase to "—nice woman for how many weeks now? Her hubby's dead now. So now you're a free agent. Now all you gotta do is call her up."

Going into Benny Smooth mode in the blink of an eye, Benny tried the soft approach. "You know? Give her a shoulder to cry on. 'Hi, Angie. Sorry about your husband, but...'" And changing to full Benny mode, he dropped into, "What more you gotta do than that?"

Sighing out of his exhaustion, Gabe tried wearily to correct him again, now knowing it's not going to make a bit of difference. "Her name is not..." Gabe started, and then deciding against even trying, threw his hands up and continued walking towards the office.

W

With Benny now in pursuit, Gabe muttered, "It just doesn't seem right."

As Gabe went into the office to clock in, Benny squeezed in past him, walked over to the phone and picked it up. "What's the number?

I'll call her for you."

Grabbing the receiver forcefully out of Benny's hand and slamming it back down into the cradle instead of clocking Benny with it, Gabe decided to take a different tack with him.

"Right," he told Benny. Miming picking the phone up, Gabe continued "'Hi, Angela, remember me? Now that your husband's dropped, what say I come over and fuck your lights out?'"

Glaring at Benny, he leaned in with, "Not even you, Benny—" he started to say.

"Look. I know you're the sensitive guy an' all that shit and I'm the stupid fuck. But you gotta do something. Call her, forget about her. Either way dude, it's eatin' you alive."

Pacing now and ready to walk out, Gabe started muttering to himself again, becoming infected with the Benny Bug.

"His funeral's probably in few days, so maybe I can somehow go and get her attention..."

A triumphant Benny chimed in with, "Aw, right. Makin' a man's decision. Maybe there's hope for you yet."

Turning to look at Benny and suddenly really feeling about ready to end their friendship with a big bang, Gabe caught himself and shook his head instead.

"God help me if I'm making the wrong one."

With the sun shining brightly again, the mourners had begun filing out of the Church doors. Walking in line past Angela who was now dressed in all black, Gabe saw several women standing with her who looked like Frank's mother and sisters. And another woman close by who looked like she was Angela's younger sister.

After the majority of the mourners had left and gotten into the various limos and town cars, the last of the funeral party gathered and walked towards the family funeral limo.

Watching from where he sat in his Malibu across the parking lot from the church, Gabe turned the car on, preparing to follow when the funeral cortege began pulling out.

At a safe distance of course.

Gabe had never been in Arlington National Cemetery before. Of course he'd seen it on TV over the years, with various other funerals and of course, from the other side of the river when he'd once upon a time, played volleyball and went to picnics in Potomac Park.

It took up a large part of the hillside just outside of Rosslyn, Virginia, with the starch-white tombstones stretching for what seemed like miles in contrast to the shiny new towers of downtown Rosslyn close by.

With the funeral party spreading out on one of the longest driveways, Gabe pulled up on an adjacent drive, placing himself behind a large copse of trees to hide as best as he could.

Still questioning himself as to how good of an idea this was, he was kicking himself inside for having listened to Benny about this at all. He knew it was one of the worst ideas he could have entertained.

Goddamn it, Harrison. This is ridiculous. And stupid. If she sees me...

Well, I'm here, for better or worse. He looked around and figured to let the Malibu drift a little further into the shade before parking it and getting out. He closed the door ever so gently, so the rust bucket wouldn't shout out his location, and began making his way down as close as he could.

Several news vans were parked off to the other side of the funeral party, filming from an appropriate distance. It suddenly occurred to Gabe it wouldn't do to have his illusive figure seen in some camera shot on the evening news.

Nor would it be in his best interest to be attracting the attention of the Secret Service who were obviously in great profusion all around with their stony stares, hands folded in front of them at the ready, silently scanning the area behind their sunglasses and ear pieces.

There were also dignitaries arriving and getting out of their respective limos. And even more obvious Secret Service agents also hovering on the outside of this new crowd.

Gabe carefully began making his way towards the funeral party, maintaining a good distance from the Secret Service. Without any mausoleums in this cemetery to hide behind, he remained in the shadows, praying to not be seen.

Later, after the casket was being lowered into the ground, a number of mourners were leaving, getting into their respective cars and limos. As the number began declining and the contingent of Secret Service thinned considerably, the rest of the mourners gathered in closer.

Gabe figured it was down to family and close friends, and he felt safe enough to begin creeping out of the trees to get a better view. Angela and her in-laws, along with the woman Gabe thought was probably Angela's friend Maddy, were still at the grave side. Being comforted by one of her husband's sisters, Angela suddenly looked up over her shoulder in Gabe's direction.

He could see Angela stiffening, and looking distressed even at this distance. As her sister-in-law pulled away at Angela's reaction, Angela merely shook her head, saying something to her, and the woman pulled Angela back into an embrace.

Giving him a sharp look over the other woman's shoulder and shaking her head discreetly, she released her relative and turned her back on Gabe as the family began walking over to and getting into their respective limos.

Before stepping into hers once everyone else was safely inside, Angela turned in Gabe's direction to give him one last excoriating look, shaking her head and mouthing an emphatic "No!" this time.

Shaking her head in disgust, she dipped into the limo that most likely she and he had "done the nasty" in so many times before now. But by the look in her face, that was all obviously now very much in the past.

Definitely a bad decision, he thought, sighing.

That does it, Benny, Gabe thought, as he turned once more towards his car. Closing his eyes and hoping he didn't stumble on one of the lower headstones, he muttered to himself, "This doesn't look good."

Slowly getting into the Malibu again, Gabe paused for several seconds, taking in the stupidity of what he'd done. Grabbing the steering wheel, he pounded his head on it, slowly at first and then harder and harder, not feeling the pain.

THIRTY-ONE

Greeting all of her non-family well-wishers in her living room, Angela was a million miles away. Having a reason for it that was obvious to others was her only comfort now.

Angela had been in a state of shock since having gotten the phone call from the Senate floor informing her of Frank's collapse. She had managed to call Henry to rush her to George Washington Hospital, hoping to get there in time to at least say goodbye.

But before she had managed to reach it, Henry had pulled over and taken the call on the limo phone from the DC Police escort following the ambulance informing her of Frank's having died in transit.

The shock had only been compounded and she was surprised to find it deepened, at the further shock of seeing Gabe hiding in the shadows at the funeral. She had almost fainted, but found her shock then leavened with anger rising out of the ashes of the moment.

How could he? she thought to herself during the limo ride home. But she was also cringing at the other thought that intruded now, that she and Gabe had had sex numerous times, right here in this very limo that she and Maddy and her family were currently riding in from her husband's funeral.

Of course she hadn't thought of that at the time. All she had thought of then was how exquisite she was feeling, and for perhaps the first time in her life.

On this ride however, she only felt disgust at herself at what she had allowed herself to do. *How could I?* she thought to herself again, hoping that her feelings of inner revulsion weren't showing on her face.

She looked around herself at the other women (yes, there were no men in this party, as the men were riding in another limo), but saw that each of them were deep in their own inner musings. No one saw what she could only imagine what was playing over her face right now.

Except Maddy, of course. Angela looked over at her friend, and saw Maddy had the most benevolent and comforting of expressions on her face, as she obviously had some idea of what was going through Angela's head during this ride.

Or did she? Was she just being her usual comforting self? Angela would have to wait for much later to have that discussion.

Once she was home however, her mind was consumed by the task at hand, both giving and receiving comfort in the moment for her and Frank's family's loss.

She worked the crowd without feeling now. As much as she didn't like the effect, she had been a public person for most of her marriage, and she was now taking care of the needs of others and postponing her own needs. Comforting the older women who were part of her former circle; being there for Frank's family; playing both hostess as well as grieving widow.

She needed to be the politician's wife now, being the ambassador as much as the grieving widow. And she most definitely couldn't let any of her feelings show of having been distanced from her husband in the last few years.

She would have to grieve and sort out all her conflicting feelings much later, in private or with Maddy.

Much later, she was at the front door escorting the last of the church ladies out. Her family had already left earlier, and this was the last of her duties.

The last farewells were being traded, along with the ubiquitous and perfunctory assurances of "We must do lunch sometime" that echoed hollowly in Angela's mind.

Closing the door on the last visitor, Angela turned to find the sole person remaining: Maddy, always her rock, far more than any of her family ever had been. Maddy, whom Angela had forgotten was still here.

Maddy was there to take the suddenly falling apart Angela into her arms to comfort. As she guided the now sobbing Angela towards and into the side study, closing the doors behind them, Maddy walked them both to the large ancient leather sofa inside.

Maddy had grabbed a large box of tissues earlier and deposited them here, knowing the storm to come once the audience had gone. After a while of holding Angela, Maddy gently pushed her friend into an upright position. Compassionately taking Angela's chin in hand, Maddy asked sternly, "What else is it, my dear?"

Not catching the implication, Angela answered in a thoroughly drained voice, "I'm exhausted."

"Yes, I know," Maddy said, giving Angela an expression asking a silent "And?" already knowing the answer.

"Gabe came to the funeral today."

"Yes, I know."

Angela looked horrified. "You—"

Sitting for a moment in silence as she decided how to approach all the matters at hand she needed to, Maddy then gently told her, "Well...Let us say that I suspected rather than knew. That is, when your attitude changed in the limousine."

With eyes already red from earlier crying, Angela's eyes turned bleak. She asked, "It wasn't obvious, was it? I mean..."

"To your family? No. But they don't know you like I know you. And besides," Maddy said, "they have no idea of what all of this means to you. They have their own grief to deal with, and they would interpret anything they see in you as part of that grief process."

As she continued to think about all of this, Angela found herself turning from grief to cold anger. "He's turning into a stalker now," she said, with more vehemence than she expected.

"Oh no, my dear," Maddy told her solemnly. "I'm afraid it's much worse than that."

Confused now, Angela paused before asking, "What do you—"

With a glint in her eye, Maddy stated the obvious. "He's hopelessly in love with you."

Already at the point of exhaustion, Angela was feeling really ready to cry now. Knowing in her heart that she would have to deal with this at some point, it was all too much now, all at once.

"Oh, Maddy. I just never thought it would come to this." Reaching over to the end table and attempting to grab a box of tissues there, "I really—"

Her hand reaching the already strategically placed box, Maddy grasped it and handing the box to Angela, continuing with, "There are other things in all of this to consider as well."

"Excuse me?" Angela was getting deeper into a state of loss at "all of this" the more they talked.

"But, Maddy. What am I going to do with Gabe? Should I call the police? How should I—"

"The police? My dear, how melodramatic you can be."

"But—"

"But, nonsense," she pshawed, instead asking her friend, "Do you love him?"

Unable to handle anything else at this point, Angela was about to say "No." She couldn't consider continuing anything with Gabe. It would tarnish her husband's reputation after the fact.

Plus she was appalled that he would do such a thing as he had done. Surely this represented that she had severely misjudged him and his mental state.

She had suspected that there was a reason that he couldn't commit to any of the women in his past. This only solidified those suspicions that had begun forming in her mind.

She couldn't possibly be in love with someone like that. Could she?

"No," she said firmly. "He was a mistake that I made. He has to stay in the past," she said, with a part of her reeling from this decision inside.

"Do you love him?" Maddy asked her once again, even more forcefully.

"How can I love someone I haven't known for very long?" Angela asked, knowing that Maddy would have a ready answer.

"I asked you, 'Do you love him?' Not whether you should love him, or whether you could. I asked you, 'Do you?'"

Awash in too many emotions to handle at the moment, Angela tried shaking her head "No," and was perturbed to find that it was changing in mid-shake to a wobbly and muddy "Yes."

"No," she said defiantly.

Maddy gave her a stern look, but said nothing further for now. "Well, first things first. First we need to get you prepped to take over your dear lately departed Franklin's Senate seat."

Sobering up considerably at this, Angela felt her face go slack in further shock, as she asked incredulously, "Frank's Senate seat. Maddy. This time surely you must be joking."

"Nonsense," Maddy contradicted her firmly. "Was I joking regarding your having an affair?"

Taking Angela's hands firmly in hers and locking eyes with her, Maddy continued, "Of course you're going to fill Franklin's seat. I would think that that is a given," in Maddy's usual "take no prisoners" voice.

"But—" Angela objected. This was all too much.

On a roll, Maddy kept up, "Besides, you have a number of precedents here. Mary Bono is a wonderful woman — despite her politics. And let's not forget that woman from Missouri — what's her name, taking over her husband's seat."

Trying desperately to control her rising confusion, Angela interjected with another feeble, "But—"

The steamroller was engaged, and Maddy forged on with, "Now. About your friend Gabriel..."

At this, Angela was brought back to herself forcefully, "Now you are joking." And then looking at her friend asked desperately, "Aren't you?"

As if she hadn't heard her, Maddy said, "No one has to know that you have known each other...Biblically, shall we say? Before now. That we can construct for later."

"But, Maddy—"

Maddy continued relentlessly with, "Do you love him?" once more.

Not really trusting where this was going, Angela tried interrupting her with, "Maddy, I don't—"

Not taking no for an answer, Maddy said, "Of course you do. I've seen it in your eyes, and read volumes in your silences."

"But, Maddy—"

Like some sort of super hero, Maddy announced with a comic character voice, "Never fear. Madelaine Lightfoot is here."

Looking dumbfounded, Angela began opening and closing her mouth several times, before finally closing it firmly.

Relaxing into a state of surrender and knowing that Maddy could become unstoppable, Angela finally allowed herself to ask, "Ok. What are we going to do?" And corrected her question with, "About the Senate seat?"

Glad that her young friend was not going to fight her on her future, Maddy looked into Angela's eyes and told her very nonchalantly but insistently, "First, I'm going to call in a few favors."

"Ok," Angela said, finally surrendering to the sense of this Maddy inevitability.

"And then, we're going to get you into that seat of power which you've so richly deserved these last few years. And then," pausing for a dramatic flourish, Maddy continued with, "You're going to live happily ever after." Smiling warmly, Maddy waited.

Looking at Maddy as if she was crazy, Angela told her reluctantly, "I don't know about this, Maddy. Especially about Gabe. And shouldn't I take time to grieve my late husband's demise?"

Now taking a very serious look, Maddy leaned in and told her bluntly, "My dear, you've been mourning the loss of Frank, long before he actually passed away. And he could have told you about his condition, but he didn't. And what I have already set in motion will take time, so that yes, you will have the proper time to mourn your late husband. You are still in a state of shock, and as soon as that breaks, the healing will begin."

Drawing a now-weeping Angela into her embrace fully, Maddy said, "Trust me. I haven't been around this place for all these years without earning it."

After a few minutes, as Angela began drying this round of tears, her smiling mentor suddenly started her strategizing patiently with, "Now, here's what we're going to do."

Shaking her head wearily, Angela's eyes begin glazing over as Maddy continued her lecture on ascending the throne of power. All she knew at this point was that she couldn't trust Gabe. That much she knew about her future.

After Maddy left, Angela climbed the stairs to her bedroom. She was exhausted beyond anything she could have ever imagined herself to be previously.

Reaching her bed that she now realized would be cold for a long time as she threw herself down on it, not bothering to even take off her funeral dress, she found that she could care less what happened to her now.

She had listened to Maddy prattle on about how she, Maddy, was going to help her attain the seat that Maddy had never had the possibility in her day of taking over from her then newly deceased husband.

Maddy had become very much the political maven in recent years, Angela had gathered. She had worked behind the scenes in ways that Angela hadn't even been able to imagine before.

Maddy knew people, knew things *about* people, that apparently those people were afraid to let leak out. Those things, while not specifying what she knew, Maddy only insinuated.

When Angela awoke several hours later, the light outside had faded to evening. There was a hushed silence to the city outside belying the rush-hour traffic she knew was driving there.

As she sat up, she knew what she had to do. Whatever Maddy had planned for her ascension to Frank's seat would be fine with her. She had imagined many times one day running for office herself. But that thought had slid away from her mind many years ago. She would deal with that later.

But Gabe? She knew she had to cut that off immediately.
hat Gabe had done this afternoon had almost given her a heart attack, to see him there off in the distance, skulking like some kind of pervert lurking in the trees so close to those she knew and loved.

She also knew that they would no doubt cut her off from any contact at all, if they had suspected what had been the case with this strange man.

But part of her was screaming inside to not cut this man out of her life. And another part of her was truly frightened that she had let

Maddy talk her into this reckless decision about Gabe in the first place.

But all of her knew that it had to end now. (Or at least, that's what she was working to convince herself of.)

After pacing back and forth for what seemed like hours, she finally made the decision she thought that she had to. Going over to the phone and picking it up, she dialed Gabe's number and hoped that he wasn't at home so she could leave him a message. She would have to call the phone company in the morning to block his number so he would be out of her life for good.

She waited as the connection was ringing through. She was just about to hang up when, the connection made, she heard his voice on the outgoing message on the other side.

Once again thinking of hanging up and not responding to his outrageous act at all, she was startled by the loud beep.

She paused for a second before feeling the full rage that she had felt earlier rising full force. "Gabriel! I don't know what the hell you were thinking. How dare you show up at my husband's funeral? I don't appreciate it one bit. If I didn't— If I hadn't—"

And with an ominous long silence during which she felt like hanging up, Angela instead continued with a hushed, "Don't ever call me or try to see me, ever again. Do you understand? I...don't know...don't," and purposely let the phone drop into the cradle as loudly (and finally) as she could.

"There. It's done," she told herself, trying hard to feel satisfied with having ended it.

But she couldn't. She suddenly felt the tears and crying rising up from deep inside of her once more. All the years of self-denial that had been ended in the arms of this man she had just sworn off for good. All the ambivalence and grief from two sources of pain, began flooding her mind and heart.

She threw herself on her bed and cried as she never had in her life, as she realized that she was having to grieve two deaths in one day.

THIRTY-TWO

Walking in the front door of the Globe afterwards, Gabe was immediately confronted by Benny. "So, the funeral go all right?"

Immediately sitting down in stunned silence, Gabe put his head in his hands. Not sure of who he should despise more now, he looked through his hands at nothing.

"I shouldn't have gone," he said to himself.

And then, looking up at Benny with what was obviously not a good look for Benny to see, Benny blanched a silent Woah.

"I wish I'd never thought of it," Gabe said darkly. And then, as if having a Benny-like brainstorm, he said, "Oh. No, wait! I didn't think of it. You did!"

Gabe had a direction to turn his anger in other than himself. "Of all the stupid fucking things for you to suggest to me to even think of doing, you suggest I should go to the funeral."

Miming having another Benny Thought, Gabe asked, "Why didn't I think of that? Because it was one of the absolutely stupidest, Benny-shit things I could have thought about. That's why."

"Hey! Don't blame me if you manage to fuck everything up—"

Standing up now in a way that felt very threatening, Gabe suddenly drew up to his full height, towering over Benny.

"Maybe," Gabe cut him off. "Maybe, it was the suggestion that was fucked up. Maybe? Dontcha think?" Gabe asked Benny harshly. *I should just haul off and hit him now, knock a few teeth out and get it over and done with,* Gabe thought, steaming with anger.

Walking away now disgusted at both of them, Gabe ceased listening to Benny's insistent "Hey! Hey!" objections trailing off behind him.

"Now I really need a drink," he said to himself wearily.

Hours later the sound of the key entering the lock broke the silence again. Gabe, now obviously plastered and four sheets to the wind, managed to stumble inside, also managing to leave the key in the lock as he tried unsuccessfully to close the door.

After several attempts to close it, he finally opens it and found the keys clanging in the lock the reason he couldn't shut the door. "Fuck," he mumbles, and started trying to drunkenly wrangle them out of the lock.

Finally managing to get them free, he shuts the door — successfully this time. Wheeling around and heading straight for the bedroom, he bypasses the flashing light on the answering machine.

THIRTY-THREE

The regulars were filtering in from their day on the Hill, as the evening news was once again playing on the TV as a general background noise. As the evening rush at the Globe was starting, it was the lull of the afternoon crowd swiftly turning into the night crowd in full swing.

The closed captioning was on even though the audio was on as well, and the new bartender was passing back and forth "slingin' and swingin'."

One of the segments on world affairs was finishing regarding the latest budgetary crisis in Congress with the model-gorgeous Announcer speaking as the sometimes on/sometimes off again captioning was scrolling across the bottom of the screen, trying to keep up.

"And now, on a lighter note..." the announcer continued, switching moods like a new outfit. "Only six months after being elected to the seat that was vacated by the death of her late husband last year—"

A lone hand stopped his slinging and swinging to come out of the frenzy, reaching for and hitting the volume button on the remote, raising the audio in mid-sentence. "—Senator Angela Treworthy of Connecticut—" she continued bouncily.

On the screen they were now showing the official Senate portrait of Angela (much like the earlier portrait of her husband). A little more ironic than Frank's portrait, Angela's was showing her still looking stiff and unaccustomed to the attention. With only a hint of her smile to come showing.

The announcer continued perkily droning on, "—has not only found herself in a seat of power... but has also now found love. This of course has set the gossip mills in the halls of Congress spinning furiously."

With a shot of Angela from earlier in her Senate seat voting on a bill, the announcer began amping her voiced intrigue higher. "After a whirlwind romance with an interestingly much younger Hill staffer she met on her third day on the job—"

Switching to a shot of Angela and Gabe descending the steps of the church where they had just been married (and Frank had been given his send off), "—the newlyweds are off! It's a much shortened weekend cruise before Senator Treworthy returns to DC, and back to the current budget battle."

Shuffling to new papers on her desk, the perky announcer shifted her style yet again in the blink of an eye, returning to playing the serious anchor.

"In other news..."

Hitting the volume button again, the sound of the TV began receding into the background with the din of the crowd and their clinking glasses replacing it.

Benny was now the one standing behind the bar. With the remote still in his hand and with a very un-Benny-like faraway look in his eyes, he returns to "Slingin' and Servin'.

"Straightened up and flew right," Benny was telling one of (his now) regulars when they made a comment about where Gabe was finding himself now. He was kind of meaning himself and not Gabe, but Benny being Benny still, wasn't about to admit it.

Saying to himself now and admiring his ex-friend more than he wanted to, "Attaboy, Gabe. Always knew you'd do it."

But this being the Globe and the beginning of evening rush, his reverie was soon interrupted with a shout from one of his customers down the bar. "Hey, Benny! You going to wake up, or what? Where's that drink you been promising me?"

Smiling good-naturedly now, Benny just shouted back, "Yeah, yeah, yeah. I'm coming already. Hold your ever lovin' horses you know what, will ya?"

THIRTY-FOUR

The morning sun was glinting off the gentle seeming waves being created... several stories beneath them by the massive cruise ship El Carribe they were on.

Capitol Hill seemed so far away right in this instance, as they were passing through the warm waters off the Bahamas. Bright sun, high clouds, and the clear bright blue sky were being mirrored by the water as far as the eye could see in a forward direction.

Cradling a closed-eyed Angela in his arms as the wind is once again blowing her hair around them, Gabe is both relaxed and happy. The rest of the passengers are all blissfully cavorting around them, paying no attention whatsoever to the newly minted happily, just-married couple on their way to becoming the newest power couple in DC. But Washington and the Capitol Building were now far, far away.

"So," Angela was whispering to Gabe. "Here we are, all above board, on board, and I've never felt better. Even the years with Frank are disappearing behind me."

"Like the ships wake?"

"Yes. Now I'm awake."

Turning around in his arms, "So, how are you doing Mr. O'Connor?" she asks.

"I'm doing fine, Mrs..."

Putting her finger on his lips before he can say it, she whispers solemnly, "I'll always be Mrs. Treworthy, Gabe," she says.

Looking up at him, she smiled much less solemnly. "But you'll never be Mr. Treworthy. I hope that you can understand that I'd change my name, but I need to... No, I want to keep it.

"For Franks sake. After all, I really did love him for many years."

"I understand," Gabe said, suddenly grinning ear to ear adding, "Senator." Smiling an even broader smile, he plants a big kiss tenderly on her forehead, asking, "So is this what happily ever after feels like?"

Nuzzling deeply into his neck, she sighs and whispers, "Oh, God. I hope so." Laughing lightheartedly, she looked up and returned to gazing into his eyes for a second, shaking her head lovingly. "Oh, I do hope so."

Turning them both around to gaze ahead over the railing, Gabe returns to cradling his new wife and letting that cloud of hair envelop him once again.

"And although I wouldn't use it in a Novel," he said. "And they both lived happily ever after."

"Here's to clichés," she said, snuggling even deeper.

THE END

ABOUT THE AUTHOR

Robin Chappell is a Writer and Fine Artist/Photographer (among many other creative outlets), living in Los Angeles. Originally from Missouri but having lived the majority of his life in Washington, DC and environs, he moved to LA in 2005 to work in the Film Industry.

His book "The Synergy Design Group" (a "lookbook" detailing his Art, Design and Architectural work) will be coming out in September. And he also has a technical project in Planning (and Seeking Funding) to address the Drought Conditions in Southern California and other Countries around the world.

His Novel "shadows and LIGHT" (a Metaphysical Science Fiction/Horror story) will be coming in October of this Year. Others of his Novels will be rolling out over the following years to come!

And coming in the next two years, look for Robin's first Television Series (along the lines of "shadows and LIGHT")! He is currently working on the Pilot Episode and the Series "Bible" (the book with all of the character and plot elements for the first Season and hopefully more) of that Series (further details and Title TBA) now.

www.ingramcontent.com/pod-product-compliance
Lightning Source LLC
Chambersburg PA
CBHW072025020726
47501CB00006B/1952